Praise for

My Way to Hell

"This amusing urban fantasy romance brings together a lead pair that fans of the saga will appreciate . . . Fans will enjoy that Marcella is back burning tamales and peanut butter as only a retired sexagenarian former demon could when she becomes a not so average woman in love."
—*Genre Go Round Reviews*

"A hysterically touching sequel . . . Marcella is the kind of protagonist who gets readers rooting and keeping their fingers crossed for the next book . . . A quick page-turner for even a novice to Cassidy's fast-paced fiction."
—*Fresh Fiction*

Kiss & Hell

"A fun, lighthearted paranormal romance that will keep readers entertained. Ms. Cassidy fills the pages of her book with nonstop banter, ghostly activity, and steamy romance."
—*Darque Reviews*

"Delaney, with her amusing sarcastic asides, makes for an entertaining romantic fantasy with a wonderful mystery subplot . . . Readers will relish this lighthearted, jocular frolic."
—*Genre Go Round Reviews*

"Cassidy has created a hilarious lead in Delaney Markham. Readers will run through all types of emotions while enjoying laugh-out-loud moments, desperate passion, wacky and fun characters, pop-culture references, and one intense mystery. The book's charm is apparent from the first page, but the twisted mystery tangled throughout will keep the pages turning."
—*Romantic Times*

continued . . .

The Accidental Human

"I highly enjoyed every moment of Dakota Cassidy's *The Accidental Human* . . . A paranormal romance with a strong dose of humor."

—*Errant Dreams Reviews*

"A delightful, at times droll, contemporary tale starring a decidedly human heroine . . . Dakota Cassidy provides a fitting, twisted ending to this amusingly warm urban romantic fantasy."

—*Genre Go Round Reviews*

"The final member of Cassidy's trio of decidedly offbeat friends faces her toughest challenge, but that doesn't mean there isn't humor to spare! With emotion, laughter, and some pathos, Cassidy serves up another winner!"

—*Romantic Times*

Accidentally Dead

"A laugh-out-loud follow-up to *The Accidental Werewolf*, and it's a winner . . . Ms. Cassidy is an up-and-comer in the world of paranormal romance."

—*Fresh Fiction*

"An enjoyable, humorous satire that takes a bite out of the vampire romance subgenre . . . Fans will appreciate the nonstop hilarity."

—*Genre Go Round Reviews*

The Accidental Werewolf

"Cassidy, a prolific author of erotica, has ventured into MaryJanice Davidson territory with a humorous, sexy tale."

—*Booklist*

Berkley Sensation titles by Dakota Cassidy

YOU DROPPED A BLONDE ON ME

BURNING DOWN THE SPOUSE

WALTZ THIS WAY

KISS & HELL

MY WAY TO HELL

THE ACCIDENTAL WEREWOLF

ACCIDENTALLY DEAD

THE ACCIDENTAL HUMAN

ACCIDENTALLY DEMONIC

ACCIDENTALLY CATTY

Waltz This Way

DAKOTA CASSIDY

B

BERKLEY SENSATION, NEW YORK

THE BERKLEY PUBLISHING GROUP
Published by the Penguin Group
Penguin Group (USA) Inc.
375 Hudson Street, New York, New York 10014, USA

Penguin Group (Canada), 90 Eglinton Avenue East, Suite 700, Toronto, Ontario M4P 2Y3, Canada
(a division of Pearson Penguin Canada Inc.) • Penguin Books Ltd., 80 Strand, London WC2R 0RL,
England • Penguin Group Ireland, 25 St. Stephen's Green, Dublin 2, Ireland (a division of Penguin
Books Ltd.) • Penguin Group (Australia), 250 Camberwell Road, Camberwell, Victoria 3124, Australia
(a division of Pearson Australia Group Pty. Ltd.) • Penguin Books India Pvt. Ltd., 11 Community
Centre, Panchsheel Park, New Delhi—110 017, India • Penguin Group (NZ), 67 Apollo Drive,
Rosedale, Auckland 0632, New Zealand (a division of Pearson New Zealand Ltd.) • Penguin Books
(South Africa) (Pty.) Ltd., 24 Sturdee Avenue, Rosebank, Johannesburg 2196, South Africa

Penguin Books Ltd., Registered Offices: 80 Strand, London WC2R 0RL, England

This book is an original publication of The Berkley Publishing Group.

This is a work of fiction. Names, characters, places, and incidents either are the product of the author's
imagination or are used fictitiously, and any resemblance to actual persons, living or dead, business
establishments, events, or locales is entirely coincidental. The publisher does not have any control over
and does not assume any responsibility for author or third-party websites or their content.

PUBLISHING HISTORY
Berkley Sensation trade paperback edition / March 2012

Library of Congress Cataloging-in-Publication Data

Cassidy, Dakota.
Waltz this way / Dakota Cassidy.
p. cm.
ISBN 978-0-425-24550-7 (pbk.)
1. Women dancers—Fiction. I. Title.
PS3603. A8685W35 2012
813'.6—dc23
2011044103

PRINTED IN THE UNITED STATES OF AMERICA

10 9 8 7 6 5 4 3 2 1

ACKNOWLEDGMENTS

First, a quick thank-you to Myriam Hernandez, who was the inspiration for the hero's Aunt Myriam. You rock, sistah!

I'm an insane fan of *Dancing with the Stars* and *So You Think You Can Dance*, which inspired this particular book. But it wasn't just the latest crop of TV shows that made me decide to create a heroine who's a dancer.

I loved to spin in circles as a kid, and—much to my parent's amazement—I got so good at it I stopped getting dizzy. It was my dad who found a way to put all that twirling to good use. It was also my dad who showed me the ways of Lawrence Welk and ballroom dancing.

There really was—in my young world, anyway—nothing like some Lawrence on PBS, and the sound of the words "And a one, and a two, and a three!" I loved ballroom dancing long before it was hip, and I followed that passion, along with my deep love of ballet, contemporary, and jazz for nearly thirteen years of my childhood and well into my teen years.

And I danced because my dad introduced me to the quiet, gentle beauty of a waltz; the sizzling excitement of a smoldering paso doble; the torrid passion of *Swan Lake*; and okay, the lure of floaty, swirly dresses with lots of dramatic makeup and hair that flowed down my back. He took me to endless dance classes when he was tired, and he never missed a performance. Not since I was four.

Oh, to fouetté and relevé in a pink tutu again without pulling a hip muscle. You know, that spinny thing you do while you're in fourth position? I hope I've used that correctly in a sentence. My addiction to spinning didn't necessarily require me to spell the spin.

So this is for my dad—miss you much down here.

Dakota ☺

Also note, I've obviously taken artistic license with the various titles of ballroom championships for fictional purposes. Just so all you die-hard ballroom fans and those who've practiced the sport don't take offense. Riverbend, New Jersey, is a fictional town made up in my pea brain. ☺

Acknowledgments to www.e-cookbooks.net/aprons/funny1.htm

CHAPTER ONE

The first rule of the ex-princess club? Suck. It. Up.

"Cornflake?"

Melina Cherkasov smiled distractedly at the sound of her father's voice, tucking her cell phone beneath her chin while she tried her key in the lock of her small dance studio for the second time that morning. If one more thing had to be replaced, her husband, Stan, would blow a nut. "Hi, Daddy. How are you feeling?"

His grunt, gruff and short, made her smile. "I'm fine. Jake's fine. Still shits big, my Jake, the damn mutt. Everything's fine here in Jersey. I wanna know how *you're* feelin', spaghetti and meatballs?"

For as long as she could remember, whenever her father referred to her, his pride and joy, he always used endearments that involved food. It had become a game that had made her giggle as a child, and still filled her heart with warmth as an adult. Joe Hodge was big, loud, and without censor or, as some might say, class, but he loved his little girl like no other.

Mel's stiff fingers jammed the key into the lock again and twisted hard. "What do you mean how do I feel, Dad? I feel fine." She gave a perplexed glance at the door and fought a curse word, catching a glimpse of herself in her studio's glass window. She blew out a disgusted breath.

Her brown-black hair pulled back so severely in a tight ponytail made her need for a touch-up painfully evident in the early morning sunlight. And she noted her olive complexion was looking a little wan today sans makeup. Maybe that was because she hadn't heard from her husband in three solid days, and she'd spent half the night trying to reach him.

"Where's that sissy-pants husband of yours?" her father barked.

Mel winced, giving up on the door to lean against the brick front of the old building with a huff. There was no love lost between her husband, Stan, and her father. Stan was older than Mel by twenty-two years. Something her father had made no bones about disliking from the moment he'd been introduced to Stanislov Cherkasov when Mel was just nineteen. That he was an infamous Russian ballet choreographer slash ballroom aficionado and now a national celebrity as a judge on *Dude, You Can Dance* meant squat to Joe.

Joe had often grumbled about paying for all those expensive ballroom lessons that had led Mel to three junior championships, two U.S. titles, and the opportunity to pursue her dreams in the big city only for her to end up married to a man who was as unsightly as a wart on his ass.

A geriatric wart, at that.

Joe called Stan Twinkle Toes or, while he twirled around with a finger over his head and cackled, the Ballerina.

Often. Mostly directly in Stan's face over some holiday dinner until Stan had refused to even consider getting on a plane to the East Coast to endure, in her husband's words, "the stoopid American's free turkey dinner."

She chose to ignore the possibility that her father would go off on one of his tangents about men in tights and sought a cheery approach to her husband's whereabouts instead. "Stan's in—" She paused a moment. Where was Stan, and why couldn't she get into her dance studio? "Oh! He's in Wisconsin, Dad, auditioning contestants for the show."

There was a low growl, and then, "The hell he is."

"What?" Her question vague while she dug through her purse to see if possibly she had the wrong set of keys.

"You watched the TV today?"

She chuckled indulgently. He always forgot the time difference between L.A. and Jersey. "No, Dad. It's only nine in the morning here. I just got to the studio. Besides, you know I don't do the news." Too much death. Too much sadness. Too much gossip. Gossip that, as of late, since the show's popularity had risen to stratospheric proportions, marked her handsome husband's every move.

There was a rustle and she supposed her father was repositioning himself in front of his TV. "Well, maybe you oughta find ya one. You got one in your studio, don't cha?"

"It's just an old black and white with crappy reception." There wasn't much in her studio that wasn't old.

"Bet Fred Astaire has a big flat-screen the size of my ass in his office."

Mel sighed and closed her eyes, a slight throb beginning above her right one. "It doesn't matter what Fred Astaire has, Dad. I have a dance studio where you're supposed to learn to dance—not watch TV."

"Don't matter, Mel—you need to go turn it on and watch what I'm watchin'. That *Hollywood Scoop*. You know, the twenty-four-hour access to the stars show?"

"Daddy?"

"Sweet potato?"

"First, I can't get into my studio. The key won't work for some crazy reason. Second, since when have we watched TV together—long distance—"

"Since I can't get to where you are in Lala Land before you get the news. So I wanna be sure I'm at least nearby—even if it's only on the phone."

Still not giving her father her full attention, she paused again, lifting a hand to wave at a neighboring yogurt-store owner who gave her an odd look, before quickly turning away and jamming his key into the door of his store.

At least someone's key still worked. "Third, Daddy, what have I told you about watching tabloid television?"

His sigh was long. She could picture him tipped back in his La-Z-Boy in his retirement village, his wide face wrinkling in impatience at being called to task. "You said half of it wasn't true and the other half was only mostly true," he offered, his tone that of a petulant child who'd been reminded the hundredth time in a day to stop running in the house.

"Right. So why would I want to watch *Hollywood Scoop* with you? I love you, Dad, but I won't indulge those gossipmongers. They speculate far more than they ever hit the mark. Besides, I don't have cable here at the studio. A studio I can't get into right now anyway."

There was a pause on her father's end before he asked, "Don't Twinkle Toes own that run-down, piece-of-crap building that just barely passes code you got your studio in?"

Once more, Mel hesitated. If she fed her father even a morsel of a reason to beat Stan down, he'd open wide and gnaw off her arm. Yes. Stan owned the building. Yes. It was run-down and badly maintained, and yes, it was the lowest on her husband's list of priorities. Lower still because Stan didn't love that she allowed children who couldn't afford ballroom lessons to come to her classes whether he liked it or not. "Dad, that's not the point, and I really have to go. I have to call a locksmith."

"Honey, don't go. You need to listen to me."

His somber words caught her attention, but it was brief. She was too busy trying to figure out if the lock had rusted. Mel sank to the ground to eye the door's keyhole, accidentally tipping her purse on the pavement in the process.

She rolled her eyes at the scatter of makeup, antibacterial hand soap, and receipts galore. Tucking the phone under her chin, she began to sift through the mess, searching for her other set of keys.

"Melina Eunice Hodge!"

The use of her middle name was meant to bring her back into focus and force her to pay attention. All it really did, or had ever done, was make her cringe. God, she hated her middle name, even if it was because her mother's mother was a Eunice—and someone Melina had really loved. It still sucked.

The use of her middle name also sent a shiver along her spine. Something wasn't right. "I'm sorry, Dad. I'm distracted. It's been a crazy week, and Stan's been gone a long time. So I've been a little cranky."

"Looks like he's gonna be gone a whole lot longer."

"Say again?"

"Girl, would you please sit still and just listen to me. Jesus, Joseph, and Mary, Mel! You were always a fidgeter. I need to talk to you. Now be still and quit fussin'."

Her fingers stopped moving upon command, her stomach jolted. "Stopping. Because now you have me worried. Are you sick, Dad?" Her worst fear since her mother had died five years ago was losing her father, too.

"Good, and no, I'm not sick. Not unless you count my God damn acid reflux and bursitis. Oh, and my knees. They drive me to drink."

"It isn't your knees that drive you to a Schlitz, Dad, and you know it." Mel smiled, pulling her own knees up to her chin. Well, almost up to her chin. If she could just lose those last fifteen pounds, she'd be closer to her fighting weight.

Okay. Maybe the real number for her fighting weight was twenty-five total pounds, but she was trying to remain realistic at forty. And twenty-five pounds wouldn't allow for the occasional Choco-Bliss or ranch dressing on her salad instead of the fresh juice of a lemon.

"Listen, breadstick, you got trouble comin' your way."

Just as those words sank in, Mel heard someone yell, "It's her!"

Her head popped up at the thump of feet on the pavement, coming from across the street. A throng of cameramen and smartly dressed reporters headed her way like a pack of salivating dogs.

The paparazzi. Here?

Huh.

She wrinkled her nose in total distaste. Shitty bastards. How had they found her? Stan kept her dance studio like some would a dirty little secret. She suspected he let her keep the studio open to keep her from complaining about his long stints away from home.

Stan had little tolerance for what he called her wish to save deprived children with a silly waltz. He'd declared the caliber of dancers she was drawing beneath him in almost as many words.

While Stan had been a well-respected, famous choreographer in the world of Russian ballet, he wasn't a household name until *Dude, You Can Dance*. Now everyone wanted a piece of him, and anyone who was directly related to him. They especially wanted a piece of the woman who was married to him because Mel fought so hard to stay out of the limelight. She was an enigma and a constant source of speculation.

Not that Stan was all that interested in having her share his limelight. He didn't want to do that with anyone. He especially didn't want to share it with Mel because he said lately she looked like she'd eaten too much borscht.

Which had hurt. But then, even if she wanted Stan to love her for who she was on the inside, Mel had to admit, the outside was a little like a can of freshly opened dinner rolls—sort of oozy in some places.

Lightbulbs were suddenly flashing, and microphones were shoved in her face as she attempted to slide to an upright position in the midst of the chaos. "Melina! What do you have to say about Stan and Yelena?"

Her father's squawking fell on deaf ears as her phone slid from beneath her chin. She shoved it into the pocket of her ankle-length sweater.

"So what do you have to say about Yelena?" someone repeated.

Yelena. Like the newest choreographer Yelena from *Dude, You Can Dance* who had a body so hard even a wrecking ball couldn't crack it?

Like the Yelena with no last name, Yelena?

What could Mel possibly have to say about her, and what did she have to do with Stan? Other than the fact that he was her boss as executive producer and head judge of the show?

Mel's breath quickened when a male reporter she vaguely recognized from *Hollywood Scoop* turned to the crowd, froth but a bead of saliva away from forming in the corners of his mouth, and yelped, "Holy shit! She doesn't know! Back off, you bunch of piranhas. I got her first!"

Not to be out-frothed, a salivating blonde from another tabloid show with makeup too harsh for daylight hours gave the *Hollywood Scoop* guy an elbow to the ribs and jammed a microphone into Mel's face.

There was a flash of pity in her overly charcoal-lined eyes, and then she went all viper. "How does it feel to be left for a woman almost half your age? Have you seen this? It was taken by a fan of the show." She shoved a picture of Stan and Yelena in Mel's face.

At some Wisconsin cheese festival. At least that was what the banner said. Holding hands while Stan swallowed Yelena's lips whole.

It was clear they'd been caught off guard. Stan's eyes were wide with surprise in the shot.

The ground beneath Mel wobbled and shifted, her vision becoming blurry and distorted. Thankfully, her tongue neither wobbled, nor blurred.

She forced her shoulders to lift in an indifferent shrug. Like it was no big deal Stan was sticking his tongue down Yelena's throat while experiencing the splendor of aged sharp cheddar. "How does it feel to spend a good portion of your paycheck from Satan on all that peroxide?"

The blonde's eyes narrowed for only a second before she regained her composure. Just as she was gearing up to lob another question at Mel, another reporter shoved the blonde to the side while yet another crowded her up against the building until she almost couldn't breathe from their close proximity.

Fighting down a sob of rage, she stooped, hoping to gather the rest of her things and run as far away as she could, but they had her packed too tightly against the building.

Fuck her antibacterial soap. She grabbed at the important stuff, her wallet and her keys, her fingers scraping the concrete as she did. Mel rose, sucking in a harsh breath at the head rush that assaulted her, and in stoic silence, began to push against the cluster of hands holding microphones, her heart crashing out a painful rhythm in her ears.

Some of the neighboring store owners had begun to gather along the sidewalk, their obvious curiosity stung just as good as any sharp slap across her face. Their whispers made her sad. No one made a move to help her fight her way out of the throng of cutthroats.

And she'd once thought they were all sort of like neighbors. Like the kind that always had each other's backs when vulture reporters were breathing down your neck? Nice neighbors, the lot of 'em.

Definitely not Mr. Rogers approved.

Biting her lip, while making a conscious choice not to let the scourge of humanity get one single word from her, Mel went at them headfirst, bulldozer style.

Her yelp was warrior-ish and meant as a warning when she lunged into the crowd, caring little if she stepped on toes.

Then Tito Ortiz, twelve, and on his way to a brilliant Latin ballroom dancing career if his father would get over the "dancing is for girls" thing and let him, grabbed her hand. "Ms. Mel! Hurry, follow me!" He gave her the last yank she needed to break free. Mel crashed into a cameraman, hissing when their shoulders made hard contact as Tito tugged her to freedom.

She clung to his sweaty hand, tripping on the edge of the sidewalk while trying to keep up. The distinct crunch of her toe, encased in canvas slip-ons, forced her to bite the inside of her mouth to keep from crying out.

"I know a shortcut, Ms. Mel! Run faster, they're catching up!" he yelled, dodging and ducking until they reached an alleyway she was unfamiliar with. Tito stopped short at the end of it, gasping for breath in unison with Mel.

He took her forearms in his hands and squeezed them. His dark eyes, filled with concern, pierced hers. "You stay here, Ms. Mel. I'll get Mama. She'll bring you home, okay?"

Mel nodded mutely, letting her head fall back on her shoulders while she fought to catch her breath. Her toe throbbed with a hot ache, but it didn't match the throb of humiliation or the sharp stabs of pain to her heart.

"Wait right here, Ms. Mel. I'll make sure they don't find you." Tito's words, so sweet and reassuring, brought her reality into focus.

Stan was schtupping Yelena.

In Wisconsin.

During a cheese fest.

The bastard would pay.

Then a thought hit her. No. He wouldn't pay. Not in houses and diamonds anyway.

A tear slipped down her cheek. She swiped at it in an angry gesture when it fell into a patch of sunshine pushing its way through the two buildings.

It was such a nice day. Wow. It truly sucked to find out your husband was banging some hard-bodied choreographer on such a nice day.

News like that should only come on rainy days.

~ℓ~

"Daddy?" Mel sobbed into her dying cell phone almost ten hours and a hair-raising escape with Tito's mother from the alleyway later. Hating how weak she sounded, she stiffened her spine and clenched her teeth.

"Ah, pork chop, I thought you'd never call back."

The gruffly gentle, sympathetic tone of her father's voice made a fresh batch of tears fight to seep from her eyes. "I think I need to come home now. Do you have room for me and Weezer?"

"I always have room for you, Grape-Nuts. You come on home and we'll make everything all right. Together. Just like we used to."

Like they used to. As if a banana-split sundae could make this better. Well, maybe it could. If it had sprinkles. The chocolate ones. She shook her head at the memory. Her breath shuddered on its way out of her throat, her pride shattered. "I think I need to borrow money to . . . buy a ticket . . ."

There was a grunt on the other end, a familiar one of angry discontent. "That sonofabitch!"

Oh, if he only knew the half of the sonofabitch Stan was, Mel thought, taking one last look at her house in the Hills, her *locked* house in the Hills, before getting into her friend Jackie's SUV, giving Weezer, her Saint Bernard a nudge into the backseat. "I . . ." She couldn't speak.

"You just get to LAX, Mel. I'll make sure a ticket's waiting for you and Weez. A ticket and a big hug from your old pop when you get here."

Mel choked on her gratitude. Jackie grabbed the phone from her. "Mr. Hodge? It's Jackie Bellows, Mel's friend here in L.A. I'll make sure she gets to the airport, and I'll have what that asshole left her, which wasn't much, by the way, shipped to your house. Don't you worry about anything but catching her at the other end." Jackie nodded at the phone, then ended the call with a short goodbye.

Mel curled up in the passenger seat, pressing the side of her face to the window while she watched her house turn to a tiny dot among hundreds and simmered.

Jackie reached a hand over the console, squeezing her knee. "Stan's a fuckhead-fuckwad."

Mel nodded. He certainly had the "fuck" part covered—in all contexts of the word.

Jackie shook her head of spiky, platinum blond hair. "You need a good lawyer."

That got a reaction out of her. "For?"

"He locked you out of your house, Mel, and took the studio away. How can he do that shit? No warning. No nothin'? He just blindsided you. Not okay. Not legal by California law, either. This is a community property state. You need a lawyer to straighten this out."

Mel let her head sink to her hands. Where had this come from? Stan might not have been the most supportive, loving husband in the world, but he'd never been cruel.

Jackie slapped her hand against the steering wheel. "But it is legal—if you signed a prenup, that is. You didn't . . ."

Oh, but she had. "I did. At the beginning of our marriage. I thought you knew that."

"Then we got trouble."

Mel's smile was watery and grim. "Right here in River City."

"You could always come stay with us, Mel. We have plenty of room." And they did. Jackie and Frank had eight thousand square feet, a guesthouse, four kids, two rabbits, a snake, five dogs, and a tarantula. All on three glorious acres.

Helpless rage sank to the pit of her stomach. "And do what? I have nothing, Jackie. No money. No job skills. I don't suppose you know of anyone hiring chubby one-time ballroom and Latin champions, do you?"

Jackie grunted at her. "You let that shit make you think you're fat. I've only told you a thousand times, Mel. You're not fat. But Stan is a fathead. Yes, that fucker is."

Yes. That fucker was.

"And you don't have to work, honey. It's not like we'd charge you rent. It's not like we're not filthy rich, you know. Why don't you just come to the house—let me baby you for a little while. I'll make pasta alla vodka," she cajoled, mentioning one of Mel's favorite dishes. "In the meantime, maybe Frank can talk to one of his lawyer buddies while they play the stupidest game on earth, golf, and we can figure out a way to squeeze something out of Stan's pocket. Nothing's iron-clad anymore."

She used the corner of the collar on her sweater to wipe more tears from her eyes. "I think I just need to see my dad, Jackie. But I appreciate the offer." No way was she leeching off her rich friend while she hunted for a job at Target and planned Stan's homicide. The fewer people involved in the crime, the less she'd have to worry for their safety.

"I can't believe he put his shit out there on national TV like that. I didn't like Stan from the moment I met you two, and you know it, but I never thought he'd do something this craptacular."

That much was true. Jackie had never hit it off with Stan when they'd met at a function twelve years ago for a children's cancer charity. She hadn't been afraid to share that they'd never do couple things together, but she and Mel had been almost inseparable since.

"Do me a favor, would you?" Mel asked her friend.

"Just ask."

"You'll probably travel in the same circles as Stan, you know, being married to a big television producer. The next time you see Stan at some party or charity event, flip him the bird for me. In fact, use both hands when you do it."

As they pulled into LAX, Jackie growled, "You got it, BFF. Now you do me a favor?"

"Because I have so many to give."

"Don't rule out coming back to L.A. Living with your dad in a retirement village is not the place for a forty-something, beautiful woman who has hips that should have been registered as lethal weapons back in the day. I'm just not a Jersey, The Situation, Snooki kind of girl. New York I can do—there's shopping. But I'm not sure I love you enough to fly to Jersey just so we can grab a hamburger and margaritas at some diner for BFF night." Jackie followed her joke with a warm grin.

Mel wanted to chuckle. She just couldn't. "I'd say I'm hurt, but I'm pretty sure there's nothing left on me to hurt." Mel popped open the door before Jackie could feel any sorrier for her, reaching back in to grab Weezer's leash and her wallet. The first step she took made her teeth clench.

Jackie was out and around the car in seconds, wrapping her slender arms around Mel's neck. The scent of her perfume made more tears sting Mel's eyes. "Make sure you ice that toe—it's broken. It's broken because of that fuckly fucker," she snarled.

"It'll be fine. I've broken worse than a toe before."

"Yeah, but now you're old and fat. Takes longer to heal," Jackie joked.

Mel gave her one more squeeze, forcing back the bitter flow of tears threatening to fall. "Thanks, Jackie. I don't know what I would have done if you hadn't come to check on me."

Jackie leaned down and gave Weezer's big head a scratch. "You take care of Mommy, 'kay, pal?" Then she whipped around, her finger pointed. "And you," she yelled to a man, hovering in the departures area with a camera around his neck. "If you take that picture, you'll find out how yoga gives this woman a strong core." Turning back to Mel, she said, "Hurry up and get out of here before I have to embarrass Frank all over Tinsel Town."

Mel gave her a quick kiss. "I'll call you."

"You'd better."

She gave Weezer's leash a tug, hobbling behind him before turning one last time to wave goodbye to Jackie.

And every single thing in her life as she knew it.

CHAPTER TWO

Six months later . . .

"Myriam Hernandez!" Mel skidded to a halt at the exit door of Leisure Village South's rec center, wincing when her still-sore toe caught on one of the vacant chairs left at table number nine. Her breathing was irregular, and her heart beat a dance in her chest so harsh, she thought it might pound out of her.

She really needed to build her endurance back up—or maybe actually move occasionally. When a seventy-year-old could beat you in a sprint from one end of the room to the other, it was time to reevaluate your mattress time versus your upright and awake time. Taking a gulp of air, she bellowed, "Myriam!"

Myriam's silver head cocked at the sound of Mel's voice for only a moment, clearly considering an escape route, then she made a break to pop open the door and flee her bad behavior.

But Mel was too quick for her. She planted herself in front of the steel door on a stumbling skid, crossing her arms over her chest, and cocking an eyebrow in inquiry.

Myriam gave her a brief guilty look, but her thinning, coral-glossed lips said she knew her sharp tongue was going to have to atone. She narrowed her dark eyes at Mel, preparing her defense. "Who was it? Damn Nancys, the lot of them," she grumbled.

"You mean who nearly knocked me over to tell me your latest madcap entry to the Pillage and Plunder Diaries?"

Myriam grunted, her smile begrudgingly tinted with a hint of admiration. "You're funny."

"You're work." Mel blew a lock of her hair out of her face with a tired breath and fought a smile. Stern. She must not feed the beast in Myriam. If she let Myriam know her razor-sharp tongue and lightning-fast wit made Mel chuckle herself to sleep at night—she was doomed.

Myriam cackled, slapping her on her arm. "I like that you're a 'take no horseshit' gal."

"Good. Then you won't mind giving me no horseshit. You know, sort of as a gift for all the prior horseshit you've given me?" Mel teased.

"C'mon," Myriam cajoled. "Who was it?"

"Who do you *think* it was?"

Myriam shrugged with indifference, hoisting her prim shoulder bag with the butterflies on it to the front of her body in a defensive stance. "I don't know. There're at least a dozen stoolies in this place. Bunch of namby-pambies, they are. Could have been anyone who ratted me out."

Mel hid a smile, one of the first genuine smiles she'd experienced since she'd come to Leisure Village. "So, what you're saying is, you didn't tell just one available male senior, but a dozen, they had wilted winkies and couldn't handle the likes of all your womanliness?"

Her bottom lip curled with indignation. "I did not say 'womanliness.' I said 'my feminine curves,' and I'd bet my Celebrex it was that sissy Norm Peterson. He's always talkin' like it's the size of a blue whale's—those are the biggest winkies on record, by the way"—she made a wide gesture with two hands—"but Mildred Stein says different."

Mel sighed. She just wanted to go home and sit with her dad and Weezer and watch *Yard Crashers*. "So why do you antagonize? If you keep being so cantankerous, I've heard talk about a petition to ban you from all social activities. Tonight it's senior speed dating—last week it was sunset shuffleboard. You can't just whack someone over the head with your shuffleboard stick and expect to get away with it. Do you know how many complaints I got in the suggestion box after that? In fact, it's not even a suggestion box anymore—it's the 'What Myriam Did to Me Today' box."

"Bet no one put their *name* on the suggestions," she sneered, cracking a sinister smile like she was head gangster senior and the resident seniors were all her gangster minions.

Which wasn't totally off the mark. Myriam Hernandez struck fear in the hearts of all Leisure Village seniors. Mel was responsible for policing all of Elder-Landia, and Myriam didn't make walking this beat easy.

"That's because they're all afraid of you." Mel shook her finger under her most difficult senior's nose. "Now, this can't go on, Myriam. I have people to answer to if I have any hope of keeping this job, a job I can't afford to lose." She winced, fighting a tone of desperation.

Trying to keep her private life private was virtually impossible, not just in the Village, but in town—at the Krispy Kreme, at the diner, in the Stop & Shop. The list went on and on.

"Because you're married to a crusty wiener."

Her stomach turned. "Well, technically, I'm not married to him and his crusty wiener anymore." It just felt like she was still married to him because the press wouldn't let her not be married to him since he'd informed her they were getting divorced.

On television.

In an exclusive interview.

After he'd been caught in a picture taken by a random fan, kissing the fabulously rock-hard Yelena with no last name.

At a cheese fest.

"Shoulda taken a cue from me and hit him with the shuffleboard stick. Woulda served him and his Ring Dings right."

Heat flushed Mel's face. Yeah. His Ring Dings definitely needed checking. She'd spent many nights watching reruns of *CSI* in the hopes she'd find the perfect way to kill Stan without getting caught. "Violence isn't the answer, Myriam."

"It is if you want to win at checkers."

"Yeah. Speaking of checkers—what's this about you taking all of the red checkers from the rec center, anyway?"

"Nobody would let me play."

Mel gave Myriam's arm a squeeze to soften the blow. "Nobody lets you play because you get angry and throw things. Now, enough's enough. No more hijinks—no more hitting people with that suitcase you call a purse and absolutely no more mocking some man's"—she leaned in to Myriam and whispered—"penis. Okay? How about we make a deal. You play nice for the next month—not a peep—and I'll pretend I never saw the zillion suggestions to boot you to my boss lady Max. I'll throw them all away." She stuck her hand out, likely making a deal with the devil herself. "Deal?"

Myriam took it and gave it a firm shake. "Fine. But if Norm brags one more time, I'm gonna give it to him but good."

Mel pushed open the door, ushering Myriam out into the warm August air. "No. You're going to ignore him and smile secretly to yourself because you know he really doesn't have a penis the size of a blue whale."

"Really, who does have a penis the size of a blue whale these days? I hear it's rare," a man's voice remarked with a hint of laughter in it from behind Myriam. "Aunt Myriam?"

Mel's eyes moved from Myriam's small frame upward to the larger one blocking out the floodlights of the rec center.

"Ah! There's my boy!" Myriam, usually sour of face unless she was in the height of a prank, softened until she was almost unrecognizable. She introduced him like he was visiting royalty, there was such pride in her voice. "Mel, *this* is my nephew. Honey, meet Mel with the stupid last name and our part-time social director here at the Village. She's helping Maxine. You know the lady who married that sweet piece of booty Campbell Barker?"

Mel covered her mouth with her forearm to keep her snort to herself.

A tall, broad-chested man with a navy blue T-shirt and faded jeans stuck out his hand after sending his aunt a look of warning. "Nice to meet you, Mel with the stupid last name."

Myriam snickered, latching on to her nephew's thickly corded arm.

She gave him her hand. "Do you have a stupid first name?" she inquired sweetly.

"I do." He smiled then—a smile that was dashing. The white of his teeth gleamed, the bronze of his skin glowed. "It's Drew. Drew McPhee."

"A fine Irish name," she commented, refusing to be awed by his thick, chocolaty hair with sun-kissed gold highlights and his light blue eyes in a shade so unusual they held her mesmerized.

"He's only half Irish," Myriam snorted. "The other half of him's Puerto Rican—just like his aunt."

He let go of Mel's hand, and she realized her palm had become sweaty when the humid breeze hit it. "Aunt Myriam's still holding a grudge that my mother married a McPhee instead of a Lopez or a Suarez. Any ez'll do, right, Aunt Myriam?" he said on an indulgent chuckle, squeezing Myriam's hand, then giving it an affectionate pat.

Myriam made a face up at her nephew. Clearly, her discontent with the male population at large extended to family, too. "Selena marrying your father is all-out war as far as I'm concerned. No good Puerto Rican wants to marry an Irishman. None."

"A war that's lasted forty-four years now," Drew said with a wink. "C'mon, Aunt Myriam—Mom's waiting for you to come over and help beat Dad up. It *is* Saturday night, the night when all good Irishmen get a beating from their Puerto Rican sisters-in-law. It's fast becoming a sport."

Myriam reached up and pinched his lean cheek. "You were always funny. Hey, you know, why don't we invite Mel over, too? She's got nothin' better to do on a Saturday night, bein' *divorced* and all. She might have to wait forever to get a date because she's so old, and I'm sure she'd love some of your father's crappy corned beef and 'fart all night long' cabbage. Whaddya say, Mel?"

Mel refused to let slip a horrified gasp and instead lobbed the ball back at the feisty senior. "How do you know I don't have a date, Myriam? Maybe I have some hot stud just waiting on the edge of his seat for me to leave senior speed dating and join him for our secret rendezvous." She fluttered her lashes.

Myriam guffawed as though Mel had just told her she had a date with Robert Pattison. "You don't, either. You hole up at your dad's and lick your wounds every night. You know it. I know it. Every senior from here to eternity in the Village knows it. So instead of crying in your beer, you should just date my Drew," she decided.

Mel dragged the door of the rec center shut and chuckled with a shake of her head. "Oh, I don't think so, Myriam. What if we got married? Then you wouldn't just have a half-Irish, half–Puerto Rican nephew, but a half-Italian, half-Polish, divorced-from-a-Russian niece. I think the world would collapse under all those countries, foreign and otherwise. Besides, I have a hot date with my dad tonight, and Weezer needs to be walked. No one wants Weezer to potty in the house, especially me."

Myriam gave her a mocking smile, but her eyes were kind. "That's fine, dear. You go home to your very exciting life with your dog and your cranky old father, and I'll go home with my handsome nephew without you. See if I ever impose you on any of my family again." She threw up a hand to wave a dismissive goodbye before heading off into the darkness toward the parking lot.

Drew rocked back on his heels, crossing his tanned forearms, which had a thick dusting of hair, over his chest. "So if I said she was a handful and we all try to keep her in line but she's like corralling greased cats, would that make whatever she's done tonight better?" Drew asked with an amused grin that left deep grooves on either side of his mouth.

"What makes you think she's done something?"

"My Aunt Myriam's always doing something, and it's usually not nice."

The corner of her mouth lifted. "I like her spirit."

"We'd like it more if it didn't always involve hand-to-hand combat."

Mel found herself with her second genuine smile of the night on her face. "Okay, that would probably make my job a lot easier, but even with the shuffleboard showdown and tonight's wholly embarrassing poke at the size of Norm Peterson's, ahem, man parts during senior speed dating, she's pretty funny."

"She's a terror."

"That's a fair adjective," she responded, forcing a bland expression. His bigness made her uncomfortably aware—of everything. The way he smelled. The way his jeans molded against the muscles of his thighs before giving way to long calves. The way his eyes crinkled in the corners when he smiled. The way he towered over her, making her five-foot-two frame feel very small. Mel swept around him, making her way down the rec center's entryway.

"Let me walk you to your car."

Mel smiled then frowned at the shiver his voice created. That'd be nice. To be walked to her car by someone as deliciously fine-looking as Drew. But you had to have a car to be walked to. "I'm fine, thanks. I walked."

"You live here?"

Among the scent of mothballs and liniment. Oh, yes, at the ripe, old age of forty, she lived at home. In a retirement village. Like the crazy cat lady, sans cats. "For the moment. With my dad," was her cool reply.

"And Weezer."

"Right. Weezer, too." His steps echoed hers, moving in heavy clunks toward the parking lot.

"How about we give you a lift home?"

"But then you'd be late for corned beef and 'fart all night long' cabbage. Really, I'm fine. I could use the exercise." The moment she said it, she realized she'd given him permission to scan her goodies—which were aplenty—to discover if she really needed crunches.

"Said who?"

Her ex-husband. The tabloids. Every show from here to *Ellen*. "My scale," she remarked dryly.

His eyebrow, a darker brown than his hair, cocked upward. "You're scale is as stupid as your last name—which I didn't get, by the way."

Mel stopped at the end of the sidewalk and looked up at big, handsome, smiling Drew. "It's a mouthful."

"A mouthful's plenty, if you ask me."

Mel blushed hot red. "Cherkasov." She waited while he made the connection between her and Stan.

Yet, he surprised her when he said, "So, Mel Cherkasov, since Myriam can't convince you to come have some dinner with almost total strangers and I can't talk you into a lift back home, will I see you around the Village? I do a lot of shuffling back and forth with Aunt

Myriam. She's the driver from hell—so we avoid letting her do it, if we can."

He'd see her only if it meant there was money to be had in leaving her father's house. It was the only thing that could remotely motivate her to breathe outdoor air or, for that matter, get involved in anything other than a can of chocolate frosting with sprinkles and some salt-and-pepper kettle chips. "Anything can happen."

"Good to know. I hope anything happens again soon." He grinned before taking long strides toward his truck.

Her heart jumped a little only to settle back into her chest with indifference, which was exactly the position it belonged in. "Say good night to Myriam for me," she called, heading in the opposite direction.

That direction being without purpose.

Or meaning.

Or hope.

Or a foolproof plan to murder Stan.

Yet.

Maybe she was missing a crucial detail in all those reruns she'd been watching. That meant more *CSI* reruns and definitely more chocolate frosting.

~᥊~

Drew slid into the truck, turning the key in the ignition and eyeing his aunt in the passenger seat. "So who is she, this Mel?"

Myriam shifted to set her penetrating gaze on him. "Do I hear the voice of interest there, kiddo?"

"You hear the voice of a man who wants to know who all your victims are so he can apologize to them when someone knocks you off."

Myriam's cackling filled the interior of the truck. "I like Mel. She doesn't know I do, but I do. I give her a hard time at every turn, and still, she has a smart aleck answer for everything. That's gutsy. She's had a bad time of it lately. Her ex-husband's some kinda idiot."

He kept his comment noncommittal, while massaging the back of his neck. "Interesting."

"Wanna know why?"

"Do I?"

"Don't answer a question with a question, mister. She's that Stan Cherkasov's ex-wife."

"Nuthin' but a hound dog, I take it?" Drew quoted an Elvis song, one of his favorites.

Myriam scoffed. "In spades. I can't believe you don't know who Stan Cherkasov is."

"I'm stumped."

"Don't you ever watch TV, boy?"

"When do I have the time for TV with my job at the school and Nathan running me ragged all the time with his after-school clubs?"

"He's a smart one, my Natty."

Pride welled in his chest for his son, a genius. Literally. "You'd better not let him hear you call him that. He's decided now that he's twelve, he's Nate or Nathan. Period."

She pursed her lips in displeasure, tucking her chubby fingers into her purse. "He'll be whatever I say he'll be and like it. Now back to Mel. Poor Mel. Her ex-husband's a big time choreographer on that show *Dude, You Can Dance*. A Russian—the swine."

"Dude, what?" What kind of a ridiculous name for a show was that?

"*Dude, You Can Dance*," she reiterated with impatience. "The show where they find kids who can dance, and then they throw them on stage and let the viewing audience judge their performances. It's a big hit in reality TV. Bet if you ask my Natty, he'll know what it is." She gave him a sidelong glance like he was an idiot for not having a clue what she was talking about.

Drew sighed in search of patience. His aunt loved gossip, especially Hollywood gossip. He found himself wondering if Myriam had grilled poor Mel and tried not to visibly cringe at the notion. "I don't watch much TV, Aunt Myriam. I definitely don't watch some dance show."

"That's because you're a buffoon with two left feet and no appreciation for the art," she said, giving him an affectionate slap on the knee. "Anyways, he got caught doing the dirty with another, much younger choreographer from the show named Yelena. She has no last name. Least ways not when they introduce her. Caught by a fan that took a picture of it and sold it to the highest bidder. Poor Mel found out he was cheating on her from those nasty reporters on the television show *Hollywood Scoop* when they showed up like vultures at her failing dance studio."

He remained silent, unable to identify with a situation resembling some scene in a movie—though, he did experience a twist in his gut for the kind of humiliation that must have stirred up for Mel. Instead, he let his mind wander back to Mel's mouth, wide and generous, and her hips, supple and round, while his aunt continued to talk.

"Poor thing. She was all over the TV, her big eyes all wide with surprise when the one reporter asked her how it felt to be left for a younger woman. Even though I just know she tried to hide it, she had no idea. Her husband, that Stan, blindsided her, the jack-off. I don't know the exact details, but I can get 'em, if you want 'em. The story around these parts says he took everything from her—even her little dance studio—and she had to move back here with her dad, Joe Hodge, because she has no money. She's workin' part time in the Village for Maxine. You remember Maxine, don't you? She's got that employment agency—"

"Trophy Jobs Inc., right?" Drew interjected, pulling into his parents' neighborhood, the familiar street lined with oak trees that

would soon change color. He'd seen Maxine here and there when
he'd come to pick up his aunt from the rec center, but he didn't know
a whole lot about her other than she organized the events at the Village his aunt attended and often created chaos at.

"That's the one. Bunch of the retired seniors who had big, important jobs before they retired donate a lot of their time there to help
women who up and get dumped by their old husbands for younger
women because their boobies are saggin'."

Drew barked a laugh. It didn't look like Mel's boobs were sagging
from the quick glimpse he'd tried to snatch while she avoided his
invitation for a ride home. In fact, they'd looked damn fine under her
purple blouse with the white buttons. "So the 'trophy' in Trophy Jobs
has significance?"

"Yep. Maxine called it that because she was a trophy wife who
was dumped and left with shit for Shinola. She's famous in the Village. Everybody loves Max, me included. Nowadays, she helps other
women that were married to jack-offs and have no job skills that're
marketable. Mel's sort of her part-time assistant in the Village."

Drew grunted his disapproval. He had no regard for lazy women
who didn't want to do anything but stay out late club hopping. "So
Maxine has an employment agency for women who've done nothing
but sit on their asses unless they were shopping or ordering room
service? Is her employment agency just a waiting room where they
can have their nails done while they wait to find the next rich man?"
He knew that kind of woman. The kind who loved anything that had
a ridiculous price tag on it just because it said some fancy designer's
name.

Myriam whacked him on his shoulder, making him wince. "Don't
you go sayin' that about Mel. Not in front of me, mister. She's not that
way—not even a little. She's a nice girl, a nice-lookin' girl who can
dance, from what I hear. She used to be a ballroom champion till she

gave it all up to marry that cheater. I love ballroom dancing. Did I ever tell ya about me and your Uncle Ernesto?"

Her smile took on that distant quality it always did when she reminisced about his late uncle. "When we were dating, we used to go over to a place called Dickey's Dance Lounge in Brooklyn and really cut a rug. Boy, my Ernesto could do one helluva cha-cha." She clucked her tongue for emphasis.

He'd heard the story a million times, seen his mother and his aunt fool around in the kitchen together doing a salsa, but he and a dance floor were like sworn enemies. Not gonna happen—no matter how often his mother and his sisters taunted him.

Drew pulled into his parents' driveway and turned off the ignition in his truck. "So she's a professional dancer?" No wonder she couldn't find a job. There wasn't much call for that in Riverbend, New Jersey.

"Yeaaah, buddy," Myriam drawled with a tone that told him he'd better tread lightly when referring to her precious Mel. "A former champion ballroom dancer. Quit sayin' it like she's got the bubonic plague. She was one hot piece o' work back in her day, and nobody as nice as Mel deserves to be dumped and left with nothing. 'Specially seein' as she's stuck with the crazy bunch of seniors like we have at the Village."

"Excluding yourself from that equation, I suppose."

"Damn right, I'm excluded. I'm ornery, not crazy," she twittered with a grin full of dentures and mischief.

Drew jumped out and made his way to Myriam's side of the car. He opened the door, his curiosity over the hot Mel piqued. "How could he leave her with nothing? Didn't the divorce laws protect her?" Christ knew they'd protected his ex-wife. Those laws took a huge chunk of his paycheck to pay her alimony, which she didn't exactly use for her greater good.

"She signed one of those prenups everyone's always talking about gettin' when you marry somebody rich. And to think, they'd been married for something like twenty years. I tell ya this, kiddo. If I ever see him, I'll spit on him and his fancy girlfriend Yela-whoever."

Drew gave her his arm and helped her out of the car. "Wow. Where'd all this love for Mel come from? You don't like anyone, Aunt Myriam. Better not let Dad hear you all warm and fuzzy like this over some stranger. He's been in the family for almost forty-four years, and he still gets no respect. He'll get jealous."

Myriam snorted in the darkening night while they made their way up the slate walkway to his parents' front door, lined with colorful mums just waiting to bloom. "Your dad's an old coot. And I like Mel. She's a sassy-mouth. I like anyone who won't take my crap."

Yeah. Even he had to admit, he admired a woman who could handle his aunt.

His son, Nate, threw the front door open to reveal the typical swarm of family that gathered. Saturday night was a tradition at the McPhee household, one Drew hated to own up to treasuring but did nonetheless.

Saturdays meant wall-to-wall kids from toddlers to teens. It meant his three sisters and their spouses all crowded into his mother's kitchen for corned beef and enchiladas with flan for dessert. It meant Tito Puente with some Irish folk music in the mix.

It meant family. How the two had ever managed to blend such completely different cultures was often a topic of conversation and much laughter.

"There's my Natty," Myriam cooed, holding out her arms to him.

Nate, almost five-five now, rolled his eyes, but reluctantly let his great aunt envelop him in a hug. Myriam kissed him on the top of his dark head before plowing toward the kitchen to begin her sarcastic inspection of the night's feast.

Nate knocked knuckles with Drew, who gave his son a grin of affection. "Hey, Dad. I found an awesome website about quantum physics."

His son's genius left him ever in awe. "Quantum physics, huh? I don't think I've ever been as excited as I am right now," he teased. He and Nate had an understanding. Nate could be as smart as he wanted to as long as he didn't expect Drew to match his IQ or his interest in everything Mensa.

Drew didn't pretend to get most of what interested his son, and Nate was okay with that. They found other things to do with each other.

Nate laughed, his blue eyes so like his mother's, giving Drew the amused-bored look he'd perfected since he'd turned twelve and had gone purposefully aloof.

Drew clapped Nate on the shoulder. "Hey, you got your laptop?"

"I didn't find a new website on quantum physics by magic." Nate snickered.

"Can you look something up for me?"

"Sure."

"You ever heard of a show called *Dude . . .* something?"

Nate made a face. "You mean *Dude, You Can Dance*?"

Drew shrugged with an outward show of indifference, hoping Nate wouldn't question his interest in something so damn girlie. "Yeah, that's it. I promised Aunt Myriam I'd look it up."

Nate nodded, moving his way through the throng of people to a corner of the living room. His lanky body folded into a corner chair by the arched windows in the dining area and he reached equally lanky fingers out to grab his laptop. "Aunt Myriam loves *Dude, You Can Dance*. So does Gram. Most girls do."

Drew watched his son type the words in on Google and caught a quick glimpse of a picture of Mel with those wide eyes of surprise his aunt had mentioned before Nate clicked on the website for the show.

What a shitty way to find out your spouse had been unfaithful. Again, there was a familiar sting of understanding for Mel in his gut.

"What do you want to look at, Dad?" Nate's sharp eyes lanced his.

What the hell had Aunt Myriam said Mel's ex-husband's name was? "Who's the guy that runs the show? Do you know?"

"Stan something," Nate replied, clicking on the choreographer's name. His picture appeared along with a loud blast of the show's theme song.

"Turn that down!" Drew ordered, his eyes scanning the crowded room. All he needed was for his meddling family to find out he had just a little interest in a woman, and it would be on. They'd never let up. Especially his sisters.

But it was too late.

Myriam pinched his sides from behind and snorted with laughter. "She's a looker, that Mel. Knew you were interested."

Yeah. She was interesting.

And just recently divorced in a public and ugly way.

Which made her a little less interesting.

Unless you counted her mouth and her hips.

Those remained interesting.

In fact, they left him all shook up.

CHAPTER THREE

"Hey, Pop Rocks. How was senior speed dating?"

Mel flopped on her dad's rust-and-red-plaid couch with a deep groan. "Not so speedy." Weezer sauntered over from his bed in the corner to impose his big head onto her lap. She absently rubbed his ears, loving their soothing velvety softness. Jake hopped up on the couch and put his paws on her, his eyes begging for attention.

Her father chuckled. "Well, we're old. Speed's not on our résumés anymore. That cranky Myriam give ya more trouble?"

Thinking of Myriam reminded Mel of her rakishly handsome nephew Drew. And then she stopped herself from thinking about him because that would only lead to trouble.

Mel rolled her head from side to side to ease the mounting tension in her neck. "Myriam is the very definition of trouble, but she brings with her a good cardio workout. You should've come. You would have had fun."

Her dad grinned from his La-Z-Boy, a copy of *The Divorced Woman's Guide to Healing* in his lap. Joe propped his glasses at the end of his nose. "I can't show off all my best moves in front of my kid. You don't wanna hear your old pop lay a line on a woman, do ya?"

Mel winced and chuckled, planting a kiss on Jake's head, then rose to head to her father's small kitchen. "Okay. Stop there. You're right. I don't want to hear you make the moves on some poor, unsuspecting seventy-year-old."

"Hey," he called from the living room. "You're not gonna eat chocolate frosting for dinner tonight, are you, young lady?"

"Actually, I was considering vanilla. You know, because it's made with a bean and beans are technically vegetables," she halfheartedly joked, pulling the can from the fridge.

Joe was suddenly in the kitchen, filling it up with his large frame, his thick hands buried in the tops of his suspenders. "That's funny. Gimme that." He grabbed at the can of frosting, successfully stealing it from her grip. "Now before you go wallowin' like a pig in mud in that can full of sugar, you got a phone call while you were out."

Mel grinned, swiping at his hands to make him give the can up. "Jackie?" She was the only person who called her lately. Ever. The few friends she and Stan had made as a couple were now Stan and Yelena No Last Name's friends.

Bitter. She was just a little bitter about that.

Joe held the can high, daring her to jump for it, a game they'd often played when she was younger and trying to develop strength in her legs. "Nope. Maxine."

Her steam ran out and she sank to the floor in a pile that left her knees creaking. Mel got the feeling Maxine was lying in wait for her to come to her senses and allow Maxine to preach her divorced words of wisdom.

Maxine had minions, too. Minions Mel had mentally dubbed the Hare Krishna's of Single, banging on their tambourines while they spread messages of self-love and empowerment. "She say why?"

Her father pitched the frosting over her head and into the garbage with a remarkably deft shot for someone who was seventy-two. "She said you gotta meet her tomorrow at Trophy, nine o'clock sharp. Which means no sugar for you or you'll be up all night with the jitters. Can't have that. I made you a nice salad and some pasta. Just like your mom used to cook. No more junk or you'll rot your teeth."

"My teeth will survive. I had them all capped at Stan's request. My butt, on the other hand, probably could use less frosting."

Joe chucked her under the chin. "You knock that off. I won't have you wanderin' around the house callin' yourself fat anymore. You're not fat. You're beautiful. No daughter of Joe Hodge can be anything but. Just like your Mama was. Now quit buyin' into all that crap Stan the Ballerina fed you. What does he know about beautiful when he's porkin' a woman who looks like the skeleton I hang on my door at Halloween?"

"Dad!" Her father and the word "porking" were too much after tonight and all the seniors' sexual innuendo she'd heard while she'd drifted from table to table. Who knew you could utilize a walker like *that*?

Joe's face held no apology when he shook his head at her, the wrinkles in his face deepening. "It's true. I don't know who you are anymore, little girl, but you ain't the kid I sent off to New York all those years ago who told me she was going to pursue her dream whether I liked it or not. Even after your mother and me argued with you about it for weeks before you left. Remember that?"

Mel's eyes fell to the floor in self-disgust. No. She wasn't even a mere shadow of the girl he'd sent off to New York to audition for a Broadway play she couldn't even remember the name of now. This was somewhere Mel didn't want to go. The place called "Who Mel Used To Be."

Her father grabbed for her, pulling her into a bear hug and kissing the top of her head. She buried her nose in his shoulder, inhaling the scent of Old Spice and spaghetti.

"Hold your head up, meat loaf. I'm tired of seein' you staring at the floor all the time. You got nothin' to be ashamed of, Mellow-Yellow. You were a good wife to that shit. He was a bad husband. Stop beating yourself up about it by abusing your body and eating all that garbage."

Mel tipped her head up, tears glimmering in her eyes. "Have you been going to some sort of therapy I don't know about, or did you get that from the divorce books you've been reading?"

Joe chuckled and ran his knuckles over her scalp. "I'm not above watching those doctors on TV or reading a book so I can find a way to help my kid. You're eating all that garbage because you're depressed. That's gotta stop, and you have to get to bed at a decent hour tonight instead of sitting up and watching *Hoarders* all night long. You're not getting enough sleep. You're not eatin' right. You're not dancing. You're worrying me, Mel."

She gave him a squeeze and a pat on his broad back. "Don't worry, Dad. Please. I promise my will to live will come back. I'm just not sure when that'll be," she joked.

Though these days, since her life had changed so dramatically, she wasn't sure that was really true. She'd been drifting since she'd arrived in New Jersey—going through the motions because she wanted everything to be all right again.

It just wasn't. She had a hole in her soul and nothing to fill it up with.

She missed her rundown studio. She missed the children who'd attended her dance classes. She missed her house and her bathroom with the antique claw-foot tub. She missed the ballet barre Stan had installed in their basement.

She missed.

Oddly, in all of the things she missed, Stan didn't so much factor into the missing she was doing as of late. Stan and his lies were something she definitely didn't miss.

So many lies. Lies she'd so foolishly bought. She no longer knew when he'd begun to lie or if he'd always lied and she'd just been too stupid to know. The rumors were endless, and while it didn't take away the sting of his public betrayal, it made missing him an item at the bottom of her list.

"Listen to your pop. Being the newly informed guy I am, I've learned something about your divorce, and not just from TV and a book. From Maxine, too."

Mel pushed away from him, placing her hands on her hips. Maxine . . . the Zen to all things divorced. If you listened to her father, Maxine's ex-trophy wife advice to divorced women was considered on par with the soothing chants of Tibetan monks.

Just the idea that she'd been labeled an ex-trophy wife by the press made her want to dig a hole and climb in. The label implied she'd never done anything but shop and drip diamonds, which was totally untrue. Sure, she'd had some diamonds and credit cards with no limit, but most of her time had been dedicated to teaching her kids to dance and staying out of Stan's critical line of fire.

"Oh, more Maxine insight. I'm on tenterhooks." At her father's request, when Maxine had hired Mel part time in the Village, she'd also given her the Trophy Job Employment Agency pitch.

A pitch filled with uplifting messages and words Mel would rather gag on than utilize. The divorce journal being high on her list of gag-worthy suggestions. Writing was never her thing—all her creativity flowed through her limbs—not a pen and some paper filled up with emotions she didn't understand well enough to describe in meaningless adjectives. In fact, she'd come close to failing English her junior year.

Joe's gray eyebrow rose in disapproval. "Maxine knows where you are because she's been there, too. I remember what she was like when she first moved here, and she was just like you. Don't put her down for doing something about it. She scooped—"

"Poop. Jake's poop. Big poop. I remember." Mel heard the pride in her dad's voice when he spoke of Maxine. He made her sound like she'd saved the world in her Donna Karan dresses and Louboutins instead of just surviving an ugly divorce.

Joe ignored her pettiness. "I've learned that you should be sad your marriage is over. Especially after the way it ended, so sudden and all. But you should have lots of other things that fill you up and make you happy, sweet face. Things that help you get through the sad. I've figured out, you don't have them. All you had was Twinkle Toes—he was your priority, and that's a cryin' shame."

Her throat clenched tight. That wasn't entirely true. "I had the studio, and the kids . . ."

"Yep—all owned by that shit of an ex of yours. He pulled all the strings, and he only let you keep the studio because it looked good in the press for his wife to teach kids people considered underprivileged. But he complained about it all the time, didn't he? No, don't answer. I know he did. When he decided he didn't want you to have those things anymore because he wanted out for a younger chippie, he yanked the rug from under you and took it all away. You let him have all that control. Not a good thing in this day and age."

Mel sank to the captain's-style kitchen chairs, resting her elbows on the table. If Stan having all the control meant he had his business manager, Jerry, handle everything financial, then, yes, he'd been in control. If never making it her business to know what that included was at best naïve, then stupid her.

Yet in all the years they were married, Stan had never withheld money—he'd never threatened to take away her credit cards because she'd overspent. Though to her credit, she wasn't much of a shopper to begin with. Her studio had been her passion.

"I think you should stop watching all those talk shows. It's easy for Oprah to say, 'Have your own checking account apart from your spouses, ladies' because Oprah probably owns at least ten financial institutions. It wasn't like Stan would have told me I couldn't. I just didn't feel like I needed control of our finances because Stan never, ever made money an issue."

And he hadn't, which made leaving her with nothing so much more painful. She'd been a good wife—supportive, low maintenance. A real Suzy Sunshine in a world where wives of rich men spent more on Botox injections than they did on a year's worth of groceries.

"Don't you defend him, young lady! I think you don't like hearin' the truth, but that's too bad. Twinkle Toes stiffed you the first opportunity he could." He shook his stout finger at her.

"I . . ." Yeah. Stan had stiffed her. There was no defense she could summon for the truth. No matter how good he'd been to her in their marriage. In the end, he wasn't living with her father in a two-bedroom retirement home.

Joe gave her a pointed look. "Exactly. So now you have to go out and get your own life, Mel—and your own checking account—and start all over, but in the process, I don't want to see you mopin' around. You never leave the house unless you have to walk Weez or help Maxine at the rec center. I know it's been tough trying to find a full-time job in this economy with no work skills, and I know you and Maxine have been lookin', but there are other things you could do in between—things you enjoy."

She had agreed to let Maxine do some job searches for her and make inquiries into some college courses she might be able to take in order to find a job. God, being broke sucked, and even if she had money, she was still a little fuzzy on how to handle it without Stan's accountant.

That was another reason she didn't want to attend any of the group meetings they held at Trophy Jobs, because the titles alone for each self-empowerment class made her feel pathetically naïve.

"Discover Is the Name of a Credit Card—Not a Shopping Journey: How to Establish Credit in Your Newly Single Life Without Falling into the High-Interest Trap."

"I don't have any money to spare to enjoy anything right now, Dad. I have just enough to buy Weezer's food and contribute for some groceries."

Clearly, her Father was accepting no excuses. "You don't need money to take a walk in the animal park. You don't need money to go to those singles get-togethers they have at the VFW hall every month. You don't need money to dance. But you don't dance anymore, Mel. I remember when I used to have to climb over you to get past you doing all those stretches in the living room of our old house. I haven't seen a single stretch since you got here. Won't you lose all those pretzel moves you do, if you don't keep those muscles limber?"

Who cared if her muscles stayed limber? She had no students to be limber for. So her muscles could just eff off. "Listen, Mr. Answer for Everything, I'm still trying to adjust to not being half of a couple. Almost all my adult life I've been half of a couple. I don't know how to be any other way. It's kind of taken the wind out of me, and somewhere along the way, I can't find a reason to dance, okay? And not a chance I'm going to some singles get-together."

Her father went to the fridge, pulling out a plate he'd covered in cling wrap. "That's part of the problem. You're not supposed to be half of anything. You have to be a whole you all by yourself." Joe dropped the plate in the microwave and pressed some buttons.

"I think you should quit hanging around Maxine." *Please, please, please quit hanging around Maxine.*

"I think you should quit bein' resentful because she has it together and you don't," he retorted with a stern tone and a frown.

Ow. Yet, there was a niggle of truth to what he said, and she found herself resenting the hell out of it. She'd heard all the stories about how Maxine had one-upped her ex-husband and begun her employment agency. She was legend here in the Village, and if Mel was honest with herself, a nice lady and easy to work for. "I'm sorry, Dad. I'm being petty."

"You sure are," he agreed, dropping the plate of soggy noodles slathered in red sauce in front of her. "Now eat something decent for a change, or you'll hurt my sensitive feelings. I'll get your salad."

Mel twirled her fork in the pasta and, while her father wasn't looking, held it under the table for Jake, and then Weezer.

You couldn't drown your sorrows properly in soggy pasta—even when it was made with love and the wish for you to hurry up and heal.

Chocolate frosting made everything almost bearable.

That it had so generously given her back the ten pounds she'd been down just before her divorce was neither here nor there.

Who cared what her ass looked like?

～ℓ～

Maxine Barker smiled her perky, meant to inspire motivation smile at Mel as she made her way across the tiled floor of Trophy Jobs Inc. "Mel! I'm so glad you came. I love that color on you." She pointed to the deep turquoise of Mel's sadly pilling sweater. "It's starting to get chilly enough for a sweater. Can you believe it's this cool on the last day of August?"

Mel contemplated Maxine, trying to remember her father was her biggest fan, but was hesitant to show anything in the way of enthusiasm for fear Maxine would take it as a sign she was an all-systems-after-divorce-therapy go. "It's definitely cooling off."

Max hitched her jaw to the left, putting a relaxed hand in the pocket of her tailored taupe slacks. "Let's go talk in my office."

Without waiting for an answer, she took confident strides toward a door along a white hallway strung with pictures of seniors from the Village who donated their time to Trophy.

One plaque in particular made Mel pause momentarily to stifle a laugh at the absurdity of it all. It had a cracked tiara on it and read "Suck it up, Princess."

Max ushered Mel in, waving her hand at a pair of leather chairs. One was filled by a woman with wavy auburn hair and a chubby baby in blue overalls slung over her shoulder. On the couch positioned at the other side of the room sat the most perfect female Mel had ever seen—and coming from L.A., she'd seen.

"Mel? This is Frankie Antonakas, her baby Nikos Junior, and Jasmine Jones. Both Trophy Jobs success stories."

Well and fuck. This was one of those ambush interventions, and she'd walked right into it like someone had told her there was a case of Suzy Q's in Maxine's office.

Mel didn't know what to do. Because she loved her father, she didn't want to be rude to these women. She also didn't want to be harpooned by the divorce spear and left to bleed out on the shore while they chanted their speeches of empowerment and danced around her fat ass in a circle.

"You want me to block the door while you run interference, Frankie?" the beautifully surreal creature named Jasmine asked. "She doesn't look like the kind who'd take out a woman with a baby, but you just never know." Her bright red lips, the perfect color to compliment her creamy features, curved into an amused smile.

Frankie tipped her head full of gorgeous auburn hair back and laughed, stirring the baby who stuck a thumb in his mouth and nuzzled against her neck. "Come sit down, Mel. What you suspect is right. We're here to help. All you have to do is listen. If you don't like what you hear, you can go back to sulking and pouting. We've all done it. It was all kinds of awesome. Well, except for the smell. I thank God every day Max made me finally shower." The women all giggled together while Mel frowned, perplexed by her comment.

Maxine sat behind her desk and motioned for Mel to sit, too. The clink of Maxine's bangle bracelets sang in the air that had become suddenly oppressive. "Sit down, Mel, and relax. I know you're reluctant to participate in anything, much less listen to a bunch of women who you think want to advise you on how to Krazy Glue your life back together, but that's not the only reason I asked you to come."

Mel slid into her chair, her glace at Max wary. Maxine was her boss. She didn't have much of a choice but to sit and listen if she hoped to buy Weezer more food. Saint Bernard's ate buttloads of food. "Does it have to do with the Village and the rec center?"

"It's better," Max declared, flashing Mel another brilliant smile and folding her hands on top of the files on her desk.

Well, what could be better than herding seniors with attitude on a part-time basis? "Okay . . ."

Frankie rolled her eyes while laughter slid from her lips. "Quit looking like we just invited you to join our coven. Sit down and at least listen. If you don't like what you hear, then you can go home to Joe and be honest when you tell him you at least heard our shtick, okay?"

"But the catch is, you absolutely have to listen," Jasmine added, uncrossing her graceful legs and straightening the multicolored scarf she had draped elegantly over her shoulder.

"What exactly am I listening to?"

"The speech I give all ex-trophy wives before I hook them up with potential employers," Max said.

Mel's spine stiffened. "I hate that label. Ex-trophy wife," Mel muttered. It implied she'd married Stan for all the wrong reasons—like money reasons. Absolutely untrue.

Had she been blown away by his interest in her? Definitely. Had she fallen madly in love with her Svengali-like mentor? Unequivocally. Had she devoted her every waking moment to him? Yes. Had he asked her to? She couldn't remember. It had just happened. Still, the term made her squirm in her chair.

"Well, that's unfortunate," Jasmine interjected with a drawl, pushing her long blond hair from her face. "But that's what you are.

A beautiful woman who married her much older, very rich husband at a tender age and got ditched when her goodies got stale. Own it."

"I didn't marry Stan for his money." She said that a lot lately—in defensive mode. She'd said it to the seniors, the pet store manager, and the drive-thru cashier at Wendy's when she was getting a chocolate Frosty with the change she'd found in her father's couch cushions.

Jasmine waved a hand with perfectly polished nails in the air. "Whatever. Most of us truly fell in love. Doesn't change what society calls you. Though, now I'm an ex-trophy wife slash cougar. Again, own it." Jasmine's smile held no malice—she was simply a straight shooter. For someone who hadn't been able to scream her rage at Stan while she hunted him down with her sledgehammer and night-vision goggles, Mel admired that trait.

Max waved a finger of admonishment at Jasmine, her hair catching the light from the window when she shook her head. "Easy on the newb until we break her in. Anyway, it's like I said. I have a speech I give before I hook you up with a potential employer, and tag, you're it."

Mel was remiss in hearing the part about potential employers and instead focused on the speech. "The speech?"

"Yes. The one where I give you a packet with all sorts of information in it that you'll make faces about behind my back before you consider pitching it in the garbage. The packet includes, among other things, a divorce journal—typical and cliché, but believe it or not, a way to really vent instead of letting things build up. It's also the speech about not letting this disgusting piece of shit you were married to own the rest of your life by suppressing your reasons to live."

Mel's eyes widened at Max. Now, ex-husband bashing she could probably get on board with. Maybe these were the women to trust with the Hefty bags and bleach after she killed Stan in the most heinous manner she could concoct.

Max winked a lovely green, perfectly coal-lined eye in response.

"Yes. I called him a disgusting piece of shit. It's unprofessional and only allowed once in the 'speech' conversation. After that, we go all adult on you and tell you not to hold grudges because they're unhealthy."

"I love the 'piece of shit' part of the speech," Jasmine murmured her delight, her eyes twinkling.

"Nah, my favorite part's the part where you find a way to beat down the piece of shit by being self-sufficient and confident all by your lonesome. Sometimes, Max swears in that portion. I love to hear her say the word 'fuck'—it cracks me up," Frankie snickered, running soothing hands over Nikos Junior's back.

Mel's head had been sinking into her chest with disinterest until she caught sight of Frankie's face in full view. "You're—"

"Mitch in the Kitchen's ex-wife. That's me." She grinned like she wasn't at all displeased by Mel's recognition.

"I loved his show . . ." Mel mumbled, then caught herself. Frankie's freak-out on Mitch's show was infamous. There were YouTube spoofs on it, *Saturday Night Live* had had a field day with it, and the late-night talk show hosts had used her for fodder for months afterward. Instantly, she regretted her words. "Damn, that's probably not appropriate. I'm sorry. How rude of me."

"Don't be sorry, Mel. Just be glad to know you can find your way out of tabloid hell with me as your guide." Frankie rose, slender in her skinny jeans and layered tank tops, to pass the baby to Jasmine, who cooed her appreciation and ran her nose along the baby's cheek, inhaling his scent.

Frankie sat back down and faced Mel, her warm eyes and smile reassuring. "Here's the score. Your husband had the upper hand when you were married. You did whatever he wanted, gave him every last fiber of your being, accepted whatever explanation he offered, and then he took a dump on you by taking the one thing you really love, your dance studio. In one way or another, we've all been through it and come out the other end realizing it was never about the cars and the jewelry or the limitless credit cards we had. It was about not being able to breathe on our own when we lost it all. It's sad and maddening all at once."

Mel looked down at her feet covered in her old black ballet slippers with shame in her eyes, her heart tightening in her chest. "That's it," she choked, refusing to cry in front of strangers. "I don't know how to breathe anymore. I can't get comfortable in my own skin. Everything feels unfamiliar." Everything, everything.

"That's because Stan owned your skin, darling. But he doesn't anymore. He chose to find new skin," Jasmine pointed out, cradling Frankie's little boy against her perfect breasts. "Look, we all know what it is to suffer through a high-profile divorce, Frankie being the expert here. We all also know what it's like to be tossed to the curb and lose everything. Your friends, your house, your clothes, your world. We know what it's like to have to start over with nothing while trying to understand some of the most basic of life's lessons like balancing a checkbook and interest rates on a credit card. It's like wandering around in a foreign country where the countrymen don't speak Gucci."

Mel felt her lip tremble. She hated that words of fear were tumbling from her lips, but there they were—tumbling in an outpouring of pathetic. "I went straight from my parents to marriage with Stan. I don't know the first thing about surviving on my own. Everything was handled either by Stan or his accountants, business managers, maids, and drivers. I feel like an idiot." *Nay. You define "idiot."* She fought a groan.

Max snorted from behind her desk. "I get it. Are you ready for this? When I was in the middle of my divorce and living with my mother, I'd finally made enough money to contribute to the groceries. She took me to Walmart. I actually hadn't been in a place where you could buy things at discount in almost as many years as I was married. How's that for pathetically sheltered? I was pitiful. Look, I know you think all the gurulike stuff I spout is silly. You're not some trendsetter there. I have all sorts of analogies and euphemisms for being an ex-pampered princess that are laughable. I had oodles of time to think while I job-hunted and took the place of one senior or another at the Village, teaching classes at the rec center. But if you at least give them a look, I think Jasmine and Frankie can tell you from personal experience, they work."

Frankie nodded, twisting a strand of her hair around her finger in thoughtful contemplation. "I hated Maxine's hokey advice—at first. But she taught me to suck it up. She made me shower. She helped me get a job. She encouraged me to come to the meetings here at Trophy where I met Jasmine, where I learned how to stand on my own two feet. I had no job skills other than being Mitch's bitch. No one in the industry would hire me because Mitch blackballed me. If it wasn't for Maxine, I'd still be at my Aunt Gail's, buried under the covers."

"And you'd really smell," Max said on a chuckle.

Frankie nodded. "Yeah. There's that."

"Is your aunt Gail Lumley?" Mel asked. She remembered Gail backing up her dad when he talked about the kind of help Maxine offered, but she'd blown her off because she wasn't receptive to anything but a bag of salt-and-pepper kettle chips at the time.

"That's her."

Mel felt a smile lift her lips. "I like her. She's pretty feisty."

"Indeed, she is," Frankie confirmed. "She's also who called Max to intervene. Just like your dad called us. He wants to help, Mel. So do we. So there's really only one question, Mel—are you ready to suck it up and take back your life by learning all the things you would have if you'd lived on your own and found out exactly who Melina Cherkasov was before you devoted your life to that jerk?"

Without warning, tears, hot and stinging welled in her eyes again. She made a frustrated swipe at them. "Maybe."

"Well, it's time you figure it out, Mel," Max said, only this time it was without the cajoling warmth in her tone, which was replaced with a sharper edge.

"But it's only been six months . . ." Which was a perfectly good excuse. Drowning your pain in junk food because you were divorced surely had a longer grace period.

Jasmine sighed, shifting on the couch. "It's not like we're asking you to hurry up and sleep with someone. We're asking you to get off your ass and get back in the game. We don't just mean earning a living either. Do you know what you like to do aside from dance? Maybe you like to spelunk, and you wouldn't know it because you never took the time to figure it out. Those six months you've been mourning that dick are six months you can't get back. I don't know about you, but Stan the Dancing Man wasn't worth six minutes of your life let alone half a year."

Yeah. A small crack in Mel's reluctance rippled inside her. "So what do I have to do? Is there a ritual ex-princess hazing?"

Max shot Mel a sympathetic look. "Your hazing began when you went to your studio and found out it was locked because Stan didn't want you to have it anymore, honey. When he took you from the kids who so obviously loved you. You've been hazed enough, in my opinion, and of all of us, you at least began to try and get it together more quickly than we did. You might be filling the gaping hole of your depression with junk food, but you multitasked and did it while you looked for a job. At least it wasn't booze and cheap sex. Those are messy interventions."

She and booze had never worked well together. Too much to drink made her either cry or sing. Both of which no one wanted to endure. "Is there some type of award or maybe a merit badge for my chaste nature and sober state?"

Max's laughter tinkled. "No awards. Your reward is you haven't slid all the way down the slope. I thank God at the very least I didn't have to drag you out of bed like I did Frankie. So here's the score. Take this." She held out a manila envelope in Mel's direction. "Look at it. Mock. Look at it again when you're past rolling on the floor in fits of laughter. In the meantime, I have good news for you."

Mel took the envelope with a shaky hand. Max was right. She didn't want it, and if some of the crazy catchphrases her father had picked up from Maxine were included in the divorce packet, she would indeed mock. "Thank you. So the good news?"

Max beamed. "You have an interview for a full-time job!"

Frankie and Jasmine clapped their hands.

But Mel was instantly skeptical. "People in Riverbend are hiring women who can spin without getting dizzy?" There really was a job for everyone.

"I saw your old competition videos on YouTube. You were truly beautiful to watch, Mel, and your partner, Neil Whatever, from *Celebrity Ballroom*—hellooooo," Frankie commented with a sigh of exaggerated lust. "You were both so sexy at such a young age. Very sultry. Maybe sometime you can teach me how to roll my hips like that. I'm sure Nikos would appreciate it."

"Were." "Was." All words that contributed to her *now*. Neil was part of her was. They'd kept in touch over the years and made a point of seeing each other whenever possible, but his job and her life with Stan didn't always allow them the kind of time she wished they had together. Still, he would always be one of her best friends.

Max sighed just as breathy before saying, "Actually, yes. You have an interview at Westmeyer."

Mel was taken aback. "The private school for boys who're Mensa candidates?"

Max grinned. "That's the one. God, I can't tell you what it's like to be around all those little geniuses. I feel like a total idiot. In fact, I *am* an idiot compared to them, but I can't wait until you meet Dean Keller."

Mel gave her a confused look. "Is this a private lesson? Does the dean want to learn how to samba?" She didn't want to dance. Strike that. She didn't want to move. She'd only agreed to Waltzing Wednesdays at the Village because she needed the money. As it stood, as the condition of her body stood, she was better off working at a Container Store.

"He might after he sees your hips in action," Jasmine snorted.

Maxine laughed. "No. Westmeyer has a tradition. All the boys must learn to ballroom dance to hone their sorely lacking social skills. Most of the boys who attend Westmeyer are introverts with their noses always buried in a book. They don't work well with others and are typically more awkward than your usual tween with girls. As you know, twelve and up is an age of *discovery*."

"Oh, I love it!" Jasmine snarfed. "Hormonal smart kids who can waltz."

"The tradition goes back as far as the early forties and is attributed to the woman who opened the school—Leona Westmeyer. Her love of ballroom dancing and the traditional, in particular, was what led her to insist the boys learn how to dance. According to Dean Keller, the boys' reluctance to socialize with anything other than a petri dish worried her enough that she mandated they all learn to dance and have fun. Lightening up being the key goal here. Back in those days, ballroom dancing was common. Everyone knew how to dance. Its resurgence on TV seems to please Dean Keller."

"Leona *Smith* Westmeyer?" Mel asked.

Max looked down at her papers then nodded. "Yep. You know her?"

Mel clutched her hands in front of her, trying to remember what she knew of Leona's history. "I know of her. She's legendary in American smooth ballroom dancing. I had no idea she had a school for boys, let alone one for geniuses."

"Her son was one, and he was who inspired her to open the school."

"So what good does it do for me to teach boys to dance with one another?" She didn't want to dance. God, she really didn't.

"They have a big dance in December just before Christmas break, and then again in the spring with an all-girls private school—Thurston's the name, I believe. Anyway, Westmeyer's dance instructor retired at the beginning of this school year. Westmeyer begins earlier than public schools to allow for the heavy load of classes those boys endure. They've had a lot of trouble replacing the last teacher. It would seem there aren't many ballroom teachers in Riverbend—you're it."

Lucky, lucky boys. "But what about the Village classes?"

"I'd appreciate you staying for a while at the Village—just on Wednesdays. You're going to be hard to replace there, but I have someone in mind to take over your other duties."

"But I haven't danced in . . ."

"In six months. I know," Max confirmed. "Your father told me. But it's your best skill and the one that's most marketable. This is a helluva lucky break to find something so well suited to you, especially considering it's not a common profession. So if you want a job that's full time and has bennies, dust off your leotards and suck it up." Max smiled before glancing at her wristwatch. "And now we have to get going—you have an interview to get to."

Mel clutched the envelope under her arm, her knees suddenly weak with fear. She'd never been on an interview. "I don't . . . I mean . . ."

"You've never been on an interview. I know. Me neither before I was divorced, but I can tell you this, I got really good at begging. Just ask the manager of the Cluck-Cluck Palace, and then thank God I nabbed you an interview doing something you love instead of one that involves the mindless task of shredding cheese." Max grabbed her purse and a light jacket.

"Don't panic, Mel," Frankie soothed, rising to give her arm a squeeze. "You'll be fine. By the way, take my number, Jasmine's, too, in case you ever want to talk. The three of us meet at my husband's diner, Greek Meets Eat, once a week on Tuesdays, if you're up to grabbing meat loaf and some coffee. Drop by."

Mel took the slip of paper from Frankie and shoved it into the pocket of her skirt. Frankie's husband. She'd remarried after that fiasco? Talk about the will to trust. No way was Mel ever getting married again. "Thank you . . ." She gave Frankie a faint smile of gratitude, trying to hide her curiosity about Frankie's husband.

Jasmine handed the baby back to Frankie and reached out to smooth Mel's rumpled sweater, then took hold of Mel's shoulders and turned her toward the door of Max's office. "Come hangout with us on Tuesday. You won't regret the diner's meat loaf. Now, go get 'em, tiger. Grrrrr."

Mel sucked in a breath of air and followed Max out the door with trembling legs.

She rooted through her purse, praying she'd remembered to throw a couple of Hostess CupCakes in it before she'd left for Trophy.

Instead, she came up with a Ziploc bag full of carrots and celery with a note taped to it.

It had a smiley face on it and read,

Sugar rots your teeth, SpaghettiOs.

Love,
Dad

Shiny.
Oh, and grrrrr.

CHAPTER FOUR

Dear Divorce Journal,

Stupid. That's what this divorce journal is. How do you like that, Maxine Barker? Huh? Oh, and suck this, *Princess*.

"I hate to say it, but this looks like Frankenstein's summer house," Mel remarked as she and Max drove toward the imposing brick structure of Westmeyer on her first official day as ballroom instructor.

Max's laughter filled her car. "It is kind of gloomy, but the foliage is gorgeous, don't you think? I love when the trees begin to turn."

Max's words drifted to her ears. She just hadn't had enough time to sit with this job thing. A career, as Max called it. It was bigger than she was right now. "That's the 'always look for the silver lining commandment,' isn't it?" Mel joked, folding her arms under her breasts in a protective gesture.

"It is. I knew you couldn't resist my pamphlets. No one can."

A glimmer of a smile wrestled with Mel's lips. So, yeah. Guilty. She'd skimmed the contents of the packet Max had given her last night over a salad and a piece of grilled chicken. She'd even tried the divorce journal writing thing. You had to laugh at some of the crazy things Maxine must have spent hours and hours thinking up. It was only right she honor the effort and the job Maxine had found for her.

"And yes, before you say it, it took a long time to come up with some of those witty words of wisdom. A writer, I ain't." Max gave her a knowing look and a raise of her eyebrows.

"You're like a mind reader at a carnival. Spooky."

"I have to be. If I don't anticipate the cruel jokes you'll make about my divorce advice, I can't be prepared to fire back, now can I? So, how do you feel today? Did you get a good night's sleep? Eat something nutritionally balanced and not slathered in chocolate?"

"All while I memorized your pamphlet as if it were the new Bible."

Max pulled into a parking space and patted Mel on the back. "I'm glad you have a sense of humor. You'll need it with a bunch of preteen boys who'd rather have lobotomies than learn how to dance."

Mel looked down at her hands, clutched together in a ball. "I don't want to dance. How can I expect them to want to?"

"You'll find it again, honey. I know you will. Someone who danced like you did can't have lost all of that joy. It's just buried under a pile of shit that's become more important—like survival. But dancing was once your life, and the pleasure you took from it isn't stupid or insignificant. It's not trivial."

Mel's head shot up. That was exactly how she felt. Dancing seemed superficial and a ridiculous skill to have when she could have been a shop teacher or a garbage man. "How did you know?"

"I know because being a housewife was to me like dancing is to you. Okay, maybe that's a shitty analogy, but you get the meaning, right? You think to yourself, 'Jesus, what good does it do me to love to dance when I don't want to get out of bed. Who cares that I was, at my peak, once a champion in the sport?'"

Mel nodded her consent, the deep regret for her lost youth stung like vinegar on a fresh wound these days. "I knew the hazards going in. I knew making a living as a dancer was at best a huge risk and at worst a pipe dream. But back then when I met Stan and he was full of so much praise for my work, I thought nothing could stop me. Youth, right? But then his work took precedence. I became more of an assistant to him, and I stopped pursuing auditions because his work always took us all over the globe. When I think about how glad I was that he decided to do the show because it meant we'd stay in one place for an extended period of time, it makes me want to drive to Hollywood and choke him." But only after she cut out his heart.

Max clapped her thigh. "Good! Angry is good. It beats indifference. That's death. Trust me. Look, everything you once loved looks very dull and drab to you right now, but I promise, it gets shinier once you dust it off and give it a good buffing. This is your opportunity, Mel. No one who danced like you did can stay dormant forever. No one."

Nervous anxiety skittered along Mel's spine. "Suddenly, I'm a nervous wreck." Since she'd snared this job yesterday, her attitude had been one of unsettling indifference. It didn't feel like the coup of the century. It didn't feel lucky. Maybe she just couldn't feel anymore?

Though, it certainly should feel lucky, considering her complete lack of marketable skills. She was going to make a semi-decent salary and she had benefits. In a few months, she and Weez could stop leeching off her father.

Max had told her how Frankie and Jasmine had struggled. That her struggle was a far shorter journey should be a reason to be grateful. She'd only been broke a few months instead of close to a year like Maxine.

Instead, last night, after her boring dinner and only a half of a spoonful of some refrigerator-hard frosting, she'd gone to bed without a single worry about her new employment.

She was too caught up in how much she missed her other students, students who weren't reluctant participants and who wanted to learn to dance, and the ongoing plan to finely hone Stan's perfect murder.

But this morning, as she haphazardly made an attempt to cover the dark circles under her eyes with concealer and applied a light gloss to her pale lips then packed a lunch of apples and a bologna sandwich with mustard, her stomach had twisted and heaved.

When Max, who'd been kind enough to give her a lift because her father had a podiatrist's appointment, had pulled up, Mel had almost turned tail and run.

She was no Hilary Swank in some remake of *Freedom Writers*. These kids wanted to dance as much as she wanted to wax her legs.

But it turned out Max was a hard taskmaster who took no shit. So here Mel was on the way to start her new career.

Max turned in her seat. Her green eyes so warm it made Mel's heart thaw a bit. "Just keep your eye on the prize, Mel. A paycheck. A pretty good one, too. One that will afford you a place to live eventually—and plenty of chocolate frosting. And self-sufficiency. There's nothing like that for your wounded pride. You taught in L.A.; you can teach in Jersey. I know you were good at it because I saw that interview on *Hollywood Scoop* with the little boy who said he missed you."

Humiliation flooded her cheeks in the shade of red. How that reporter from *Hollywood Scoop* had conned Tito's mother into letting him do an interview left her speechless. Not to mention, pissed. "Tito. He was a great kid."

"These kids will be, too," Max soothed. "Now get a move on, teacher, or you'll be late."

Like it was her first day of kindergarten, Mel slid from the car with reluctance. "All right," she offered dejectedly.

"Don't forget your lunch." Maxine tossed the brown paper bag at her and waved. "Have an awesome first day, Mel!"

Mel watched Max drive off like her mother had just abandoned her at the 7-Eleven. She wanted to run after Maxine and cling to the bumper of her car. Beg. Plead. Cry.

Deep breaths. Deep breaths.

She paused when she was unable to relax.

Okay, deeper breaths.

"Hey! Mel, right?"

Mel stopped her breathing exercise cold, turning to block her eyes from the sun as a tall man approached.

He lifted a broad hand in her direction, the scent of his spicy cologne drifting to her nose on the early morning breeze. "Remember me? Nephew to Myriam the Hun?"

Oh, she definitely remembered. How could she forget so much hot? Her heart skipped at least two beats when she peered at him through the sunlight. The curl of his hair around the collar of his casual jacket made her knees weak. "Drew, right?"

He grinned and she wondered why he appeared so pleased she'd remembered his name. "That's me. C'mon, I'll walk you in."

Everything seemed brighter suddenly when he placed a light hand to her waist. She didn't feel as much like she was headed to the guillotine with Drew taking long strides beside her.

Not until she saw her reflection in the school's doors anyway. Her thick, kinky-curly hair, always difficult to contain no matter what product she used, flew around her chalky face in tangles, pulling out of her ponytail, and her wraparound skirt was wrinkled. Much to her delight, she'd also missed a button on her sweater, leaving it uneven.

Ah, but she'd remembered her bra. The miracle one. God was good.

"Do you have a son who attends Westmeyer?"

"Me? No. No children here. I . . . I teach here." That's right. She was a teacher. Teacher, teacher, teacher.

"You're a teacher? I thought you were a dancer." He stopped at the wide double doors of the school, looking down at her with his dreamy eyes.

Mel's eyebrow cocked upward. How had he known that? "Well, I wasn't born knowing the steps to the tango. I had a teacher who taught them to me."

He chuckled, his white teeth flashing for a moment. "Right. What I meant to say was what do you teach?"

Mel cocked her head, running a nervous hand over the length of her messy ponytail. "Ballroom dancing."

Drew's dark eyebrow's slammed together. "Say again?"

"Ballroom dancing."

"Here?"

"It seems so."

"And who hired you?"

"The dance fairy?"

She'd meant to make him smile again, because it was so nice, but he wasn't smiling. "Was it Dean Keller?"

"Yes. Why?"

"God damn it," he spat, shoving open the doors and stalking through them.

Mel followed close behind, forcing her eyes away from his ass encased in the jeans he wore like a second skin. "Wait! What did I say?"

But he waved her off with a quick flip of his hand, leaving her to stand in the middle of the school's imposing foyer while curious boys in starched black uniforms milled around her.

Well, then. Yay, teaching.

Mel glanced at the clock on the wall and realized she'd better find out where her class was going to be held. She stopped a short young boy with thick round glasses and a pristine black jacket with yellow piping. "Can you tell me where Dean Keller's office is?" She'd lost her bearings after yesterday's blur of hiring and paperwork.

He pointed behind her. "If you take this hall approximately

twenty-two point three feet then make a hard right, walk another
fifteen point six and a half feet, you'll find his office. His name's on it.
It says Dean Keller. D-E-A—"

"Thank you," Mel cut him off, frightened by the idea he'd actually
measured how far the dean's office was from the entry.

She slipped between the boys and pressed forward twenty-two
point three feet. Ah, there it was. Just like Young Einstein had said.
Just as she raised a hand to knock on his door, she heard yelling.
Drew's yelling.

"You told me my son was coming here to get an education—not
dance like some fairy! There was nothing in the welcome package
about ballroom dancing and leather pants, Keller!"

Mel's eyes went wide. She clapped a hand over her mouth to keep
her gasp from escaping her lips.

"Men," someone muttered.

Mel whipped around to find Dean Keller's secretary, Mrs. Willows. She'd met her yesterday while she'd filled out insurance forms.
"I'm sorry?"

Hawklike gray eyes on a gaunt face assessed Mel. "Don't be sorry.
I said 'men.' They all react the same way when they find out the boys
have to learn to dance. They make such a big deal out of it when it's
really not that big of a brouhaha. So, yes. Men. Especially a man as
manly as Drew McPhee. Now, he's all man, a man who's probably
going to be your worst nightmare while you teach his son, Nate."

Like she didn't know nightmares. Mel squared her shoulders. She
was offended by the very notion that if a man danced, he was some
sort of slight to Neanderthals everywhere.

Sure, there were lots of gay ballroom dancers. There were lots of
gay flight attendants, too. They just didn't wear costumes that sparkled when they left Newark airport. Dancing was healthy—it was

incredibly good exercise and some of the strongest men on the planet
were dancers. So enough already with the stigma. "Well, he'll just
have to suck that up, won't he?"

Whoa. Had that been a spark of passion in her tone?

Heh.

Mrs. Willows began to laugh, the wrinkles on her neck bobbing
up and down. "I like you, and yes, he will if he wants his son to attend
Westmeyer, especially on a scholarship."

"The hell I'll see my son dressed in some tutu!" Drew shouted,
storming out of the dean's office and heading right toward Mel. His
face no longer held that easygoing expression, but a hard mask of
fury. His nostrils flared in angry fits of snorts.

Hoo boy. She put her hands behind her back, clamping her fingers
together. "Um, if it's any consolation, there aren't many tutus in ballroom dancing. It's mostly Lycra pants and those skimpy tight shirts."

Drew's blue eyes narrowed to slits in his head. "Let me make
myself perfectly clear. I didn't send my son here to learn how to do
the twist—"

Mel flashed him a sweet, totally disingenuous smile. "Oh, I don't
know how to twist. Though, I'm sure I could learn."

His lips thinned while his gaze left her feeling like the antichrist.
"Look, lady. I didn't send my kid to this fancy private school to do the
sumba!" Drew's words sizzled from his mouth.

Mel popped her lips in obvious mockery. "That's a rumba, or a
samba, depending on the meaning of your jumble of inept words, and
you're right. There'll be absolutely no rumbas and no sambas—or
even a sumba. Not a one. You'll be so relieved to know, I'm teaching
traditional ballroom dancing. You know—the girlie waltz. Maybe a
nice sissified foxtrot."

He dragged a hand through the luscious thatch of hair she now wanted to pull out of his head. "This is the most ridiculous rule I've ever heard of."

"Yeah. Coordination and exercise are all that and more." Suddenly, and for the pettiest of reasons, she wanted this job. She wanted to show Mr. Manly Man that dancing was hardcore work. It took more than just some jazz hands to lift a hundred and twenty pounds of sparkly rhinestoned woman over your head.

"He gets all the exercise he needs throwing a football around."

Mrs. Willows gave Drew an elbow to the ribs. "Now, be fair, Drew McPhee. You know darned well Nate hates sports. And you better get going. Ms. Cherkasov has a ballroom class to teach." She left them with a snickering chuckle that pinged around the hallway.

Drew jammed his hands in the pockets of his worn Levis. The tightening of his jaw left her very aware of the effort he was making to hold back. "Have I said this is ridiculous?"

She contemplated him from heavy-lidded eyes. "With zeal."

"Nate came here because they don't have the facilities to keep up with his genius in public school. He didn't come here to *dance*."

"Did you have some sort of dancing trauma that's led you to so vehemently hate all things dance-ish? Did some angsty teenage girl break your dancing heart at the prom? Mock your technique, maybe?"

"I don't hate dancing. I hate that my kid's going to be forced to do something he hates."

"And what brought you to the conclusion that he's going to hate my classes? Because I have to tell you, I'm taking this exceptionally personally. I'm a good instructor. In fact, most of my students came back year after year to attend my classes when I had my own studio. So, why don't you stop fobbing your silly, knuckle-dragging perceptions off on your son before he's even had the chance to experience his first class. And now, I have to go fluff my tutu. I don't want to be late for my first day." With those parting words, Mel stomped off to Mrs. Willows's office to locate her classroom, leaving Drew McPhee and his blatantly discriminatory bullshit to rot in the fiery pits of hell.

~ l ~

All right. So maybe she'd been a bit hasty when she'd decided for Nate that he'd love ballroom dancing.

From the looks of the forlorn faces who'd much rather be measuring the drips per nanosecond of a ketchup bottle, she was not the Hannah Montana of Westmeyer.

Reluctance took on a whole new level when she'd asked them all to loosen their ties, roll up their sleeves, and put their laptops in the corner of the room.

She'd never had students who didn't want to learn how to dance, but after Drew's sharp, biased, stupid freakin' words, she was determined.

After teaching them how to stretch their muscles, and almost pulling one of her own, Mel plastered a smile on her face, addressing the group of ten boys, her first group of seventh graders for the day. "So, I'm Ms. Cherkasov and I'll be your ballroom instructor this year. Why don't we start by telling me your names? You first." She pointed to a bland-faced, confused boy with white-blond hair and strawberry-kissed cheeks.

His bright eyes took everything in as though he were mentally calculating the amount of footsteps it would take to make a break for freedom.

He shuffled his feet encased in black shoes so shiny, she could see her reflection—which still looked flustered and mussed. "Johann Finklestein."

She was just about to move on to the next boy when Johann snapped his hand in the air. "Yes?"

"May I just make an observation, Ms. Cherkasov?"

Manners. Nice. "Because you asked so politely, hit it."

"Do you have any idea how many low IQ bullies are going to have a field day with this when they find out we're learning how to waltz?" Johann's cheeks turned a brighter shade of pink, making his platinum blond hair appear whiter.

"Do you have any idea how many bullies you'll be able to lift over your head when I'm done with you? Ballroom dancing takes strength and control, gentlemen. Have any of you ever watched *Celebrity Ballroom*?"

Three boys raised their hands, including Nate, who'd been identified for her by Mrs. Willows. "So then some of you have an idea what ballroom dancing is all about. Have you ever seen the muscles on some of the men who teach the celebrities to dance? They're strong and in top physical shape."

"And they wear ruffled shirts. Polyester, I'm guessing. My naked eye tells me the thread count isn't high enough for cotton," one boy with dark hair and sharp cheekbones commented.

Mel smiled encouragingly. "You are?"

His eyes instantly went to the shiny hardwood floor. "Emilio Benito Salazar."

She tapped beneath his chin. "Look up when you speak to me, Emilio, please. A strong dance partner always holds his head up and his back straight, and it's nice to meet you." Mel winked at him to reassure she wasn't singling him out for his bad posture. "Now, who's next? How about you?" She pointed at Nate, tall for his age with midnight black hair and an expression of apathy on a face that was an exact replica of Drew's.

"Nathan McPhee."

"And how do you feel about ballroom dancing?"

He shrugged his slender shoulders. "I feel like I don't have a choice."

Instead of reprimanding him for his sulking attitude, Mel laughed. "Nope. You sure don't. But I remember when I was your age, I had to go to pre-algebra because I didn't have a choice."

Nate frowned as though the thought were inconceivable. "You were still in pre-algebra at twelve years old?"

Mel nodded, moving toward the lockers on the far side of the room to pull out the broomsticks the former instructor had left. "I know. You guys did that in nursery school, right?" Her comment managed to illicit some chuckles, lightening the atmosphere of the room. "So let's continue with introductions while I pass out these broomsticks."

Jordan, Ahmed, R.J., Kendrick, Samuel, Anders, and Hank Wong made up the rest of the group of ten boys.

She handed them the broomsticks while they all made faces. "These are for your posture. And today we're going to learn the basics of a waltz. So put these in front of you like this." She demonstrated by putting the stick over her raised arms and letting it rest there. "This will make your backs nice and straight while you learn to be the frame for your partner."

"I know what that is," Ahmed chirped, his dark, chubby features breaking into a smile. "The man is the frame and the woman is the picture, right? The frame can't ever leave the picture. Or something like that." Clearly embarrassed, he looked down. "My mom loves Richard Gere. She watches *Shall We Dance* over and over. I just heard Jennifer Lopez say it when I was making crème brûlée in the kitchen. I didn't really watch it or anything lame like that."

R.J. threw his broomstick over his head, narrowly missing Jordan's shoulder. "Sure you didn't."

Mel eyed R.J., planting her hands on her hips. "And what if he did watch it?" There would be no taunting another student on her watch. She'd taken a lot of heat as a kid for her love of an art that hadn't always been in the public eye like it was today.

Instantly, R.J.'s eyes grew wide at being called out. "I was just saying."

Placing her hands on the middle of R.J.'s chest, she tilted his torso back. "Then say it with respect, please. Now here are my rules. You all have to take this class whether you like it or not. I know some of you don't like it, and that's okay by me. I'm not exactly a fan of genetics, either, but I respect those who can sit still long enough to learn about it. I'd like the same respect from all of you. By the end of this semester, you'll know how to do a smooth waltz. You'll be graded on your posture, the rise and fall of your feet, how well you direct your partner, and last but not least, your artistry and interpretation of the music."

Groans permeated the air.

"I know, I know. I suck, right?" She grinned, feeling a little more like herself. "But here's the thing. This can be fun. I *insist* you have fun. It might not be as fun as thermonuclear bombs, but I promise, we'll end up laughing. Now, if you all don't straighten up and fly right, I'll make you wear ruffles for your finals."

All ten boys instantly stood erect and clamped their mouths shut.

She smiled again and brushed her hands together. This was going to be work.

A deep sigh escaped Mel's lips as she let her left leg drape over the ballet barre and arched her arm over her head to stretch. The tight pull of skin over her ribs ached, making her flesh itch.

The day had been long. Each set of students showed her the same kind of love she'd gotten from her first class.

None.

She let her cheek rest along the top of her thigh and winced. Her father was right—her pretzel-like abilities were slipping. She'd better get it together if she hoped to endure eight solid hours with a bunch of boys she was hired to motivate.

She still had to get home, shower, and change for yet another round of dancing with the seniors for Waltzing Wednesdays at the rec center. The idea that she couldn't just go home and drop face-first into bed after consuming a can of Betty Crocker's finest wasn't appealing.

But at least the seniors wanted to play with her.

"Are You Lonesome Tonight?" tinkled on the sound system. Perfect for a waltz. Not to mention, a sad musical tribute to her new status in life.

Single.

Something she'd remain forever if she continued to look like the dishrag she saw in the wall of mirrors in her classroom. Her eyes stared back at her—tired and dull.

She snorted. Pretty.

Dropping her leg, Mel grunted when it hit the floor. Her eyes scanned the room for her purse and as she crossed the room to gather it, she did a couple of 3/8 reverse turns then tripped from the sting in her big toe, falling to the floor.

Mel let her head fall forward, tears welling in her eyes.

Fuck.

Fuck a full-time job. Fuck her disinterest in the only thing she'd ever truly felt free doing.

Oh, and fuck Stan.

~ℓ~

"What kind of dance teacher is *that*?" his father remarked when his new teacher tripped and fell on one of those 3/8 reverse spins she'd talked about. He'd found his dad watching her through the window to her classroom with a small smile on his face.

His dad didn't smile all that much when it came to girls, but he was smiling watching her. The harsh tone he'd used when Ms. Cherkasov fell meant the exact opposite of his rude words, too, which set Nate's mind to working a mile a minute.

"Though, she has good taste in music," his father commented absently, eyes on Ms. Cherkasov.

His father liked the new dance instructor. If he was honest with himself, so did he. She was nice and really pretty—if you liked women who were middle-aged.

He totally hated dancing.

Totally. But he got it. He knew he got it because he'd caught Ms. Cherkasov watching him in all those mirrors with approval in her eyes. He'd picked up the fundamentals of a waltz with ease.

Lame.

It was probably from being forced to watch those dance shows with his grandmother and Aunt Myriam. He did have a photographic memory.

"Hey, Dad. Who you talkin' to?" he asked, playing dumb.

Drew planted a hand on his son's head and gave him an affectionate squeeze. "Nobody. Just muttering. You ready to hit it, pal?"

"Yeah. We have to hurry up, too."

"For?"

"Don't you have to pick up Aunt Myriam at the rec center in the Village tonight?" Nate knew he didn't, but he also knew Ms. Cherkasov was going to be teaching the seniors tonight. He'd heard her tell Mrs. Willows at lunch.

"Shoot. Did I forget again? I thought I didn't have to go get her until Friday night so she and Gram can play canasta."

Nate shrugged his shoulders, hurling his backpack over his head and began to walk toward the exit doors. "I could've sworn she said Wednesday. I thought I saw it circled on her calendar," he said, looking away from his father's eyes. He'd never been a very good liar, but he wasn't lying to save his skin or keep from being grounded.

He was lying because his dad needed to spend time with adults who weren't related to him. Or at least that was what Aunt Myriam said.

"Well, I guess you'd know with that photographic memory. Your Aunt Myriam's gonna kill me with her social schedule at that Village lately. I'm beat, but it's better than her driving. I was thinking we'd grab a pizza and watch some TV while you figure out how to save the world. Maybe Aunt Maura could pick her up tonight?"

Crap. "No! I mean, Aunt Maura's got cheerleading practice with Macy tonight, and pizza's bad for me. I'd rather have some of Grandpa's Irish stew and soda bread."

Drew stopped walking.

Now he'd done it. He'd pushed the lying thing a little too far.

"Did that Ms. Cherkasov teach you some dance move that made you knock your head?"

Nate laughed. "Nah. I'm just messing with you. Grandma always makes me a meat loaf sandwich on Irish stew night. They're my favorite—even over pizza."

Pushing the doors open, a cool stream of air hit Nate's face, lifting his hair. He swatted at it, pressing the strands back over his forehead. He didn't need for his father to see he had the beginnings of acne. They'd be at the Proactiv kiosk in the mall in two seconds flat. Acne was a natural ailment for a teenager. His father overreacted to everything where he was concerned.

Drew beeped the truck and climbed in, waiting until Nate was settled in the passenger seat to ask, "So how'd you feel about ballroom dancing?"

"Wow. What's that about, Dad?"

"What's what about?"

"That tone in your voice when you say the word *ballroom*. Like it smells like toe jam."

"No tone. Just a question."

"Nuh-uh. I heard tone. I know you don't like to dance, but . . . I do." If hell really did exist like Aunt Myriam said, he hoped they had Internet because that's where he was headed with all these lies.

He watched his father squirm for a minute, then waited while he chose his words carefully. Nate always knew when his father was taking caution before he spoke. He had a tic in his jaw that pulsed in time with the vein in his forehead. "You liked it?"

"I really did. Very cool." Keep it simple, he reminded himself.

"No kidding?"

"Nope."

Nate smiled to himself while his father warred with whether to ask him a personal question about his sexuality. He knew his dad would be okay with whatever answer he gave him, but it was stupid on his father's part to assume that if he really did like to ballroom dance, which he didn't, that he was gay.

Nate didn't quite understand why some of his father's generation still struggled with the thought that just because you liked to dance, you were light in your loafers. In some cultures, dancing was just a form of expression and no big deal. In India, men danced together all the time. But he decided to clue his father in just to set things straight. "Do you know Madison Nickels?"

Drew paused, giving his son a sidelong glance. "The young lady in 12-C?"

Nate smiled. "Yeah. That's her. You mind if we study together some nights? She says she sucks at biology. I've already done all that stuff. I can tutor her."

Now his father grinned. "You think she's *preeeeettttyyyy*?"

He focused on the look he'd perfected lately. Bored. "Maybe."

"Then I don't mind at all. As long as you behave like a gentleman and follow her mother's rules."

Nate sat back in his seat and hid another smile of satisfaction.

All systems go.

CHAPTER FIVE

Dear Divorce Journal,

On this business of sucking it up: I can't believe I'm doing this. I mean, *can't*. But I need an outlet for self-expression because my other outlet's on the fritz—so here goes. I hate everything. Every—little—thing. How's that for an expression in sucking it up, Maxine?

"Oh! Nice, Mr. Ledbetter. Look at you," Mel praised with a giggle when he managed to dip Mrs. Ledbetter without letting her drop to the ground like he had two weeks ago. "I can't believe how good you have gotten. I'm not worthy."

Mel made a bowing motion to the Ledbetters before circling the rec center floor of couples practicing the basic steps to a foxtrot, fighting back a yawn. Today had worn her out. Her legs were as heavy as her eyes.

And her ass.

Depression. It had to be. She'd worked long hours at her studio in L.A. There was no excuse for this kind of exhaustion. Not even the swell of "Moon River" lifted her spirits.

A tap on her shoulder from behind made her whirl around to find the movement made her dizzy. She put out two hands to steady herself, planting them on a hard chest.

Callused hands reached for her, solid and steady and maybe just a little bit exciting. "Mel? You okay?"

Her vision blurred for a moment then cleared. Oh. Look. It was the dance police. The one and only Drew McPhee. It was hard to deny the raw physicality of a man blessed with the best of both worlds from his ethnic background.

If she were in a better place, he might have taken her breath away with his chocolaty hair and bronzed skin. His thick fringe of black eyelashes made his blue eyes almost sapphire. The steel blue of his fitted shirt, hugging defined pecs and falling on a tapered waist, was the perfect complement to offset the tight black jeans.

So instead of lavishing Drew's beauty with drool, she reminded herself all her breath was reserved for starting her life over. It was going to take a lot of breath.

Mel yanked her hands back and instantly took two steps away, narrowly missing a dancing couple. She found her hand going to the hair she'd never bothered to brush to smooth her fingers over it any way. When in the presence of such chiseled hardness, one should least be tidy in appearance.

Drew's hand went to her elbow, and he repeated, "Are you okay?"

"Fine. Just tired. What brings you here tonight? Did you come to your senses and realize real men wear tights?" she asked, folding her arms under her breasts.

His eyes were filled with the kind of amusement she imagined only the devil could display. "Absolutely. In fact, I went right out and bought a pair in every color of the rainbow because I never want you to mistake me for anything but a *real* man."

Like that would ever happen. "I feel like you're just shy of grabbing your crotch with that statement."

"Never let it be said I wouldn't make the effort upon request."

"You'll never hear those words from my lips."

"So I suppose I owe you an apology."

Mel's eyebrow rose upward in her best disapproving teacher expression. "You suppose?"

"My son said so."

"Is that similar to your mother making you do it?"

He held his thumb and index finger together. "Very, very close."

"I await."

Drew rolled his tongue along the inside of his cheek before he spoke. "I was harsh today."

Mel cocked her head at him, fighting the peculiar shiver of awareness his presence sent slithering up her spine and along her arms. "That doesn't even rhyme with 'I'm sorry.'"

"Look, Nate is at the school on a partial scholarship. I had no idea he'd do anything other than study to be the rocket scientist he almost already is. I want him to focus on his studies, not learn whatever that dance you said was."

"It's the waltz. Own it, and that's still no excuse for being so rude."

His grin was playful. "I *was* rude. The rudest."

"Well, that's settled."

"I'd like to make it up to you."

Now her grin was playful, and she found, not as uncomfortable as one would think when you felt so disjointed and disinterested. "Do you have cash?"

Drew pulled the wallet from his back pocket and held it open for her to see. "Only two singles and a five."

Mel waved a hand at him. "Then forget it. I like big bills or haven't you heard? I was a kept woman."

He regarded her with eyes that revealed nothing, shoving his wallet back in his pocket. "I heard. How about I make it up to you with a drink or even some coffee?"

Uncomfortable returned in one fell swoop. He was asking her out.

A man with a crappy attitude about one of the most intimate creative venues in her life was asking her out. She couldn't go out with someone who felt the way Drew McPhee felt about her one true passion in life.

Was this single? Jesus, what was single? She'd never been single long enough to know. No dates. Not for a long time. "How about we just chalk it up to your lack of knowledge and Stone Age beliefs, and let it go?"

"Here's the problem with that. I don't know if I can sleep at night if you don't let me buy you a cup of coffee. There's also Nate to consider. He'd be very disappointed if he found out Ms. Cherkasov refused make-up coffee."

Her eyes turned to avoid his steady gaze and focus on the seniors she was supposed to be teaching to dance. She slowed Mona, Maxine's mother, and Gail Lumley, who'd both deemed no man in Leisure Village South worthy of a dance partnership with them, to correct Gail's hand at Mona's waist as they took another turn around the dance floor. "I like a man who uses his son to get his way. Admirable."

Drew's shoulder bumped hers when he laughed with ease. "Dirty pool's the name of the game."

Her palms grew sweaty when his shoulder touched hers. "I get the impression, with all the guidelines and rules at Westmeyer, dating a student's father is out of the question." *Good save, Mel.*

"I never said a word about dating. That's the plural use of an event we haven't even had a singular of."

Shut up, Mel. She tucked her chin to her chest, praying the stain of red that rushed to her cheeks blended in with her sweater. Mel sidestepped away from the heat of Drew's body, hoping that would help the breathless, headiness of his presence. "Touché."

"But you're right. Westmeyer does have rules about dating students' parents. Though, seeing as I'm an employee as well as a parent, one has to cancel out the other, don't you think?"

"You work at Westmeyer?" Was the ruler of the universe on an extended vacation? How was it that such a biased, narrow-minded man who was sexier than sin itself would end up being in her immediate vicinity every day?

"Yep. I'm the resident fix whatever's broken engineer."

"Does this mean you'll be breathing down my neck all the time about the choice of color for Nate's pending tutu?"

He barked a laugh, deep and hearty. "Hot and heavy."

"Things to look forward to."

"So a drink? Coffee?"

Mel's tongue warred with her teeth in a sluggish refusal. Drew McPhee probably wasn't used to being turned down. "I don't think so. I'm still ugly bitter about my divorce and men in general. Which means I might act out in ways uncharacteristic of a lady."

"Oh, I'm bitter, too. You're not the only divorced person in the world, you know. In fact, you can believe I'll act out due to past bad experiences in my relationship with my ex-wife. But I say we should act out together. I'll be your wingman. You be mine."

Mel's irritation sparked at his tenacity—which was ridiculous. It wasn't like Drew wasn't crazy good-looking. He was. That's part of what irritated her.

The first person to ask her out on a date in her post-divorce melancholy should be someone she would have easily turned down and not second-guessed her choice to stay away from in the shallow end of the dating pool. He should be someone with bad breath or dirty fingernails—or something that totally turned her off and made him unworthy of a date with her.

But no. Instead, there was a perfectly handsome, virile man asking her out. Mel sighed, unsure how to proceed. She should have read Maxine's stupid pamphlet with less mockery and taken a more studious approach.

Maxine had an answer for everything in that damned packet of lame euphemisms. Surely, she had one for this, too. "Look, Drew. I appreciate the offer, but I don't think I'm in a place . . . that's . . . I mean, it's only been a few months since . . ."

"Since your messy, ugly, newsworthy divorce?"

"Yeah. Since that. But thanks for summing it up so well. I don't think I've ever heard the words about my divorce spoken so succinctly until you," she said, allowing her sarcasm to drip with each word.

He shrugged his wide shoulders. The crisp rustle of the fabric of his shirt brushing against his skin rang in her ears. "I'm just calling it like I see it. That's what happened. It apparently sucked. But it's over now. You know, all those healthy clichés like shouldn't you be moving forward and dipping your toes in the dating pool?"

Because? By hell, for sure, the next time she left the house, she was definitely bringing Maxine's stupid guide to divorce with her so she could refer to it when she didn't know what to say.

Nudging her shoulder with his again, Drew said, "Are you saying you don't find me attractive and the idea of coffee with me makes vomiting all night long, followed by a case of the hives more appealing?"

"No." She paused and pretended to reflect. "Wait. Maybe."

He winced, the skin on his brow wrinkling his otherwise smooth features. "Ouch. If I were a less secure guy, I'd be hurt. But just so you know, I'm pretty secure, and you'll regret the choice not to entertain having coffee with me." He winked at her, letting dark lashes fall to his cheek.

Reminding herself that Drew wasn't just some guy who wanted to take her for coffee, but her student's father, she decided to change the subject, hoping he'd let it drop. "So what brings you here tonight? You didn't come all the way over to Leisure Village just to ask me out, did you?" She let her eyes go innocent. Poke, poke, poke. *Take that, you arrogant, overbearing ballroom-dancing hater.*

His eyes scanned the dance floor of milling couples. "I came to pick up Myriam. Where is she anyway? I haven't seen her float by."

Mel let her eyes stray back to his face, admiring the sharp angle of his jaw with a hint of stubble. "Myriam's not here. She was ordered a one-week timeout by the Village committee for using foul language because another senior wouldn't dance with her."

"Are you sure?"

"Sure she uses bad language? Uh, yeah. I'm sure. I know it's wrong, but I secretly think it's pretty funny when she yells at Frank Johnson for pretending to need a walker just to avoid dancing with her."

"Did he?"

"Bring a walker with him just in case he was paired with Myriam? Yes. I'm ashamed to say, he did. But it really was in self-defense. He was paired with her three weeks ago, and she really beat him up for being such a crappy imitation of Fred Astaire."

Drew chuckled. "She can be a real warrior. I can't say as I blame Frank. Tell him next time he should break out the serious hardware and bring a wheelchair."

"In truth, I don't blame him either. Sometimes Myriam—"

"Mel!" someone yelled from behind her.

Her head swiveled in the direction of the voice—familiar and so welcome.

Neil Jensen, her old dance partner rushed up to her, pulling her into an embrace and whirling her around.

Mel clung to his neck, planting a kiss on his cheek with a grin so wide, her face hurt. Being in Neil's arms was like coming home. A piece of her scattered jigsaw puzzle of a life instantly fell back into place, tucking into a corner, right where it should be. "What are you doing here?" she asked, breathless and giddy as she ran a hand over his thick head of blond hair, giving it a hard scrub of her fist.

Neil kissed her hard on the lips and grinned back. "I came to save you from yourself, Mel's Bell's. Your dad called me and told me to grease my white horse to save the damsel in distress, and here I am."

Mel buried her face in his neck with a sigh of relief and a giggle of complete joy. "I'm so glad to see you! You have no idea how glad." Without fair warning, a tear stung her eye. Neil represented so many happy memories. Their friendship was one she'd treasured since they were paired together way back at Miss Gina's School for Dance when they were ten. They'd worked together, won several titles together, for almost nine years until the lights of Broadway and Stan had lured her away.

Neil's brown eyes, soft like dark chocolate satin, were sympathetic. He pressed a finger to her cheek to thwart her escaping tear. "I know all about it, lead foot. I watch TV, and your dad told me what little I didn't know. I tried getting in touch with you, but finding you was like trying to find the Holy Grail."

Mel clung to his neck. "I know. It's . . ." She shot a sidelong glance at Drew, who hovered but kept his eyes averted. "We'll talk later. You will be here later, right?" Worry saturated her words. Suddenly, Neil's presence was like a lifeline to a world she had lost her way in, and she wasn't ready to let go of it.

Neil nodded. "The show's on hiatus until January. I have more time than a prisoner in solitary on my hands. I'm all yours for as long as you need me."

Mel wasn't sure if she saw Drew's eyes roll or if it was just a trick of the now-dimmed lighting for the free dance.

Either way, it was rude not to introduce them. "Neil Jensen? This is Drew McPhee. I teach his son, Nate, at Westmeyer—my new job, which I'll explain later. His Aunt Myriam's a senior here in the Village. Neil's my old dance partner from way back in the day when I was competing. He's a choreographer on *Celebrity Ballroom* now. You know, the show that takes celebrities and turns them into ballroom dancers?" She shook her head with a chuckle. How stupid of her to think Drew would watch anything but *American Choppers* and the Playboy Channel. "Forget it. You wouldn't know what I mean."

Neil extended his hand and Drew took it, giving it a hard shake that made Mel frown in confusion. But Neil's good nature, always a buffer, took over, and he either ignored Drew's brash attempt at showing off his manhood or didn't care. "Nice to meet you, Drew. Your son has the best ballroom teacher in all of Jersey," he said on a smile then turned his captivating grin on Mel. "Speaking of ballroom—wanna show them how this is done?" he thumbed over his broad shoulder at the crowd of dancers, holding out his right hand to her. "Good meeting you, Drew," Neil said with another smile, throwing his hand out to Mel.

As it was, and always would be, placing her hand in Neil's was a homecoming—a swell of familiar excitement rose in her chest at the idea of dancing with Neil again.

And it was more than good to know that part of her, the part that sought solace on a dance floor when everything else was falling apart, wasn't entirely dead.

~ℓ~

He'd been dismissed. As summarily as if he'd never been.

Drew lingered in the back of the rec center as Neil twirled Mel around to the tune of raucous clapping and whistles from admiring seniors and the song "Moon River."

So Neil could dance.

And if he was the kind of guy who was into admissions, he'd admit that Neil didn't look at all like a man in a tutu when he spun Mel around while she clung to his underarms and her long legs splayed out behind her. Her head lay against his chest in a way that made Drew's eyes narrow with discontent.

Clearly, it took a certain amount of strength to do that and make it look like it was no big deal. But he'd bet dollars to donuts Neil didn't know jack about a band saw and a drill.

He'd also bet dollars to donuts that Mel didn't really care that Neil didn't know a piece of knotty pine from a two-by-four.

Which meant they were worlds apart.

She was never going to build a house, and he was sure as hell never going to dance a waltz. Turning him down was probably the best thing to happen to him in a long time. Mel came from high-maintenance living. He knew that lifestyle, and it was one he wanted no part of. Simplified was the way to go.

Yet, that didn't keep Drew's eyes from straying to her face, serene in the low lighting, soft and so feminine it left his gut aching. It didn't make him take himself out the door either.

Instead, he watched, fixated by how lovely she was, admiring the swell of her hips pressed to Neil's and the long length of her leg when she sent it upward in an arc of graceful air to let it land behind her with her toe pointed at the floor.

She stole the breath from his lungs, and he wasn't sure if it was because her love for this thing called ballroom dancing was so evident, almost something he could taste, or because of the way she moved across the floor like a goddess even with mussed hair and frumpy clothes.

He couldn't tear his eyes away.

"Jasper was right."

Drew jumped at the sound of his aunt's voice. "About?"

"He said you were over here moonin' over Mel. Called me right up on his cell phone to tell me, he did."

He felt suddenly spiteful and it leaked into his words. "I'm not mooning. I was here to pick you up. Or at least I thought I was. Where have you been, lady?"

"Can't pick someone up who ain't here. I was banned from 'Dancing with the Waitin' on Their Room in Heaven' crowd for a week. So you must be here for Mel." Myriam thumped his shoulder. "She's somethin', huh? Pretty as a picture. Too bad you don't dance, Drew McPhee. Sure looks like whoever that hottie is dancing with her is enjoying himself." She cackled her characteristically evil laugh.

He willed himself to tear his eyes from Mel's luscious body and focus on his aunt's craggy face. "Nate said you needed a ride back to Mom and Dad's after Mel's class."

"And that's why you dressed up and put some cologne on? For me?" She tugged at his fitted shirt. The one he wore for special occasions and on Sunday if his mother forced him to go to church with her.

"I was dirty after work."

"You were horny after work, pal," she said dryly.

Drew hid a smile. "You're a dirty old lady, Myriam Hernandez."

"And you're a besotted middle-aged man, Drew McPhee. Own it, bucko. Nothin' wrong with likin' a pretty girl. And Mel *is* pretty. And I don't need a ride—you read the calendar wrong."

"Then I'll take you home." With reluctance, he turned away as Neil and Mel's dance ended, wanting to be anywhere but in the rec center when the lights went up.

"Sorry about the mistake, but I don't need your ride, boy. I'm waitin' for Jasper. We got a date. Why don't you wait for Mel? Maybe she needs a ride."

Mel didn't want to be waited for. That much was apparent from the dreamy look she gave Neil when their dance ended. "As long as you're okay, Aunt Myriam, I'm out." He turned to make his way to the door while fighting his ridiculous resentment for Neil Jensen.

"Chicken," Myriam taunted after him.

He was no chicken. He'd asked her out and she'd turned him down. Mel's Bell's apparently wasn't interested in a man who wasn't schooled in the arts and didn't have more money than brain cells.

He could take rejection.

Even if he had to spend every day of the school year with Ms. Rejection.

Shit.

Mel sat across from Neil at the Greek Meets Eat Diner while she picked at a Caesar salad, and he consumed a plate of spaghetti and meatballs. "Don't they feed you in Hollywood?" she commented with a grin.

"I'm catching up on my carbs," he joked, shooting her one of his dashing smiles. "I can't eat like this during the show because it weighs me down, so every once in a while I indulge. Nothing beats Jersey diners. So when in Rome." He slipped another mouthful of pasta between his lips and wiggled his eyebrows.

"I lingered a little too long in Rome." Mel grimaced when she pinched a small roll of fat lying directly under her ribs.

Neil gave her a thoughtful glance. "What happened, Mel? Why the hell didn't you call me? You know I would have come and gotten you and Weez. You could have stayed with me."

"And done what when I got to your place, Neil? I had no money . . . no . . ."

He held up a hand and made a face of disgust. "Oh, I heard. I heard it all—through the *tabloids*. Which really pisses me off. I should have heard it from you, Mel. I felt like total shit when I found out. And I could have gotten you something on *Celebrity Ballroom*."

Mel's face flushed with shame. "I was so humiliated I didn't know which way was up, and I get the feeling no one who watches *Celebrity Ballroom* wants to see rolls of flesh seeping out from beneath my feathers and rhinestones. Besides, all that spray tanning has to be a lot to keep up with."

Neil laughed, a laugh she'd missed. They'd only seen each other occasionally over the years, and it was almost always when Stan wasn't around. Mel had never understood the tension between the two men, but it was palpable and uncomfortable and had kept Neil away often over the years.

Yet, when she and Neil were together, it was always like old times—like they were still meeting at Miss Gina's five days a week to practice. "It's a damn good paycheck and a consistent one to boot, especially at my age. I'm grateful to have work. Work I love, and you're not fat, Mel. I didn't have any trouble lifting you tonight. Just like the old days."

When she was ninety pounds soaking wet? Right. "The hell you didn't. I heard you grunt. Thank God for deaf seniors and loud music."

"Okay, so you put on a couple of pounds, but it looks good on you. All you need is a little toning up. I still think you're more beautiful than ever."

Mel put her fork down and toyed with the edge of her napkin. She and Neil, once they'd hit their hormonal fluxes at thirteen or so, had always known they'd never be anything but friends. His compliment, while a stab at comforting her bad body image, was ludicrous. She flicked a finger under his nose. "I don't need you to whitewash what I look like. I see it in the mirror every day."

Neil shook his shaggy blond head, his mouth a thin line of anger.

"No you don't. You see what Stan told you to see. I've shut my mouth for a long time out of respect for you about that asshole, but not anymore. Stan's a jackass for doing what he's done. Did he really take the studio and not leave you a penny?"

Terror gripped Mel's stomach for a moment then eased when she remembered she had a job and a pending paycheck.

So, fine. A big thumbs-up to Maxine for being right about at least the relief that security brought. "He did, and I haven't spoken to him since just after he left for auditions for the show. Everything after the press informed me he was doing Yelena was done through his lawyers. I didn't have one because I couldn't afford one, and I wouldn't let my father pay for one. So I signed papers because despite the fact that I did love Stan once—or thought I loved him—I don't want a cheat and a liar. There was nothing else to say because of the prenup, so that was that."

Neil's fist clenched, the veins in his hand pulsing. "Jesus Christ, Mel. That's brutal."

"What I don't get is why he was so cruel about it in the process. Stan wasn't a horrible person, despite your deep dislike for him. Yes, he was self-absorbed and impatient, but he was once very good to me. If he'd come to me and asked me for a divorce because he'd fallen in love with someone else, yeah, that would have hurt, but to turn it into a tabloid fiasco by letting me find out from a reporter and then enforce that stupid prenup I signed, like I would have taken all his money from him and left him bankrupt, leaves me baffled. And hurt. So hurt I almost couldn't breathe from it for a while."

Yet, as she spoke the words, she realized Stan's betrayal didn't hurt as much as it had for the first couple of months. It still hadn't stopped her from wanting to know why he'd let the press have at her in such a vicious fashion and afterward would only speak to her through his lawyers.

Someday, if she ever had the courage, and she could get past his brood of angry security guards and locked gates, she'd like an answer. For now, it was okay to avoid any sort of drama. She was up to her eyeballs with drama.

"So it's true? The reports on *Hollywood Scoop* and in the papers? The prenup's really ironclad?"

"Locked up tight like a virgin in a nunnery."

"The fuck." He threw his napkin on the table and sat back in the booth.

"That seems to be the sentiment."

"The least the asshole could have done was leave you something. You know, because he's filthy rich? Christ, it isn't like you didn't devote your entire life to him. If nothing else, he should have given you something out of decency. What a selfish, egotistical prick," Neil sneered.

"I didn't want his money, but the dance studio . . . that definitely hurt." God, it had hurt as surely as if he'd stabbed her over and over.

Neil reached across the table and rubbed her knuckles. "Did you still love him when this went down? Or more appropriately, do you still love him now?"

Mel's grainy eyes ached. "I loved who he was as an artist, but I'm beginning to wonder what I'd find if you took away all the wide-eyed surprise because someone as famous as Stan fell in love with me. If what I felt for Stan was anything more than a crush on my childhood idol that I, in all my youth, mistook for real love, keeps me up at night lately. I'm not sure I understand the concept of love—or even what it means to find the 'one' everyone talks about. I thought I had, but Stan and I grew apart probably as early as five years into our marriage. I began to want to settle down, and Stan loved roaming the world. I kept hoping it would change, and it never did. So I settled because I took vows—and I took them seriously. The glue that held us together was our love of the craft. We just loved it differently."

Neil's eyes were distant. "You were definitely starstruck. Don't think I don't remember all those gushing phone calls after that first audition in New York for his Off-Broadway play."

She remembered. Or more aptly, she remembered the gushing phone calls filled with screams of excitement when Stan began to woo her. The deep emotions she'd thought she'd experienced, clearly clouded by admiration for Stan, weren't as easily summoned today. "I just couldn't believe someone like Stan could fall in love with some-one as unlikely as me."

Neil squinted in her direction. "Well, the rest of us could. You're a beautiful woman. I hate to tell you this, but back in the day, not many rivaled your ass. It was mesmerizing, and Stan wasn't getting any younger."

"Unlike in the here and now where it's just lumpy."

Neil's anger, though she appreciated a good BFF high five for Stan's ass-o-holic behavior, was a vibe she literally felt roll off him when he spat, "Lay off the self-flagellation with me, okay? This is me. Neil. It's bullshit, and I'm not going anywhere until you see it's bullshit. I've rented a furnished efficiency here in town, and I've got three months of nothing but time on my hands with the occasional charity appearance back in L.A. till the show starts again after the New Year. So guess what we're going to do?"

Her lips lifted in a smile. Neil was here. Finally, somebody had decided she needed a break. "I hope it involves canned frosting. Chocolate's my favorite, but I'd settle for vanilla."

Neil frowned at her. "Nope. It involves you getting your ass out of bed every day at five and running with me before you go to work. It also involves lots of vegetables and yogurt and the occasional trail mix. I need a workout partner to keep me on track while the show's on hiatus."

"So you're telling me you couldn't possibly maintain that rock-hard physique without my love and affection in the mix?"

"And your jiggly thighs."

She sputtered on her water with lemon. "How can you afford to leave your life to save mine?"

"Because you're my oldest friend, and I wasn't doing anything important anyway."

Neil's aversion to long-term relationships had always baffled her. He had so much to offer, and he understood a woman like no man she'd ever known. Yet he fell into one affair after the other like he was just biding his time instead of investing in a future that meant he wouldn't be alone someday.

"Don't you have a girlfriend, playa? Someone who's going to be royally tweaked that you're spending all this time with your ex-, now-fat, dance partner? I don't need some angry, totally in shape and capable of kicking my ass twenty-three-year-old hunting me down because I stole her man. You do remember Mary Swarofsky, right? It was a good thing my knees were so strong or she'd have taken me out in the parking lot at school. I don't have that in me these days. I just can't duck as quickly."

Neil laughed when he nodded. "I remember, and nope, no crazy bitches hell-bent on revenge. I'm free as a felon whose charges were dismissed."

"How do you manage to keep all those hot L.A. women at bay? I don't get it. You're a good-looking guy. No, you're a great-looking guy who's on a hit TV show with every variety of woman imaginable drooling over you. But here you are, forty and single."

Neil's expression darkened for a brief second, leading Mel to believe maybe somewhere along the way, there had been someone and it had left him with a lingering ache, but then he shrugged casually. "Chalk it up to every cliché you can think of. I'm a ramblin' man. I get bored easily, and let's not forget, I'm probably as self-absorbed as Stan was. I'm just not as much of an asshole. I'd have left you a couple of bucks for all those years of devotion."

Something didn't ring true in his words. She didn't doubt Neil was and always would be one of her best friends. But to up and leave L.A. when he could be taking on other choreographing jobs in his downtime from the show? That wasn't like the Neil she knew. "Okay, so now tell me the real reason you're here. Why are you doing this?"

"Because I owe you, Mel."

There was that fierce tone in his voice again. One she didn't grasp the origins of. *"Owe me?"*

"I can't tell you how many times I've regretted not trying to keep you from marrying Stan since this all went down. Can't sleep for the shit he's put you through. Hell, I danced at your wedding and drank that Dom like I didn't have objections. I did. Major ones."

Mel ran her finger around the rim of the glass as she called up the memory. "I remember. You made a little bit of a scene at my shower, as I recall. But you were drunk—so I forgave you."

Neil nodded, his face lined in misery. "I was drunk, but I wasn't wrong. I knew it then, and I regret the hell out of it now. I should have made you listen to me."

"No one could have stopped me, Neil. Not even my parents' objections stopped me. I was an adult—even if I was only a newer one. I made my bed. Now I'm lying in it."

"Well, you're not going to lie in it while you consume kettle chips and cake batter."

"Frosting."

"Whatever. I'm here, and you have to go home and go to bed because five's gonna come early, *dancer*," he taunted, throwing some money on the table and lifting his perfect body out of the booth.

A rush of gratitude overwhelmed her and more tears stung her eyes. "I love you."

"You love me right now, but tomorrow at five in the morning? Probably not so much. Move it, pretty lady." He swatted her ass on their way out the diner's door.

Mel giggled, feeling lighter than she had in months.

Well, her spirit felt lighter.

Her thighs still had a big question mark hovering over them.

But for the first time in months, she wanted to get out of bed in the morning. Maybe not at five, but she wanted.

Wanting anything other than the cover of her shame and pain was a start. That thing Maxine kept saying would happen just might have begun.

With his hand at her waist, Neil gave her a light pinch. "Hey, isn't that your friend from the Village giving us the evil eye," he asked as they made their way to Neil's Corvette.

Mel glanced in the direction of Neil's gaze and nodded up at him, shooting a twiddle of her fingers in Drew's direction when they passed in the parking lot and avoiding the curious butterfly that had taken flight in her stomach at the sight of him.

But Drew only glowered at her. Someone was still holding a grudge about being turned down, reinforcing her first thought that no one turned down Mr. McPhee.

Neil opened the passenger door and poked his head in with a question on his face. "You like?"

Yeeeessss. "No. No, I do not like. And he doesn't like me either.

He's of the ridiculous mind-set that teaching boys to dance is girly. He was really pissed when he found out I was his son's ballroom instructor at the school. Too bad you couldn't show him what manly is all about, huh?" She pinched Neil's lean cheek with affection.

He pursed his lips. "Yeah, too bad."

CHAPTER SIX

Dear Divorce Journal,

In light of sucking it up: five in the morning should be outlawed. In fact, there should be no numbers on a clock before, say, nine a.m. The other day I hated everything. Now all of my hate's directed at Neil. I'd forgotten what a Jane Fonda–ish exercise dick he is. And I don't care if my caboose will eventually look like I bought the Booty Pop when I finally can fit into some skinny jeans. I. Hate. Neil. I also hate crunches and third position in ballet.

I'd also forgotten how much third position strains a girl's flabby thighs. Oh, and there's one more thing I hate. Drew McPhee. Okay, maybe not him per se, but all of his luscious fantastical-ness. Yes. That I hate. I mean, Jesus Christ and a tango—a girl says no to a date with a guy and then not only is he suddenly every-where, but to make matters worse, he's all she can think of? What kind of special hell is that?

Neil watched his best friend in the world, the only friend he'd ever almost completely trusted wander off into the lit interior of West-meyer a week after he'd arrived in Jersey and gritted his teeth.

He loved Mel as much as he loved any family member. Maybe even more.

And he'd done something so unforgivable, she was now broken, penniless, and so sad, it hurt him to look at her for very long without wanting to find Stanislov Cherkasov and beat the Russian out of him for mutilating Mel's life this way.

To see her with so little interest in a passion they'd shared and worked so many years to find fruition in, almost broke him.

But Stan would pay.

It would hurt.

That made Neil smile as he left Mel to make some phone calls.

⁓

Mel limped toward her first class, attempting to hide the agony she was in, but her thighs just wouldn't go down without a screaming match. Oh, God. How was she going to teach a class when she couldn't move without squealing like a pig?

Damn the Neil-a-nator and his endless taunting about hip-hugging bikinis and muffin tops. The relentless bastard; she'd never said word one about her desire to be a cougar. She'd grown crazy-fond of her soft, doughy middle.

Clinging to her classroom door, she dug her fingers into the door-frame and groaned at the thought of warming the boys up with stretches.

"Did someone show off just a little too much doing the waltz last week?"

Mel's head popped up.

Drew smiled down at her—smug and arrogant, a tool belt around his lean waist.

If her arm could move more than two inches above her hips without protest, she'd yank that hammer out of it and club him to death—spiky end up. "You remembered the name of the dance. I'm impressed. Bet you can't spell it."

She'd managed to avoid him for a week now, but for the occasional passing in the hallways. Him with a sour expression of distaste on his gorgeous face when he walked past her classroom, and her counting the planks of wood on the dance floor to avoid his cranky. Just because she'd said no to coffee didn't mean they had to have a Mexican standoff each time they were in the general vicinity of one another.

And that was another problem altogether.

As vehemently as she'd denied the wish to date was as often as Drew's handsome face and sinful grin popped up in her mind's eye. From almost the moment she'd said no, she'd done nothing but think about him.

He'd put some sort of voodoo curse on her—maybe made a Barbie Mel doll he stuck pins in every night to make her painfully aware she'd said no to him. He was sticking them in her unmentionables, too. Two nights ago, she'd awoken with some very impure thoughts about Drew McPhee and red-hot cheeks.

And lady bits . . .

He leaned into her, his lips so close, Mel almost sighed. His breath had the faint smell of mint, and his shampoo was definitely something manly. Such a surprise. She straightened at the sound of his slight chuckle. "I'm here to fix the loose boards on your dance floor, queen of the waltz."

"But I have a class in five minutes."

"And my time is limited. I have a plumber coming in about the water heater in an hour. So it's now or never, and I know you don't want to compromise the safety of the boys. If one of them tripped and fell, you'd have one less tutu to fill. We couldn't have that."

Damn safety precautions. "Fine, but could you hurry it up? The boys can't dance if you're banging around. It'll throw them off tempo." God knew they couldn't afford that.

"That would, indeed, be a travesty," he remarked with another smug grin, heading toward the right edge of the floor to assess the loose boards.

Mel gingerly made her way to the ballet barre, gripping it so it was behind her and praying it would hold her weak, overexercised body up. Even her fingernails ached. She watched from her place at the barre as Drew kneeled on the floor and popped up one board to examine it.

Her eyes fell to his ass and then the strain of thick muscles in his thighs. They flexed and rippled while he reached forward and lifted each plank. The angles and rigid planes of his body under the sunlight streaming into the classroom made everything about his deliciousness magnified.

Or was that just because she was exhausted and that made her hypersensitive to everything Drew related?

Mel gulped, closing her eyes to shut out his frame. What was that old saying—sometimes you get what you wish for? What had she been thinking when she'd wished Drew away? What was a little difference of opinion when it came to the arts?

But it wasn't like they disagreed on political parties or genres of music. He'd slammed the one true love of her life. Her livelihood. Her world.

However, seeing him, hearing his voice, watching his deft movement with a hammer made a drink and those big strong thighs pressed against hers in a TGI Friday's booth somewhere not such an unappealing thought now.

Then she caught herself. She was doing it again. Getting all caught up in a man when what she should be caught up in was her and this new life she had no choice but to lead. Isn't that what Max and the divorce minions had said? She should find out who she was and whether she liked to spelunk or scuba dive—or whatever.

Yes, that's what they'd said, and instead, for the past week, she'd spent her time thinking about a man. God, she was pitiable. She wouldn't know a healthy relationship if it cha-cha'd right over her. She had to have a healthy relationship with herself before anyone else. She needed to learn what her boundaries were—her lines in the sand.

And that meant she absolutely would stop focusing on Drew.

Just then, Drew glanced over his shoulder and caught her looking at him. "No. Don't say it. I have a way with wood. I can tell by the way you stare. Your admiration comes off you in waves," he teased.

Mel scoffed, pivoting on her sore heel to face the barre and begin plies. She bit her lip hard to prevent the high-pitched scream she wanted to wail at the tearing of her inner thigh muscles. But the hell she'd show any signs of weakness.

"Morning, Ms. Cherkasov," Johann said, rushing into the room just seconds before the bell went off. As the boys filed in, Mel asked them to line up.

Today was the day they'd dance with a real partner.

Her.

Her in all her muscle meltdown. Fighting the wince her heel hitting the floor brought, she glided toward them. "So are we ready for today? It's your first pop quiz."

Moans—lots of them. She'd grown used to their moans. They always followed the mention of a quiz. "Oh, quit with all the moaning. I bet you don't moan when Mr. Linky says it's time to dissect the lifespan of the cockroach or calculate the distance between here and Jupiter."

"I know the answer to that," Emilio said.

Mel couldn't help but chuckle. "I bet you do, but the real question is do you know the steps to the waltz because that's your test today, and guess who you're going to be lucky enough to dance with?"

"Strippers?" Hank Wong shouted then looked embarrassed. She'd noticed that Hank had a habit of speaking long before he thought.

Another chuckle followed from the other end of the room, deep but muffled.

Mel gave him her stern eye even as she wanted to laugh until she cried. "Hank Wong, you know that was inappropriate, but I'll give you it was a little funny, too. Now no more stripper talk. You're dancing with me, gentlemen, and I'm no stripper. Line up, prepare your frame, and remember to count in your heads, not out loud. Soon, the waltz will be second nature."

Shuffles of reluctant feet dragged across the floor, forming a line. Mel nodded her head to signal R.J. to begin the music. Holding her arms up, she awaited her first victim, Nate, fully aware his father's eyes were on her back.

At least she hoped it was her back—not her ass. That was a tragedy in her wraparound skirt and V-neck, royal blue leotard.

Nate took her hands in his, pulling his spine upward from his core. Mel, at five-two, was almost four inches shorter than him. Yet, Nate's carriage, the way he took command without even moving, gave him the illusion of someone who stood six foot.

When the first beat of the music began, Nate's innate ability to lead his partner at such an early stage of the game brought a genuine grin to her face. As their movement began, and this tall, skinny, sometimes even awkward boy took command of the floor, Mel's mouth fell open.

Nate had an amazing musicality to his movement, his rise and fall with each step so beautifully in sync with the music made her heart thump with the possibilities he presented. His posture began to slump for a brief moment, but she didn't have to remind him. As though he knew he'd made an error, he instantly caught it, then smiled a question at her.

When he was able to navigate a small turn and still end up on the correct foot, Mel felt a tear sting her eye.

It meant he'd been paying attention. That he had a rare, inbred gift for dance was secondary right now. *Someone* in her classes had been listening, watching, instead of calculating mathematical problems in their heads to amuse themselves in their boredom.

A petty thought also occurred to her—Drew had just witnessed his son dance a waltz that was better than some who'd practiced for weeks just to get the basic steps. Drew McPhee's son could dance. He didn't just go through the motions because he had to, he *danced*. He felt the music. He allowed it to take over when it should and held back when it shouldn't. His dancing had shades of light and dark she'd never experienced in her years of teaching.

Score.

When the music stopped, hope swelled in her. The hope that at least just a little of the joy dancing could bring had rubbed off on the boys—on Nate.

The room filled with a silence and then all at once, the boys were sound and motion, clapping Nate on the back and guffawing like he'd just scored a winning touchdown. "Dude, you almost looked like one of those guys from *Celebrity Ballroom*," Ahmed praised in his stoic, even tone.

Mel stole a glance at Drew.

If her mouth had fallen open in surprise before, Drew's could catch softballs. Mel instructed the boys to practice their box steps before striding across the room. She clucked her tongue at Drew. "Tell me. What color tutu do you think would really work for Nate? I say a sky blue. It'll enhance his eyes, no?"

Drew shoved a hand into his thick hair, ignoring her jab. "I don't know what to say."

"Say he did a terrific job, and you're proud of him. He has an intuitive gift for interpreting music and gorgeous natural lines. That's rare."

"I don't know where that comes from."

"Clearly, not you, caveman," she muttered under her breath so her students wouldn't hear her. "Do me a favor, okay?"

"No tutu."

Mel smiled up at him cockily. "We don't need your stinkin' tutu. Don't quash this, Drew. Please. Don't make him feel like he's putting on makeup and a skirt, okay? Scratch that. Even if he was putting on makeup and a skirt, make sure he knows you love him. Nothing beats that. I had parents like that. So, keep your archaic thoughts about girls and dancing to yourself. If you beat him up about just how good he is, you'll beat the fun right out of it. You'll embarrass him if he thinks you disapprove, and I won't have it. Got that? Love him for who he is."

Drew's nod was slow, his eyes still fastened on his son. "There was never any question."

"Then my work here is done."

Mel turned back to the class and clapped her hands. "Okay, guys. Let's focus. That was good, but we have a long way to go. Nate," she said once the ruckus had died down, "nice job!" She followed her praise with a curtsy. "That's the way it's done, guys. Johann, you're my next victim." She pointed to the floor in front of her and smiled.

Johann took her hands in his, his palms sweaty, his tongue slipping nervously along his bottom lip.

As the music started back up, it brought with it a new sense of purpose, making her forget her aching shoulders and sore calves.

Nate could dance. It just took one student. She'd done something right.

Boo-yah.

───❧───

Drew caught up with Nate just as the last bell of the day rang. He clamped a hand on Nate's shoulder, spinning him around in the middle of the crowded hallway.

"Hey, Dad. You ready?"

Drew looked down at his boy. A boy who'd glided across the dance floor with the alluring Mel Cherkasov like he'd always been doing it, and pride swelled in his soul. Sure, he'd like it if Nate could throw a football to victory—or hit a homerun. Those things he understood. He didn't understand this dancing thing.

He only understood, his son excelled at it and appeared to actually like it. Mel was right. Whether Nate was a garbage man or a brain surgeon, he needed to know his father loved him.

"Yeah, I'm ready, kiddo. But first, *niiiiiice* job out on that dance floor. Knuck it up, pal." He held his fist forward.

Nate shot him an irritated look and rolled his eyes, craning his neck around the corner. "Knock it off, Dad. Everyone's looking."

Drew let his fist drop. "So? You should be proud of what you did in there. You're pretty good."

"How would you know? You hate to dance." Nate said it with no malice, his tone simply matter-of-fact.

Drew smiled at him. "I know because Ms. Cherkasov said so. I know because even someone who doesn't get it could see you were good at it."

Nate's slender shoulders lifted with nonchalance. "I was just okay. I almost stepped on her sore toe because I started on the wrong beat. But after that, it was no big deal."

"So you like it? Sure looked like you liked it."

Nate gazed up at him, his eyes pinning Drew's as they walked. "Yep. You think she gives private lessons?"

Drew stopped mid-stride. "Seriously?"

"For serious."

"I guess we could ask."

Nate's eyes were skeptical. "I bet you'd rather pay for football lessons, huh?"

Drew stopped him in the hall, keeping his voice low so as not to do the unthinkable and embarrass his kid, he said, "I don't care if you want to learn to plant tulips, bud. So long as you're happy doing it, I'm happy, too."

Nate snorted. "I like daffodils better."

"Fine, then plant daffodils."

"So you're okay with it? I thought you'd be mad."

"Dogs get mad. People get angry," he corrected, using a line his own father had used when he was a kid.

"Angry, whatever. You'll ask her?"

"I'll ask her."

"Cool."

"Yeah. Cool." His heart tightened. And it wasn't just because he was proud his son wasn't afraid to pursue a hobby other kids would laugh at him for.

It had a little something to do with the possibility he'd be seeing one sexy ballroom instructor—a whole lot more if he had his way.

Boo-yah.

Jasmine and Frankie waved to Mel from a corner booth at the diner they met at every Tuesday night. Frankie's husband, Nikos, the owner of Greek Meets Eat, opened the door for her.

After that morning and the utter bliss she'd experienced when she'd realized Nate had been paying attention in class, her day had gone downhill.

She had not one, but two Band-Aids on her toes, and an ice pack in her purse for her eye—which David Hockenmeyer had bruised when he slipped and his head smacked into her face.

But she had her first paycheck in the brand-new account she'd opened. What better way to celebrate than hangout with the divorce guru's minions?

"Heeey!" Frankie said with a smile, scooting over to invite her to sit. "What happened?"

"Dance-class accident. I'm fine. Believe me, I've had worse," Mel assured her.

"So, you decided we're more fun than a can of chocolate frosting? That deserves a toast." She held up her glass of wine and clinked it with the beautiful Jasmine's.

"So how goes it, dance teacher?" Jasmine inquired, her gaze zeroing in on Mel.

Even her bruised eye and sore toes couldn't thwart the smile on her face. "I never thought I'd be this excited, but I got my first paycheck today, and I opened my first checking account, and it's all mine."

Jasmine clapped her hands and held up her hand for Mel to high-five. "Give it to me, sister!"

Mel clapped hands with her. "I feel ridiculously independent over something as simple as a checking account and a debit card. That's stupid, isn't it?"

Frankie shook her head of lush auburn curls. "No, sweetie, that's empowerment. Damn invigorating, huh?"

A rush of pride settled in her chest. Yeah. "I can't tell you how good it felt. Who knew?"

Jasmine poured Mel a glass of wine. "We knew, darling. So tell us about this job. Is it all kinds of awful? Are the kids snotty little know-it-all's?"

"They're definitely smarter than a fifth grader. It's a little intimidating, and they hate to dance. Almost every one of them."

Frankie leaned forward, her elbows on the table. "Then why do you look so happy?"

Mel shrugged, taking a sip of her wine before speaking. "I think it's because I feel like I'm actually doing something. I'm exercising again and eating better. I just feel better."

Jasmine arched her eyebrow. "We heard there was a man involved in the better."

"A man?" Did the divorce minions have mind-reading skills, too? How could they know about Drew? What was it with these women?

"Oh, my God—yes, a man. Only the sexiest man ever," Frankie cooed, twisting a strand of her hair with her finger.

"Hey!" Frankie's husband, Nikos, dark and gorgeous, gave her a playful tap on the head from the booth behind them, where he and his brother sat with the baby. "I thought I was the sexiest man ever?"

Frankie tilted her head back and blew him a playful kiss, leaving Mel with a lingering stab of envy for their obvious affection for one another. "You are, honey. But the second sexiest man ever is on TV. You know, *Celebrity Ballroom*? Neil Jensen?"

Jasmine purred. "Nom-nom. How do you know him, Mel? If I wasn't already wildly in love and newly married, I'd sink my cougar claws into a piece of that."

Mel laughed, hiding a sigh of relief they didn't know about her new obsession with Drew. "Neil's my old partner from my competition days. He's here to beat me back into submission."

"I'd let him beat me into anything," Maxine commented, slipping in beside Jasmine and giving her a quick peck on the cheek. She gave Mel a pat on the hand. "You look terrific, Mel! I've heard only great things from Dean Keller and the rest of the staff. I'm so glad it seems to be working out."

Mel couldn't help but grin. Today's coup with Nate couldn't be tarnished by a swollen eye. "The boys are awful dancers. They hate every second spent in my classroom. I know they'd rather be finding the cure for cancer, but I'm actually kind of getting into the swing of it—even with all the bitching and moaning."

"So this Neil—is he the reason for the happy? Any chance of a little romance in the air?" Frankie asked.

Mel placed her order with the waitress and shook her head. "Never. First, I'm not ready for anything more serious than a hangnail. Second, Neil and I will always be nothing more than friends. We've always known that. He's like a brother, and lately, the reason I hate five in the morning. How did you know he was even here?"

Maxine laughed, handing her menu to the waitress. "Nothing gets past the Villagers. Surely you didn't think you could wow the seniors with your fancy footwork and it would go unnoticed? My mother and Gail gushed about that demo you gave them until I was almost compelled to hit Arthur Murray's and never look back. I won't even tell you what she said about Neil and his back end. It isn't fit for polite company."

"I'll tell you what Gail said about Neil," Frankie offered with a sly grin. "She said, and I quote, 'Bet a man like that doesn't need a penis pump.'"

"Well, so far there've been no complaints, but I'm not getting any younger," a voice drawled from over Mel's shoulder.

Frankie hid behind her napkin while Maxine's face turned red and Jasmine, unabashed, stared Neil down. "Oh, look, a yummy man," she snickered, motioning him to pull up a chair.

Neil held up his hands, shaking his head. "You ladies carry on. I'm just here for some of that infamous takeout meatloaf."

"Oh, c'mon, Neil," Mel chided, tossing her napkin at him. "There are three gushing females here. You don't want to pass up the chance to add more admiring fans to your posse, do you?"

Neil smiled his dazzlingly white Hollywood smile and chucked her under the chin. "I'm afraid I have plans, girls. Maybe another time?"

"You're here in Jersey two minutes and you already have a date? Jesus, Neil." Mel whistled.

"Neil—Neil Jensen?" a young man, dressed in a dark suit with a plaid tie called from across the diner, making his way toward them.

Neil stood in front of Mel in a defensive stance. "That's me. You are?"

"I'm Fierce Parker, the entertainment reporter from *Jersey Every Morning*. Do you mind if I ask you some questions about your ex-partner, Melina Cherkasov?"

Mel shrank behind Neil, praying Fierce wouldn't see her. He'd called her father's, looking for her side of the story about her and Stan's breakup a few months ago.

Thanks to Jackie and her anonymous tips to one gossip venue or another, no one had found her yet. Frankie shot her concerned eyes, while Max narrowed hers in the reporter's direction.

"In fact, I kind of do mind, Fierce," Neil said affably. "I have no comment."

Mel slid farther down in her seat, her feet numb and her empty stomach lurching.

Fierce's alert eyes scanned the faces at the table, looking past Neil while Mel cowered, her hand over her face. "Just a couple of questions. C'mon, Neil. Help a guy out."

"I have nothing to say about Melina Cherkasov. Now, Fierce, I'm going to be as polite as I can when I ask you to please leave myself and the ladies alone while we enjoy our dinner."

Mel heard the tension in his voice, knew it well from the hundreds of times they'd had to smile and nod at a critique of their work Neil didn't necessarily agree with. She prayed Fierce would take the hint and go away.

Like praying had done her a whole lot of good lately. "Have you seen her recently? Do you know where she is? Did you know Stan's asked Yelena to marry him? Does *she* know?"

Neil's sigh was ragged and growing impatient. "Again, I'm going to ask you to move along, Mr. Parker. No comment."

But Fierce was, after all, a reporter. If he could blow one small word out of proportion, inflate one tidbit of gossip, he'd find a way to get a quote from Neil.

Neil couldn't afford even a whiff of bad press that might jeopardize his job on *Celebrity Ballroom*. Mel wouldn't allow his reputation to be blighted defending her. "Is it true that she's living in a homeless shelter?" Fierce pressed, his gaunt face studying Neil's.

"No . . ." Mel whispered at first, but Neil waved her off from behind his back. "No!" she yelped, both in defense of her supposed homelessness and Neil's signal to keep quiet. "No! That's not true," she yelled, jumping up from the booth, making the bottle of wine they'd been sharing wobble.

Shit. Hadn't she learned anything being married to superstar Stan? Never give the press anything. Never confirm or deny.

"Melina." Fierce, his eyes hungry, surveyed every inch of her, including her swollen eye and the rumpled clothes she hadn't had time to change out of. "Can I ask you a couple of questions? Don't you want everyone to hear your side of the story?"

She licked her lips, pushing a protesting Neil out of the way. "No. You can't ask me any questions. Please leave me alone." For all the good asking nicely would do when some cub reporter, desperate for ratings, was who she was asking.

He placed a hand on her arm to keep her from stepping around him. "But this is your opportunity to tell the world what happened," he coaxed, a smile on his thick lips.

Mel gulped hard, her terror over being found a huge lump in her throat. "I said, please leave me alone," she repeated, pulling her arm back, forcing herself to calm.

Yet Fierce was one tenacious bastard. As she tried to inch past him, he blocked her by shoving his sleazy face in hers and placing his hand back on her arm, faking an expression of sympathy.

At that very moment, when all good knights in shining armor should rear up on their white horses, a fist out of nowhere shot over her shoulder and landed a punch that cracked so loud, it made everyone in the diner drop their silverware.

The owner of the fist whispered in her ear, creating havoc with her already roiling belly. "What color tutu do you wear for an occasion like punching a guy out?"

CHAPTER SEVEN

Dear Divorce Journal,

So there's something to be said for having a man stand up for you, even when the man is Drew "Dancing Is Stupid" McPhee. And yes, I feel compelled to make it up to him. Maybe while he's naked and I lick something fattening off his concrete abs. Oh, this has to stop. If it's the last thing I do, I'm going to purge myself of this obsession with Drew like a priest at an exorcism. Off to find my Holy Water and Bible.

In the commotion, Mel was hustled out of the way, dragged to a nearby corner by Frankie and Maxine while Jasmine gave Fierce a hard crack of her purse to his head before stepping over him and heading in Mel's direction. "You okay, honey? Wow and wow. Who is that and where can we bioengineer three hundred more of him?"

Mel was too shocked to answer her. Instead, she made a beeline for Drew just as he was reaching down for Fierce.

"Did you hear the lady, Parker?" Drew yanked the dazed reporter to his feet. "She said to leave her alone. No means no, Fierce. Didn't your mother teach you that?"

Mel placed a hand on his back to stop him, caught briefly by the luxurious feel of his muscles beneath her palm, before catching herself. "Drew! Stop. Let him go."

Fierce wiped the back of his hand across his nose with angry eyes. "You animal! I'm just trying to do my job."

Job? Mel's temper flared. Since when had being an asshole become a job? Her privacy was at stake here, and she was ready to defend it at all costs. "By trying to force me to answer your questions?" Mel hissed up in his face. "Pay close attention, *Fierce*. If I were answering questions, or felt like I had any reason to answer them, it definitely wouldn't be for some loser reporter who's on some lame morning show no one but the people who pay for basic cable watch because they don't have a choice. Now get out of my face, or I'll make that fist in your nose seem like a day at the spa!"

Fierce's face distorted. "I bet the basic-cable crowd would love to hear about your new boyfriend here."

Now it wasn't just her privacy, but the anonymity of Drew and Nate and all the children at Westmeyer. Mel lunged for him, launching herself like her legs had springs. She latched on to his tie and yanked his head down to her level. "If you even *think* my name, I swear by all that's holy, I'll—"

"Back off, you vulture," Drew bit out, taking Mel by the shoulders and planting her beside him. He cornered Fierce, his stance threatening. "I think you and your threats better leave, or I might mess up your pretty suit."

Mel intervened, putting her hand on Drew's chest. She wouldn't allow him to become mixed up in the mess her life had become. "Drew! Don't. Let it be."

"Fine," Drew said on a huff of angry air. He brushed off Fierce's shoulders and handed him a napkin from a nearby table to wipe the blood from his nose. "Good as new. Now leave the lady alone, Parker, and if I ever catch you even five hundred feet near her, I'll beat you up and take your lunch money. Got that?"

Nikos, Frankie's husband, came up from Fierce's rear, placing a hand on the reporter's shoulder. "Make sure you tell all of Jersey on your show tomorrow morning you got your ass beat at the Greek Meets Eat Diner, pal. Spell it right, too. Now, leave, and don't come back, or I won't just take your lunch money—I'll beat your 401K right out of you."

The reporter's eyes narrowed to small slits in his head as he wiped the blood from his nose. "I could press charges," he sneered at Mel.

Drew's fists clenched. "You definitely could, but when you're pressing those charges or blogging about this or whatever it is you snakes do, make sure you tell everyone you put your hand on the lady first. And there are, oh, I'd say, probably thirty or so witnesses to attest to that fact, right folks?" Drew's eyes looked to the astonished customers for acknowledgment.

Customers that began to clap and cheer in response to Drew's request.

Fierce shoved his way past Drew and Nikos with resentful eyes and a red face, stomping his embarrassment to the door.

"Byyyye, Fierce," Drew drawled. Then all of his attention was immediately on Mel. He put a hand to her cheek. "Did he do that to your eye? I came in at the back end of it, saw he had his hand on your arm and wouldn't let you go, and reacted. My apologies for behaving like the caveman you expect me to be."

Mel leaned into his hand, closing her eyes to fend off the sudden attack of the girlies. "No. He didn't do this to my eye, and thank you. You have no idea how terrified I am of the press . . . Anyway, thank you."

He smiled, infuriatingly handsome. "You on your way out?"

Realizing she'd just created a scene, her appetite was suddenly gone. Frankie appeared out of nowhere with a carryout box. "I'm sorry, honey. I never saw him coming and by the look on your face, I know you just want to crawl into a hole now. But you have to eat in your hole. Take this with you, for me. Eat when you get home and you're not so upset."

Jasmine pushed a stray strand of Mel's hair from her face, cupping her cheek as Maxine rubbed her arm. "Let's have lunch on Saturday, okay? All four of us. I have a kitchen that just begs for someone to cook in it, and Simon would love nothing more than to have three gorgeous women to flirt with. I'll call you tomorrow with directions. Now, let the nice hunk, um, man walk you to your car. You are a nice man, aren't you?" Jasmine gave him the evil eye.

"The nicest," Drew replied in return.

Neil draped an arm around her shoulders and leaned in to whisper, "Oh-m-gee. Mel's got an admirer. You gonna be okay with him?"

She patted his hand and gave him a quick kiss on the cheek. "I'm fine. He's fine. I just want to leave so everyone will stop staring. I'm sorry, Neil. I'm so sorry. Stupid me to think they wouldn't eventually catch up to me. I'll see you tomorrow. You know, when all humane people are still asleep?"

Neil nodded, planting a quick kiss on her cheek.

Rattled, Mel whispered her apologies to everyone, especially Frankie, whose place of business had been turned upside down then let Drew lead her out to her car.

He took her hand in his as they made the short walk to her father's truck in silence. She backed up against the truck's door, still holding his hand, warm and callused against her cold skin. "What are you doing here?"

"Men who don't dance eat, too." His thumb caressed her palm in maddening circles.

Her laugh was nervous. "I'm sorry. I mean, I'm glad you were there. I knew I couldn't hide forever, but I'd hoped eventually all the speculation about me would die down. But it seems the more elusive I am, the more everyone wants the dirt."

"No kidding. Does that happen often?"

Instantly, she worried he feared for the safety of Nate and the boys at Westmeyer. "No. This is the first time since the divorce. I'm sorry you were involved."

"I'm not. I had to find a way to show off my manhood. Knocking some cocky reporter out was as good a way as any."

Mel laughed, gazing up at him with shy eyes. "Either way, thank you. I appreciate you running interference." On impulse, she rose on her toes to plant a kiss of gratitude on his cheek when Drew turned his head and the side of her lips caught his.

The world did something funny then. Something it had never done before, and while she might have only been married to one man all her life, she'd kissed a lot of boys beforehand.

The world sort of fell out of focus before righting itself, making her swoon.

Swoon.

Their lips disconnected, but Drew didn't move away. Instead, he let his mouth linger at the side of hers, achingly enticing. "Gratitude and you make a nice combination. Who knew the dancing queen doesn't just have a smart mouth, but a kissable one, too?"

Her breath shuddered when he spoke, her body leaning into his. She shivered and knew she couldn't blame it on the cool evening air. Drew revved her engine, floated her boat, and made her lady parts do handstands. "Who knew a Neanderthal could be so noble and gallant and worthy of my gratitude?"

Instantly, Mel pulled back, flattening against the truck. Who was this Flirty McFlirt? "Well, anyway, thank you. I get so tongue-tied when it comes to the press that it makes me an easy target."

Drew let a hand rest on the doorframe of the truck, loosely pinning her in position. "Funny. You don't seem to have that trouble with me."

Her breathing was becoming choppy at his close proximity.

"That's because I'm not concerned you'll write some story that mis-construes every word I say and turn it into something ugly and com-pletely untrue."

"What a shitty way to live, Mel. I'm sorry."

Was that genuine remorse or just the generic condolence every-one offered? "I managed to stay out of it for a very long time, but since my divorce . . ." Mel clamped her mouth shut.

"Yeah. Most of us get divorced and generally no one cares but your immediate family. Your divorce has been a circus that's involved the entire world."

Mel's breath hitched when Drew's cologne drifted to her nose. Had he seen the reports on *Hollywood Scoop*? Had he watched all those undernourished female reporters, wearing designer-label dres-ses, speculate about her whereabouts and if she was taking her meals in a soup kitchen or living on Johnny Depp's secluded island while she lapped up his pity?

The coy flirting she'd indulged in moments ago slipped away and was replaced by the heavy air of her humiliation. Knowing he'd prob-ably seen more personal details about her life with Stan than she'd reveal to someone she hardly knew made her hope the ground would open and swallow her up—now.

Pity was not something you wanted from your obsession. It served as a mood killer for all those naughty thoughts. "It was definitely a circus. Complete with elephants and a sideshow freak." Her temple began to throb. "Look, I have to go. I have to be up early, but thanks again." Mel slipped under his arm, turning her back to him to look through her purse for her keys.

But Drew took her arm in a light grasp. "Don't run away. I was just making an observation. I was sympathizing. Something I'm sure you think I'm incapable of, but I was nonetheless. I'm divorced, too. It had a sort of suck-i-tude to it. Granted, it wasn't as global in the

sucky department as yours, but it sucked just the same. Even us com-
moners feel pain."

His body, sheltering her from behind, and his words, spoken with
a quiet decency, struck the chords of her heart. "It did suck, and I'm
sorry yours sucked. But it's over now, and I'm really trying to move
forward. Reporters like that Fierce just make it difficult."

Drew's breath was back in her ear, making her fight a soft sigh and
the impulse to lean back against his wide chest. "I bet I can help you
move forward."

Mel hid her smile, finally locating her keys and pulling them out
to beep the truck door open with shaking fingers. "Really?"

"Really. Moving forward always involves getting out and experiencing new things. At least that's what my family told me when I got
divorced. So I say you experience coffee with me—in the spirit of
moving forward. Consider it therapy from one of the former walking
wounded. You know, like a sponsor-type thing. Nothing serious. No
commitments, just some coffee."

Breathless, she popped the door open when something occurred
to her. This was a chance to purge herself of Drew McPhee. She'd
berated herself for a week now for turning him down, and since that
day, he'd become the object of her desire. That couldn't be healthy.
What she had to do was prove to herself he was no big thang.

Drew wasn't someone she'd idolized since her childhood like
Stan had been. He was just a man.

Yes, he was an amazing specimen of man, but if she'd learned one
thing about her qualifications for amazing, it was that she was unqual-
ified to make smart decisions about exactly what constituted amazing.

But she and Drew were equals, neither of them any more knowl-
edgeable about any one thing than the other. Stan had had the upper
hand because he was older and his expertise in the field of dance was
respected and legendary.

Drew was just a good-looking guy. A good-looking guy she couldn't stop thinking about.

Emotionally, she was still an insecure wreck—which could be why she couldn't get him out of her head. It had been a long time since a man had shown any interest in her, and that included Stan. A little spark of attention from anyone of the male persuasion was bound to be something she clung to at such a vulnerable stage, when she felt fat and ugly.

Yet, Mel recognized that would only be moving from one unhealthy Stan habit to another. Drew wasn't the only man in the world. Maybe once she'd experienced him, she would discover that, and she could do this forward motion thing everyone raved about like it was the next best thing since Bare Lifts had been invented.

Turning around, she summoned her dancing skills—more specifically, the skills she'd used in a tango, which required her to convince the audience and judges she was hot on the hunt for her partner. A tango was often a story of seduction, one she'd told endlessly with Neil in competition. The dance where she was the seducer, luring a man into her web with her sultry hips and smoldering eyes.

Mel tried a confident smile on for size, squaring her shoulders and holding her head up to find Drew's eyes gazing down at her. "Okay, when?"

If he was stunned by her acceptance, he didn't show it. "Friday?"

"Where?"

"The club for swingers. You know, in the next town over? I thought we could dabble in bondage. There's no better way to get to know someone than when they're tied up on one of those spiky tables, if you ask me."

Mel laughed, her giggle floating from her lips. "If I thought we had nothing in common before, I'm sure of it now."

"Damn. How could I have pegged you so wrong?"

"It's those pesky assumptions. So where?" She tapped a finger on her carryout carton, waiting.

Drew's brow furrowed like he hadn't expected her to say yes. Maybe he was more about the challenge than the actual coup? "How about that new café in town? Daisy's, I think it is."

"Time?"

"Seven?"

"Date."

His eyebrow rose in surprise. "What—no fight? No protests? Just 'date'?"

Mel smirked at him, tipping her jaw over her shoulder. "Should I have presented more of a challenge than I already have?"

His expression was cynical. "There's a catch."

Mel shrugged her shoulders, feigning indifference. "No catch. Your words of wisdom made me realize you're right. I should begin to experience life again. It may as well be you I experience my first date with. You know, so I can oil all those rusty spots for my future dating health. I'll work out all my awkward, insecure, haven't-dated-in-twenty-years vulnerabilities on you. Some lucky man will thank you someday for breaking me in."

He crossed his arms over his chest, hitching his jaw at her with a grunt. "So now I'm the date guinea pig?"

Mel smiled, liking the turn this had unexpectedly taken. All of a sudden, she felt in control. And it was good. "That does have a certain ring to it. Besides, you were the one who wouldn't take no for an answer, knowing full well I'm emotionally a shit wreck and probably not ready to date. I did tell you that. Yet, you persisted. Now that I've called your bluff, are you chickening out?" she challenged, feeling the stirrings of the Mel who'd once floored judges by trading her off the dance floor sunny disposition for a blistering hot temptress in the tango.

Ah, yes, she knew this costume, and as she tried it back on for size again, it was a little tight in some places, but it still fit. All right, some of her rhinestones had fallen off, but she still had it, if she was judging his reaction correctly.

The small tic in his jaw twitched, delighting her enough to make her grin. "Chickening out? *The. Hell.* I'll tell you this. It'll be the best date you've ever been on. I'll make you eat those words."

Tipping her head back, she flashed him a look of cynicism by giving him her best haughty, yet come-hither, glance. "Well, seeing as I haven't been on any dates almost ever—you won't have much expectation to live up to."

"I guess we'll see about that, Ms. Cherkasov," he gritted, clearly realizing she'd thrown down an imaginary gauntlet and had all but dared him to show her a good time.

Mel climbed into the truck, ignoring her aching thighs, flashing him another flirty, slow smile. She turned the key in the ignition and pressed the button to the driver's side window down. "Fine. Daisy's. Friday at seven. Bring your best game." She flicked her fingers at him as though she was dismissing the very notion, calling upon the thousands of times she'd had to give Neil a dramatic, choreographed shove.

Drew frowned again. It was obvious he was now unclear who'd won the first round of this battle she'd secretly created. His face hardened, turning all those muscles in his jaw into clenched bits of flesh. "You're on, lady. Friday at seven." He turned away from the truck with a scowl, taking big strides in the other direction of the diner's parking lot, the dark night swallowing him up.

Mel's hands shook as she backed the truck up and she was able to drop the performance of a lifetime. She came down hard; unaware her body had been so coiled in tension.

But then, as she drove back to the Village, she remembered

Drew's handsome face and how he'd fought to hide his uncertainty at her acceptance, and it made her giggle. Her total one-eighty had taken him by surprise. Good.

If Drew McPhee wanted a date, then by all that was holy, he was going to get a date.

With the Mel who, at one time in her life, on a dance floor anyway, had been as confident as any man-eater.

Insecurity be damned. She was going to don her inner spray tan and sparkly rhinestones and wash Drew and his nuclear brand of sexy right out of her hair.

~ℓ~

Mel breezed into her father's house, dropping her dinner and her purse on the table with a careless clunk.

"Hey, how was your day, Swedish meatball?" her dad called from the kitchen, his large frame covered in his favorite flannel bathrobe. He was scooping ice cream into a bowl while Jake sat at his feet.

"Guess what?" she asked, reaching for Weezer's leash and patting her thigh to encourage him to come. He lumbered toward her, his soulfully droopy eyes held a smile always reserved only for her. She leaned down to drop a kiss on his massive head.

Joe's head popped around the corner of the kitchen. "What?"

"I'm going on a date." She threw the words out like she was a bullet aiming for a target. "I figured I'd better tell you before Myriam Hernandez tells all the seniors and brands me the Village whore."

Joe's nod was slow, when he pushed a spoonful of ice cream into his mouth, his eyes hesitant. "Okay. That's nice. I'm glad you're gettin' out."

Mel arched her eyebrow in surprise, irritated that he wasn't prodding her for more information. Now that she'd consented to her obsession's request for a date, she wanted everyone to bear witness to her moving forward. Maybe she'd buy a billboard with the slogan "Mel's Moving Forward" for all to see. "Don't you want to know with who?"

"You make it sound like I should . . ."

"Drew McPhee." Yeah. That's who.

"Who's he?"

"He's Myriam Hernandez's nephew," she virtually spat as though saying it out loud was a contemptuous act of heinousness.

Joe held up his spoon. "Question?"

Latching Weezer's leash to his collar with a huff, she said, "Fine."

"Why does this date sound more like an upcoming boxing match? Don't dates make girls all happy and glowing? Or nervous and silly?"

"I suppose some dates do. This one is a test."

"A test? What kind of a test?"

"The kind where I prove to myself the man who asked me out is no big deal, and I move on to all these shiny things everyone says I'm supposed to find."

"Shiny things?"

"Yeah, you know all this self-discovery you and Maxine and clan preach."

"Seems to me, you're going in with the wrong attitude, ladybug. You got some chip on your shoulder."

"The point is I'm going. Isn't that what you want me to do? Get out? Meet people?"

Her father looked down at her legs. "You gonna shave your legs before you get out and meet people? I won't have them calling you 'Clan of the Cave Bear.' It'll besmirch your mother's fine name."

Mel stuck her tongue out at him. "No. On behalf of all women who want to be loved for who they are on the inside, I'm revolting against shaving my legs. I'm an as-is package."

"So, do you even like the young man who's asked you out? Even a little?"

"He's a jerk."

Her father blinked. "Which is a perfect reason to go on a date with him."

"Exactly. I'm pretty good at picking jerks. Just look at Stan and how starry-eyed and stupid I was over him. I've decided the best defense against picking another jerk is a good offense. Sort of like exposure therapy. You know, like on that show *Obsessed* where the therapist makes you sit with whatever your obsession is and wait until your anxiety levels lessen?" So, she'd sit with Drew until her need to do things she couldn't even pronounce passed.

"This isn't exactly the same thing as washing your hands or turning on and off light switches, Mel."

"It's an obsession just the same. A good-looking man compliments me and all of a sudden, I'm breaking out the latest issue of *Modern Bride.*"

Joe chucked her under the chin and chuckled. "Why would you go out with someone you know isn't good for you?"

"Because I need to get him out of my system." Out, out, out.

Joe grumbled. "He's been in your system? I'm not sure I like the sound of that."

Mel shook her finger at him. "I just mean he's all I've thought of since I met him, and it's ridiculous. It's like Stan all over again."

Her father's broad shoulders lifted in defeat. "Is he another touchy twinkle toes? Myriam never said her nephew danced."

"No, he's not a dancer, Dad. He's the handyman at the school. I just mean I'm pretty sure I've managed to make him into something he's not. Just like Stan. He's cute. So what? Is that a reason to spend all my free time thinking about him? I've been down that road before. I'm not devoting all of me to someone who isn't going to do the same in return. I decided if I give him what he wants by going out with him, I'll find out he's not such a superstar after all. I know the signs now. Well, I know most of them."

"But you already said he's a jerk. How much more proof do you need?"

Mel flapped a hand at her dad. "I just meant his attitude about boys dancing was sort of jerk-ish. That's why I called him a jerk. I don't know if he's a jerk-jerk. Okay, so he picks Myriam up and carts her all over town, and he's got a pretty solid relationship with his son, but that doesn't mean he's intimate-relationship worthy. How could I know that when I haven't even gone out with him? The only thing I do know is he can't possibly live up to the rock star I've turned him into in my head." The rock star that was a sexual terminator in bed. She clenched her teeth. Damn. Him.

"Is it any wonder men are from Mars and women are from Venus, peanut butter cup?"

Mel gave Weezer's leash a tug toward the door. "Never mind, Dad. You can't possibly understand. You had Mom. She was awesome. Your marriage was awesome. You picked right the first time."

"Yep. It was mostly awesome. But it wasn't awesome all the time, Mellie. We had some rough patches, too. That's what marriage is about. Highs and lows and ridin' 'em out."

"Well, you didn't ride the rough patches out with another woman, now did you?"

Joe chucked her under the chin. "Don't be bitter, kiddo. It's ugly on such a pretty girl."

"Am I being touchy and negative?"

He pointed to the ceiling. "And reaching a whole new level while you do it."

"Better safe than sorry, right?"

"Maybe sorry is what you have to be so safe is something you value."

Drew McPhee was anything but safe. He was a big, yellow hazmat sign to not only her libido but her penchant for choosing a man who would swallow her whole. Mel stood on her toes and gave her dad a kiss on the cheek. "I'm just a mess of jumbled emotions I have to sort through on my own. I'm sure I'm going about it all wrong, too. Go to bed, Dad. I'm going to walk Weez and hit the sack, too. Promise."

"You know I'm here if you need to talk. Even if I don't know what in the hell you're saying."

She chuckled, opening the front door. "I do, Daddy, and I appreciate it. Night now." Mel trudged out into the cool night, pulling Weezer along behind her. They walked in companionable silence for a time, her kicking the fallen leaves along the sidewalk and Weezer trotting happily beside her.

"We got trouble, Weez. I've made a date with the devil."

Weezer stopped, staring up at her with a snort.

She gave his enormous head a loving scratch. "Okay, so maybe he's not the devil, but he can't be as incredible as I've made him in my mind. I'm setting myself up for a fall. I've done it before . . ."

And she didn't ever want to do it again. The next serious relationship she went into wasn't going to involve any kind of hero-worship, and it certainly wasn't going to be based on the kind of lust she felt for Drew. That was all this was, her long-neglected hormones reacting to a man that was decidedly attractive.

That had no substance. Sex was easy.

Mel winced at her attitude. Not only was she defensive but she was behaving as if one date would determine the rest of her life.

Weezer woofed up at her.

"Fine. Maybe I am defensive, but I have to be careful, pal. I'm too easily swept off my feet, and I don't like where the sweeping left me. I'm just being cautious. I mean what if Drew and I ended up getting involved, and he did the same thing to us that Stan did? Do you really want to live with Jake for the rest of your life?"

Weezer whimpered, placing a bear-sized paw on her foot.

"Exactly my point. I feel better already. So I go on this date, Drew blows it by picking his nose or forgets to trim his nostril hairs and I get so turned off I want to yark. End date and all of my erotic dreams about him. Who has erotic dreams about a guy who picks his nose? Stan had this horrible habit of cleaning his ears at the table, then inspecting the Q-tip. It was disgusting. Had I investigated instead of running off to a chapel with him because he said I was a great dancer, I might have known that."

Weezer moaned, driving his head against her hip.

"TMI, Weez? Sorry. Forget I ever said the word 'erotic.' It'll all be over after Friday and we can forget I ever even mentioned it. He'll be toast by Saturday."

Steering Weezer back toward her father's, she nodded her head, reassuring herself. Yes, by Saturday morning, Drew and his scandalous body and good looks would be toast.

End of.

~ℓ~

"So guess who's got a date?"

Myriam snorted. "Your mother? That's a good sign, dating outside your marriage. Means the Irishman's on his way out the door."

His mother guffawed but frowned in her sister's general direction in honor of his father.

Drew chuckled in her ear as she stood at his mother's sink, rinsing the dishes. "No. Me."

His aunt swatted his arm. "You nabbed Mel, you middle-aged dog?"

Drew pretended to be hurt. "I don't think I like the surprise in your voice, Aunt Myriam. Didn't you think I was capable of nabbing Mel?"

"Who's Mel? Is she *the* Mel, Myriam? The 'finally dragging my son out of his six-year dating dry spell' Mel?" his mother asked, a look of mock surprise on her face.

"Hey! I've dated. Not in serial fashion, but there've been dates."

His mother waved a chubby finger under his nose. "Making a date with that poor Lisa Masters, then chickening out at the last minute is not dating. It's waffling."

Myriam clucked. "She's *that* Mel, Selena. The one I been tellin' ya our Drew here's got the naughty thoughts about. She teaches dance classes at the Village. The one who was married to the rusty pecker on TV."

"Whoa." Drew held up his hands in innocence. "Who said anything about naughty thoughts?"

"Your eyeballs did. They were all over her when she was dancin' with that Neil," Myriam accused playfully, turning the water off and facing him, a spatula in hand.

His mother pinched his cheek with damp fingers. "She's so *pretty*," she crowed approvingly.

"And cranky," he added, giving his mother a kiss on her cheek.

"She's been hurt. You remember that kind of hurt, don't you, son?" his mother searched his eyes, looking for the signs all the traces of hurt were gone.

He remembered. "I remember. I'll tread lightly." Though, after Mel's sudden about-face tonight, he wondered who should have the lighter tread. She'd all but challenged him to make this date the best date ever in some sort of weird duel.

Myriam shook her head of gray curls. "I'd be cranky if my husband told me we were getting divorced on the television, too."

"Your husband was too smart for that, Myriam. He took the easy
way out and died instead," William McPhee said with a cackle, sticking his nose back in the newspaper and ducking when his wife shot a
damp towel in his direction.

"Speaking of taking the easy way out—that ex-wife of yours
called. She wants Nate this weekend. I told her we have family plans,
but she said the courts say she can have Natty." Drew's mother made
a face of disapproval, her rounded cheeks flushed with indignation
when she brushed her hands off on her stained apron.

There was no love lost between his mother and Sherry, his ex-wife.
The only time his mother even attempted to hide her fury was when
she was around Nate, and she did it because Drew demanded she do it.

Sherry was a crappy mother, but he wouldn't allow those words to
come out of anyone's mouth in front of Nate. Regardless of Sherry's
love affair with a bottle of booze and some pills, one that kept her
from giving Nate the mother he deserved, Drew wouldn't tolerate
anyone disrespecting her.

"She does have that right, Mom." He hated it as much as his mother
and the rest of his family. He worried every second Nate was with her.
Not quite the way he had when Nate was younger and didn't know how
to fend for himself, but worry he did.

"What kind of judge gives a booze hound like her visitation
rights?" his mother hissed in a whisper. "She doesn't care about
Natty. She cares about Jack Daniels and Miller Light."

Drew put a finger to his mouth. "Shhh. Nate will hear you, Mom.
I don't like it any better than you do, but it's court mandated. She's
supposed to have him every weekend. Let's just be glad she's usually
too busy with a bottle in some bar to be sober enough to remember."

His mother scrunched her face in residual anger over the judge's ruling. "You just remember what I told you, Drew. If she ever hurts my Nate because she's had too much to drink, I'll kill her myself."

William was instantly on his feet at the mention of Drew's ex-wife. He reached out for his wife, placing an arm around her waist to soothe her. "Now, Selena. Let's not invite the bad in by saying it out loud. She'll probably forget she called when Nate calls her back. Or she won't answer the phone at all like she always does." His father winked at him. "So tell us about your girl, Drew."

The light Irish brogue his father had retained after living in America for over seventy-two of his seventy-four years was always a balm to Drew's ears. "She's a dance instructor at Nate's school."

"A dance instructor you were rude to when you found out she had to teach Nate to ballroom dance," his aunt accused.

He rolled his tongue along the inside of his cheek. "Okay. I was a little rude."

Myriam planted a hand on her rounded hip "That's not what Dean Keller's Uncle Hiram said. He said you yelled like some kinda caveman."

"I was caught off guard. I thought I was sending Nate to learn— not dance. But I must not have been that much of a caveman because she agreed to go out with me." So there.

Although, he still was unclear about why Mel had agreed to go out with him in the first place. Her acquiescence had been anything but sweet. It had been more like determined. As if going out with him was like facing her worst fear head on.

"You're going out with Ms. Cherkasov?" Nate asked, coming around the corner of his grandmother's blue and mauve kitchen with her collection of different variations of cows in wood lining the upper cabinets.

Drew had never considered it might be awkward for Nate. Damn. He didn't want to make trouble for his son. He'd had enough garbage in his life. "You okay with that?"

Nate shot Myriam a quick glance before responding. "Yep. It's cool."

"You sure? I don't want to cause trouble at school for you."

"Seriously, Dad, how much more trouble could there be when I'm the best dancer in her class? You don't think that's trouble with a bunch of nerds?"

Drew's mother laughed, pulling Nate to her and rocking him in a tight squeeze after planting a kiss on his forehead. "I'm so proud. You take after your grandmother, you know."

"So you taking her dancing, Dad?" Nate gave him a fiendish smile.

He wrapped an arm around Nate's neck and gave him a gentle scrub with his knuckles to the top of his head. "You're a funny kid. Not a chance. We're just having coffee."

And if he'd heard her right, it better be spectacular coffee.

He had to hope she didn't expect it to be on some private jet.

CHAPTER EIGHT

Dear Stupid Divorce Journal,

Did I really think Drew would be toast by Saturday morning? I'm pretty sure I didn't think we'd be *eating* toast. Together. In his apartment. I am a dirty, dirty whore who clearly doesn't know the distinct difference between a compliment made out of kindness and an offer to quench my sordid desires.

Though, he did say I was sort of sexy. The next time I hear those words, I swear, I'm running in the other direction instead of misinterpreting them to mean, "While I'm accusing you of being rude in a dark café parking lot, let's have sex in seven different positions on as many surfaces, so we can really get the Drew virus out of your system." Swear it.

Love,

The Dirty, Dirty Whore.

"So here I am." Mel gave Drew a condescending glare, much like the one's she'd launched at Neil when they depicted the push-and-pull of a sexually tense paso doble. The glare that said, "impress me or die."

Oh, yes. She had on her dancing shoes and she was ready to rrrrumba.

Drew rose from the table he'd chosen outside the café, pulling out a chair for her when he caught sight of her, stomping across the parking lot like he owed her money. The table sat amongst the twinkling strands of white lights draped around potted arborvitaes and woven into the maple trees on either side of Daisy's.

Warm fires blazed in chimineas scented with hickory wood that surrounded the intimate glass tables scattered in clusters.

And it was all very charming, wasn't it? Bastard could take his charming and shove it up his ass.

"Hi, Mel. Glad you could make it," he said with a cocky grin.

She flopped down in the chair, throwing her purse on the table, and eyeballed him when he sat back down, refusing to acknowledge how delicious he looked in his black fitted shirt with the sleeves rolled up. He was just a man. Just. A. Man. She'd repeated that over and over as she resisted the impulse to bathe in some hot wax and dig out her clumpy mascara.

True to her word, she hadn't shaved her legs or done much else to impress him visually. "So. Wow me."

Instead of being angry that she was demanding he entertain her, Drew laughed. "There's no wow here. Just me. If that's not enough wow—then I'm wowed out."

Mel's eyes narrowed. Why wasn't he rising to the bait? How unfair that he should be a gentleman when she'd spent the last day and a half turning him into something akin to Charlie Manson. "I thought this was going to be the best date ever," she taunted.

"You know, I gave that some serious thought after your sudden one-eighty the other night. I asked myself, 'Drew McPhee, whatever could the wily Mel be up to, first playing coy, then turning into some demanding shrew?' And then it hit me that I didn't really care what you were up to or what kind of game you're playing. I'm not into games. As to the best date ever, that's a lot of pressure to put on myself for a first date, one you're determined to see fail anyway. So I figured, screw that. It's a nice night. Not too cold, but just cold enough that it's invigorating. Just right for a hot cup of coffee. So instead of wowing you with my intellect and witty repartee, I'm just going to order some plain old coffee and enjoy an evening off. You're free to stick around if a freebie's your thing. I'm still in for buying you the obligatory coffee. It's the least I can do after you drove all of two miles to get here."

Was that the sound of the reins of this date being rudely snapped from her hands? God, why did it have to be so damned sexy?

Oh, no. She was the hunter in this game of cat and mouse.

Just call her cat.

Meow.

"FYI, all talk and no action makes for a disappointing Drew McPhee." Boom, baby. Take that, you cocky, sexy as hell bastard!

Drew's eyebrow rose while he sipped his coffee, the luscious temptation of his lips wrapped around the rim of the cup made a bead of sweat trickle between her breasts.

He put the cup down and leaned forward as though he was going to tell her a secret. His grin was sly. "Trust me, sweetheart, you wouldn't be disappointed by Drew McPhee in action. He's just decided to take his action to a less demanding playing field." He said the words low and husky, shooting her another arrogant smile.

Mel fought a purr of pure lust at his alpha stance. *Must. Resist.* Instead, she raised her eyebrow back at him with as much condescension as she could muster. "So much for making me eat my words," she said with dry sarcasm.

He sighed dramatically, shrugging his shoulders before raising a finger to catch the pretty waitress's attention. "Well, you're on a diet anyway, right?"

Her eyes narrowed in suspicious embarrassment. "Who told you that?"

"Nate heard you turning down a piece of Mrs. Willows's birthday cake yesterday because you said you're on a diet."

Was nothing sacred? She rolled her eyes. "Right. A diet. So, seeing as there's going to be no wow, I think I'll head home, but thanks for the sort-of date. It's been everything I'd hoped it would be and more."

In and out. Just like she'd planned. Why she was feeling a stab of regret that Drew hadn't bothered to even attempt to wow her could be sorted out when she was at home. Alone. In her flannel pajamas and fuzzy footies.

Drew rose when she did. "I'll walk you to your car."

Nuh-uh. He wasn't going to keep flashing the decent-guy thing in her face. She'd had it up to her neck in nice guy. He could stay here and pick his nose. "Thanks, but don't bother. I've walked to my car a million times all by myself. I think I can manage. See you Monday." She whirled around, heading off into the darkness to locate her dad's truck.

Drew's chair scraped on the cement. "Oh, no, lady. I won't have word getting out that I'm some kind of slacker on a date. I'm not going to let you ruin my reputation as a gentleman just because you have some kind of stick up your ass. I'm walking you to your car—like it or don't." His strides fell in beside hers.

Mel stopped short halfway to her father's truck, her lips thinned in anger. "Hold on. Did you just say I had a stick up my ass?"

He barked a laugh filled with disdain. "I did. Did I mention it's probably pretty big and uncomfortable? I'm guessing it would have to be for you to be so damned rude."

"Rude? I am not rude." She stalked off, kicking up parking lot dust and avoiding the truth of his statement. Not to mention a public argument that could get back to Nate. The last thing she wanted was for Nate to feel any tension between her and Drew. That was probably one of the biggest reasons Westmeyer didn't encourage the staff dating each other.

And yeah, she'd definitely been rude. It was the perfect defense against Drew's force field of delicious. Go in with a grudge, whether the grudge was imagined or not, walk away unscathed and with your pride intact. There'd be no more falling for the first kind word or flirtatious gesture ever again.

But instead of leaving her and her rudeness to mate and become one, Drew stalked right beside her. "The hell you're not. Rude is showing up to a date with a shitty attitude and an even shittier outlook on something that didn't even have the chance to happen."

She waved a finger in the air in his general direction while gravel crunched beneath her angry feet. "You *were* the one who said it would be the best date *ever.*"

"After you threw down your lady gauntlet and dared me. But guess what? I decided *you* weren't worthy of my best date ever."

Mel stopped short again. "Hah! I think you just aren't clever enough to come up with something that's wow-worthy of a best date ever."

He loomed over her, forcing her feet to move backward. "Did you just call me stupid?"

Squinting at him, she glared. "I called you 'unclever.' Not 'stupid.'"

His nostrils flared, making her heart thump in uneven beats. "That's not even a word."

She craned her neck upward, rolling her head in a slow circle of "take that." "It is now. I just made it up in your honor."

"While you're making up words, why don't you make up one for a woman with a sense of entitlement so big, it rivals the state of Texas in size."

Entitlement? Hellllloooooo. Wasn't it she who'd slunk off to her corner while Stan had taken everything? "How dare you call me 'entitled,' Captain Caveman!"

His lips thinned and his eyes glittered. "Oh, I dare. You have some nerve expecting anything from anyone with the kind of goods you bring to the dating table," he said between clenched teeth, positioning his body directly over hers.

Was he making fun of her hairy legs and dejectedly grazed with a careless hairbrush coif? So she hadn't dressed up for the occasion featuring the great Drew McPhee. Who had a sense of entitlement now? "Are you mocking my appearance? How shallow!"

His mood shifted without warning when he shot her a dazzling smile. "No. I think it's sort of sexy in a thrown-together way." Then his expression returned to its original pissed off when he shouted, "What I'm mocking is your—"

She muffled the next words he planned to hurl at her with her mouth.

On his.

How they ended up in his apartment was a hazy journey of heavy breathing, lips and tongues preventing a great deal of clarity, and some mention of its location being right next door to Daisy's Café.

With the door safely shut, Drew's hands reached for her, pushing her up against the cold metal, molding her to him, crushing her body against his until she thought she'd die from the sharp pleasure it brought.

He was everything she'd been afraid he'd be and more. Mel was sure she'd regret that fleeting thought later. Right now, he was doing things to her body that hadn't ever quite been done in the way he was doing them, and her reason went the way of off-the-shoulder sweat-shirts and Duran-Duran.

His passion was an unrestrained force, palpable and filled with a heady combination of his lips and hands. Drew touched every part of her body through her clothing, making her hips jut against his to revel in the rigid strain of his cock through his jeans.

Mel's fingers plowed through his hair, devouring the slick sensation of his tongue with whimpers of delight. Sex with Stan had always had a certain amount of restraint attached to it she'd never realized until this wild abandon with Drew. She'd never felt as free as she did at this moment. Free to explore every tense muscle in his body with hands that shook and fingers that fumbled here and there in the process of relieving him of his clothing.

She heard the pop of buttons on her worn flannel shirt and groaned her approval when he shoved her bra out of the way to cup her breast with a callused hand. Pulsing-hot pleasure shot through her veins, making the ache between her legs almost unbearable.

"Wait," she gasped, forcing air into her lungs. "Nate."

"At my parents' for the night," Drew gasped back, driving her skirt upward and yanking her panties and leotard down with a rough jerk.

Mel kicked them from around her ankles, spreading her legs wide when Drew plunged a finger deep within the folds of her swollen sex. She clutched frantically at his shoulders, pulling at the fabric of his shirt until he rolled his shoulders to remove it.

When flesh met flesh, hisses of satisfaction mingled with the duel of their tongues.

Mel's knees began to crumble at the pressure of his lips consuming hers, the drive of his silken tongue exploring her mouth, demanding she return his kiss.

Drew's chest crashed against hers, scraping against her nipples, now exposed to the cool air. Mel whimpered when he pinched a nipple between his thumb and forefinger, rolling it to a tight peak.

He reached the other hand under her ass, hiking her leg up around his waist to grind against her, wreaking havoc with her senses.

Mel let her frantic fingers find the zipper of his jeans, the rasp when she dragged it downward erotic to her ears, knowing she was revealing yet another layer of Drew.

He groaned into her mouth, low and hot, sending a round of shivers along her exposed flesh. Drew's hips drove against her hand when she pulled his jeans down and enveloped his cock, thick and hot, in her shaking hands. He pressed against her hard to gain leverage, kicking his jeans from around his feet to free himself.

Grabbing her around the waist, he hoisted her upward, letting the tip of his shaft caress her swollen clit. A deep, guttural moan slipped from their lips, a sound made in unison.

Mel clung to his shoulders as he walked her toward somewhere. She couldn't focus on anything other than this blinding need to have him hard within her, thrusting, quenching her insatiable need for him.

Drew tore his lips from hers and muttered, "Condoms this way."

Vaguely, she realized it was a good thing he had some or in desperation she might have DIY'd it and used plastic wrap and twisty ties as a makeshift form of protection.

And then she forgot everything but the feel of the soft mattress beneath her back and Drew's sinfully heavy weight on her. There were no words, no sounds. There was just his cock driving into her slick passage with a force that left her dizzy.

Mel cried out, burying her face in the muscles of his shoulder, biting her bottom lip from the sheer bliss of his possession. Her hands reached for his hair, driving her fingers through the thick strands, clinging to it, and wrapping her legs around his waist to allow him to drive deeper.

Drew strained against her, slowing his driving thrusts, finding a rhythm that he seemed to realize brought her the most pleasure.

The crisp hairs at the base of his cock scraped against her clit, heightening the onslaught of new sensations. When the first wave of orgasm tore through her, she arched her neck, rearing her hips upward to meet his.

Drew gripped her hips, his fingers digging into her tender flesh, making the next rush of release that much more exciting. Heat pooled in her belly and the electric jolt of pleasure spiraled upward and out of her control.

Just as she thought she had nothing left in her, she fought a scream of unadulterated bliss when Drew drove into her for the last time, dragging another gut-wrenching climax from her body.

He collapsed on top of her, taking harsh, raspy breaths of air while pulling her close.

What had just happened between them didn't hit her immediately. She was too wrapped up in the musky scent of his cologne and the safety the warmth of his arms around her left her feeling.

In fact, it didn't hit her until the next morning.

It also didn't hit her until they'd committed more lewd and lascivious acts than two porn stars on a bipolar high . . .

She woke with the jolt of an unfamiliar bed beneath her and the scent of burned toast. Mel sat up, catching herself before she fell out of said unfamiliar bed. Her eyes brought the room into focus slowly, her blurred vision clearing in increments, her fuzzy thoughts coming in bits and pieces.

She ran a hand over her tangled hair, pulling it from the drool it was stuck to at the corner of her mouth. Bleh. Cotton mouth. She swallowed to relieve the dryness and wrinkled her nose. No doubt, she had morning breath, too.

Huh. Nice room. Lots of manly colors like burgundies and navy blue strictly meant for only the manliest of men. The bed was a dark cherry with an iron frame.

That must have been where all that clanking had come from last night.

Last night.

She gasped, putting her hand to her mouth to muffle the obnoxious sound. Why her brain was just now catching up with her nymphomaniac-ish lady parts was a mystery. It wasn't like she'd been drunk on too much coffee to know what she was doing.

Oh, Holy Mother of God. She'd thrown herself at Drew McPhee in a parking lot without even a little prompting. One minute they were screaming at each other and the next they'd landed in his apartment, tearing each other's clothes off like they were next up in a potato sack race at some nudist colony.

Mel threw back the covers then realized she was naked. In broad daylight.

Her eyes flew to the bedside alarm clock. Seven. Damn.

She dragged the sheet from the bed, wrapping it around her during a frantic search for her clothes. Where the hell was her underwear? From the corner of her eye, she caught sight of a straight-backed chair with a plaid cushion to the left of the bed. On top of it sat her clothes, neatly folded, and her purse.

She scrambled to pull her bra on, wincing when she found a tear in the pink lace. Grabbing her flannel shirt, she threw it over her head and pulled on her panties and her skirt, shoving her leotard into her purse.

Peering around, she noted there was no connecting bathroom to at least run a comb over her hair, and there was no mirror in Drew's bedroom either.

Silly. Why would someone as good-looking as Drew need a mirror? He clearly didn't need the kind of reassurance most mortals did.

Drew . . . where was Drew?

Maybe he'd gone out to leave her some dignity when she scurried out of his apartment like some cockroach caught in a darkened kitchen?

Opening the door carefully, she poked her head out and saw the front door. The one she'd been pressed so tightly against last night they'd almost been labeled a couple.

God.

She'd make a run for it and not look back. The rest she'd figure out later while she berated herself for being such a whore. Mel made a beeline to escape—the white steel door her target.

"So, was that the best date ever, or what?" a voice filled with amusement mocked.

Mel screamed and jumped, dropping her purse.

Drew came up behind her, curling a strong arm around her waist to pull her close. "So, your verdict?"

Mel bit the inside of her cheek, desperately searching for the resources she'd called upon when she'd decided to play a part she had no business playing on anything other than a dance floor. Where was your slutty dancer when you needed her most?

Drew turned her around, a piece of burned toast in his hand. Dressed in nothing but gym shorts, he made her knees weak all over again. "Uh-oh. Is someone embarrassed?" He grinned down at her.

Of course, like everything else with Drew, his breath was perfect while hers smelled like the inside of a fifteen-year-old tennis player's sneaker.

He kissed the tip of her nose. "You know, I made a discovery last night."

Yeah, that she was an unruly, out of control tramp who needed a chastity belt. Praying the words that came out of her mouth next sounded self-assured when she was anything but, she gave him her smoldering tango eyes. "What did you discover last night, Drew?"

"Dancers rock. Hardcore. I mean, I know I made fun of it, but wow—hoorah for flexibility." He dropped a kiss on her lips then asked with a cheerful voice, "Toast?" He held up the burned bread under her nose.

Her blood boiled. The nerve of this man. "I . . ."

Drew hauled her so close to him, her back arched. "You're speechless. Nice change. But I've got your back. You're wondering what I'm thinking, aren't you? When you woke up in a strange bed this morning, you thought, 'Mel, what kind of a woman insults a man she barely knows in front of the entire town of Riverbend, then sleeps with the man she barely knows like he's the last man on Earth? How can I look him in the eye after we did all those *things*?'" he drawled, mimicking a female tone.

A strand of her mussed hair fell in her eyes. She blew it out of her face.

Drew winced. "You need a toothbrush? I think I have extras."

"No, thank you."

"Where were we?"

"We left off after we did all those *thiiings*," she repeated.

He nodded. "Right. Those things. Anyway, I'm sure you assume I think the phrase, 'For a good time call Mel' is memorialized on bathroom walls across the country, right? And don't lie because I'll know if you are."

Her eyes shifted to his shoulder. "The thought crossed my mind."

"Well, you can just put that thought right out of your pretty little head. I never once thought about bathrooms."

Mel struggled to get out of his grasp by clamping her hand on his forearm. "Let me go!" Stupidhead.

He bit his toast, keeping her body flush to his and shook his head. "Nope, not until we hash this out, and you explain what the hell all that shitty attitude was about last night."

"Before or after our sexual free-for-all?" What kind of Neanderthal wanted to talk a one-night stand over?

"Don't play coy with me, Mel. You were anything but coy last night. So spill. I'm all ears, and I have coffee, which you look like you could use."

Calling all sluts! Calling all sluts! Could I get some slutty 'it was just sex' attitude here? It would really be useful right now. "What's there to talk about? We had sex." Oh. That was good, Mel. Good use of the 'indifferent acquaintances with benefits' clause.

He let his lips fall to her ear and grumbled. "Boy, did we ever. Now I want to know why one minute you were calling me stupid—"

"I didn't call you 'stupid.' I called you 'unclever.'" She remembered that much.

"And right after that you were all over me."

"Huh. As I recall, you weren't exactly not all over me right back, buddy."

"Well, c'mon. You have to admit there's a certain kind of awesome involved in being accosted by a hot woman only seconds after she's made it clear she's just not into you. Do you take meds for all that bipolar?"

She averted her eyes to her feet. "I don't . . ." How could she tell him she'd purposely set out on their date with destructive intent and an even more destructive attitude? If this was purging, it was a good thing she wasn't hoarding.

"So I suppose you're going to tell me you don't know what came over you and you don't do this kind of thing often, right?"

"Not ever!" she shouted then bit her tongue. "I mean, I've never done something like this. Not that I haven't had sex. I have. I just mean I've never had sex with someone I hardly know and don't even particularly like." She paused. "I'm rambling, yes?"

"Yes, and it's very cute. Well, until you got to the part about not liking me. What's not to like? I'm a nice guy. You can't deny I have mad bedroom skills. I was willing to pay for your coffee. What's the beef?"

"We have absolutely nothing in common." Except that thing he did when he'd been . . . Oh, God.

He scrunched his handsome face up in question. "How would you know? We were sort of at the 'a little less conversation, a lot more action' stage last night. You can't possibly decide something like that so quickly. It's presumptuous and rude. Again with the rude."

"I'm not being rude. I'm being practical. You don't like the one thing I love most."

"Do you love radial arm saws?"

"What? I don't even know what that is."

"That's the one thing I love the most, besides Nate. Do you like the smell of sawdust? Varnish? Stain?"

Mel wrinkled her nose, relaxing in his grip a bit. "Not even a little."

"And I don't like to dance. Big deal." He shrugged his shoulders to accentuate it wasn't a big deal.

"That's not the same thing."

"It is. Building things is my passion. It's part of who I am. I like to use my hands to create things. You like to use your feet. Different but the same."

"So what's your point?"

"My point is you don't know if we have other things in common. We didn't exactly talk about much because, you know . . ." Drew hitched his thumb over his shoulder toward the bedroom and wiggled his eyebrows.

Red stained her cheeks. She felt it in the hot rush that left her dizzy. "We didn't talk because we had a one-night stand. One-night stands don't talk. They—they have—you know—and go home."

"Oh, don't kid yourself, lady. This was no one-night stand. We're going to do this again," was his confident reply. A reply that irked her.

Now what could she possibly say to that? If she said what they'd shared wasn't a one-time thing, she'd be doing the same thing she did the first time around. Becoming infatuated with someone because he was good-looking, had paid her a compliment, and then upped the ante by being good in bed.

It would defeat the whole purpose of what she'd set out to avoid with Drew to begin with. Not that she hadn't already done that, to a degree anyway. To be drawn in further could potentially be history repeating itself, and she wasn't ready for that. Not only did she not want to be hurt again, she wasn't ready for any kind of entanglements, be they noncommittal sex, or otherwise.

Then a thought occurred to her—he'd never said word one about relationships and dating. He'd said they were going to "do this" again. Translation? He was down for more sex.

Just who the hell did he think he was? He wasn't that good. Okay, so he was awesomely good, but there were other men who were just as awesomely good, right? Now that she'd worked herself up, her eyes shot daggers up at him.

She pinched his forearm, making him yelp when he released her. "No, Drew," she drawled, tilting her chin to the setting haughty, "don't kid *yourself*. I'm not sure why you think you've got this in the bag, but there are plenty of fish in the sea. Fish who like to dance. In fact, I'm dating those fish. Lots of fish, pal. So remember that analogy about dipping my toes in the dating water?"

Drew's gaze mocked her, but he remained silent.

Her eyes narrowed, she tapped his chest with a finger. "Of course you don't. That was all just to get me into bed—"

"Who got whom into bed?" Drew put his hands in the pockets of his gym shorts and chuckled.

Right. She was the hoochie here. Whatever. "It doesn't matter. What does matter is you said I should dip my toes into the dating pool. Well, guess what, Drew McPhee? You've been dipped!"

Turning on her heel, Mel left him standing in the middle of his living room with all his presumptions.

As she made her way out of the maze of apartment units and back to the parking lot in huffs of indignation, she located her father's truck and beeped it open. Climbing into the cab, Mel took a deep breath and squared her shoulders.

So she'd had sex. Good sex. Safe sex, even. That didn't have to mean anything other than just that. Even Maxine said it was healthy to feed your libido.

And wow, had she ever fed in a hitting-the-buffet-line way.

What were you supposed to feel like after an encounter with a man you planned on never sleeping with again? Why did she have such an emptiness sweeping through her? Why did what was supposed to be meaningless have meaning?

Was it because this was her first encounter since Stan and she was just reacting emotionally? Would this pass once she grew used to the idea of sex just for the express purpose of putting out a fire? Was she even emotionally on board with that?

If this was healthy, to indulge in the occasional consensual liaison, why didn't she feel healthy? Or particularly happy?

And Christ and a peanut butter sandwich—how was she going to explain having her father's truck all night long?

CHAPTER NINE

Dear Divorce Journal,

This entry is to serve as a written reminder to never date men with the name Ron who have mothers with the name Florence. In fact, this should serve as a reminder for me to never date anyone who even has a single living relative. Again.

And the dating pool is definitely not heated. It's cold, people. Cold.

"Welcome, Ms. Cherkasov. I'm Winchester, Ms. Jasmine's slave for life." A regal man in a suit and tie bowed upon her entry to what Jasmine called her and her husband, Simon's, love shack.

Mel smiled at him, taking his hand. "Nice to meet you."

"No, no. The pleasure's all mine," he gushed, gripping her hand and taking her sweater.

Jasmine breezed through the archway off the enormous living room and smiled at Win with affection. "You've got a fan in Win, Mel. He loves *Celebrity Ballroom* and when we told him you were Neil's old partner, he looked you and some of your old footage up online—well, let's just say he went all schoolgirl."

Win bowed in front of her with dramatic flourish. "You're even lovelier in person."

Mel blushed. "And don't forget twenty-five pounds heavier, but thank you."

Win clucked his tongue. "You don't look a pound over twenty-two," he teased.

Jasmine hooked her arm though Mel's and drew her into the lavish kitchen filled with shiny silver appliances and miles of colorfully swirled marble countertops. "And don't listen to Win. He was Simon's slave first. I took pity on him when I married Simon. Win's never had it so good. So, c'mon, Frankie and Max are already here. You're late, young lady."

Yeah. She was late. Late because she'd been out whoring and trying to think up an explanation for her father about where his truck had been all night. There were always explanations to be made to the person whose truck you'd borrowed when you were out sharing your goodies.

Thankfully, her father had still been sound asleep when she'd come in at eight fifteen to a woebegone Weezer. "I'm sorry. The morning kind of got away from me."

Because you see, I spent it freaking out about all the repercussions my hormones have created, so I lost track of time while I was counting them.

"Hey, Mel!" Frankie called with a smile and a wave, eyeing her over the rim of her wineglass.

Jasmine patted a bar stool at the wide island countertop beside Maxine, and Mel slid into it, keeping her eyes on the Caesar salad, cheese and crackers, and French bread in the center.

Max nudged her with her shoulder. "You gonna look us in the eye and tell us you had sex, or do you want to do it from behind the bathroom door?"

Frankie and Jasmine laughed when Mel let her head fall to her arms with a groan. "How could you possibly know? And don't you three dare feed me the line about glowing. If I'm glowing, it's the bright fluorescent glow of my shame."

"Okay, so we won't talk about your glow," Jasmine said, pouring Mel a glass of white wine and pushing it toward her. "Instead, let's just talk about the guilt. The guilt that I smelled all over you the minute you walked in. Guilt I totally don't get, but I got your back, if you need to make justifications."

"So who was he, and why so glum?" Frankie asked with a grin, lifting Mel's head from her arms with the heel of one hand and holding out her wine with the other.

Mel made a face at her, taking the wine. "He was someone I work with, whose aunt I work with at the rec center, and I'm glum because it was a huge mistake. I don't even know how it escalated to the point where we ended up—you know—at his . . ."

Maxine waved a finger in the air with a smile of triumph. "Aha! Myriam Hernandez's nephew! The hottie who saved you from that disgusting Fierce Whatever. I knew it. We all did. You could tell just by the way he looked at you that he was interested. Oh, and he's delicious—all rugged and rough around the edges."

If only she could count the ways he was delicious. There were too many to list. "Drew McPhee . . ." she murmured as if saying his name out loud would make what happened between them any less real.

Jasmine winked, rubbing her hands together. "So was it good? And don't bother to play coy. It's just us, and it's okay to say it was good. In fact, say it a lot—out loud in the mirror."

Mel swallowed a gulp of her wine for courage. "Is this the part where I own my sexuality? Because I've never done anything like this before in my life."

"What exactly did you do, other than have sex for the first time since your divorce with a man who's utterly gorgeous?" Maxine grinned, taking a crouton from the salad and popping it in her mouth.

Frankie shook her head of auburn curls and held up her hand. "Forget all that, I just want to know if it was good?"

Mel let her head hang again. "Yes, yes, yes! It was good. It was the best sex I've ever had. Though, I'm not sure if I'm a good judge of the best sex ever because I've only slept with two people, last night being my second, but yes—okay? It was good. Great. More than great."

"Then you're one step ahead of millions of divorced women who have their first sexual encounter and it blows big, fat chunks. So I don't get the problem unless it's got something to do with the ground rules. Like he said this was strictly about the sex and you thought that meant flowers and candy, and now you're hurt. Or is it that you're worried it'll never happen again," Maxine offered with a grin, biting a cracker, her green eyes amused.

That shame she'd been feeling washed back over her again in a hot wave. "No! It can't ever happen again."

Jasmine crunched on a piece of lettuce. "Why the hell not?"

"Because I didn't mean for it to happen in the first place."

"So what you're saying is, this was a one-time encounter and you're not interested in anything but the sex? Because if that's the case, go, you. I say you should try every variety of candy in the candy store and never settle for one piece unless you're ready to," Frankie provided on a chuckle.

Mel groaned, sliding down on her barstool. "I don't know what I'm saying. The only thing I do know is I can't believe I let myself get so carried away. It's not like me to be so impulsive."

Jasmine tapped her arm with a pink fingernail. "You know what, Mel? Maybe it is, and you just didn't know it."

"So I was always a closet slut?"

Jasmine's laugh was dry and throaty. "Does sleeping with two whole men in your entire what, forty years, make you a slut? If that's the case, call me head slut. This is what I'm saying. It's okay to experience new men without feeling guilt. You got your groove on, and it was good. I've said this before and I'll say it again. All those formative years, while you should have been out partying and being young, you were married. You didn't date. You didn't discover who you were as a person. I know that sounds hokey, but it's the truth. What you thought was great at twenty, isn't always what floats your boat at forty. If you ask me, having a casual encounter with a man here and there is all part of the discovery process. As long as the rules are clear, it's all cake."

"The rules . . . I think the rules are the problem," she blurted out then shoved a piece of French bread in her mouth to shut it.

Maxine cocked her head and pursed her lips. "They weren't outlined going in?"

"How can anything be outlined when you have your tongue shoved down someone's throat after you behaved like a complete ass?" Oh, Jesus. Had she just admitted that out loud?

"Ohhhhh," Frankie cooed. "I bet it was angry sex."

"What are you women, psychic?" Mel complained, her appetite taking a sudden turn for the better. She reached for a triangle of the Brie and stuffed it into her mouth.

"You act like you're the only one who's ever gone through this, Mel. I know it feels like that, but you're one of millions, honey. Don't go thinking you've got the market cornered." Jasmine's admonishment left Mel feeling less alone. "That's why Maxine has all those support groups going on at Trophy. So you'll be able to talk to others who have the same fears."

"Damn, I'm good at this. I knew it was angry sex. So, tell us what the hell happened?" Frankie coaxed.

Mel relayed every tiny detail while consuming not one helping, but two of Jasmine's Caesar salad. Clearly, one night stands left you starving. "Anyway, that's what happened, and I don't want it to happen again." Maybe that was a lie. Fine. It was a lie.

"I call bullshit!" Jasmine cried, pointing her finger at Mel. "You do so want it to happen again. What you're afraid of is becoming too deeply attached to someone again. I just don't get the impression you're the kind of woman who can leave her emotions out of the bedroom, but I've been wrong before. Either way, remember this: just because you had sex doesn't mean you have to wear his high school ring, Mel. If you've discovered that, own it, baby. You had sex. It was good. You want to do it again, but you don't want anything more than that."

Mel shook her head with a sigh. "But that isn't exactly how I feel. The problem is, I don't know how I feel. One minute I'm embarrassed that I behaved so out of character, the next I'm grinning from ear to ear because . . . Look, here's what I'm really afraid of. I clearly don't know the difference between infatuation and true love. Lately, when I think of Stan, I almost wonder if what I felt for him was just an intense crush that would have passed if I'd let it play out instead of signing on for life. I didn't know it at the time, because I was so blown away by the great choreographer Stanislov Cherkasov paying me so much attention, but when I began to examine it more closely after our divorce, I found that none of the things I wanted most in a relationship are the things Stan gave me. It never, ever occurred to me to look elsewhere. I stayed because I took vows. Period. I think that's just who I am." When she said those words, Mel realized, that was who she was. Her core was loyal, and she'd never break a promise if it killed her.

She let her head fall to her hands. "I was in awe of Stan, and I'm in lust with Drew. That can only lead to disaster if I'm not on the same page. Though, there is one thing I'm definitely sure of. I behaved like an idiot when all was said and done, and I stomped out of his apartment."

Maxine sputtered on her wine. "Oh, I can identify with that. I was every kind of idiot come Sunday with Campbell. It happens to us all because most of us, Jasmine aside, hadn't dated in forever. You don't know the rules. You aren't familiar with the lingo. It's just as foreign as getting divorced."

Frankie nodded her agreement while sipping her wine.

"So now the question is, what are you going to do about it?" Jasmine asked.

What was she going to do about it? "If you want honesty, sure, it would be great to do it again, but it's pretty clear, I suck at leaving my emotions out of the bedroom. I don't want to do the one-sided thing or go into it hoping I'll be so magical I'll change his mind and make him fall madly in love with me. I don't even know that I want him or anyone to fall in love with me. I'm definitely honest enough with myself to know I'm not tough enough yet to be hurt again, and that's exactly what will happen if this goes any further and his intentions end up different than mine turn out to be. Add in the complications of our working together and it's just better to let it go." Again, there was that twinge of sadness that had no business tweaking her heart.

Jasmine nodded, brushing her hair over her shoulder and popping another hunk of cheese in her mouth. "It's like I said, maybe it is too soon for you, and maybe you're right, maybe he does just want to have sex and nothing more. Though, the way he looked at you that night in the diner didn't at all look like just lust, but you'll never know unless you ask."

"Couldn't you ask him for me? I just don't have the kind of Ring Dings you do," Mel said on a nervous laugh. Jasmine's confidence was daunting. Of course, she was gorgeous and probably didn't have to ask questions. One could assume, if they had eyes in their head, no one turned Jasmine down.

Jasmine's eyebrow arched. "If only it was that easy, kiddo. You're a big girl. You have to take charge. That's if you really want to know the answer. I don't think you do. I think you'd much rather hide from such an intense attraction because it scared you. You behaved in a way that was what you think is out of character for you. So leave it alone and let's focus on something else."

"Like?"

Jasmine shot Maxine a secretive glance. "I think Mel's the perfect guinea pig, don't you?"

Frankie clapped her hands. "Oh, she definitely is!"

"Mel," a male voice called, followed by the click of something Mel couldn't place. "If I were you, when you hear the words 'guinea' and 'pig' from these three mouths, hit the ground running."

Jasmine's face lit up at his entry. This must be Simon, Jasmine's husband. He certainly was big enough to be an ex-pro football player. Big, blond, and handsome, he had an impish quality to him that made him appear as if life was just one big ride on a tilt 'o wheel he had no intention of getting off.

Jasmine wrapped an arm around his waist and he tucked her to him possessively. She pinched his chin, giving it a kiss. "Oh, honey. You'd hit the ground just because you're blind. Now stop scaring the newb. Mel? This is my mouthy husband, Simon. Simon? Hold out your hand to the lady."

Simon took Mel's hand with an uncanny sense of direction and gave her a warm smile. "Nice to meet you. Now hurry," he motioned with his cane over his shoulder, just missing Frankie's head. "Run as fast as you can! I'll cover you."

Jasmine chuckled like he'd said the most clever thing ever, her eyes filled with such obvious affection, it left Mel with an acute loneliness for all things couple-ish. "Didn't I tell you, this is girls' lunch? What are you doing out of your man-cave?"

His blue eyes twinkled when he plopped a kiss on the top of Jasmine's head. "Call it like it is, wife. It's my cage. That's where all wives lock up their poor, blind husbands," he teased, making his way to the fridge using his cane as a guide.

Jasmine swung back to face Maxine, her eyes shiny with excitement. "So whaddya think? I think Mel's the perfect candidate."

Mel narrowed her eyes at the women. "For?"

"I'm telling you, Mel, get out while you can," Simon called.

Jasmine chuckled. "Oh, hush, or I'm moving the bottle of Tums and switching it for some Ex-Lax." She winked at Mel who instantly felt at ease with their banter. "Just ignore him. He might not be able to see, but he makes up for it in mouth. So, Max?"

Max put her chin in her hands and perused Mel. "I think it's a great idea."

"Good, then it's settled. Lemme get the laptop, and we'll hook her up." Jasmine floated out of the kitchen.

Frankie rubbed Mel's shoulders and smiled. "I'm so excited, and remember, if this works out, it was my idea."

Mel gave them a blank look. "Um, guinea pig here. Can someone please explain the experiment to the test subject?"

Jasmine breezed back in with the laptop and popped it open, typing in a URL. The page that popped up instantly made Mel give them each a questioning glance. Whatever TrophyMatch.com was, it couldn't be good. "Is that what I think it is?"

Maxine's eyes gleamed now, too. "Uh-huh. And you, my friend, are ripe for the picking!"

Mel let her head fall to her hands, still on the steering wheel of her father's truck in the parking lot of Chester's Bovine and Swine, careful not to muss her freshly styled hair. Because God forbid she should mess up her new hairdo in favor of banging her head against the car door.

She rolled down the window with the press of a button and took deep gulps of the cool autumn air.

A date.

She had a date.

At this particular moment in time, she wasn't sure if a one-night stand with Drew had been easier. It had been sudden, and without warning, and there had certainly been less primping involved.

As far as she was concerned, Spanx were overrated, and the Kymaro was like a slingshot just waiting to unload her tightly bound breasts on some unsuspecting innocent.

Maxine had assured her that everything was on the up-and-up with this dating-site thing. The men were all carefully screened by retired therapists and psychologists, as were the women.

They went through rigorous testing and answered a million questions about everything from their hobbies to their sexual likes and dislikes. Everyone was screened and screened again. Maxine's new site had everything but the goopy eHarmony-like commercial with a happily in love couple dancing around to Natalie Cole singing.

Businesswoman that Maxine was, a commercial with a happy-clappy couple like she and her husband, Campbell, probably wasn't far down the pike.

And three weeks ago, when they'd suggested, nay, insisted Mel maybe find a different way to get her infatuation for Drew out of her system, she'd gone willingly like some lamb to slaughter.

Now this lamb had serious doubts she was going to find her mint jelly through this venue. Hold up. Maxine had said not to go into it like her life depended on it. It was just dinner.

Maxine said. Maxine this. Maxine that.

Unfortunately Maxine, who had an answer for everything, was usually right. So, in light of that, here Mel was, meeting Ronson "Everyone Just Calls Me Ron" Benedetto. A six-foot, two-hundred-ten-pound blond Sicilian who liked spur-of-the-moment road trips, animals, and the show *Chuck*, and who was just looking for someone to maybe see a movie with. Nothing serious. And he danced. When she'd read that in his profile, she'd silently sent Drew a *neener, neener, neener.*

Ron was an X-ray tech who had a full-time job and bennies he was very proud of. At least according to the six or seven e-mails they'd shared since he'd been chosen as one of her likeliest matches.

His picture had been nice enough—though he was no Drew.

That's because he's Ron, Mel.

Right. She'd do well to remember that and knock off the comparisons. It had taken everything she had in her to avoid Drew at school and at the rec center when he picked up Myriam, whose ban from social events had been lifted.

So far, so good. The occasional glimpses she'd caught of him in the last couple of weeks were brief, making it clear to her, what she'd suspected his words meant all along were true. Drew had just wanted to have sex. Now that she'd discovered she wasn't able to put sex in a compartment without involving the emotions tied to it, it was just as well she'd stomped out of his life.

Yay, discovery.

A sharp knock on the passenger window of the truck made her jump, cracking her head against the door. She rubbed the spot as she looked out the window.

"Mel?"

Mel's eyes went to the right side of the truck where a petite woman with pink foam curlers poking out from beneath her orange-and-brown-polka-dotted scarf stood, her purse hanging from the crook in her elbow. Mel pressed the button to put the window down. "Yes?" She squinted into the darkness to see if the woman was a senior from the Village, but it wasn't anyone she recognized.

"You're Mel? The Mel who's supposed to meet my Ronnie?"

Mel cocked her head. "Do you mean Ron Benedetto?"

She grinned, patting her square purse to her body. "That's my boy. Well, c'mon then, he's in there waiting."

Awesome. Maxine didn't have instructions on what to do if your

date showed up with his mother, now did she? Mel hesitated, scanning the parking lot. There had to be an escape route. If she backed
up carefully, yet with precise haste, she'd probably only take out
Ron's mother's toes. Who needed toes in this day and age?

"Well, hurry up. He's ordering pigs in a pig blanket for us—you
know, those hot dogs wrapped in bacon—and they'll get cold," she
chastised with a frown, pulling up the elastic waist on her jeans.

Bacon. Mel perked up. Everything was better with bacon.

But then she caught sight of Ron's mother's frown. Putting that
much pressure on bacon was unfair.

Mel let a reluctant hand pop open the door, sliding out to put even
more reluctant feet on the ground. Maxine would die for this. Painfully. Slowly.

"You pick out that dress?" Ron's mother asked when she came
around the front end of the truck to give Mel a critical eye.

Mel gave a quick glance to her red wrap dress with the black
flecks and forced a smile to her lips as they began to walk toward
Chester's. "I did."

"They have a different color?"

"I'm not sure, why?"

"Just think you'd look better in blue's all."

She'd have to remember that the next time she was due to date a
man and his *mother*. Mel held the door to the restaurant open for
Ron's mother. The scent of brisket wafting to her nose might have
been pleasant had it not been for the fact that she was sharing it with
her date's mother. Trailing behind her full-on assault into the crowded
room, Mel asked, "I'm sorry, I didn't catch your name."

"Florence, but you can call me Mother."

No-nonsense woman that she was, "Mother" headed straight for a
table in a small alcove that was empty but for the pitcher of iced tea
and three place settings. Mel went to the back of the table, figuring

she should probably at least sit near Ron when she told him she only swung one way and it wasn't Flo's before she left like she was on fire.

But Florence clucked her tongue in admonishment. "You're here." She pointed to the solitary chair.

Ah. Isolate the enemy. Mel bit the inside of her cheek and took her seat. "So where's Ron?"

"Oh, my poor baby. He was so nervous about meeting you. I bet he's in the bathroom. You understand." She lifted her flowered shirt and rubbed her midsection. "Upset tummy and all. First-date jitters."

Mel clenched the edge of the table, summoning patience. "Do you always go on all of Ron's dates with him?"

"Only with the girls he says he wants to marry." She dug through her purse and pulled out a plastic accordion wallet, letting it drop to the floor. "Look, there's my Ronnie at his fifth birthday party." Florence pointed to one of probably fifty pictures of Ron at various stages of his life. "He was petrified of the clown—that's why he's crying. He's still scared of 'em to this day, but he mostly doesn't cry anymore."

Where was a clown when you needed one? Mel smiled distractedly while trying to locate the bathrooms in search of Ron.

The waitress approached their table; her hat, a combination of a pig's face and snout on a cow's body, swallowed almost all of her forehead. "You ladies ready to order your entrée?"

Florence gave her a stern look that turned her eyes into beady dots in her head. "Not yet. My Ronnie's still in the loo."

"I'd love a glass of Chardonnay," Mel said, forcing the pleading tone out of her voice.

"Wait!" Florence intervened, tugging on the waitress's uniform. "We got perfectly good iced tea here. A whole pitcher. That costs money."

Mel sent her a conciliatory smile. "I don't really care for iced tea." *Or you. Or Ron, whom I haven't even met. Or dating. Or Maxine—who I really hope likes dark trunks in big sedans. Oh, and cement shoes and water. Deep, deep water.*

Mother's face became disapproving, her lips pinched together. "Me and my Ronnie don't drink. Your profile said you weren't a drinker either."

"Oh, I'm not a drinker-drinker. What I mean is, I don't plow through a twelve-pack every night. I just like the occasional glass of wine. Tonight seemed like a perfect reason to have one." Mel turned back to the waitress. "So just *one* glass of Chardonnay, please." Or an IV line and the whole stinkin' bottle.

Florence snorted, shifting in her chair with a grunt. "Make sure you put that on *her* bill."

Mel glanced at her watch. Whatever was troubling Ronnie's tummy must be leaving quite an impression in the men's room. He'd been in there for ten minutes. Five more, and she was out.

"Ms. Cherkasov?"

Her ears perked. She knew that voice. It was the voice that belonged to the feet that waltzed a waltz like a dream come true. That voice also had a father who looked like a dream come true, but only wanted to have sex—which wasn't a dream come true—no matter how dreamy the sex was.

Nate. Shit. If Nate was here, she could only pray it was with someone else's family.

Shifting in her chair, she turned to greet Nate and found Drew, Myriam, and two other people right behind him. That was it. She was giving up prayer for good. Along with dating.

She smiled regardless. She couldn't help but smile when she saw Nate. Mel purposely focused all of her attention on him, ignoring Drew like she had for three weeks. "Hey, Nate! You here for some cow?"

He laughed, the dimples on either side of his mouth deepening. "Yeah. You already know my dad and Aunt Myriam, but this is my Grandma and Grandpa." He hitched a thumb over his shoulder and his grandparents waved.

Mel stood and held out her hand, reaching around Drew. "Hi, Myriam! And lovely to meet Nate's grandparents. Nate's one of my best students."

A round woman with hair the color of midnight and patches of silver gave her a warm smile. "I'm Selena McPhee. I've heard lots of nice things about you, Ms. Cherkasov." She smiled wider, like she had a secret.

"William. William McPhee," Drew's father said with a light brogue to his words. He took his ball cap off and shook her hand, then planted his fingers on top of Nate's head and squeezed with a smile. "He's a good dancer you say, Ms. Cherkasov?"

Mel's smile grew. "The best. I've never had a student who's as easily taught as Nate is—or picks up the steps quite as well."

Myriam thumped Nate, whose face was red, on the back. "That's because he's like his Auntie Myriam," she crowed with pride.

Nate winced. "Hey, Dad? Can I go play the video games before dinner?"

Drew dug in his pocket for some singles and handed them to Nate who skipped off to the game room in the front of the restaurant. "Ms. Cherkasov. You didn't say hello to me," Drew whispered close to her ear.

"How did such lovely people spawn you?" she muttered back, turning her attention to Flo and the still-missing Ron's empty chair. "Everyone, this is Florence Benedetto, she's . . ."

"Her *date's* mother," Florence muttered, her face pinched, clearly due to the disruption.

"Right," Mel said on a cheerful nod. "Florence, this is Nate's family, the McPhees. Nate's one of my students at Westmeyer."

Myriam snorted her disapproval at Florence's grunt of acknowledgment, giving Florence that look Mel knew. The one that said Myriam was the bull and Florence was the human with the red flag. Latching on to Mel's hand, she asked Florence, "Are we interrupting, Flo?" This was a dare. A dare for the crabby, disapproving Flo to challenge her.

"No!" Mel added with haste, squeezing Myriam's hand to keep her from charging. "Don't be silly. We're just waiting for Ron. Uh, my *date*." She emphasized "date" in Drew's cocky direction.

"What kinda man keeps a girl as pretty as you waiting?" William teased. "If I was him, I'd never leave the table. Would you leave someone as pretty as Ms. Cherkasov alone where some guy could come along and steal her up, Drew?" He gave his son a pointed look.

"*Ne-ver*," he answered with a purposeful enunciation of the word and an arrogant grin at Mel, an amused glint in his eyes.

Right. Drew couldn't possibly leave a woman alone at a table because he didn't sit at tables with women. He only sat in beds with them.

Selena swatted her husband playfully with her hand, then put her arm through her husband's. "Let her be, William. Now let's leave the pretty Ms. Cherkasov to her meal and her date, and hurry it along here. I'm in the mood for a full rack of ribs."

"Mel?"

Whirling around, flustered from Drew's presence and the new male voice, Mel caught the edge of the tablecloth with the cheap ring she'd found at Walgreen's on her hand.

Surely all that sloshing hadn't come from just one little ole pitcher of iced tea?

CHAPTER TEN

Dear Divorce Journal,

Fine. So some of Chester's Bovine and Swine's infamous choco-
late cheesecake can put you in a wholly different frame of mind.
I'm working hard to remember it was just cheesecake. Just.
Cheesecake.

There was a long, stunned silence filled with only the occasional gasp.

And then there was a lot of screeching from Florence's side of the
table. Somewhere in there, Mel heard her name, and so what if it was
in vain? She'd been called worse.

"Oh! Florence, I'm so sorry!" Mel sprung into action, diving for
the napkins at the empty table next to theirs and rushing to sop up
the mess.

"What have you done to my mother?" Ron whined with a hint of
outrage in his tone, pushing Mel out of the way and snatching the
napkins from her with a yank so rough it made her jerk on her high
heels and stumble backward into none other than Drew's hard chest.

Myriam was next in the fray, poking a harsh finger in Ron's arm.
"Don't you put your hands on her again, buddy, or I'll kick your can
from here to Louisville!"

"Myriam! No!" Mel hissed, pushing out of Drew's steadying grip
to reach for her and tripping over the purse she'd put by her feet on
the floor.

Mel crashed into Ron facefirst, her purse tangling on her shoe and dumping its contents across the floor. Ron fell like a tree that had been leveled minus the shout of "timber," tipping over three chairs when he went and bellowing his pain as his head thwacked the floor.

She clung to his sports jacket, falling with him to hit the ground with a bone-jarring *thunk*.

"Get off of my Ronnie! He's got a bad back!" Florence yelped, pulling at Mel's arms, and dripping iced tea in brown splotches on her.

Drew extracted Mel, pulling her up and out of Florence's reach while holding Myriam at bay. Drew set her down with a hard drop and scooped Myriam up into his arms while she struggled, shooting daggers from her eyes at Florence whose nostrils flared in huffs.

Ron rose with a wince and a moan, and indeed, he probably was six foot tall. Though, to say he had blond hair was probably generous, considering he didn't have nearly as much as he'd had in his picture. "Look what you did to my mother! What's the matter with you?" he roared in outrage, the flap of his comb-over shooting upward.

If the entire restaurant wasn't already gawking at them as a group because of all the commotion, they were now, and all eyes were on Mel.

And a little something slipped in Mel's wiring. Whoa, whoa, whoa, Nellie. What she'd done to his mother?

Her mouth fell open, just before it snapped shut, and she gave him the kind of hell she'd been saving for a rainy day.

Mel leapt over the fallen chairs, catching her nylons on one, ignoring the loud rip and more gasps, and pointed her finger up at him. "What I did to *her*? What's the matter with *me*? Me? You brought your mother—your *mother* on a date! I think the question here is what's the matter with you? Who, at forty-two years old, brings their

mother on a date, I ask you? Then spends almost all of it in the bathroom with a nervous stomach while I sit out here with Florence the
Hun and her disapproving, pinched-mouth glares! Serial killers,
that's who! I bet you live in her basement, don't you? Is that where
you hide the bodies that you're going to skin and wear like last year's
Versace, too? How dare you misrepresent yourself as a strong, confident single man when in reality you're just a mama's boy!" Mel spat.
"This date is officially over, Ronnie 'Everyone Just Calls Me Ron'
Benedetto—and don't you ever e-mail me again or did mommy write
all your e-mails for you? Arghhhhhh!" she jumped up and yelled in
his face, making him wince and pale.

"Come on, Ronnie," Florence cooed, patting Ron's arm and giving Mel a look that screamed crazy. "Sure enough, you picked another
doozy. From now on, Mother reads all of your e-mails so we can
weed out the nuts!"

Myriam went for Flo's throat just as William McPhee stepped in
front of her. "Now cool your jets there, Myriam. Selena? Why don't
you go to the table and get us something to drink. Get something for
Ms. Cherkasov, too. She looks like she could use it." William also ran
interference with the manager who'd come to see what all the yelling
was about.

Stooping to gather the contents of her purse, she clocked heads
with Drew who was on his haunches helping. "One word from your
mouth, McPhee, and I swear, this compact and you are going to mate
for life. Got it?"

"Far be it from me to remind you how cold the waters of the dating pool can be."

Mel clenched her teeth, rubbing her head. "Shut. Up."

"Should have gone on a date with me. I would have at least left my
mother at home. Though, I can't say Myriam wouldn't make it more
interesting."

Her pent-up rage, her frustration at being this close to him again and liking it, even after she'd found out he was a total worm, all were factors in her next words. "You can't date someone who only wants to screw!" That's right. There it was—all out in the open.

Drew sat back on his haunches, delicious, sexy, dangerous, and gave her a blank stare. "Say again?"

Composing herself, she took a deep breath and repeated her words. "I said you can't date someone who only wants a bunk mate."

"I never said that."

"You did, too."

"I did not. I said it was no one-night stand, and that we were going to do it again."

Duh, caveman. "Exactly. What had we just done, Drew?"

He smiled at her and winked. "Made a little whoopee."

"So what would 'do it again' lead you to believe? We were going to prom?"

His look was of disbelief, like he'd just discovered the answer to the meaning of life. "So *that's* what's been up your backside all this time?"

"Nothing's been up my backside," she denied, though admittedly, pretty badly.

Drew rose on enticing thighs she knew intimately, pulling her along with him. "Oh, the hell, lady. You thought I just wanted to do you, and that pissed you off, so you've avoided me whenever and wherever you can."

"It did not piss me off. But yes, that's what I thought."

"It did, too, and why didn't you ask for clarification instead of giving me the cold shoulder for three solid weeks?"

Mel raised a freshly plucked eyebrow. "I didn't know you'd counted the passage of time."

"You mean since we bumped uglies? You bet I did."

His honesty made her want to smile. But not yet. "Why didn't you ask for clarification?"

"How can I ask about something I didn't even know was a misunderstanding? I thought you just used me and my awesome bedroom skills to quench your insatiable post-divorce lust. I felt cheap."

Mel's eyes narrowed in suspicion, even if her lips were fighting a curve upward. "Did you read that in *Cosmo*?"

He grimaced, the lines on his forehead forming a frown. "I think it was *Vogue*. I can't remember. It was all they had to read at the urologist I took Myriam to."

God. He drove Myriam everywhere. It was clear his family was close. He was good to his son and his aunt. It made her heart tighten and retract.

Maybe he wasn't a pair of feet waiting to wipe themselves on her doormat of a forehead. Maybe. "Well, the fact is, you didn't ask for clarification either, nor did you beat down my door to ask me out again, did you?"

"You sure didn't behave as though you wanted to be asked out again, now did you?" he countered. "Was I supposed to know you were angry about something I didn't even know you'd misinterpreted? I'm a straight shooter, Mel. Instead of hiding all over Westmeyer to avoid me, you could have just called me on all those cruel thoughts you had about me." He pouted comically for good measure.

Mel rolled her eyes up at him. "Men really are from Mars."

Drew grinned. "And women really are from Venus. So what do you say we align the planets, and you join my crazy family and the homicidal Myriam for dinner? We'll start all over again."

Mel let out a sigh. "It's been a long twenty minutes in Internet-dating hell. I don't know if I can keep my eyes open for any more."

"Oh, I bet if I offer to pay for your pig, you can manage it."

Her reserve was cracking. "Does that include the salad bar?"

He paused, as though contemplating his finances. "Fine. But no dessert."

Mel made a mock expression of outrage. "What kind of date are you? How can you ask me to give up Chester's cheesecake? I'm not sure I'm up to another cheapskate like Flo and Ron."

Drew put his arm under her elbow to lead her to his family's table. His broad chest sheltered her, leaving her fighting a sigh. When they caught sight of them, they all waved. "I'll tell you what. Maybe I can con my father into paying for the lot of us, and then you can have cheesecake. How's that?"

Mel finally couldn't hold back her chuckle. It slipped out just as they reached the table and William McPhee jumped up to pull out a chair for her. "Devious, Mr. McPhee. Very devious. I like how you think."

Mel took the seat William offered with a smile, her heart a bag of mixed emotions that left her confused and anticipating . . . something.

As she sat with Drew's family, passing baskets of cheesy garlic bread, watching when they lovingly teased one another about anything and everything, smiling when they ate off each other's plates, she realized she wasn't only happy, but comfortable.

And when she recognized and identified that emotion—she let it be just that.

Comfortable.

~ℓ~

Backing up against her father's truck, Mel waved to the McPhee's once more when they drove out of Chester's parking lot, taking Nate with them. She turned to look up at Drew who smiled down at her. "Never let it be said the McPhee's can't show a lady a good time."

"It *was* a good time. Thank you." Dinner had been a rousing success after such a disappointing beginning. Her stomach was full and her spirit renewed. She was officially in love with the McPhee's in all their chaotic madness.

Drew shot her a confused look. "Who are you?"

"Someone who just had a really great meal with your even greater family. Don't spoil it, caveman," she teased.

Drew rested the heel of his hand on the truck, once again sheltering her with his body, creating delicious havoc with her senses. "Yeah, they are pretty great, huh?"

"I enjoyed every minute of it. But I especially enjoyed the chocolate cheesecake."

He drew a thumb over the corner of her mouth, the rough tip of it making her have to work to control a visible shiver. "I can tell. You still have a little chocolate right here," he murmured, his eyes roving her face, glittering in the parking lot's lights. Her breathing stopped when he leaned in so close she could smell the beer he'd had with dinner on his breath. "So you wanna do it again?"

"Have dinner with your family? In a heartbeat. Nothing beats your father's stories about what a klutz you were in fifth grade." It was all she could do not to spit her food across the table when William had told the story about Drew tripping, falling, and completely trashing the history project he'd worked on for three weeks straight. It was easy to see where Drew's sharp wit came from.

Pressing his mouth to her cheek, he whispered, "You know what I mean."

Mel plastered herself against the truck to keep from melting into him. "We are not having sex."

"Is that all you ever think about?"

She planted a flat hand on his tightly muscled chest, willing her fingers not to knead his flesh. "I'm beginning to think it's all you think about."

Dragging his lips over her cheek, she heard his chuckle, low and thick, felt the brush of his hair whisper on her skin. "I meant, do you want to go out with me again, you wicked woman?"

Oh. Oh! Here she was again, jumping to conclusions. "It depends on where we're going. I'm worried if it's without your father, I won't get any cheesecake. So forgive me if I have my reservations."

Cupping her chin, Drew hovered over her. "Every week my family has an Irish slash Puerto Rican night. You know, red beans and rice, corned beef and cabbage. There's gonna be flan," he enticed. "I know how fond of sweets you are."

"How do you know?"

"I saw you stuffing that Ho Ho in your face outside at lunch the other day."

She faked a loud gasp of shock. "Were you watching me?"

"I was."

She shivered, but decided flippant was her best cover. "How stalkery and kinda creepy."

"Or LOL funny, considering the great lengths you went to in order to hide while you were eating it."

Her laughter trickled from her lips. "I was hoping not to get caught by Neil. We've been working out in the wee hours of the morning, and no matter where I am, I always feel like he's hiding around some corner, ready to yank my favorite dessert in plastic wrap from my mouth."

"Yeah, that Neil, huh?"

"Do I detect a question about Neil in there?"

"What's the deal with the two of you?"

"You know what the deal is. He's my ex-dancing partner."

"Were you two ever involved?"

"Nope. We've always just been friends. In fact, he's one of my best friends and always will be."

"Well, okay then. See how easy that was? I ask, you answer. Over."

"I promise the next time you use the words 'one,' 'night,' and 'stand,' I'll ask the true meaning."

His thumb caressed her chin in a maddening circle of sensuality. "Funny. So funny. So how about Saturday night at my folks' place? It's total mayhem, wall-to-wall kids, but the food's great, and obviously, you can't help but enjoy the company."

"Oh." She gave him a dejected look. "So what you're saying is, if I come to dinner Saturday, you'll be there, too?"

"*I'm* the enjoyable company."

"Sorry. I totally thought you meant your mother and father."

Leaning down toward her lips, Drew dropped a light, yet lingering kiss on them. Soft, but sizzling, her brain began that meltdown it had experienced when they'd last been this close. "Still funny. So do we have a date?" he asked, letting his hips graze hers with just enough pressure to assure her he was a man.

Mel bit back a groan of longing. "Date. But . . ."

"Stipulations, Ms. Cherkasov? Special requests? Like do you prefer your forks hand-washed in rose petals and pressed-linen napkins?"

Mel giggled. *Giggled.* Lord. "No. I just want to be clear we're on . . . you know . . . the same page."

"Is this the part where you tell me I should pack the condoms I bought in bulk and save them for a rainy day?"

"Well, maybe you could leave one package out . . ."

His smile was disarming, making her belly quiver. "I get it. What happened between us was something you weren't ready for. Or at least didn't expect. You want to get to know each other better if I ever hope to see you do that thing with your leg again. Am I hitting a nerve?"

She let out a small sigh of relief. "I think we should find out if the only thing we have in common is that thing I do with my leg."

"Oh, ye of little faith. Okay. No hanky-panky until I know what you like on your hamburger and what your favorite color is. So, date?"

"Date."

In an instant, there was nothing but the chilly air between them when he backed away, leaving her wanting. Drew smiled, popping open the door of her truck, and waving her in. "I'll pick you up at six—you'd better be ready."

Mel climbed into the truck, tucking her dress under her legs to give him a saucy look. "I might even shave my legs—it is your parents', after all."

Drew wiggled his eyebrows. "A vast improvement since we were last naked together. I'll have to tell my parents how highly you think of them."

Mel was glad for the dim light in the truck. It hid her non-shaved legged shame. "I'm going home now before you spoil this lovely occasion with your despicable lies."

Drew's laughter made her stomach do somersaults. "Bye, Mel."

"Bye, Drew."

He shut the door with a wink, and it was all she could do not to throw the door back open and beg him to kiss her good night properly. Turning the key in the ignition, she drove away before she was forced to show him she hadn't shaved her armpits.

Drew spent the drive back to his apartment grinning like he'd just scored a prom date.

A grin he couldn't seem to wipe off his face.

Somehow he'd managed to turn the debacle of their romp a few weeks ago around. When he'd gone over their final conversation in his mind after she'd stomped out of his apartment, he'd been pretty hazy about what had made Mel so angry with him.

Then he'd chalked it up to artists and their crazy sensitivity, and it had made him angry that he'd fallen into the same trap again without even realizing it. Creative women and he just didn't mix. They were temperamental, flighty, and worst of all, moody.

As the week went on and Mel had done everything but wear dark glasses and a hat to school to avoid him, he'd found himself alternately perplexed and experiencing that horrible emotion associated with the word "used."

At first, he found he was pretty hacked at the potential that he was just another body—even though his gut warred with the idea Mel was a friends-with-benefits kind of woman. Naturally, being a man, it never occurred to him he'd said something Mel would take so literally. Knuckle-draggers never did.

When he'd discussed his confusion about Mel, leaving out the sexcapades, his mother and sisters had reminded him that he was just an insensitive man and Mel was a newly divorced, probably rubbed-raw woman. They'd ordered him to give her a break.

Given a little time and distance, and the fact that she was all but hiding in the faculty bathroom, though he still didn't understand what she was angry about, Drew had to concede and had set about giving her a break. While he gave her that break, he'd thought up a thousand different ways to get her to go back out with him.

Seeing her up close tonight instead of just the backend of her as she ran away from him had prompted him to try again.

Simply because he couldn't get her out of his head for more than a minute or two before his thoughts strayed right back to her supple skin and soft lips pressed against his in the dark of his bedroom.

Because he couldn't forget how she looked with her dark hair spread across his pillow and her long thighs wrapped around his waist. Because when he was buried balls deep in her, it was different than any other woman he'd ever experienced.

168   Dakota Cassidy

Making love to her had been insane. Incredible. After much thought, he was more than sure their encounter was something she didn't do often, if at all. When he'd had time to analyze it, Drew recognized the signs. It was in the way she couldn't meet his eyes the next morning, and the wild, glazed-over look of disbelief on her face.

Still, knowing she was fresh off a divorce, definitely vulnerable and touchy, he wanted more. But it wasn't just the sex he wanted. He wanted her to look at him like she looked when she danced. He wanted to touch whatever place was so deep inside her that it made her eyes flash fire and reflect the kind of passion he'd tasted on the tip of his tongue.

He had no answer for why he found Mel so enticing. It wasn't all about that petite, rounded figure and her unruly head of curls. It was something else, something he tried to put his finger on, but it eluded him nonetheless.

He'd decided not to question chemistry. It either was, or it wasn't.

Now that he was certain Neil wasn't in the picture and he wasn't treading somewhere he didn't belong, he intended to set her Bunsen burner on fire.

───── ༄ ─────

"Well, where the hell is he, Theresa?" Neil yelled into his phone, cracking the door to his rental in the parking lot of Westmeyer where he was due to pick up Mel for a late-afternoon workout.

His personal assistant didn't deserve his ire.

Stan did.

But no one could find Stan. He'd had Theresa use every single contact he'd made in his time on *Celebrity Ballroom*, but to no avail, and it was driving him insane.

The only information he'd gathered on Stan's whereabouts was he was holed up in Europe in some cottage somewhere with that conniving bitch Yelena while the show was on hiatus. To suggest that information was reliable was shaky at best.

"Look, Theresa, I'm sorry. I know I'm being a class-A asshole, but someone has to know something. He can't have just disappeared. Do me this, call me if you hear even what you think might only be a rumor, okay?" With a defeated nod, he hung up just as he caught sight of Mel with a pretty blonde talking just outside the school doors. Her dark head was nodding at something the woman was saying, and then she laughed, lighter and more carefree than he'd heard it in a long time.

He swept up the steps, controlling his rage and slapping a smile on his face. "Ladies! Great day, huh?"

Mel gave the blonde a quick look before addressing Neil. "Neil, this is Gwen Timmons. She teaches something really smart that I think I've already forgotten how to pronounce."

Gwen giggled girlishly, brushing back the strands of her bob when the wind picked up. She plucked it from her pink lipstick and said, "I teach biology. It's nice to meet you."

Neil went directly into charming mode. It usually happened without him even realizing it, but today, he needed to slather on the good-natured when he was feeling anything but. "Ah. Pretty and smart. A lethal combo." He smiled his *Celebrity Ballroom* smile.

Mel slipped her arm though his, giving him her I-have-an-idea eyes. Shit. That was always bad for him. Her eyes were coy and hooded. "So I was thinking, maybe you and me and Gwen can grab some lunch sometime. You know, talk dissecting frogs or something."

"What all good lunch discussions are about, right?" he joked, evading Mel's request, yet knowing exactly where this was going and hoping to nip it in the proverbial bud. It was either that or wrap Mel's pretty scarf around her mouth to shut her up.

She meant well. She wanted for him what she thought everyone wanted. He wanted it, too. It just hadn't worked out that way, and Mel forcing women she thought were his perfect match on him wouldn't change that.

"So lunch, then?" Mel encouraged, nudging him just below the ribs with a discreet elbow.

Gwen waited with such anticipation in her expression, Neil's gut twisted, much the way it always did when he was backed into this particular corner.

He fought back a sigh of exasperation and instead turned up his charm meter. "I have to fly back to L.A. for a charity gig, but maybe after?"

Gwen's face brightened. "Sounds like a plan."

"Good deal. So, you ready, princess? The crunches, they call." He looked to Mel, staving off the desire to throw her over his shoulder and lunge for his car.

Mel groaned her displeasure. "Who's ever ready for crunches?"

"Oh, I love to work out," Gwen chirped. And it showed in her slender figure covered in a slim skirt and her toned arms, stemming from the blue shirt she wore that complemented her eyes.

Mel stuck her tongue out at Gwen. "Look at how much the two of you have in common. And as an aside, I'd much rather be eating a box of Twinkies. So c'mon, you Jane Fonda wannabe, let's do this. Gwen, I'll see you tomorrow."

Neil waved to her and led Mel down the steps. When they were out of earshot, she tweaked his arm. "She's pretty, right?"

"Adorable." Keeping his interest in this Gwen to a minimum was crucial to his surviving Mel's matchmaking.

"So I did good, huh?"

"Mel, here's a crazy revelation. I don't need any help getting women."

"No, what you need help with is getting the *right* woman."

"What's your definition of 'right'?"

She shrugged, jumping into the passenger seat and putting her seat belt on. "You know, the kind who want to settle down, have kids, a mortgage."

"Whoever said I want that kind of woman?"

He caught her wincing out of the corner of his eye. "Did I over-step?"

"If I told you yes, would it make a shit's worth of difference?"

"Not a lot. I'm always going to want you to have—"

"What you want," he finished for her.

She shot him a deadpan look. "I don't want a wife and a mortgage."

"Me neither," he confessed.

"So no Gwen?"

He heard the hope in her tone, and the last thing he wanted to do was trash her efforts. Clearly, she'd talked him up to Gwen, who'd fairly waited with bated breath for Mel to bring the idea of lunch up. "Fine. Gwen. When I get back from L.A. Maybe next week, okay?"

"Sweet. I knew you couldn't resist her. She's too adorable."

His cell phone rang, cutting off any further discussion of Gwen and lollipops and rainbows for now. He noted it was Theresa again. "Hey, T. Flight change?"

As Neil listened, he kept glancing in the rearview mirror to be sure his expression remained unmarred by the words he was hearing about Stan.

That sonofabitch.

CHAPTER ELEVEN

Dear Divorce Journal,

Dating a man who has a child should be a challenge, right? There's always the issue of acceptance, and usually, that involves a long road of defiance on the child's behalf before the light at the end of a tunnel. At least that's what I've read. But I have to say, hands down, ex-wives are a much bigger challenge, and shall, hereafter, be dubbed major craptacularness.

Drew knocked on Mel's father's door at exactly six sharp, dressed casually in black jeans and a heavy brown and beige sweater, his dark goodness never failed to make her insides feel like the consistency of a slushy.

Joe had insisted he answer the door, partly because Drew was Myriam's nephew, and that had struck fear in his heart for her safety, but mostly because he'd told her there'd be no repeat of Twinkle Toes, if he had anything to say about it.

"Mr. Hodge?" Drew stuck out his hand with a smile. "Good to meet you, sir."

Joe accepted it, but didn't return Drew's smile. Instead, he used his scowl from the rare date she'd had in high school. "That's me. Did you bring your tutu?"

Drew chuckled, obviously not at all offended by her father's sense of humor. "I left it in the car. It's just so big and fluffy."

Joe obviously warred with a smile, then beat it down for a stern expression. "So you're that crazy Myriam's nephew."

"Her reputation precedes her, I see. Has she been responsible for any untoward acts on your person?"

"She's responsible for so many untoward acts, I lost count. So what are your intentions with my Pop-Tart?"

Drew's eyes danced with amusement. This was a test to see if not only Joe could hack Drew's sense of humor, but if Drew could hack Joe's. "Well, first I thought we'd rent a hotel room. You know, like over at Larry's? They have an incredible hourly rate. I bought in bulk, just to be safe. Then, you know, after we wear out the quarter massage machine, I figured we'd have a pretty hearty appetite. So I thought we'd check out the gas station to see if they still have that 'buy one microwave sandwich, get the second free' deal. I don't just dole out a fancy Happy Meal on the first date. It takes time to earn those kind of reward points in a relationship."

Joe's eyes narrowed. "I can't believe you didn't consider the moonlight miniature golf. It's only a buck a game on Saturday nights and if you bring a guest, it's free. Whole lot cheaper than Larry's quarter massage machines." Joe made a face of disappointment. "I've lost all respect for you, son."

Their unified cackling followed by chummy slaps on the back made Weezer bark. He pushed between the two men at the front door and knocked his hip against Drew's thighs, showing him who was the alpha male. Mel grabbed him by the collar, but Drew stopped her with a hand to her arm.

He knelt down and sat at eye level with Weez, rubbing his ears. "You think I should have done the miniature golf, too, don't you?"

Weezer licked his face, making both of the men cackle louder.

Mel nodded her head, grabbing her purse and slinging it over her shoulder. "All right. It's clear my well-being is a total joke to the two of you heathens. Let's get out of here before my father talks you into double coupon days at the Stop & Shop. I can't believe I shaved for this."

Drew turned to Joe and stuck his hand out again. "Pleasure to have met you, sir. I promise not to let Mel spend too much time with the massage machine."

Joe slapped him on the back with a grin. "You two have a good time."

Drew took her hand, enveloping it in his, and pulled her out the door into the cold night air. Leaves in orange and brown scattered the ground, crunching beneath their feet.

He scanned her white crepe fitted shirt with the pleats on it and her plum skirt with a flare just above her knee all the way down to her low-heeled black pumps with a strap, and gave a smile of appreciation. "I like your hair down." He reached up and grabbed a curl, twisting it between his fingertips and giving it a light tug to straighten it. "I didn't realize it was so long."

She brushed at the strands that fell to the middle of her back with her hand. "It's unruly, hard to control, and impossible to manage." But she'd fought with it like it was a saber-toothed tiger for almost two hours in preparation for this date.

"It says something that you went to all this trouble for me."

Mel fought a blush. "It says I couldn't find a scrunchie."

"Is that what the purple eye shadow and pink lip gloss were about, too?"

"No. That was to impress your family. You don't want them thinking you date bag ladies, do you?"

He chuckled. "You look pretty hot, Mel. So you ready?"

Drew opened her door for her, and she hopped up into the truck, giving him a questioning gaze. "For?"

"For the onslaught of people. There's a lot of us."

"If they're like your mother and father, I'm in. Give me names to work with."

As they pulled from the curb, he ran off a list of his sister's names, their husband's names, and various nieces and nephews while Mel quietly listened.

"You're really quiet. Did I overwhelm you in sheer people alone?"

Mel grinned. "Don't be silly. I'm just paying attention. You know, *listening*. Key to our dating, as I recall."

Drew winked. "Right." He flipped the satellite radio in his truck to an Elvis station. Okay, so they had one thing in common aside from their incredible chemistry. She loved Elvis.

They drove out of the Village while Mel stole glances of him from the corner of her eye, relishing his strong jaw and the light stubble littering it in the fading sunlight.

"So I've been meaning to ask you . . ."

The look she gave him was wry. "If you ask how I got into that position where I do that thing with my leg—you can turn right around." She made a circle with her finger.

Drew's laughter filled the car, husky and low. "I wasn't going there. Just remember who tapped that first. I was going to ask if you give private lessons."

She shifted in the seat, turning to face him, enjoying their easy banter. "In how to get your leg to do that thing?"

"Later. For now I was wondering if you give private ballroom lessons."

"I knew it! I knew it wouldn't be long before you came begging me to teach you how to tango." She clapped her hands.

"Still as funny as ever. I mean for Nate."

Her ears pricked. "Nate?" She got the impression Nate did what he had to do in class. Though, he did it beautifully and he executed everything like some sort of learning machine, she didn't get the impression he liked doing it. Who was she kidding? None of the boys liked her class—they endured it until they could get their hands on a dead frog.

"Seems the kid likes to dance. He asked me if he could take lessons aside from your class."

"Did you talk him into this as a way to worm your way back into my heart? Because if you're using your son to woo me—wow, what a way to make a move."

Drew held up his long-fingered hands when they hit a stoplight, releasing them from the wheel. "Swear it was all his idea. He asked me before we—you know—tried that thing with your leg."

"I think I'm flattered."

"I think I still wish you taught baseball or something."

Her defenses went up. "Is this going to be a problem? Is this going to make you miserable because he's not learning how to score a touchdown? Because I charge a lot of money per hour to teach privately. I don't want you grumbling while you write the check."

"How much is a lot?"

"I don't know."

"You just said it was a lot of money."

"I was basing that on what I've heard the going rate is for private lessons. I've never actually taught them."

"I thought you had some fancy studio in L.A.?"

Mel shook her head, biting the inside of her cheek to quell the ache missing her kids brought. "I taught a lot of mostly underprivileged kids. Some couldn't pay at all. They just loved to dance, and I was somewhere safe they could come and let loose with. I guess that's why Stan shut the studio down, because it wasn't like I was making money. In fact, Stan probably put out more money than he gained from it. I just loved the kids, and they loved to dance."

His expression changed as the lights from the cars passed by. "I had no idea."

"You thought I was shallow and only taught the cream of the crop, didn't you?"

"I think I did."

That was the impression most everyone had about her it seemed. Except some of the seniors in the Village. If Maxine had done anything, she'd paved the way for understanding not all ex-trophy wives missed being rich. "Here's a thought. Just because Stan's rich and I was married to him doesn't mean I was a snob. Despite our cache of houses and cars, or the number of staff we had, I lived rather modestly. I spent most of my time at the studio. I wasn't interested in movie premieres or award ceremonies, so I didn't need designer dresses or makeup artists. I didn't need much but some leotards and a fresh batch of dance shoes."

"I'm sorry I unfairly judged you." His tone was somber and quiet without a hint of sarcasm in it.

Mel guessed, when Drew said he was sorry, he meant it. "Apology accepted. I can tell you this: it definitely made the transition from mansion to retirement village a whole lot easier. Though, I really do miss my bed. It was Swedish and big. Weezer and I together in my father's second bedroom in a single bed just doesn't allow for as much breathing room."

She didn't realize it, but they'd turned onto a tree-lined street, brilliant in fall color, even in the fading light. Drew turned a sharp right and pulled up to a big white ranch with red shutters and pumpkins and mums lining the cracked walkway. A house well loved, she noted. Just like the one she'd grown up in.

He shut off the ignition, turning to gaze at her. His hand cupped her chin, making her heart thump. "I meant it. I'm sorry. It was wrong of me to assume you were spoiled and pampered."

"Oh, don't get me wrong. There were lots of luxuries. Like I can't remember the last time I was in a grocery store. Stan had everything delivered. All I had to do was write a list."

"Do you miss them? The finer things in life?"

Her voice threatened to hitch, but she took a deep breath. "Not as much as I miss the kids and my friend Jackie. Okay, sometimes I miss the workout room we had in our basement. It had a pretty rad dance floor and ballet barre." She forced a smile.

But Drew didn't appear to fall for her bravado, and it made her uncomfortable enough to squirm under his scrutiny. "You miss those kids."

His reiteration almost made her falter. "I do. How about we don't talk about this anymore? I have new kids now. I need to focus on them."

Pulling her chin toward him, he dropped a light kiss on her lips, delicious and as though he'd always kissed her. "I like you, Mel."

Oh, everything about me likes you, too. "That's good to hear. I'd hate to have to go in there and make your family love me more than they love you. It's good to know you have my back."

Without another word, Drew got out of the car and came around to her side to help her out. Music seeped from the front window and more lights than a Christmas tree lit the house. The smell of something wonderful hit her nose the moment Drew opened the front door.

Selena saw her first, pushing her way through the throng of children on the floor playing a board game. She wore an apron that read, "Emeril Is My Homeboy" on it, her salt-and-pepper hair caught up in a clip on the top of her head.

She held out her arms, enveloping Mel in a warm hug scented

with something spicy that mingled with her jasmine musk perfume. "I'm so glad you came, Mel! I told Bill he cinched the deal by buying you that cheesecake, but he was convinced Myriam had run you off for good."

Mel returned her hug with a smile. "I'm not afraid of Myriam," she teased, catching sight of her stepping over children.

"I can't figure why that is either. I'm pretty scary," Myriam joked on a snort, giving Mel a quick kiss on the cheek. "You ready to get your hands dirty?"

Mel gave Myriam and Selena a suspicious eyeballing, planting her hands on her hips. "No one said anything about getting my hands dirty. I'm a dancer, not a cook. I think I've been bamboozled."

Drew put his hand at her waist, steering her around his mother and aunt. "You didn't think this was a free ride, did you? Get in there and stir something, woman."

Her head tipped back when she laughed, making it bump into his chin. Nate waved from the huge, round kitchen table, his laptop open. "Hey, Ms. Cherkasov," he mumbled without lifting his eyes from the screen.

William tugged a piece of Nate's hair. "Is that any way to greet your teacher, Nathaniel?"

Nate leveled his eyes with hers. "Sorry. Hi, Ms. Cherkasov."

She smiled at his reluctance to tear himself away from whatever he was so intent on. "Hey, Nate. So your dad tells me you want to take private ballroom lessons. Is that true?"

There was a flicker of something on his face Mel didn't quite catch, but then Myriam was right behind him, giving his shoulder a nudge. "Tell her, Nate. You wanna dance like your Auntie Myriam."

Nate nodded, securing his gaze with Mel's. "Big time."

Mel's head cocked to the left, not entirely convinced. "Really?"

He nodded his dark head. "Really."

"Well, okay then. I'll talk to your father about setting something up."

"Cool."

Myriam held out her hand to Mel. "C'mere. I'll introduce you to Drew's sisters while we make flan."

Mel headed into the fray, losing track of Drew while she narrowly avoided the chaos of careening children who ranged in age from infancy to fifteen or so and met Drew's sisters, Maura, Kathleen, and Delia.

Corned beef simmered in a huge pot on the stove, full of cabbage and potatoes, and in another, red beans and rice. Enchiladas by the dozen lined baking trays on the counter, plump with melted cheese right alongside Irish soda bread.

Someone handed Mel an apron, and it was like she'd always belonged to the clan known as McPhee. She cradled babies with varying shades of dark auburn to blond hair, stirred corned beef, wiped runny noses, washed toddlers' hands, filled sippy cups, and laughed when Drew's sisters told her stories about him being the only boy in a houseful of women.

Dinner was served buffet style, chock-full of noise and chaos. When she finally located Drew again, it was to find him stuffing his mouth full of one enchilada after another.

His smile in her direction from across the table made her heart beat harder in her chest as she had a second helping of red beans and rice. Her extended family was small, but she loved the feel of this big one. The constant vibe that said they always put family first.

It fit a place in her heart she didn't even know existed until this moment.

While she watched them interact. Share food. Tease each other.

And that scared the shit out of her.

It was an odd feeling to have so early on, but she chalked it up to the fact that you couldn't help but love the McPhee's. It went without saying they were hardworking, genuine, but above all, happy.

Stranger still was the odd sensation that crept over her, warm and sweet, when she caught Drew rocking his sister Kathleen's baby Felicity. It did something peculiar and fluttery to her stomach to watch the tiny infant curl her fingers into her uncle's hair and press her round-cheeked face against Drew's wide shoulder.

It did something even funnier when Drew nibbled on her chubby fist.

The blare of a familiar Latin tune took her attention away from the warmth Drew was creating in her. She smiled as Selena and Myriam got the older boys to move the kitchen table out of the way so they could dance.

Mel had leaned into the doorway to watch them when Nate yelled, "Hey, Grandma, bet Ms. Cherkasov could show you a thing or two."

Myriam and Selena rolled their hips, moving their feet in her direction to the rhythm of the music. Myriam wiggled her finger at Mel in invitation while she held her arms, bent at the elbows and shook her shoulders in the best ever imitation of Charo Mel could claim having seen. "C'mon, Latin champion. Give us hell!"

Mel blushed and shook her head, feeling Drew's eyes bore into her back. "Oh, no. You two are too hot for me."

Selena did a pretty good imitation of a samba roll with Myriam, gyrating her hips comically at Mel. "Show us what you got, dancer!" She let go of Myriam and grabbed hold of Mel's hand, pulling it in the air and twirling around.

The rhythm thrummed through her veins, making it hard not to allow her body the freedom to interpret it.

"Is that the best you got?" Myriam shouted with a devilish grin.

"I thought you were some kind of a champion? What happened to that infamous hip action?" she taunted.

Mel kept her movements reserved. She wrinkled her nose at Myriam. "You're baiting me, Myriam. You don't want me to show you up, do you?"

Myriam shook her hips in a challenge, rolling her neck in Mel's direction. "You bet your bippy, I do!"

"C'mon, Ms. Cherkasov!" Nate yelled, clearly enjoying the rivalry the two older women had created. "Show them that thing you did in class the other day."

Mel blushed. The hell she'd do the bootylicious in front of Drew.

Myriam danced around her in a challenge of hips and feet, and when the music changed to "Sway," Mel couldn't resist showing Myriam and Selena a thing or two about all that hip action. She lifted the edges of the skirt she'd bought just for her date with Drew. A frilly purple chiffon with a small slit in the fabric that reached two or three inches above her knee.

Mel used it like she would in a paso or a tango, stomping her feet to challenge Myriam and Selena right back. Her face split into a grin when Myriam gave her a defiant gaze.

Her hips had a will of their own, gyrating to the rhythm, sultry and quick. Someone whistled when Mel grabbed Myriam's hand and her feet automatically took over the familiar steps to a salsa.

Mel shimmied her shoulders, twisting her body, pulling Myriam with her into a cha-cha, purposely accentuating the lines of her body by pointing her toes and keeping her chest thrust forward.

When she spun past Drew, she felt the heat of his gaze consuming her movements, his eyes dark, and it empowered her, compelling her to draw on the sensuality she'd always saved for only the dance floor.

Joy pumped through her veins. Her heart thumped and while she fought to keep her movements low-key and fit for children, her body warred with her common sense. Her breathing came in familiar huffs, her veins hot with blood running through them while the music carried her feet away.

And this—the laughter from Myriam and Selena as they tried to mimic the quickness of her steps, the smiles as some of the smaller children attempted to do what the adults were doing—the freedom to communicate her one true love, was why she danced.

It bubbled inside her, making her feel well and truly alive for the first time in a long time.

When the song ended, everyone clapped, whistling and catcalling.

Everyone but Drew.

But she chose to ignore him and instead curtsied and made a big deal out of clapping in Selena and Myriam's direction, praising them for their impressive salsa and cha-cha knowledge.

"Did you see that, Drew?" Myriam yelped. "Can you believe she's not Puerto Rican the way she moves those hips? Phew!" Myriam fanned herself.

"Drew!" Selena yelled over the noise. "Phone."

Mel watched as she handed the phone to Drew and the expression that passed between mother and son. Drew took the phone, handing over the baby to his mother.

His lips hardened to a thin line while his head nodded. His expression had gone from doting uncle to a mask of disgust Mel didn't understand.

He hung the phone up and tapped Nate on the shoulder, hitching his jaw to draw his son out into the living room.

Headlights hit the front bay window in the living room, followed by a sharp screech of brakes that had everyone up and on their feet to see what was going on.

Mel stood at the back of the crowd of Drew's relatives, her stomach twisting when a hand crashed against the front door.

A hush fell over the room, and again, the hand banged on the door, relentless and angry. "Nate! You tell your scum-sucking father to open this door right now!" The words from behind the door were slurred and choppy, but whoever it was, it was a woman.

Alarm bells sounded in Mel's head when she saw Nate's face fall. Threading her way through the children and adults, Mel came up behind Nate and put a hand on his arm.

She felt a slight tremble in his shoulders before he said with resignation, "It's okay, Dad. I'll go with her."

Drew held up his hand to prevent Nate from moving. "Like hell."

"Damn this woman," Selena muttered, moving to stand on the other side of Nate.

"Open this door, Drew! Open it now. You can't keep me from my son!"

Mel's stomach sank like someone had attached an anchor to it.

Nate's mother.

Dread filled her when she realized, Drew was going to open the door.

Just as the woman began to screech again, Drew yanked the door open and made a move to keep her from coming in the house, but she ducked under his arm, wobbling in a zigzag toward Nate.

She threw her arms around him, tripping on her ripped trench coat, and nearly toppling him. "There's my baby." She slurred the coo of words at him.

Mel had to put a discreet finger to her nose to stamp out the stench of alcohol. Horror welled inside her.

Nate's mother was drunk.

When she caught sight of Mel, clearly a new face in the crowd of

McPhees, her face distorted. "Are you here with Drew?" she asked, clinging to Nate who hadn't moved an inch.

Mel didn't answer her.

"What are you? Deaf? I said, are you here with Drew, slut?" she shouted just before she lunged for Mel.

CHAPTER TWELVE

Dear Divorce Journal,

I'd leave this blank, but when I open you each night, I find myself compelled to scribble at least something so when I look back on this divorce journey of mine, I'll have entries as a reminder of how far I've come.

But this entry I'd almost rather forget. It makes me cry. For Nate. I'll only say, in all of the things Stan has done to me over the last months, I'm so grateful none of them involved substance abuse and a child.

Mel refused to allow her shock to show, but then Sherry lost interest altogether in her. Rather, she was too busy focusing on Nate who she still clung to.

Nate stood ramrod straight. He didn't rebuff her embrace, but he didn't welcome it either. Mel's eyes sought Drew's and found them blazing with anger.

"You can't take him, Sherry."

Sherry, petite, porcelain skinned if not a bit green around the gills, shot Drew a look of disgust with her wide blue eyes. "Can, too. The judge said so, didn't he, Nate?" She lifted a wobbly hand up and threaded her fingers through Nate's hair in a gesture of affection.

When Nate finally moved, it was to step backward with a shrug out of Sherry's reach.

Drew stepped in front of Nate and Mel, crossing his arms over his chest. "The judge said you have to be sober. You will *not* take my son from this house in your condition."

"He's *our* son!" she cried with a warble, stumbling in her heels. "You can't keep him all to yourself!"

The eerie calm of Drew's reply settled in Mel's bones. This wasn't just angry. This was infuriated on a level that surely only a parent can feel when one's child is in a potentially dangerous situation. "I can and I will if you've been drinking."

Sherry swatted a hand in the air with a dismissive gesture. "I only had one drink. Just one." She waved a shaky finger up at him. "You can't prove I didn't. It's my turn to have Nate. Give him to me!"

Drew grabbed at her arm, but not before she stumbled and reached out again in her drunken stupor to Nate, latching on to a handful of his shirt and ripping it.

Still Nate didn't move. Not when everyone gasped, and not even when Selena called Sherry something in Spanish Mel guessed wasn't kind. His face was blank, his young body stiff. It was as if he thought because she was his mother, he had to endure such horrific behavior.

Not on her watch.

Mel put Nate's hand in hers and quietly tugged at it, hoping to remove him from the situation, but Sherry caught sight of it and shoved past Drew. She launched herself at Mel in an awkward, crab-like thrust, catching Mel in the jaw with her flailing hands.

"Who's the slut, Drew?" she accused, spit flying from her mouth, her lips curled in a snarl. "Did you think you were going to get a new mommy for Nate because you're in charge of everything? You don't own everything, Drew, and she can't have Nate! None of you can," she seethed, piercing everyone with hateful eyes. "You bastards—all of you are bastards, trying to keep my son from me!"

Mel winced, but she refused to let go of Nate's hand. Instead, she gave him a hard yank, pulling him back against her. Though he was taller than she was, she thrust him behind her, taking a defensive stance by putting her body in front of his.

If there was going to be a rumble in the jungle, the hell she was coming out the loser.

"That's enough, Sherry!" Drew roared, wrapping his arm around her waist and propelling her toward the door while he pulled his cell phone from his shirt.

Sherry screamed her rage, twisting her body against Drew's while he literally carried her out the front door.

Maura's husband slammed the door shut the moment Drew walked through it, blowing out a heavy breath while everyone else gathered together, muttering terse words.

But Mel wasn't paying attention to anyone but Nate who'd silently slipped out the back door off the laundry room and out into the backyard.

Myriam was the first to react, throwing a kitchen towel at the sink with a yowl. "Ohhhhhh! That woman is a filthy, filthy creature!"

Selena ran her weary hand over her forehead and patted Mel on the back. "I'm sorry, Mel."

Mel was torn between going to Drew and finding Nate. "Forget me. What will Drew do?"

"The same thing he always does," Delia said, pulling a hat down over the ears of her son Patrick who squirmed and giggled. "He'll call her a cab and lodge his millionth complaint with the courts about that drunk floozy. Then tomorrow, because he's the salt of the earth, he'll drive her car home for her and check to be sure she's not dead of alcohol poisoning."

Kathleen, dark and gorgeous, and a complete dichotomy in coloring to the fair Delia, scrunched her face. "And it'll be the millionth complaint they ignore because she's Nate's blood. That they won't terminate her visitation until she gets sober stuns me speechless."

Mel was horrified. "How can it be okay for her to show up plastered and try and take Nate? Clearly, she shouldn't be driving with him in the car. What kind of law allows that?" Mel asked, outraged that Nate was subjected to something so ugly and so detrimental to his safety.

"Oh, she can't. She absolutely has to be sober, but that doesn't mean she can't try. It also doesn't mean she can't make a scene that Nate has to be a witness to time and time again. In the end, she's his mother. That's what the court says," Maura's husband, tall and lanky, spat.

A tear slipped along Selena's pudgy cheek. One Mel was sure she'd shed many times before. "It was her Saturday. I should have known she'd show up here and try to assert all those rights she flings around at us when she gets done at the bar with whatever man she's managed to weasel into buying her drinks."

Kathleen put her arm around her mother, and kissed the top of her head. "C'mon, Mom. I'll make you some tea before we go."

While everyone cleared dishes and soothed Selena, Mel made her way to the laundry room to take a peek out the window at Nate.

The backyard light shone on his lone form, sitting on one of the yellow plastic swings, unmoving, his torn shirt flapping in the subtle breeze.

Mel dug around on the washer where the coats were piled and grabbed the one she'd seen him wear at school. Tightening her sweater around her neck, she headed out the back door into the inky evening.

Nate's eyes glistened, tearing at her heart. It almost made her want to hunt down Sherry and club her to death with the broomsticks she gave the boys to use for their posture.

But not enough to ignore the pain Nate was so obviously in.

She held out his jacket to him with a smile, then sat in the swing next to him. "Guess you don't want to talk."

He shrugged into the jacket, wiping the corner of his eye on it. The wet film of his tears glistening on the black nylon fabric left Mel gritting her teeth to keep from reaching out and hugging him. Nate didn't want pity. That much was clear from the determined set of his jaw. And he was twelve. If anything, he'd rather give up his Xbox 360 than cry in front of her. "Not really."

She shrugged her shoulders like it was no skin off her nose, taking the swing next to his and rocking it by using her toes. "Okay. I can just sit. Or I can go back inside. I hear there's flan, and we both know how I feel about dessert."

"Sorry," he mumbled.

"For?"

"My mother. She's not a bad person—mostly. But when she drinks, she has a pretty bad temper, and sometimes she says things that are rude."

"No sweat."

"She hit you." His voice hitched just enough to let his embarrassment leak into it.

Which meant she had to go out of her way to prove to him she didn't care what his mother did. It was no reflection on him. Mel began to pump her legs. "Hah! That was nothing. You should have seen the time Neil slugged me in the eye during a particularly intense tango. That was something."

"You don't have to be nice."

"I'm not being nice. I'm being factual. There's a difference."

"You have a bruise."

Mel ran her finger over the lump forming on her jaw. "Do I? Huh. Didn't even feel it."

"Did my dad take her home?" The worry in Nate's voice shredded her, but she refused to allow him to think she was affected or put off by him because his mother was an alcoholic.

"Not sure. You want me to go see?"

He shook his head hard "No! I mean. No," his tone softened in his typical showing of respect. "Please don't. She'll only get angrier if she sees you."

Mel nodded her understanding. "Then I'll stay put."

"I don't get her. She doesn't want my dad, and she doesn't want to be married to my dad, but she doesn't want him to be around anyone else. That's why she acted like that when she saw you. I'm sorry she called you a slut."

Mel tried not to let Nate see how that information affected her, and she didn't want him to think she'd use him to pry. Nate was letting off steam, and she had to show him she respected that. "How about you quit apologizing for someone else's behavior? And let me tell you about the competitive world of ballroom dancing. That word is cotton candy compared to some of the words I've been called. No one can ever top what Joanna Lucille Vega called me. She was dreadful." Mel wrinkled her nose to show him how dreadful.

"What'd she call you?"

Mel snorted at the memory. "Ladies don't repeat such things. Suffice it to say, it wasn't nice and it was exceptionally unsportsmanlike."

"Nate?" Drew's voice came out of the darkness, making them both stop their swings.

"Did you call her a cab?"

Drew approached them, his mouth set in grim disapproval, his hands shoved deeply in the pockets of his jeans. "I did. She'll be fine."

Nate rose from the swing, his expression sad. The light from the backyard glimmered in his eyes, sharing his unshed tears. "She's never going to be fine. You know it, and I know it."

Nate's adultlike acceptance of his mother's alcoholism left a cold chill Mel couldn't shake. Shouldn't he at least be hopeful Sherry could overcome? But knowing Nate, he'd looked up the statistics of beating such an ugly disease, weighed reports, and factually calculated his mother's fate based on her past behavior.

If Sherry was the kind of repeat offender she appeared to be, Nate's sense of hopelessness was warranted. Being a genius gave Nate a logical mind, and surely he'd drawn logical conclusions. But logic didn't always allow you to dream.

Drew sucked in a breath. When he let it go, he blew out a puff of air, cold with condensation. "I wish I could say that wasn't true, son."

She had to fight to keep her rising anger in check. If Drew didn't at least leave Nate with some hope his mother could recover, then who would? "Hold on," Mel intervened, unable to relinquish the idea that nothing was impossible. "Nothing's impossible, right? People do it all the time."

"Right. Ever watched *Intervention*?" Nate asked sarcastically.

"I've watched marathon after marathon," Mel responded. "I've seen a lot of recovery in there along with the failures. Nothing's impossible."

Drew popped his lips together, shooting Nate a glance. "Son? Why don't you go inside and help Grandma with the clearing up. I'll be in in just a sec."

"You're mad at Mel," Nate assessed in his oh so logical way. "Don't take it out on her, Dad. She's just trying to be hopeful because she doesn't know."

"Inside," Drew commanded with the hitch of his thumb.

Nate shot Mel a quick look of sympathy before skulking back in the house.

Drew rounded on her the second he heard the back door shut. "How about you don't fill my kid with bullshit hope of any kind of recovery for his mother?"

Mel jumped up from the swing set, her feet cold and numb from the chilly night, knowing full well she was interfering where she didn't belong but taking the road less traveled anyway. "How about you remember he's twelve, and while it's fine to teach him reality sucks, it can be tempered with some hope?"

"Because he's my son and not yours, and while you teach him in the classroom, I think I have a pretty good handle on everything else."

"Good comeback, but his emotional well-being's just as important to me as it is to you. A healthy, well-adjusted, secure child always learns better."

"Nate knows where his mother stands. There's no point in candy-coating it."

Mel was astonished and even a little disappointed. "God forbid you should instill the possibility for recovery exists. It's called *hope,* Drew, and I don't know if you were paying close attention to your son's face in there while the woman who gave birth to him made a complete ass out of herself, but it hurts him. Does he have to be so dipped in reality he can't believe things can change?"

Drew shoved a hand through his thick hair, the lines on his face weary. "I have a lot of trouble with hope where Sherry's concerned."

Gazing up at him, Mel pursed her lips. "Yeah, I get that. It's pretty clear, but do you have to steal Nate's hope, too? She's his mother, for God's sake. He has every right to wish she'd get better. She's not my mother, and even I hope she gets better."

He pulled her to him, smiling down at her. "I'm being a caveman again?"

She brushed him off, rolling up her sleeves. "Don't turn my light switch on and off to avoid the subject, Drew. I understand preparing Nate for the worst. I'd bet my left ovary he's already done that himself by looking up all sorts of things related to alcoholism online because that's just who he is. But you can't find optimism on Google, Drew. That's an attitude, and something you should wholly participate in practicing. Sure, tell him things don't look good, but don't count her out just yet. You have no right to steal that from him until he gives it up himself."

"And then he ends up hurt because he's continually disappointed in her? This has been going on since Nate was six and Sherry and I divorced, Mel. You have no idea what you're talking about."

"I only know what I saw, and Nate's resigned to her never recovering because you are. She's his mother, good, bad or otherwise. Was she always like this? Or were there good times?"

Drew's smile grew fond—a smile that stabbed at her heart like tiny needles being thrust into it. "No. Not always. She was a good mother—at first." But that was all he had to offer, leaving Mel feeling left out.

"I don't want to pry, and you don't have to tell me what happened between you and Sherry, but I also don't want to see Nate stuff his wish for his mother's recovery away because you say it won't happen. You don't know everything, Drew McPhee, and you sure as hell can't predict the future. So with that thought in mind, I'm going to keep hoping Sherry realizes the terrific luck she has in a son like Nate, and wish for the best."

His face grew soft again. "She called you a slut."

"Is that an apology I hear in your tone for someone else's bad behavior? Like I told Nate, that can't touch some of the things I've been called. So forget it."

His thumb caressed her chin. "She also hit you. I'm sorry."

Mel raised an eyebrow. "I've broken my coccyx—and yes, in case you didn't know, that's my ass. A little lump on my jaw won't kill me."

"You broke your ass?" His chuckle was deep, rumbling and echoing in the night, breaking the tension between them.

"Well, Neil broke it when he dropped me. And don't let him tell you he didn't drop me. He dropped me like I was hot. But I try not to hold grudges."

Drew's face went grim. "I should have known she'd show up."

"I take it she does this often." Mel didn't ask it as a question, she had a horrible feeling this was just one episode in a string of them.

"On more occasions than I can count. How she can love booze more than our brilliantly funny kid always leaves me astounded."

"Has she tried to get help?" How could you not at least try when you had a son as incredible as Nate?

Drew's next words were snide and filled with residual anger. "Oh, she's been to plenty of rehab courtesy of me and at the expense of my business. And she always leaves rehab the same way she went in— drunk."

Mel let her hand rest on his arm, her eyes sympathetic. "I'm sorry for both you and Nate."

"He's such a great kid. I don't know how she can't want to be as great for him as he is to her." There was a defeated sorrow in Drew's voice—sorrow for a wrong he couldn't right for his son.

Mel remained silent. If Drew wanted to share with her, she wanted something so painful to be done in his own time.

He braced a hand against the swing set. "I guess I owe you an explanation."

"You don't owe me a thing. The only thing you do owe me is flan."

"I know everything about your sordid past."

Mel rolled her eyes, tightening her sweater at her chest. "Like you're breaking records there? Who in the free world doesn't?"

"Tell you what. I'll go get us some flan, and you meet me up there." He pointed to the tree around the corner, a tremendous oak, shedding its leaves in a colorful array of bright patterns on the ground.

"In the tree?"

"You afraid to climb?"

"Hah—go get the flan. We'll see who's afraid of what."

"I'll check on Nate and meet you back here in five."

Mel rounded the corner of the house, and when her eyes adjusted to the darkness, she saw a ladder made of rope hanging down the side of the oak. Looking up, she grinned, feeling foolishly light-hearted. A tree house.

She grabbed a handful of the rope and began to climb, hoping it was sturdy enough to hold her. As she hit the top, she threw her leg over the limb that served as the entry to the structure and slid in.

The interior had her catching her breath. Even in the dark, she could see the outlines of two small benches built into the wall of the tree house, polished and shiny. The moonlight streaming in from the window with actual Plexiglas cast a golden hue on the interior that bounced off the walls, creating a world all its own on the planked wood walls. There was a round table made of knotty pine meant for a child in the middle of the small floor, positioned by the benches with a book on it.

Mel slid in and found she couldn't totally stand up, so she inched over to the bench and grabbed a seat, marveling at the craftsmanship that had so apparently gone into this tree house. Her eyes caught the title of the book on the table—*The Forensic Science of C.S.I.*

"Nate's," Drew said, sliding a plate with flan toward her with two forks. He dropped a Thermos on the floor of the tree house and pulled two disposable cups out of his jacket pocket before angling himself upward and into the interior.

"Is he okay?"

"He's fine. He asked to go to my sister's with his cousins for a sleepover."

"This," Mel said, spreading her arms out with a smile, "is amazing. It's like a dollhouse."

"Don't let Nate hear you say that," he warned. "We don't need no one callin' this a stinkin' dollhouse. This is a man-cave, complete with manlike things, including a refrigerator that, if you run an electrical cord to the house, can be plugged in."

"Who built this? It's got the most unbelievable little details to it. For instance, the coat rack—the knobs on it look like kitchen cabinet handles. And the floor is linoleum, isn't it?"

Drew popped open a drawer just beneath his feet to pull out a candle just before sliding in beside her. He lit the candle, illuminating the small space, then threw an arm around the back of the bench. It was small, making their seating a close one. His thigh pressed against hers was warm, leaving her skin tingling. "I built this when I was thirteen."

"*You* made this?"

"Cavemen are good with their hands."

"You designed it?"

"Your tone, it saddens me. Why so surprised?"

She shrugged, eyeing the creamy dollop of flan on the plate. "Because when you said handyman . . . I guess. Never mind. I don't know what I thought, but this is incredible. When did you build it again?"

Drew scooped some flan up, pressing the spoon to her lips. "When I was thirteen. Nate and I remodeled it a few years ago so he could have somewhere to hang out. That's how I found out the only thing keeping him from being the postman's kid is our love of accuracy when measuring. Otherwise, he's not interested in building anything but maybe the next atomic bomb."

Mel laughed, savoring the sugary goodness of the flan. Taking the spoon from his hand, she dragged it through the dessert and fed him some in return. "He's so brilliant it scares me. That has to be tough for a parent."

Drew smacked his lips in appreciation. "You mean when the parent isn't as smart as the kid?"

"Yeah," she said on a teasing grin, licking the spoon, shivering at the intimacy of putting something in her mouth that had just been in Drew's. "Where did that come from anyway? Is Myriam a secret member of Mensa?"

His chest expanded with a sigh. "Actually, Sherry's the genius."

Mel kept her face placid, though internally, she couldn't help but be saddened by so much potential left to pickle in alcohol. "I see."

"You can ask, you know."

"And you can tell. But only when you're ready."

Drew settled in, leaning his head on his hand. "Sherry was an artist. She had a successful gallery in the city. Unlike Nate, it took her a long time to come to terms with her genius. She struggled in school. You know, the typical stuff when you're smarter than everyone else. Instead of burying herself in a book, she acted out, did some really stupid things: dabbled in drugs, pills, played a lot of hooky. She was part of the artsy crowd."

There was a familiarity in Drew's reference to Sherry's high school days. "So you knew her in school?"

He nodded, dragging the spoon through the now forgotten flan. "We both grew up here in Riverbend, knew each other in high school a little, but we didn't reconnect until well after we'd graduated. It took her a long time to get her act together, well into her early twenties, but when she did, she enrolled in college and she was on the fast track—a real superstar. We met again at our tenth high school reunion when we were twenty-eight. I had a fairly successful contracting business at the time. We got married within the year, had Nate, and then almost five years later, everything went to shit."

"Went to shit?"

"Yep, right after Sherry killed her brother."

CHAPTER THIRTEEN

Dear Divorce Journal,

So, this entry is a much more pleasant addition.

Tree houses. Yay!

Mel didn't even try to hide her gasp of horror. "Killed him?"

Drew shook his head. "Technically, she didn't kill him. But she thinks she did. Back then she was what they call a 'functional alcoholic.' Somebody who's built up a tolerance and doesn't exhibit the typical signs of inebriation. After Nate was born and as her gallery grew more successful, the pressure to stay on top got harder, but Sherry liked the finer things in life, and she was willing to do whatever it took to keep wearing Gucci and Prada. Growing up poor gives you a different perspective on things, I guess. Either way, the pressure was intense and she coped by drinking."

Mel's surprise was matched only by the almost-ugly tone Drew displayed when he mentioned Sherry's love of materialistic things. "Funny, I figured a caveman like you would think Gucci was a prescription sleep aide," she teased.

Drew chucked her under the chin. "Such a comedienne. I know all the designer labels and then some. Being married to Sherry was a lesson in all things overpriced. Because of her, we had the best of everything."

"And 'everything' isn't important to you?"

"*Family* is important. Sitting together at the same table for dinner, even just at McDonald's, is important. Do I really need a pair of shoes that cost three thousand dollars because they have some guy's French name on them when I can have a pair that's just as good for fifty?"

Mel gave that some thought. "Clearly, you're not a woman," she joked.

"Clearly," he said with a rueful smile.

Mel licked the spoon. "So back to your story. Did you know about her drinking?"

"Not at first. Days went by where we didn't see each other except in passing due to the nature of her ambition. We'd begun to lose touch in our marriage. She traveled a lot, art shows, acquisitions for the gallery. She was in high demand for shows. For a while, we were even bicoastal while she opened a gallery in L.A., something I hated. The more money she made, the greedier she got and the less we saw of her. But we had lots of nice things . . ."

Mel again heard that snide tone to his voice in reference to all of their "nice things," and it made her pause at his almost vehement aversion to them. "So she liked nice things and she had the power to buy them. Is that a bad thing?"

The lines of his face grew hard. "It is when that's *all* that's important to you. That and your booze and pills."

Mel winced, afraid to approach that angle any further. "So back to how Sherry became so out of control."

"I didn't realize how out of touch we were until Christmas Eve. She'd always been moody, but I chalked it up to her creativity."

Mel took exception to that statement. She was creative, but she was anything but moody. "So everyone who's creative is a brooding artist in your mind?"

He eyed her. "Maybe not everyone. Anyway, I didn't see the signs of her drinking until a holiday party just before everything went to hell. She threw back eight or ten drinks without even blinking that night while I nursed one scotch and soda. Not a slurred word or single stumble out of her."

"So she was drinking heavily when she was away, then?"

"That's my guess. Looking back, I think I just didn't want to acknowledge there was a problem. I always chalked her odd mood swings up to her artistic nature. She could be temperamental and sensitive on the best of days, and I'd had a taste of some of that going into our relationship. But as she became more imbalanced, it never occurred to me that she drank like that all the time. At the gallery, in the apartment she had in L.A., when she was driving Nate to preschool," he gritted the last words from between clenched teeth.

Turning to face her, he captured Mel's gaze. "She hid it well. If I'd known—really understood . . ." His words held such remorse that Mel found her hand straying to his, reaching out to tuck hers into it.

If there was one thing about Drew she knew was real, it was his sense of family. "Had you really understood, I think you would have done whatever you could to help her."

"Shortly after that party, everything blew up. She began to forget things, miss appointments with buyers. One day, she forgot to pick Nate up from a birthday party while I was in Kentucky on business. Thank God for Myriam. She was who tipped me off that there was a problem. When Sherry finally came home, she was pretty sloshed. She tried to take Nate for ice cream at three in the morning. Myriam called me hysterical, and I immediately demanded Sherry seek help, for all the good it did me. From that point on, everything happened so fast . . ."

The flan sat in her stomach like lead while she silently allowed Drew the time to gather his thoughts and finish.

"What I didn't know was Sherry was falling apart. Her gallery was sinking without her there to give it direction. Her painting was suffering. Her entire career was on the line. Not to mention, she'd endangered Nate, and still, she chose to drink." He all but spat the words.

"Alcoholism is a horrible disease, Drew," Mel consoled, the backs of her eyes stinging with unshed tears.

"Don't I know it. Sherry's brother intervened on my behalf. He'd come in from L.A. to help with a half-assed attempt at an intervention of sorts. The plan was to get Sherry to go to rehab. Instead, Martin ended up dead."

A shudder ran along her spine. "And I'm sensing you feel partially responsible for that?"

Folding her hands into his, he bowed his head. "You bet I do. At this point, my business was falling apart. I was afraid to leave Sherry alone with Nate, and I was worn out from trying to keep track of her. I lost countless contracts because I was so wrapped up in what Sherry needed. Everything I did was based on what kind of mood Sherry was in at any given time. I needed help. So I put all that money she made to good use and hired a nanny to keep an eye on Nate when I couldn't be around. My family wasn't happy about a stranger caring for Nate, but they had lives and jobs at the time, and when Sherry and I got married, we moved to New York. I couldn't ask them to come into Westchester every time Sherry snuck off to drink."

Her heart wrenched for the small boy she'd seen in the pictures lining Selena's walls. Smiling, cherubic, pulling a wagon, wearing a pumpkin costume at Halloween. "So you hired someone to look after Nate so you could work," she prompted.

His face was grim in the moonlight. "Yes, and Elsa was terrific. She went above and beyond the call of duty where Sherry was concerned. Anyway, this went on for several months while Sherry sunk deeper and deeper. She'd gone from a functioning alcoholic to a total train wreck. I called Martin, her brother, for help. The day he flew in, Sherry took off while I was at work. Elsa was under strict orders not to interfere with Sherry's comings and goings—it only made her angry, and I didn't want Elsa hurt or Nate exposed to any more of her brand of crazy. According to Elsa, Sherry was still gone when she left. Martin let Elsa go home early, and he was playing with Nate when he had a heart attack. I came home that night to cop cars and Nate, usually easygoing and quiet even at five, completely hysterical."

Mel closed her eyes and gulped. "Does he remember it?"

"He was who called 911."

Mel felt a sting of pride that even at such a young age, Nate was so brave. "Even then he was a genius."

Drew's eyes were far away, reliving whatever horror he'd seen that night. "But what he saw . . . his recounting of that night is that Sherry came home and she smelled 'yucky.' She and Martin got into a fight about why he'd come in from L.A. She accused him of ambushing her with my help. Nate's words were, 'Mommy and Uncle Martin had a big fight. She told him she didn't need help, and he got really mad. Then his face turned red and he fell down.' Sherry was so drunk, she passed out, and Nate called 911."

Tears stung her eyes. "Poor Nate."

"Sherry probably could have saved her brother had she been sober. After that, and her refusal to admit she had a problem or get help after the first couple of bouts with rehab, I was done. I took Nate to a therapist and filed for divorce."

"And you won custody."

"You bet I did. If I'd had to leave the country, there was no way she was getting her hands on Nate. She didn't fight me very hard about it either. She was too busy wallowing in her guilt over Martin's death and her booze."

"But she still has the right to see him? How can that be?" Mel found herself disgusted all over again on Nate's behalf. Why should he be subjected to such cruelty time and again when it could be avoided?

"She has the right as long as it's supervised. Her showing up here like she did tonight is something she's done more times than I can count. I do what I always do. Notify my lawyer who notifies the courts and then charges me two hundred and fifty bucks an hour to tell me she has every right to see Nate as long as it's supervised."

"But why don't you file a restraining order—or call the police when she shows up? Isn't there a law about drunk and disorderly?"

Drew's hands clenched into fists, his face visibly torn between Nate's love for his mother and his own sense of duty to his son. "Because Nate loves her, Mel. Because he's never anywhere without someone with him who can prevent her from taking him, and he knows better than to get into a car with her—ever. She's his mother. I don't have the heart to make this any worse for him by throwing Sherry in jail. But that we have all these rules about his visitation with her and precautions he has to take, like always carrying his cell phone to dial 911 if she tries to convince him to go somewhere with her, makes me want to wring Sherry's neck. No kid should have to search his mother's house to see if she's got a bottle of vodka hidden somewhere like he's some jailor."

Mel sat in cold disbelief. What a huge burden for a twelve-year-old. "I can't think of any other word for this than 'horrible.' But he does love her. I can see it." She paused, cocking her head. But what about Drew? "What about your contracting business?"

Regret shone in his eyes. "It was a shambles when all was said and done. I'd neglected it for so long, borrowed against it to send Sherry to rehab, and then the economy tanked and here I am, Westmeyer's version of Tim the Toolman Taylor." He joked, but Mel heard lingering resentment.

"So are you still angry with her? She didn't just lose everything. You and Nate did, too."

"Well, I still have Nate, but I'm past it now. All of the expensive furniture and ridiculously pricey art we had meant nothing to me. I'm a simple guy who needs a bed and a refrigerator. I did everything I could think of to help her when we were married, but jeopardizing Nate was too far. Though, I am resentful where Nate's concerned. I won't allow anyone to speak ill of Sherry in front of him, but I'd like to wring her neck because of what having her for a mother does to him."

"To fall so far . . ."

"She lost everything, and even more ironic? I pay her alimony—which is just booze money to her. Watching that decline was brutal for me, but for Nate, it was excruciating. There was a time when Sherry was as devoted as any mother, and Nate being Nate, remembers it."

Mel's sigh was shaky. Now she recognized she'd gone too far. "First, I apologize for laying into you about your lack of hope where Sherry's concerned. I understand why it seems hopeless. After hearing that, I feel hopeless. Still, I'm convinced there's always hope, and you shouldn't take that away from Nate, keeping a realistic slant on it. It should be for him to decide when he's given up on her. As long as he's not in danger, taking that from him would be unfair, but I'm sorry I spoke up before I knew the details. Second, I'm not going to tell you not to blame yourself for your brother-in-law's death because I can see it's pointless. But for the record, you can't be everywhere, Drew. It sounds like you had people who relied on you for their livings."

"If I'd gotten home an hour earlier . . ."

"'If' is a huge word, one that can be applied to almost anything. If I'd pursued my dream instead of marrying Stan, maybe I wouldn't be a candidate for world's most pathetic ex-trophy wife. But I didn't.

And here I am. I don't want to diminish your tragedy by comparing it to something as frivolous as my former lifestyle, but you get the meaning."

His mood lightened like someone had turned on a light switch. Drew moved in closer to her, pulling her back against his chest and wrapping his arms around her waist. "Do you like where you are?"

"You mean right now? Or in general?"

He let his chin rest on the top of her head. "Right this very second."

Mel grinned, adjusting to the sense of contentment she felt in Drew's arms. "Well, it beats being on fire."

"You're not on fire?" He sounded surprised.

"Should I be?"

Turning her around to face him, he smiled. "Because if you're not on fire, I'm not doing my job," he muttered before hauling her to him and cupping either side of her face. He dipped his head, taking her mouth in a demanding kiss.

Her groan was a hush of pleasure when Drew's lips separated hers, letting his tongue caress hers, creating that hot rush of excitement in her. Mel melted into his chest, letting her breasts press against it, relishing the tingle of heightened awareness it left between her thighs.

Drew's arms went around her, molding her to him, pulling her down on top of him until they lay on the bench. The sinful grind of his hips against hers left her clinging to his shoulders. In an instant, she was indeed on fire, desperate to allow these new sensations to consume her.

Their kiss deepened, their tongues stroked and tasted, the sounds mingling with their sighs. Mel held in another moan when Drew's fingers brushed the underside of her breast, caressing it through her clothing. His other hand strayed to her leg, drawing his fingers along her skin, cupping her ass, kneading the flesh until there wasn't an inch of space between them.

When he skimmed the top of her panties, Mel fought a scream of frustration. She wanted him. Hard. Hot. Now. The sharp, sweet sensations Drew created made it hard to remember their agreement. If she knew anything, she knew this wasn't the way to get to know someone. They knew each other like this.

She tore her mouth away from his on a harsh pant. "Okay, officially on fire. You're work here is done."

His eyes glittered in the dark. "Don't you think we should put out the fire?" he asked, like he didn't have the answer. His lips found their way back to the sensitive flesh of her neck just below her ear, his hand cupping the back of her head.

"You agreed we could get to know each other before, you know . . ."

"Wasn't that just me who purged all over you a few minutes ago?"

She gasped when he nibbled her earlobe, wrapping her arms around his head at the sheer delight of his teeth on her skin. "But you still don't know my favorite color."

"Bet I can make you see colors," he enticed, his voice husky and thick. In a swift move of hands and strength, Drew lifted her upward, sliding between her legs.

Her hand went to the back of the bench to steady herself when he pulled up her skirt.

Mel's heart crashed against her ribs at the mere thought of what he intended and almost stopped when Drew hooked a finger in the leg of her panties and pulled them aside.

The first dip of his tongue against her aching flesh left her dizzy. His moan, intimate and sinful, made her writhe. He stroked her with wet swirls, delving deep between the lips of her sex then withdrawing until Mel had to bite her tongue to keep from screaming her anticipation.

Heat coiled in her belly, electric and needy as he inserted a thick finger into her passage and drove it upward.

Colors were definitely involved, streaking behind her eyelids while she pressed down on his hard finger, desperate for the lashes of his tongue. Her hips rocked, gyrating against the hot flicks he lavished on her most intimate part, crashing against his mouth when he pulled her flush to his face and kneaded her ass.

Mel's head fell back on her shoulders, and she clenched her teeth when orgasm threatened to rip her apart. Her breathing grew ragged, a harsh rasp in the silence of the tree house as the mounting pressure of climax exploded with the wet ministrations of Drew's tongue.

She bucked against him, the sharp heat he evoked assaulting her flesh in wave after wave of fiery relief.

Sensing her release, Drew's strokes slowed, his hard hands gripping her hips now softened and released her slowly. He slid back upward, pulling her back down to press her head under his chin and cradle her near.

Mel couldn't find words for what had just happened. It was clear from the rigid line in his jeans he was as aroused as she'd been. Her head popped up, guilt and embarrassment left her stumbling on her words. "I—"

"I know. I'm awesome." His grin was easy and confident.

"But—"

"There was nothing you could do. I returned my boxes of condoms in bulk. Costco's employees have officially dubbed me a failure."

Her chuckle was lighthearted. "I told you to keep at least one," she chided with a finger to his chest.

Drew planted a kiss on her lips, lingering for only a brief moment. "We did make a deal. What kind of guy would I be if I didn't keep my word?" He settled her back down in his arms, massaging her back with firm hands.

Her smile was shaky against his chest when she whispered, "What, indeed?"

Mel's heart shifted just a little left of her chest, as she lay with Drew in a tree house while the moonlight streamed through the Plexiglas window, and she savored the warmth of his secure embrace.

The more she learned about Drew, the more she discovered how wrong she'd initially been about him. He wasn't just easy on the eyes.

He loved his son and his family with fierce integrity. He worked hard, and he was decent enough to be kind to a woman who loved booze more than her own son and had torn his life apart.

That was good to the core. It was honorable.

It was heart stopping.

Mel gulped.

No.

She couldn't be.

She refused to be.

Yet, here she was. Fighting not to fall in love.

~ℓ~

"Look who's glowing."

"Look who waited up way past his bedtime to be sure his daughter met curfew."

Joe snickered, pulling his glasses from his face to tuck them into the pocket of his bathrobe. "I figured you'd wanna know Jackie called, and you got a very serious-looking envelope in the mail. It's on the table in the kitchen. And now, your old man's going to bed." Joe rose from his chair, grunting when his knees creaked. "And in case you were wondering, I like Drew. He has a fine sense of the funny."

Yeah. Apparently, she liked Drew, too. Her lady parts *really* liked him. "He's very witty."

"And he sure likes you."

Mel fought the urge not to gush when she asked, "Really? Says who?"

"Says the way his eyes gobble you up like you're chocolate cake. That's who says. The ballerina never did that."

The ballerina never made her feel quite the way Drew did either. "Well, don't you go making reservations for doves and VFW halls just yet. He's only the first man I've dated since my divorce. I feel like maybe I've locked myself into one particular brand of candy instead of foraging the candy aisle."

"Good candy's hard to come by. Count yourself lucky you haven't had to eat a lot of cheap brands to get to the good stuff. Sometimes you just hit it right. Night, Milky Way," he said before kissing her on the top of her head and ambling off to bed with Jake in tow.

Mel plunked down in the chair at the kitchen table and smiled at Weezer who buried his broad head in her hands. "Buddy—we got trouble."

He groaned his acknowledgment, his droopy eyes sweet with understanding.

She slid to the floor and Weezer sat beside her, putting his heavy paws in her lap. "I think my original assessment about Drew was wrong. He's not just another good-looking guy. He's deep, Weez. He's kind to the elderly. He's a good father, even if his views on dancing are archaic. He has a terrific family, and he's got an ex-wife who could drive even the meekest to homicide. Yet, he won't hurt her if it means hurting his son. What do you suppose I should do about how I feel, Weez?"

Weezer snored, sound asleep on the floor beside her. She stroked his enormous head before rising to catch a glimpse at the envelope her father had mentioned on the table and throw it in her monster-sized purse to look at later.

There were more important things at hand right now.

Like how she was going to keep her feelings for Drew on the slow track. If this was going somewhere, she didn't want to rush it.

Looking back, she realized she never really knew Stan the way most married couples knew each other. She'd known his persona, and she'd fallen in her version of love with it.

She'd fallen in love with someone who'd only existed in her girlish fantasies. There were no knights in shining armor because by the time you hit forty, your armor was riddled with the dents from the slinging arrows of life. But she was realizing, tarnished armor, while it had pockmarks, also had characteristics that could only be acquired from life's battles, and your scars either made you or broke you.

If this thing with her and Drew went any further, she was going to view it with the kind of realism he seemed to want Nate to see his mother with, minus the lollipops and unicorns.

Because unicorns could really yutz you up the ass when you choked on your lollipop.

CHAPTER FOURTEEN

Dear Divorce Journal,

Sorry I've been on hiatus. I know, a month's too long to hold back a good whine, but lately, I haven't been whining as much as I've been doing more productive things. For instance, dating—chastely, of course.

You'll be happy to know, Drew's been a perfect gentleman and hardly ever cops a feel. Which, BTW, is going to be the death of me. I know I'm to blame. I did say I wanted to go slowly and get to know each other.

So, his favorite color is orange, but I've never seen him wear it. He hates broccoli because he says they look like miniature trees. He loves anything that involves sweat, a ball, and chicken wings with beer. Oh, and Elvis. Loves Elvis—which is fine. I'm all about some blue suede shoes.

He hates reality TV, but loves *Medical Mysteries* and *Ice Road Truckers*, which, when we watch, in turn makes me want to do two things: Google every little ache and pain I've ever had, or scream, "What are you, a moron?! Ice isn't meant for trucks that weigh hundreds of tons!" Chicken chow mein and steak are two of his favorite dishes. But he'd give those up forever for a big bowl of garlic mashed potatoes.

His favorite breed of canine is a bulldog because they're manly but cuddly and he's not opposed to cats. Now I ask you, what else do I need to know so this man will discard my stupid request to go slowly and take me like I'm his love slave?

Neil gave Mel's ass a sharp snap with his towel as they finished up their workout at the rec center. "Wow. Hardly any jiggle, lady. What a difference a month makes, huh?"

Mel curtsied and winked, wiping the sweat from her brow with the towel around her neck. "That's because you stole my jiggle. My can of chocolate frosting would like it back, please."

"Not on your life. So tell me what's new? How's *Drewwww*," he cooed his name.

Mel turned her back to him, smiling secretly to herself. "Drew is fine."

"Just fine?"

"He's very fine."

"Do I hear that giggly thing women do with the tone of their voices when they have the stupids for a guy?"

Hands on her hips, Mel gave him a condescending look. "You hear nothing of the sort. You hear a woman who's treading carefully into this relationship with both eyes open and two ears peeled if she hears a single note of discord."

Neil pulled her to him with a sharp yank, arching her backward so she was forced to look up at him. "Bullshit. I think you've got a crush, my lovely."

Planting her hands on his chest, she smiled. "I've got a like. There's a difference."

"Well, it's not a very big one in your case. It's written all over your face every time anyone says his name."

Grabbing her water bottle and her apple, she took a bite out of it. "I'm that obvious?"

"Oh, obvious is an understatement, and you know what? Good for you. You deserve someone in your life who makes you this happy."

"We don't have a lot in common. Except making out. We're aces at that." In the car, after school, in his apartment during a movie when Nate was at a friends. At the Beef Barn's drive-thru, and once even in the janitor's closet. Oh, the making out they did.

"Ah, but are you learning to enjoy new things you never thought you'd discover because you're so different?"

Her smile was ironic. "I have to admit, putting on a Giants jersey and screaming, 'Knock that mother effer's legs off' while we eat chicken wings, sliders, and weenies in a blanket, then wash it all down with a beer can be therapeutic."

Neil's smile was wide when he brushed her hair out of her face. "So two worlds collide, huh?"

"Well, he's not doing a samba, that's for sure."

"But there are other concessions on Drew's behalf?" Neil nudged.

"He sat through an entire showing of *The Nutcracker Suite* on PBS and didn't squawk once. Okay, he dozed once or twice, but he was mostly present. Plus, he drove me to the mall to buy a dress for the staff cocktail party next week and even helped me choose the color."

"So explain to old Neil how this isn't a relationship? The mall is commitment, dancer."

She made a face at him. "It is not. It's the food court where they have waffle cones. I had to buy him one when he got antsy once we hit the shoe department at Macy's."

"It's okay to fall, Mel."

Her hands wrung together, fear steeped like a teabag in her gut. "We haven't known each other long enough."

"So does someone send you a memo when the allowable time frame to fall in love has passed?"

"No . . ."

Neil pursed his lips in disapproval. "There are no rules to this, Mel. Sometimes a connection happens, and sure, you can wait until the rules of society say it's okay to make your feelings official. You can wait until Mercury is in retrograde. You can wait, wait, wait. Or you can give it a go just because it feels good and right."

If only Neil knew the half of good and right she was feeling. "I'm afraid."

"I see that. I also see the reason you're afraid. You're afraid that you're doing the same thing all over again with Drew that you did with Stan. Too much, too quickly. But I think there's a huge difference now. You're a different person compared to the girl who married Stan. You're newly independent. You make your own financial choices, and soon, you're going to have your own place. Maybe making all those rational, responsible choices means you can rely on yourself to make smarter choices in other areas of your life, too."

"We've only been dating a little under a month. I'm definitely not thinking about anything else but day by day." And that wasn't easy. What she really wanted was to get to the day when they nailed each other again. Soon.

"Well, that's good to hear," a familiar voice said.

Mel spun around, her face splitting into a grin. "Jackie!" She flew at her friend, squeezing her tight. "What the hell are you doing in Jersey? Didn't you say you weren't a 'Situation' kind of girl?"

Jackie hugged her hard. "I did, and I maintain Snooki and I will never be friends. I just can't get my hair to bump the way hers does. However, seeing as you never answer a phone, and I was feeling like I'd just die if I didn't have some diner food, here I am. Surprise!"

Mel squeezed her again. "I'm so glad to see you!"

Neil poked his head between them, sticking out his hand. "Neil Jensen. The other BFF."

Jackie laughed and took his hand. "Oh, I know all about you, buddy. I've heard the stories. So it looks like someone's been working out." Jackie gave a wink of praise while her eyes scanned Mel's length.

"Courtesy of the other BFF," Mel offered. "He's killing me."

Neil chuckled. "Yeah, but look at those abs, huh, Jackie? If you run your fingers down them, you could make music on 'em."

Jackie grinned at her. "You look amazing, kiddo. And did I hear talk of a boyfriend? What a difference eight months makes, eh?"

"He's not my boyfriend. He's someone I'm seeing."

"A lot," Neil interjected with a wiggle of his eyebrows.

Jackie hooked her arm through Mel's, the scent of her expensive perfume wafting to her nose and bringing with it comfort and familiarity. "So do you have time to talk now? Or do you have work? Have I mentioned how proud I am of you for nailing a job? So proud."

Mel gave a quick glance at the clock and nodded. "Yes. Work calls, and I have to shower first, but why don't we do dinner tonight and we can talk then."

"Totally on me, of course, and bring the boyfriend. He needs a good Jackie once-over."

Mel chuckled, taking her by the arm and leading her out of the rec center toward Neil's car. "I'll see if he's free. And where are you staying? Last I checked, there's no Four Seasons in Riverbend."

Jackie gave a mock sigh, her lean face sharper in the sunlight. "Tell me about it. I'm at the Marriott where I'm making sacrifices—big ones, in the name of BFF-dom. They don't have twenty-four-hour room service. Heathens," she joked.

"Make it snappy, kiddo. No time for girl talk now. Disgruntled geniuses await. Nice to meet you, Jackie," Neil said, before getting into the car.

Jackie waved then pulled Mel close to her and whispered, "Have I got something to tell you."

Mel's stomach lurched. "Please tell me it's not about Stan. I told you in our last conversation, I don't want to know anything about him unless you have a firm location on him and some bleach and Hefty bags."

Jackie tightened her turquoise scarf around her neck. "Fuck Stan. No one knows where he is. It's like he's fallen off the face of the planet, the coward. That's not what I mean. I mean, I've got something we need to discuss. So bring your man-friend with you tonight because I'm dying to meet him, and I'll leave you a voice mail with the name of the restaurant. God knows they have to have something that's overpriced and isn't called the Cluck-Cluck Palace in this town. If there is one, rest-assured, I'll find it. I have a reputation to uphold."

Mel hugged her friend hard again and planted a kiss on her cheek. "I so missed you."

"Yeah, yeah. Off with you now—to your job. *Your job.* Have I said how proud I am?"

"You did, and know what? I'm proud of me, too." Mel grabbed the handle of the car door and popped it open. "See you tonight."

Hopping into the car, Mel waved at her friend, grinning.

Jackie was here.

Mel could only hope Drew was ready for the Jackie once-over. Jackie was anything but subtle.

So tonight would be a real testament to Drew's sense of humor.

And his cojones.

⁓℮⁓

Drew straightened his tie, uncomfortable as they stood outside Arthur's, indeed, the most expensive restaurant in town. He frowned, pushing at the sleeves of his suit jacket.

He wasn't a fan of overpriced restaurants that served steaks he could just as easily get at Chester's for less than half the price. If memory served him, you paid for the experience.

His idea of experiences didn't include waiters who scraped the crumbs from your table with a special scraper. This smacked of times better left behind him, and he was fighting the instinct to just let Mel and her friend have dinner while he watched the game and ate some chicken wings. With everything in him, he battled the issues of his marital baggage and forced a smile to his face.

"Everything okay?" Mel tilted her head up at him.

"I hate monkey suits."

"But you look so handsome, monkey," she whispered when he leaned down to give her a quick kiss. She brushed at the lapel of his dark suit, letting her hands come to rest on his pecs.

"Not as handsome as you. That's quite a dress." He gave her an approving eye, tilting her hips to meet his in their embrace.

"You like?" she teased. She was sexy and flirty in the dress she'd claimed she'd bought at a thrift store. It was slinky and black, hugging her newly toned curves and falling to just past her knee. She'd accentuated the dress with silver heels that made her legs look longer than they really were. Her hair fell down her back in tight ringlets she told him Jasmine had taught her to tame with some new hair gel, and she'd used red lipstick instead of her clear gloss just for tonight.

"I definitely like. I say we talk about how much I like at my apartment after dinner—what say you?"

Mel shivered against him. "I say let's get dinner over with. Don't linger. Ixnay on the appetizers."

Drew pulled the etched-glass door open with a chuckle. "Not a stuffed mushroom shall pass these lips. After you."

The maître d' greeted them with a dramatic bow. "How can I help you?"

Mel smiled into the dimly lit interior of the pricey steakhouse when Drew placed a hand on her hip. "We're meeting Jackie Bellows."

The maître d' turned sharply on his heel. "Right this way."

"This is pretty fancy for some steak," Drew muttered behind her.

Mel waved a dismissive hand. "That's Jackie for you. She always says Frank has money for a reason. The reason being her. She once told him, if she can find a way, she'll spend his money in the afterlife. Jackie makes no bones about the fact that she's rich—it was one of the first things I liked about her. She has no pretense."

Right. Jackie was her rich friend from L.A. He tried to remember all the information Mel had given him in a rush on the phone when she'd asked if they could swap their date at the diner for Jackie's surprise visit dinner. "So who's she married to again?"

"Frank Bellows. Big Hollywood producer. More money than Onassis. But none of that matters. Jackie's one of my best friends and she wants to meet you." Mel paused halfway to the table and whispered, "Gird your loins."

Jackie jumped up when she saw them, giving Mel a hug. Her blond hair was platinum; her skin lightly tanned with a healthy California glow. She wore an abundance of rings on the fingers that squeezed Mel's, mostly diamonds. Her red silk blouse and black, slim-fitting skirt screamed money. She elbowed Mel. "So introduce me to the hunk."

Mel grinned, slipping her arm through Drew's. "Hunk, meet Jackie. Jackie, hunk."

Jackie winked, pulling Drew into a hug, too, patting him on the back. "Wow. When Mel finds a boyfriend, she finds a *boyfriend*. Nice to meet you, Drew. I've heard so many good things about you. Now sit." She pointed to the red vinyl booth behind a round table with a pristine white tablecloth. "Prove them to me."

"Drew Hunk McPhee. Good to meet you, and I love a good steak with some pressure on the side," he joked, allowing Mel to sit and sliding into the booth beside her.

The waiter arrived with their menus, and while Jackie ordered a bottle of wine he knew was expensive, he ordered a beer.

"A beer drinker," Jackie commented with a grin. "Nothing says man like beer. It says solid and simple."

"Simple." The word grated on him. In Sherry's circles he'd been called simple a time or two. He buried his face in the menu, wincing at the prices while gritting his teeth. Jackie appeared perfectly nice. There was no reason to cast his aspersions of the rich and privileged on her before she'd proven otherwise.

"So what do you do for a living, Drew? Mel said something about you two working together."

He had no shame about what he did. It was honest, hard work. "I'm the on-site handyman, for lack of a better word, at Westmeyer where Mel teaches."

Jackie pinned him with hawklike eyes. Her spiky hair bobbed when she nodded her head. "Like I said. Solid. I bet you rock a tool belt. And a little birdie told me, you don't like to dance? How can this be when that's what my Mel's all about?"

"I like to watch Mel, if that's any consolation."

Jackie patted him on the arm from across the table. "Good answer. So you have a son?"

Drew smiled, relaxing a little. Nate was easy to talk about. "Nate. He's twelve."

Jackie rolled her eyes and cackled. "Christ. You don't know how you lucked out. I have three damned girls and every one of them pushing those teen years. Only one reasonable boy in the lot and he's in college now, so far gone, I've forgotten how little pain he inflicted. Do you have any idea what you've escaped by having a boy?"

Drew laughed, pulling Mel's hand into his to run circles along her wrist with his thumb. "I've heard the horror stories from my sisters."

"Oh, they have lobster!" Mel blurted, then covered her mouth, giving them both a look of shame. "Sorry, but do you have any idea how long it's been since I had lobster? Thank God for rich BFFs," she crowed. Clearly, Jackie's money wasn't a forbidden subject.

"Oh, hush. In no time at all, you'll be eating lobster every day if you want to."

Drew's head popped up from the menu he'd been only absently staring at.

Mel's did, too. "Right. Teachers can't afford lobster, Jackie. They can't even afford to read the word."

Neither could handymen. He wasn't poor, but he didn't have the kind of money Stan had.

Jackie's face beamed, her high cheekbones sharper when she smiled at Mel. "That's why I'm here, kiddo. We have some talking to do. But you have to promise to keep it hush-hush. Both of you."

"I promise to only sell the information if it means college money for Nate. Ivy League's going to kill me. I think, in all fairness, leaking information is a sin that should automatically get a pass under those circumstances." he joked.

Jackie nudged Mel. "I like the hunk. He has a great sense of ha-ha. Anyway, guess who has a new gig?"

Mel feigned surprise. "Shut up. You got a job? Is this a Frank life lesson? Like the time he made Jaynie work to pay off the water bill by weeding all nine million of your gardens because she was taking forty-minute showers?"

"Hah! Good times, right?" Jackie reflected then shook her head. "No life lessons for me. I have a job. Those damn hellions he impregnated me with. It's work."

Drew wondered how much work it could be with nannies and maids.

"I don't know how you do it without help," Mel said.

Jerk. You're a total shit, McPhee.

"Millions of women do it without help, and I do have a live-in. No way I could attend all those charity events and parties if Melda didn't help clean the toilets for me, but I'm grateful for her, and she knows it. She has a weekend house in the valley bought and paid for because I love her so much. But what I'm really grateful for is that Frank's rich enough to allow me biweekly visits to a therapist. Jesus knows I need one with three girls left to raise."

"So who got a new gig?" Mel asked, her eyes bright with interest.

Jackie leaned into her like she had a secret. "Frank."

"Ohhhh, another blockbuster movie?"

"Nope, TV, believe it or not."

Mel gasped, nibbling on a piece of bread. "Frank's stooping to TV? I thought that was all beneath the big honchos who made box-office smash hit movies?"

"Not when it's the kind of cash cow *Celebrity Ballroom* is."

Mel squealed her delight. "*The Celebrity Ballroom*? You're kidding me?"

"Would I kid you? That's part of the reason I'm here."

Mel groaned. "If you tell me this was a trip designed as a heads-up because Stan's remotely involved in this, the minute I have two extra pennies to rub together, I'm coming to L.A. and kicking Frank's sorry ass. Friendship is null and void."

"Oh, no, my pretty ballroom dancer. This trip has to do with you."

Drew watched Mel's face grow confused. She sipped her wine. "Me?"

Jackie's smile was sly. "Yeah—they need a new judge. Linda's contract's up, and she's never been very popular with the audience, so when her contract negotiations came up, they canned her."

Mel frowned. "But how does that involve me? I'm no Linda Little."

"Was Linda Little Linda Little before *Celebrity Ballroom*? No one knew who she was except those of you on the dance circuit. She was just an ex-champ. But now they need another expert in Latin—someone just like you, toots."

Mel's eyes shone with excitement. "I don't get why anyone would even mention me."

"Don't be ridiculous. You don't think Frank's got your back? He threw your name in the ring, honey."

"Seriously?"

"Oh, I'm very serious. You could be the next judge on *Celebrity Ballroom*."

Well, then. Here-here to lobster every night.

CHAPTER FIFTEEN

Dear Divorce Journal,

I really thought I was over the bitter where Stan's concerned. So I'll simply ponder this. Does it make me a spiteful bitch if I'm offered and take the job on *Celebrity Ballroom* just so I can gain access to the studio where Stan tapes *Dude, You Can Dance* and use it as a means for hunting his ass down and killing him while Yelena's screams of terror ring in my ears? I know that sounds awful at this stage of the game—because I'm doing all of that finding myself, and I really like what I've found, but there's still a small piece of me that wants to see his testicles ground to sand.

I think I still have some work to do.

"So Frank mentioned *me*? Oh, Jackie—I've always loved Frank, but after that kind of a recommendation for an unknown, I owe him at least one healthy male child."

Jackie's rings sparkled in the low light of the wall sconce when she shook her finger at Mel. "You can only sleep with my husband if it means you take the rest of the kids with you as part of the package. No way are you bagging me with your love child while you flit from party to party in Versace."

Mel's chuckle filled Drew's ears, happier and lighter than he'd heard it since they met.

"Tell the hunk we're just joking," Jackie directed. "He looks positively green."

Mel turned to Drew, her beautiful face full of mischief. "We're just joking. No healthy male child. But I'd definitely sleep with him. Frank's hot."

Now both women laughed, leaving Drew to wrestle with the illogical, totally irrational anger filling his gut at Mel sleeping with this Frank. A man who was clearly happily married to this woman Drew couldn't help but like, rich or not.

"So tell me what you know," Mel prodded.

"I just know Frank was clear he wanted you. Not to mention, this would be incredible publicity for *Celebrity Ballroom*, seeing Stanislov Cherkasov's ex-wife on an opposing network. Never forget, my husband's a shark, honey. This isn't totally altruistic, and you can always count on me to be honest with you about his motives. He was honest with me when he sent me here to ask you. The ratings would go through the roof and you'd never have to say word one about Stan. It's like a subtle smack down. Something that schmuck deserves."

Drew waited to see if Mel harbored the wish to make Stan pay, but if she was still holding a grudge, she was doing a fine job of hiding it.

"Well, that's just Hollywood," Mel replied easily. "It makes sense that Frank would make a decision based on ratings. Ratings I get. For the last year of our marriage, that was all Stan talked about. I don't begrudge Frank that."

"It's one of the reasons he is where he is. I love where he is. It means I could eat like this every night if it weren't for my spawn wanting all that nurturing I read about in books. Now, food's here. No more business, let's eat. I'm starving." Jackie dug into her steak with passion, laughing and chatting with Mel while Drew listened attentively and participated when requested.

When the evening drew to a close, he was the first to jump up and usher the ladies out into the parking lot, opening Jackie's car door for her. "You"—she pointed at Drew—"I like. You know when to talk and when to just let us run our big mouths uninterrupted. That's a skill, Mr. McPhee, a skill finely honed. You must have been married for at least five years, right?"

Drew bit the inside of his cheek and forced another smile. "I was."

"It shows," Jackie said with a smile. "So you be good to my Mel—got it? I'm a tough old bitch. I'll kick your ass if you even think about breaking my girl's heart here."

He tucked Mel to his side. "I'll remember that with the appropriate fear in my heart," Drew joked.

Jackie's mouth opened in raucous laughter. "Oh, my God, I *like* you. Okay, kids, I'm out. I fly back early in the morning because my horrible children need love and someone has some kind of recital—or something that involved me making a costume with duct-tape and a glue gun. Mel? I love you. I'll call you the second Frank has more details. Now gimme a hug and don't get all whiny with the goodbyes. I hate crying."

Mel gave Jackie a hard squeeze. "I miss you so much, and now that you see Jersey isn't so bad, you'll come back, right?"

"Hah! Not before I get you back to L.A. Love to your dad. Bye, guys." She got into her car after one last hug and drove away.

Mel wiped a tear from her eyes as she stared down at her feet. "Just give me a sec to get the sissy out of my system."

Drew pulled her into his embrace, inhaling the scent of her raspberry shampoo. "Don't make a mess of this suit with all that mascara. It's the only one I've got," he teased.

She sniffled. "I didn't realize how much I missed her until just this second."

"She's quite a character."

"She's one of the best friends I've ever had." Pulling away, she looked up at him. "She liked you. That says something."

"Really? What does that say?"

"That she won't hire someone to pick you off with all her lovely money."

Drew chuckled. "Sooooo . . ." he whispered against her ear.

Mel put her arms around his neck, tilting her head up. "Yesssss?"

"We're still on for my apartment?"

"Where's Nate?"

He loved that she was always concerned about his son. "At my mother's. It's Friday night, which means movies and ice cream. So we're good?"

She gave him a coy glance. "Only if dessert's involved."

"Oh, I got your dessert," he murmured against her lips.

She pressed a tender kiss against his lips. "Then what's the hold up, slowpoke?"

He pulled her to his truck, helping her in. When the light from the dome in the ceiling illuminated her as she tucked her legs inside, Drew had to grip the door.

Her hair fell down her back in silky ringlets of dark chocolate, framing her heart-shaped face with a seductive curtain he wanted to bury his hands in. But it was her eyes that made his breath still for the briefest of seconds.

They were as dark as her hair, smoldering black with just a glint of amber in them, and he realized, he recognized that look.

It was the one he thought was reserved only for when she danced. He'd seen it on more than one occasion while he watched her practice with the boys at school like some lovesick fool.

As his breath left his lungs—he knew.

Now he had to make sure she knew, too.

~ℓ~

Mel's heart thumped in her chest with an uneven rhythm while Drew lit candles and put a disc in the CD player. Suddenly, she was nervous. Their last romp had been unexpected. She hadn't had time to worry about what she looked like naked. Even after almost six weeks of Neil's grueling workout regimen, she still had lumps.

Lumps she'd probably rather weren't highlighted by his Glade scented candles.

Mel clenched her cold hands together in nervous anticipation when Drew loosened his tie and took off his jacket to hang it in the small closet by his front door.

It gave her a moment to reassess his apartment, which was sparse in terms of furniture and any kind of decoration. Well, except for the picture of the waterfall.

Drew reached behind it and turned something on. "See? It's just like real water, so sayeth Myriam. She told me I didn't have enough atmosphere in the apartment for Nate—so she bought this for us when she was in Atlantic City."

Mel watched the waterfall seemingly flow with real water, her mouth open in fascination. "It's as riveting as a velvet Elvis painting. I can't tear my eyes away."

Drew approached her from behind. "Let me help you with that," he whispered against her ear, wreaking havoc with her belly. Drew ran his hands over her hips, drawing her back to lean completely against him.

His muscled frame against hers, pressing into her flesh through her thin dress was intoxicating. They swayed for a bit, moving to the soft music on the CD player. Mel's eyes closed when a familiar tune came on, and she whispered, "Is that Tony Bennett?"

Drew's lips slid over the sensitive skin of her neck. "It is."

"I'd have never figured you for that type of guy."

"Then you still have much to learn, grasshopper. I was raised on Bennett and Sinatra, to name a few." He turned her in his arms, molding her to him, smoothing his hands over her waist.

"I have a confession."

"Well, I know you're not a man. What's left?"

"Funny. I'm being serious here."

"Confess," he prompted, gliding his tongue over her lips.

"I'm petrified."

He pulled his lips from hers, giving her a concerned glance. "Of?"

"Being naked."

"That must make it hard to shower."

"Again, being serious."

He chuckled low and gritty. "Sorry. Being very serious, I can assure you, you have nothing to be petrified about."

"Oh, please. You didn't see me totally naked. It was dark the last time. Now we have all these stupid candles."

"Oh, but I did. Now I have a confession. I peeked while you were sleeping. Pretty impressive backend ya got there, lady."

Mel buried her face in his shoulder, her cheeks hot. "It is not. It's flabby."

"How about you let me be the judge of that? It couldn't be that bad because I'm back for seconds. And let's not forget, I've been waiting for that flabby ass of yours to be naked for more than a month's worth of make-out sessions. Clearly, I like you, flabby and otherwise. So how about you let me prove that to you?"

Mel let him lead her to his bedroom, stepping over the shoes he kicked off. He opened his arms, and she went willingly, burrowing against the crisp material of his shirt with a sigh. His chest pressed against her cheek, allowing her to hear his heartbeat, rapid and sure.

Tilting her head up, Drew caressed her lips with his, tentatively touching them before pulling away. His hands roamed in soothing circles across her back and down along the slope of her hips, pulling her closer and closer.

She sighed when his tongue slipped into her mouth, rasping against hers, tasting like the mint he'd used after dinner. His groan of encouragement when she wrapped her arms around his neck made her back arch, pushing her breasts into the muscles of his chest.

His hands found the zipper on the back of her dress, sliding it down her spine while his lips devoured hers. The contact of his hands on her hot flesh made her gasp in hungry need to feel all of him.

When he slid her dress off, leaving her in a white lace bra and low-waist panties, Drew smiled his approval. "Were you planning to have your way with me, Ms. Cherkasov?"

Mel rolled her eyes at him, planting a finger on his chest. "I was thinking no such thing. Underwear is underwear. Why is something sexy a presumption that sex will occur? Maybe I just like nice underwear."

"I gotta tell ya, I like your version of 'no presumption of sex' underwear," he muttered, thick and low while she unbuttoned his shirt, pushing it aside to feel the heat of his skin.

Her fingers fumbled when she reached for his zipper, dragging it down, the sound sharp in her ears. As her hands made the connection to his hard abs and lean hips, she sucked in a breath.

Every inch of Drew was as good, if not better, than the last time she'd touched him. His firm flesh beneath his boxer-briefs made her fingers shake when she dragged them over his thick thighs.

Drew unsnapped her bra with ease, letting it fall off her shoulders, then hooked his thumbs into the scrap of panties she'd totally lied about choosing because they were just underwear, and slipped them off her.

And then they were naked, and it was all she could do not to cover herself from his scrutiny. It was as exciting as it was embarrassing, but Drew changed that with just one word. A word that was low and husky, matching the clear desire in his eyes.

"Perfect," he said before dragging her with him to the edge of the bed. He pulled her body flush to his face, taking a deep breath, inhaling her flesh and wrapping his arms around her waist.

Mel's hands went to his hair, raking her fingers though it, arching into the stubble that had formed on his cheeks and was now tickling her skin. Drew's lips were hot, consuming her flesh as he groaned, kissing his way along her hipbone.

Mel's gasp was sharp when he slid his palms up between her inner thighs, grazing the tender flesh. She gripped his shoulders to keep her knees from collapsing beneath her when his breath whispered over her swollen, aching flesh.

He slithered his tongue inside her, spreading her lips to caress her clit with long strokes.

Mel rocked against him, shuddering against his hard embrace, lifting herself on her toes to savor the lap of his tongue, hot and wet. Drew's hands cupped her ass, kneading it, drawing her against his mouth with force. When the first sharp sting of orgasm wound tight in her belly, Mel's breathing came in harsh gasps. She whimpered the words, "Please, don't stop," in a cry of anguish.

Drew complied, whispering his tongue along the lips of her sex, dragging it back and forth until he evoked a deep growl that began in her chest and came out a howl of pleasure. Her hips gyrated, her hands when to his wrists, clinging to them as his fingers tugged at her hard nipples.

She ground against him, pushing her body until completion came hard and fast in a crash of light and sound.

The aftermath of her climax left her falling boneless against the shelter of his strong body, allowing him to encompass her in his embrace.

Drew sprawled her across his lap, his cock pressing insistently against her thigh. Clinging to his neck, she sighed as he rocked her, giving her the time to recuperate. His lips lay against the top of her head, and Mel closed her eyes, relishing the intimate contact.

But her hands itched for other things. They itched to discover Drew and find what pleased him. She slid off his lap in a sinuous movement, slithering down between his legs to spread his thighs wide.

His stare gleamed from above her, his eyes dark with need—one she intended to fulfill. Mel let her hands explore the crisp hair on his thighs, dragging her fingers through it, luxuriating in the ripple of his muscles beneath her palm.

She leaned forward, pressing her hot cheek to his abdomen, kissing his heated skin then resting her head there while she examined what lay between his thighs.

He was long and thick, the skin stretching across his cock smooth and lightly veined. Her fingers were compelled to skim the satiny flesh, and he jolted when she enveloped him in her grasp.

Mel made a long, drawn-out pass up and then down his shaft before placing her lips on it, tasting him. Drew leaned back on his elbows with a groan, cupping her chin, tracing the outline of her lips when she finally took his length into her mouth.

His gasp was raw, his hips jutting upward, reaching, driving between her lips. His fingers found the back of her head, threading them into her hair, directing her as she pleasured him.

Then Drew's hands were on her shoulders, pushing her away. "Damn, Mel," he gritted, dragging her back to meet his gaze. "That's so hot. Your lips are like silk. I can't take any more."

Mel didn't have the time to respond before he placed both of his hands on either side of her face and pulled her into a kiss that left no air in her lungs. In their tangle of limbs, he somehow managed to locate condoms in the nightstand drawer, and Drew slipped one on just before he slid back to the edge of the bed, picked her up, and impaled her on his cock.

The movement was so swift, so intoxicating, Mel bit back a scream before placing her mouth on his again to drive her tongue into it, clenching his hair in fistfuls of the silky strands.

Drew reciprocated by placing his hands on her waist, forcing her hips downward. The heat of his cock, the sinful stretch of her wet passage, the scent of desire made her heart crash and her head swirl.

But then Drew slowed his thrusts, easing the tension, whispering into her mouth, "Christ, woman. I can't get enough of you. If we don't slow down, I'll come right now."

Mel's breath wheezed in and out of her lungs, raspy and heavy. Drew's erotic words made this crazy, white-hot need only deepen. "I'm trying," she said between clenched teeth.

Drew stilled her, holding her hips in place with hands of steel until she settled. His cock, so hard and pulsing, was a temptation she had to bite her lip not to indulge in. Instead, Mel took deep breaths, willing her body to calm.

He ran his hands along her back, massaging the muscles with a gentle caress, tracing the underside of her breasts, tweaking her rigid nipples until they stung with desperate need. He followed the outline of her body, lightly trailing her skin until she shivered from his now gentle touch.

She did the same, clenching his arms, learning each curve of his biceps, every sprinkling of hair on his forearms.

Drew slipped a finger between their bodies, spreading her aching lips and stroking her clit with his forefinger, making Mel lean back, bracing her hands on his thighs as he stoked the embers of the flame building in her belly.

His lips found her breasts, licking at her nipples, drawing them into his mouth.

Mel's moan was harsh and her hips began to rock once more, undulating their need. Drew's thrusts became more forceful when he splayed his hand between her breasts, driving his cock upward.

Perspiration dotted her forehead as she strained to take all of him, savoring every nerve-shattering inch of his shaft. That swell of sharp heat hit her again, beginning deep in the pit of her belly and careening toward out of control.

Drew hissed her name just before his head fell back on his shoulders and he grunted. Mel followed, whimpering at the sting of electric currents setting her veins on fire.

The coil of orgasm sprung loose, and Mel couldn't hold back her scream of completion. She drove downward on Drew's lap, crashing against him until she found what she sought. It ripped through her body with flashes of light and the sweet bliss of surrender.

When it passed, Mel sank against Drew's thighs, only to have his strong arms scoop her up and fold her into them. As she settled against him, her breathing eased in time with Drew's.

He cradled her to his chest once more before nudging her. "Hey, I'm old. I think my legs are cramping."

Mel chuckled, slinging her leg over and off him. "Are you calling me fat?"

"I'd rather wear a dress," he joked, taking a sip of her lips before leaving her to discard the condom.

Mel sank back to the bed, taking a moment to gather her thoughts after the most amazing sex ever. The myriad emotions running rampant in her body, as well as her heart, frightened her and comforted her in a fell swoop of confusion.

Drew tugged at her hand, pulling her up to him. "Wow, right?"

"It had a wow factor," she admitted with a giggle.

"It had all kinds of factors," he said against the top of her head.

Mel slipped her arms under his, loving the heat of his skin on hers. "It did, indeed."

Drew began to sway to the music that drifted in from the living room. Norah Jones's raspy "Come Away With Me" filtered to her ears, tender and gentle.

This moment, timeless, safe in the cocoon they'd created, left her in a state of awed wonder.

It was the exact moment Mel knew she'd fallen in love with Drew, and there was no going back.

CHAPTER SIXTEEN

Dear Divorce Journal,

Well and fuck. I went and did it, and then it went and did me. Yes, dear journal, I fell in love, and for about two whole minutes, okay, maybe it was more like two hours, I had a boyfriend. Then he turned into a total shit. Do I have a total shit magnet stuck on me somewhere I'm unaware of? Maybe it's one of those computer chip implants that seeks out total shits. Either way, Drew McPhee is a total shit. Oh, and piss on love.

A hard body molded to her back, and Mel sighed with deep contentment.

Drew wrapped his arm around her waist, nuzzling her neck. "You're awake."

She felt the smile of his lips against her neck. "I had no choice with your hot, stinky breath on my neck," she teased.

He cupped her breasts, rolling her nipples between his fingers until he made her moan. "Not so, dancer. I've been up for two hours and I brushed my teeth."

"And I see you're all suited up," she giggled, reaching behind her to find he'd already put a condom on.

"Always be prepared. It's my motto."

"Isn't that the Boy Scouts' motto?"

"I don't care whose motto it is. I couldn't stand to look at you naked anymore because I need to be inside you. Now, bend to my will, woman."

Her eyes popped open, panic-stricken. "What time is it? Nate—is he due home?"

Drew splayed his hand over her abdomen, slipping a finger between her thighs. "Relax. He won't be home for another two hours. Grandma makes chocolate chip pancakes on Saturday mornings. Nobody wants to go home."

Mel breathed a sigh that shuddered on its way out as Drew stroked her clit. Her arm went around his neck and she arched into him with a sensuous stretch. "I want to go to Grandma's if we're talking chocolate chip pancakes."

He pressed his hot cock against her ass. "And miss this?"

Mel let her eyes slide shut. Oh, this man and his decadent lips and work-rough hands. She didn't think she'd ever get enough of him. Her response was breathy. "It *is* pancakes. I'm not sure you can measure up," she challenged.

Lifting her thigh to wrap it around his hip, he drove upward into her in a single, fluid motion, dragging a throaty groan from her lips. "Are you questioning my prowess?" he teased, nibbling at her neck while his fingers dipped in and out of her swollen lips.

Mel pushed back at him, grinding her ass into him, wanting nothing more than to be as close as humanly possible without morphing into him. "I would never do such a thing," she said on a giggle that turned into an "oh" of intense pleasure as Drew manipulated her body to his will.

"Good thing, because I don't think pancakes can make you scream quite the way I do," he said on a long groan as their bodies blended.

"You've never seen me eat a pancake," she murmured, her lips pressed against his forearm to keep the scream of pleasure she wanted to yelp to a minimum.

Drew pumped upward, his shaft pulsing hot and hard in her. His lips pressed to her ear. "Christ, Mel. Every time I think I have a handle on being inside you, it's all I can do not to come."

Mel's heart fluttered in her chest at his words. That a man like Drew admitted she had the power to undo him made her feel sexy and wanton. She raised both arms, draping them around the back of his neck and pulling him hard to her.

No more words were necessary when they picked up where they left off after a long night of lovemaking. Mel's head thrashed against the pillow when Drew's thrusts became harder.

Drew's arms tightened around her in response and his harsh breaths quickened until they both reached satisfaction.

Mel flopped against him, sated, sore, and replete.

Drew brushed her hair out of her face and smiled down at her. "You want coffee?"

She smiled back. "Does it taste like chocolate chip pancakes?"

"You know, we could always go to my Mom's . . ."

Mel stretched. "In my slinky dress and heels? Is that considered appropriate attire for breakfast?"

"Point."

"I just don't want Nate to get the wrong impression. I know he's very perceptive, but to see me in something like the outfit I had on last night is like throwing the fact that I spent the night in his face." She was coming to treasure her time with Nate—in class and out. The last thing she wanted to do was upset him.

Drew's smile lit up his face. "I like that you always think about Nate. Coffee it is. Throw on my shirt and meet me in the kitchen. We'll talk about Nate if I can keep my hands off you for more than twenty seconds." He planted a lingering kiss on her lips.

She watched as he got off the bed; his well-muscled body naked, rippling and firm in the sunlight streaming through the windows made her heart clench again. He threw on a pair of sweats and winked at her before leaving the bedroom.

Oh, God. She was in love. She knew it. It was a much different love than the one she'd experienced with Stan. The connection she shared with Drew had more depth to it—it entailed a give-and-take, and she was relieved to find, it was barren of any hero-worship.

Yes, Drew was compelling and sexy and smart, but she didn't crave his approval in the way she had Stan's. She enjoyed it, even reveled in his heated words, but it wasn't the basis for their relationship, and she was finally seeing the difference between being involved with a man who was her equal and one who was her idol.

And it was hot and invigorating and a revelation all at the same time.

Top that with a possible job offer from *Celebrity Ballroom*, something she hadn't had time to dwell on since Jackie had told her about it last night, and things were looking good.

Mel slid out of the bed, throwing on Drew's shirt from last night, taking a deep sniff of the remnants of his cologne. She made her way to the kitchen, smiling to herself when she caught sight of the waterfall painting.

Drew held out a cup of steaming coffee in a chipped dark green mug.

She reached for it, but he pulled it back and grinned his heart-stopping grin. "Not before this," he said, leaning down to give her a thorough kissing.

Mel sighed into his mouth, then snatched the coffee from his hand, almost dripping it on the floor. She set it on the counter and jumped up onto it to settle back against the cabinet.

"So, Nate," he began, pushing his way between her legs to put his hands on her waist.

Mel's smile was fond when she eyed him over the rim of her coffee cup. "He's such a great kid and a superb dancer."

Drew hauled her close to him, and her legs automatically wrapped around his waist. "He is a great kid and, like you said, a perceptive one. I don't want to have to be careful about how I feel about you, Mel."

Her heart skipped a beat. "Meaning?"

Drew's hands cupped her face. "Meaning, I want him to know we're involved."

"Ohhhhh. Is that what we are?" she asked when his lips found hers again.

"Well, if last night wasn't enough to convince you we're involved, maybe you need more convincing?"

"I'm always down with more convincing, but let's be serious. Because it's Nate, and I would never want to jeopardize his feelings. He has enough to deal with . . ."

She almost hated to mention Sherry's name. They hadn't spoken of her since the night she'd argued in Sherry's favor, and while she didn't want to rock the boat, she certainly wouldn't walk on eggshells about her either. Sherry was Nate's mother—alcoholic or not—and the kind of struggle she brought would need to be addressed if her issues were ongoing like Drew had said.

"Sherry," he finished.

Mel looked him straight in the eye. "Yes. Sherry. She's his mother, and if we're going to be involved, she's a part of my life now, too. No matter how much on the outskirts of it she is."

"Fair enough. So, in light of Sherry, and the problems she's created for Nate, I want to be as honest as possible with him about us. I want to tell him we're involved, and that he can expect to be spending time with you outside of school."

"Without a doubt, I agree. So what are we calling this involved thing?"

"Do you want my high school ring to wear around your neck so that as far as the eye can see, everyone will know you're my girl-friend?"

"Can you even find your high school ring?"

"No."

She let her shoulders lift in a mock sigh. "Fine. No jewelry."

"How about a verbal agreement?"

"That states?"

"You're my woman. Which means no dates with men named Ron who have mothers named Florence."

That he even remembered Ron's name made her insides warm and gooey. "Ahhhh, you *were* jealous."

"I was nothing of the sort. I was mortified you had such bad judgment."

"What can I say? We exchanged e-mails and pictures. You can just never tell."

"Well, you don't have to tell anything anymore. Now that I'm your boyfriend and all, and you know what that means, don't you?" Curving his hands under her ass, he rubbed his rigid shaft against the cleft between her thighs.

"Does it mean I have to cook? Because no can do, pal. I only cook on special occasions."

He took her cup of coffee from her, planting it on the counter and nibbled on her neck. "This isn't a special occasion? I just asked you to be my girlfriend."

Instantly, Mel's hands went to his hair, clenching the soft strands with a soft moan. "Not special enough to make me want to cook."

"Well, let's see if I can change your mind," he cajoled, driving his hands under her borrowed shirt to cup her breasts.

Mel decided, given his skills of coercion, he probably could.

~⁓~

"Thanks for the ride home, *boyfriend*," she giggled the words—giddy and girlish.

He leaned over the console of the truck and kissed her. "Anytime, *girlfriend*. So, you wanna do something with Nate tonight?"

She gave him a flirtatious smile. "You want to go dancing, don't you?"

"Like I want to lose a limb. How about a movie and dinner?"

"Deal. Does Nate like French food? Do you? There's this new place in the town over I've been dying to try since Jasmine told me about it. I love French food."

Drew's face shifted a little, his affable expression losing some of its lightheartedness, his body growing stiff. "Your rich friend Jasmine from Maxine's employment agency?"

She was taken aback. "What does her bank account have to do with French food?"

"French food is expensive. At least the French food I've eaten."

Mel frowned momentarily then forced a smile to her face with her solution. "Well, if it's expensive, it'll be my treat."

Now his lips grew hard, forming a thin line. "No go."

Mel titled her head, confused. "What?"

"I said no go. I invited you, I pay." His tone was one that clearly brooked no argument. It also smacked of a demand rather than a request, and that smacked of the need to control.

"Said who?"

His hands gripped the steering wheel in a tight clench. "Me."

"That's ridiculous, Drew."

"It's how it is."

"What era do you live in?"

"The one where the man pays."

And that was just that? Because Drew said it, it would be? The. Hell. Her temper soared. "Well, when you decide to join us here in the year 2012, give me a call!" She pushed the truck door open and stomped into her father's without a backward glance.

Knuckle-dragger.

Mel spent the remainder of her weekend alternately angry and hurt, and angry that she'd allowed herself to be hurt. If Drew McPhee had stopped for one minute to realize her paycheck was probably less than his, he'd have realized she'd never suggest a costly restaurant.

The fact that he wouldn't allow her to pay made her irrationally angry. It was a ridiculous, archaic notion and she refused to put up with it. No one was going to take her independence from her ever again.

Not even someone who had the power to make her cry herself to sleep with wet sobs muffled by her pillow while Weezer moaned his sympathies in her ear.

No one was going to hold money over her head again either. It felt too much like a right to ownership. She was no man's little woman anymore, and her trophy-wife days were long gone. She'd worked hard these last months to get on her feet and earn her own keep.

She kept those angry thoughts in mind to keep her tanked up when she entered her classroom early, hoping the concealer and foundation she'd used to cover up the remains of her stinging heart were doing their job. Resting a hand on the ballet barre, she lifted her leg and leaned into a long stretch.

"I'm a cad."

Mel's head shot up. She pursed her lips, refusing to be drawn into the magnetic force field of Drew's handsomeness. "No argument here." She returned to her position at the barre and forced herself to dip into the stretch. No more backing down. No more letting everyone walk all over her while they did all the thinking for her.

"That French place you were talking about?"

Her spine stiffened. "What about it?"

Drew approached her, laying his face sideways on the barre to meet her eyes. "I didn't know it was just a food truck."

Mel's lips thinned. "Why does that make a difference?"

"I overreacted."

"Oh, you bet your bippy you did. Did it ever occur to you that I can't afford chic restaurants anymore?"

"Obviously not. I only heard French and remembered the places Sherry and I used to go, and the fact that your lifestyle was once attached to a man who's a millionaire."

"Billionaire, and here's a tip. I'm not Sherry, and I'm not married to Stan anymore. You know, you'd think I'd have baggage. Wasn't it me who was left with absolutely nothing but my dog and some dental floss? No job. No capacity or skills to earn my own living because all I've ever done is dance. No place to live. At least you had marketable skills. I just got lucky with this job. Stan may not have been an alcoholic, but he held all the cards, monetarily and otherwise. I've been hurt, too. Yet, I've managed to let go of most of my anger. You? Not so much. And they say women cling to the past."

Drew rose to his full height. "I admit to a certain sensitivity to situations like this, and sometimes my need to keep Nate from any more hurt becomes overbearing and stupidly overprotective."

She lifted her torso to stare at him dead on. "Don't you use Nate as an excuse, Drew."

"It's just the truth. I'm pretty cautious when it comes to him, and it's one of the reasons I haven't been seriously involved with anyone since my divorce. I don't want to make the wrong choices. I won't apologize for looking out for my son."

"And I would never ask you to. Looking out for him is one thing. Keeping him from French food *I* buy is just plain dumbass."

"I was wrong."

She said nothing, fighting a smile.

"Really, really wrong," he coaxed, his tone softening.

Mel's eyes narrowed; letting her leg fall, she rested her hand on her hip. There was something else she couldn't quite put her finger on, but she decided not to ask until she had a clearer vision of what Drew's underlying issue was with her paying for some food.

Didn't all those psychiatrists always say the argument you were having was never what the real argument was about? "You were a total ass. I think you might need some lessons in sucking it up. Maybe you should put a call into Maxine."

"I don't have her number," he teased.

"I can give it to you along with her pamphlets on divorce and letting go of your bitter baggage."

He looked skeptical. "Bitter baggage?"

"Yeah. That's her catchy phrase for hanging on to your past and judging everyone by your ex's measuring stick. I judged you that way, and then I hit recovery full throttle. I hate to admit it, but Maxine's advice, hokey as it sounds, makes perfect sense. And if I can do it, anyone can."

His look was that of genuine surprise. "You did that with me?"

Mel's smile was secretive. "No way am I feeding your ego. Suffice it to say, I worked it out. Or I thought I had until you turned into Stupidhead Man."

"I should have a cape or something and a costume with a big 'S' on it."

She giggled a snort. She couldn't help it. "I'm really pissed off at you."

He shook a finger at her. "Yeah, but you're cracking. I can see it."

"What I want to do is crack your head open."

"That would be messy, and I don't think Ernie the janitor's up for brain splatter."

"It's nothing less than you deserve."

"I won't disagree."

Mel's face grew serious. "Let me make just one thing clear. I was someone's toy for a long time. I didn't know it, and had I realized it, I would have done something about it much sooner—before I was left without even a toothbrush. I had no life but my studio, and even that was something Stan held over my head. He paid the bills, he owned the building, and when he didn't want it or me anymore, he took it away from me. Now I pay my own bills, and soon I'll have my own roof over my head. No matter what happens in any relationship I'm in, I won't be left high and dry again. I'm never letting anyone have that kind of power over me again."

"I didn't realize it was a power struggle when I said I'd pay for dinner."

"It became one when you refused to let me because you thought my penchant for the high life is something I can't give up or I miss so much I'd be willing to spend a quarter of my paycheck to revisit. I'll have you know, via Maxine and all her kooky catchphrases, I've learned to live within my means, means that are modest at best. You also stole some of the joy I seem to be reaping from making my own living, and it made me want to flatten you."

He gave her a "meant to make her laugh" sad face. "I'm sorry I stole your thunder. I suck."

She was warming. "You sure do."

He reached for her fingers, loosely entwining them with his. "Can I make it up to you?"

Mel was hesitant. "Are you hearing me? Really hearing me?" She had to know he got it, or there was no point in going any further, and as hard as it would be to let Drew go before they'd had a chance to really see if they worked, she'd do it if being with him meant sacrificing her lines in the sand. She'd hate every tear-filled, snot-dripping second, but she would.

His nod was sharp. "I'm really hearing you."

Mel relaxed then. For the first time, she was drawing up all those boundaries Maxine had talked about, and it was good. "Okay."

He hauled her near him, wrapping his strong arms around her waist and pressing a quick kiss to her lips. "So now that we've gotten our first official fight out of the way. You wanna try dinner again tonight?"

Mel melted against him, relieved and empowered all at once. "Only if it's really expensive."

Drew gazed down at her, his eyes amused. "Now who's clinging to their baggage?"

She laughed, putting her arms around his neck. "I had the best bags. Louis Vuitton. Gorgeous."

"I'm familiar with Louis."

"He was so good to me, but alas, our love affair's over."

"Good thing. I'm a jealous guy."

She gave him a flirty smile just as the bell rang. "I'd have never pegged you for jealous. Now get out of here before the boys see us and we scar Nate for life."

Drew grabbed another quick kiss before saying "Speaking of Nate, I told him about us."

Mel shot him a hesitant glance. "Was he okay with it?"

"He was awesome with it."

She heaved a sigh. "Phew. I'm glad I passed muster. Now go before they catch us."

Drew winked and smiled, then sauntered out of her classroom just as the boys filed in. They were whispering and laughing to each other, sharing sly looks as they passed Drew and slapping Nate on the back.

Here came the difficult part. Keeping her private life private and not letting it interfere with Nate's school life. "Boys? Something you care to share with me?" She was daring them to tease Nate openly.

Each pair of eyes grew wide at being caught. Shoulders in various widths, covered in staid uniforms bumped up against one another.

Mel crossed her arms over her chest and smiled. "That's what I thought. So, we need to get the show on the road because Thanksgiving's right around the corner and not long after that, Christmas break. We have a dance to attend, guys—with lots of lovely young ladies who'll want strong, confident dance partners. Let's get to work. R.J.? You're up first." She stood in hold position, waiting for R.J. to join her.

Nate stood at the back of the room, tall, handsome, and with a big grin. He flipped her a thumbs-up to acknowledge her subtle defense of him.

She smiled back and turned her attention to R.J., who summarily stepped on her toes the moment Emilio turned the music on.

Neil watched Mel from outside through the window of her classroom and took a a deep breath. If the rumors Theresa his assistant had told him were true, he had to move fast.

But the timing had to be right, and he had to do it before Stan did. The last thing he wanted to do was hurt Mel. She was happy now, probably happier than he'd ever seen her, and her life was back on track.

He'd blow that all sky high and turn her past with Stan upside down.

Shit.

"Hey, Neil, right?"

The voice from behind him was familiar from that night at the diner. He swung around to find Drew staring down at him. "Yeah. Drew, right?"

"Yep. What brings you to Westmeyer? Do you need me to get Mel for you?"

Neil put his hands in the pocket of his jacket. "I wish. I'm actually here for the biology teacher. Mel 'Won't Take No For An Answer' set us up on a lunch date."

Drew laughed. "Gwen Timmons, but you don't sound thrilled."

"Is anyone ever thrilled about having their best friend set them up on a date? But it's Mel. Who could say no to that face?"

Drew's smile made Neil more sure than ever he was as in love as Mel was. "I feel that, my friend. She's hard to turn down."

"And she's a good person." He realized once the words were out of his mouth, they'd come out insistent and a little edgy, but if there was one thing he wasn't going to do again, it was fail Mel.

But Drew didn't seem to notice. He appeared caught up in something in his head that made him smile. "She's definitely that. I gotta run, man. But nice seeing you again—and have a great date."

Oh, it'd be super-duper. Neil forced his Hollywood smile to his face. "Thanks. Check you later."

As he made his way down the hall to locate Gwen, he tried Theresa one last time, but it went to voice mail so he left a message. "Theresa. The second you get this, get me that reporter from *Hollywood Scoop*."

Mel turned around in the seat of the truck to wave at Nate as she got in. "Hey, Nate!"

He looked up from his phone and smiled. "Thanks for having my back today. I just want you both to know I'm cool with you dating, and I don't care what anyone says about it," he said, very adult, very stoic.

Drew frowned. "Someone said something about it?"

Nate shrugged his shoulders with indifference. "Some of the guys saw you two before class started. They said you were holding hands so they razzed me about it. No big deal. Ms. Cherkasov shut them up."

Drew smiled his approval at her, taking her hand as they pulled from her father's driveway. "So burgers in town tonight?"

"Can we hit Joe's Stand, Dad? He has the best chili cheeseburgers, Ms. Cherkasov."

"It might be a little cold for Mel, sitting outside," Drew warned. "She's from L.A. where it's always sunny—even at night."

Mel waved a hand at them. "Cold schmold. I'm a tough old bird, I'll have you know, I was raised in Jersey, just one town over from here, and nothing can keep me from a chili cheeseburger. I say we do it. I brought my scarf." She tugged at the turquoise scarf around her neck to show them.

"You're all right, Ms. Cherkasov," Drew said, smiling in her direction.

"I have to draw the line at kissing," Nate reminded them from the backseat.

"Got it," Mel said with a serious glance backward at him. "No kissing."

"Hey! Whose side are you on?" Drew protested, putting the car in park in front of Joe's Hamburger Stand.

Nate leaned forward, placing his arms on the back of the seats. "Seeing two adults, especially when one is your parent, kissing is gross. Research shows, it's a natural adolescent reaction. One you carry into adulthood when your parents then decide you're old enough to understand the birds and the bees, and they feel free to talk about it in front of you."

Drew pointed to the door with a bark of laughter. "Out, smart guy. Here—money. Go get us some chili cheeseburgers. I have to kiss Mel."

Nate scrambled out the door, laughing.

Drew leaned over the console. "So, Ms. Cherkasov. I need a right and proper kiss. Lay one on me."

Mel leaned over, too. "Make it quick. Kissing's gross." she teased, sighing when his lips finally met hers after their weekend-long sabbatical.

Drew's tongue slid between her lips, caressing hers, until she was breathless and giddy with need. He pulled away, but only enough to mutter, "We'd better stop now or Joe's is going to have its first indecent exposure."

Mel feigned a pout. "But we just got started."

Cupping her jaw, he nipped her lower lip with a husky groan. "And if we don't stop, I'm going to tear your clothes off right here and do you until your eyeballs cross. It's been too long."

"It's been two days," she chastised, nipping the side of his mouth, reveling in the hot heat of their lips so close.

"That's two days too long. Now out before I cop a feel."

Mel giggled. "I'm out. I'm out." She slid out of the truck and went to find Nate who was waiting on their order.

Drew went to find the bathrooms while they waited; the scent of grilling hamburgers and chili making Mel's mouth water. She put a hand on Nate's shoulder. "So you're sure you're okay with your dad and I dating, Nate? I don't want it to be uncomfortable for you at school."

Nate shrugged. "We're nerds, Ms. Cherkasov. We don't spend a lot of time caring about much else but science and stuff most people don't understand. We do the obligatory teenage things, like make fun of each other when a situation like my father dating my teacher arises, but then reason sets in, and we look up facts and statistics about adult relationships in the workplace, find a logical explanation, and move on."

Mel had to fight to keep her face straight. "Well, okay then. If you're okay, I'm okay. So how long have you been at Westmeyer?"

"Since the end of last year just when the old dance teacher left. That's when my teachers in public school told my dad I was too smart for them. He didn't want them to move me up three grades due to peer pressure he felt a twelve-year-old couldn't handle."

"Ah, you mean like dating and stuff when you're twelve and everyone else is sixteen?"

Nate's lean cheeks, red from the cold, formed a smile. "That and drugs and alcohol. He said he wanted me to retain as much of my youth for as long as I could, because no matter how smart I was, physically and in some cases emotionally, I was still twelve, and I belonged in sixth grade like every other twelve-year-old. I'd just be in sixth grade with people who are as smart as me."

Mel's admiration for Drew upped ten notches. "Your dad's a smart guy."

"He's very smart, and very protective, because of my mother and all. So I took a ton of tests to see if I qualified to get into Westmeyer's scholarship program, and he took a job there to help pay for my tuition."

Huh. She tucked her chin into her jacket, wincing at the sting of cold air to her eyes. "So you're there on a partial scholarship?"

"Yep, and my dad made a deal with Dean Keller. He'd fix up all the stuff that was starting to fall apart for a smaller salary if Dean Keller would put the rest of his salary toward my tuition."

Mel's heart tightened at the thought. She grabbed the tray that held their burgers while Nate got their drinks and paid for the food. Drew's sacrifices for Nate knew no bounds, and his complexities grew.

God, he wasn't just dreamy, but a terrific father. And deeper, and deeper she fell.

They located the table Drew had chosen and plunked their food down. Mel slid in beside Drew, pressing up against him for warmth.

Drew doled out the food. "Your nose is red."

"That's because it's ten degrees," she said, snuggling up against him.

"No, it's not," Nate disagreed. "It's forty-two degrees with a ten percent chance of precipitation. The winds are coming from the northeast at three miles per hour." He bit into his burger with relish.

"So this is what it's like to date a genius's father?" Mel teased, dabbing a fry into a mound of ketchup.

Drew rubbed her cold hand with his and rolled his eyes at Nate. "If you only knew the half of it."

As they chatted and ate, despite the cold, Mel was warm with something as simple as a cheeseburger and the two men she was growing fonder of by the second.

Deep contentment and the simple things like having dinner together were sorely underrated. All of the money Stan made, all of the chef-prepared meals they'd shared, none of them had made her this happy.

"Hey." Drew nudged her with a cold nose to her cheek. "Is that your phone?"

She dug in the pocket of her down jacket and pulled it out, seeing it was Jackie's number. "It's Jackie. I'll call her back. We're having dinner and not even Jackie's important enough to ignore fries."

"Go ahead," Drew coaxed. "We're almost done anyway."

She popped another fry in her mouth and smiled at his understanding. "Hey, Jackie! Guess where I am? Freezing my butt off, eating hamburgers with Nate and Drew. I bet you can't top that with your fancy vichyssoise soup and braised lamb chops with a balsamic glaze."

Jackie's familiar cackle shot to her ear. "Oh, don't I wish. I'm eating canned ravioli while I help the whiners with homework, but Frank wanted me to call you."

Mel's heart jumped with a jolt to her chest. She'd been so busy thinking about Drew and getting the boys ready for their big debut, she'd forgotten about the reason for Jackie's visit.

She hadn't even mentioned it to Neil. Frank probably hadn't been able to talk them into auditioning her and Jackie was calling to let her down easy. Bummer that. Yet, she found, she wasn't as disappointed as she thought she'd be.

Mel pressed the phone to her cheek, burrowing into Drew's embrace. "So you're calling to let me down easy, eh? I love that you're the kind of friend who'd call me personally to tell me I'm just not *Celebrity Ballroom* worthy. It was my jiggly butt that turned them off, right?" she joked, ignoring Drew's look of disapproval.

"Hell no, that's not why I'm calling. I'm calling you to tell you Frank wants your ass here in L.A. pronto for an on camera audition!"

CHAPTER SEVENTEEN

Dear Divorce Journal,

Did you hear that? That was the roar of my own personal empowerment apocalypse. Duck.

As Jackie droned on, Mel's heart raced. "The studio's all abuzz about you, kiddo. 'Bout shit their pants when they heard your name." Jackie covered the phone with her hand then. "Yes, I said shit, Jaynie. I'm a crappy parent. If this is the worst I ever do to you, color yourself lucky your therapy bill will be small." She came back on the line. "Kids—all about the right and wrong. Anyway, next week's Thanksgiving, but can you come over the weekend?"

Tingles of excitement swirled in the pit of her stomach. "You're not serious!"

"As a virgin in a cathouse with a prepaid Visa, honey!"

"Oh, my God, Jackie! I can't believe this. So what do I do next?" Her. On *Celebrity Ballroom*. It was insane. It was the opportunity of a lifetime. She couldn't breathe from her excitement.

"You check your e-mail on your father's ancient computer for a ticket—courtesy of Frank and the studio—show up, and wow 'em. That's it."

She gripped Drew's hand. "I can't do this, Jackie. I'm not ready. I still jiggle. I mean, really jiggle. And my hair's always a mess. Not to mention, I suddenly can't remember a single dance step. Not one.

And that guy Franz scares me. He's so mean to all the faux-lebrities."
Oh, God. She wasn't just a has been, she was a forgetful one.

"That's just nerves, sweet pea. Franz is a pussycat in real life. And
quit worrying about dance moves. It'll all come back to you, and they
have all sorts of crap to stuff you in, smooth you out, lift you up. Don't
worry about any of that. Just be you, Mel. You're beautiful. That's all
they want."

Her. How ironic that suddenly she, old in terms of Hollywood,
flabby and not even remotely star worthy was what the studio wanted.
"Okay, I've officially stopped breathing now, and I'm freezing. Oh,
my God, Jackie! Thank you. Thank Frank. Thank the kid down the
road—thank whomever's responsible for cutting me this kind of a
break."

"You go finish dinner with your men, kiddo. I'll catch you at the
airport myself. E-mail me, honey—bye!"

Mel stared at the phone for a long moment, well after Jackie had
hung up, unable to process the kind of turn her life had taken.

"*Celebrity Ballroom*. That's major, Ms. Cherkasov," Nate said,
grinning. "You should be really proud. Aren't you proud, Dad?"

"Very. How about we talk about this on the ride home? Mel's
going to lose her nose to frostbite if we don't, and you have school
tomorrow."

She helped Drew and Nate clean up, then let Drew lead her to his
truck, still in disbelief.

As they drove back to her father's, Drew said, "You're very quiet,
Ms. Cherkasov."

"It's shock," she said on a chuckle. "Can you believe my incredible
luck?"

"I can," Nate chimed in. "You're an awesome dancer."

"Thanks, Nate. You're not too shabby yourself." She slipped her
hand into Drew's, taking deep breaths.

The ride home was filled with chatter from Nate in the backseat, chatter she couldn't process fully due to her excited panic. When they pulled up to her father's, Drew jumped out to walk her to the door.

He pulled her into his embrace and gave her a quick kiss under the glow of the outside lamp. "You go do girly stuff like scream and jump up and down, and I'll see you at school tomorrow, okay?"

Mel shook her head. "I just can't believe it. Hey, thanks for tonight. I really enjoyed it." She ran a hand over his chest with a smile.

"Well, chili cheeseburgers at Joe's can't top a gig on *Star Ball-room*."

"*Celebrity Ballroom*, and says who?"

"I'll see you tomorrow?" He pecked her lips once more without much passion, but Mel chalked it up to Nate's presence in the truck.

"You bet." She turned to head in and called, "Night, Drew."

But he'd already made his way down the path that led to the driveway.

"So cool about Ms. Cherkasov, right, Dad?" Nate said when he got back in the truck.

Drew fought his irrational thoughts and forced his tone to an even calm. "You bet."

"She'd be so awesome. She's a great dancer, and she's always nice when she gives us critiques. Everybody will love her. Bet her Q-score goes through the roof."

Lights from passing cars whizzed past him in a blur while he tried to focus on Nate's words. "What's a Q-score?"

"It's how they rate her appeal to the television audience."

"How interesting."

Nate's impatient sigh filled the car. "You don't really mean that, Dad. You're pretending to care."

"I am not." *You are, too.* "I've no doubt Mel's Q will go through the roof." It had with him. Why wouldn't it with everyone else?

"It's a 'Q-score' and I wonder if this means she'll have to move to L.A. That's where they tape. If she did that, I guess she'd have to leave Westmeyer. That would so suck. She's the best teacher we've ever had."

Drew clenched his teeth. Yeah. He wondered that, too.

━━━━ℓ━━━━

"Ms. Cherkasov," Drew rumbled in her ear from behind.

She shivered, his cologne resting in her nose and making her dizzy. It had been a week since they'd last made love, and she was anxious to get this cocktail party over so they could spend the night together while Nate was at Selena's and before she had to leave for L.A. "Mr. McPhee?"

"I bring you spirits to dull the pain of watching Ms. Willows flirt with Dean Keller after only two glasses of wine."

Mel giggled, turning on her heel to smile up into his face, taking the glass of red wine from him. "I dub thee my knight in pain needing dulling."

"Have I told you, you look amazing tonight?"

Mel leaned into him, savoring the heat of his large frame and his sweet words. "I don't remember you telling me, but I do remember you showing me just a snippet of how amazing I am when you tried to put your hand up my dress in the car."

"Well, then let me make this right." He leaned into her, his voice silky soft in her ear. "You look amazing, and if I don't get you naked in the next thirty minutes or so, I can't be held responsible for dragging you out into the hall, throwing that hot body of yours up against a locker and making love to you right there in the hall. I *need* you. Soon."

Mel's breath shuddered and the sinful anticipation they'd built up all week long was threatening to boil over. She took a sip of her wine, running her tongue over the rim while she held his eyes. "Well, then. Go make the rounds and hurry it up. We can't afford to be fired because of our bad case of lust."

He groaned, winking at her before moving away to mingle.

Mel watched him from the corner of the room, supple, sleek, so handsome he made her mouth dry. He was like some beautiful animal, feral and proud, and he had no idea how damn sexy he was.

"Hey, Mel!"

She was startled from her lustful thoughts when Gwen Timmons approached her, drink in hand. Oh, hell. She'd forgotten all about Gwen's date with Neil. She was so wrapped up in her nerves about her audition and Drew, that she'd missed her workouts with him this week. "Hey, Gwen. How went the date with Neil?"

Gwen's face darkened just enough to cause a ripple of alarm in Mel, but then she said, "Oh, it was fine. I guess we just didn't connect on all the right levels."

"I'm sorry to hear that. He really is a great guy. Just hard to pin down."

Gwen rocked back on her heels. "Harder than you think."

"What do you mean?"

She waved a hand at Mel. "Nothing. Forget it. It just didn't work out. No harm, no foul. I'm off to check out the new phys ed teacher." Gwen teetered off just as Drew came back across the room.

"I have to talk to Dean Keller, and then we're outta here. Deal?"

She pouted. "But they have Triscuits and cheese in a can. I can't believe you'd make me leave before they break them out."

"I have something much better." He wiggled his eyebrows and headed out of the staff lounge to the tune of her breathy sigh.

~ℓ~

"Drew, please come in," Dean Keller said, gesturing to the chairs in front of his desk.

Whatever Keller wanted, he'd better spit it out fast. Mel, in her almost but not quite low enough cleavage-revealing dress was setting his drawers on fire. He wanted those sexy legs ending with the nude pumps on her feet around his waist while he was buried balls deep in her—ASAP. "How can I help you, sir?"

"I have some bad news, Drew. I hate to do this—especially now that the holiday season has begun."

He clenched his glass of cheap Scotch. "Is it Nate? Is everything all right?"

Keller shook his head, folding his lean hands together on top of the desk Drew had fixed just last week. "Nate's fine, Drew. It's his tuition."

Drew shifted in discomfort. "Sir?"

"Tuition's going up, Drew. The school can't afford to pay you any more than they already do with budget cuts and so on. Next semester there'll be a ten percent increase."

His stomach dropped. "I don't know that I can afford that, sir."

"I figured you'd want to know. We value both you and Nate here at Westmeyer. Your work is meticulous, bar none. We'd hate to see you leave."

"Then I'll find a way."

"You're a good man, Drew. I know if there's a way, you'll find it."

If Keller was right about anything, he was right about that.

He'd find it.

Somewhere.

～ ℓ ～

"Hey, what did Dean Keller want?" Mel asked when he brought her coat.

He looked away and held out her jacket. "More things to fix. There's always something in this creaky old place. So, you ready?"

"Hurry—get me out of here before Gwen does a stripper dance on the buffet table for Coach Gartner."

Pulling on his own coat, he asked, "Things didn't work out with Neil?"

She sighed in frustration. "No. Nothing ever works out with Neil. He's just not a one-woman kind of guy."

"Yeah. I didn't get that vibe from him." He took her hand and pulled her out of the staff lunchroom and into the deserted hall, flattening her against the wall to kiss her before she had the chance to ask him what he meant.

He made her forget everything when he slid his hand into her jacket and cupped her breast through the thin material of her dress. "Ahem. I think you'd better button your jacket and take me to your dungeon."

Drew chuckled against her lips, the rigid press of his shaft noticeable. "At your command."

They literally ran to his truck, hand in hand, the anticipation of some alone time magnifying their flight. Drew jumped into the truck, turned the ignition on to crank up the heat, and pulled her almost over the console to capture her lips in a fiery kiss. "Woman, you're going to break me being so sexy. It was all I could do to keep my hands off you in there."

Her breathing was shallow, and the place between her legs ached with heated need. "Well, now you don't have to. So get this chariot moving, huh? The faster we arrive, the faster we can be naked."

Drew took the wheel, leaving one hand on her thigh, and pulled out of the parking lot. The radio played something bluesy and soft, making Mel smile and close her eyes.

He trailed his fingers along her thigh, inching the skirt of her dress higher in slow, agonizing increments. When he reached the top of her thigh-high nylons, he cleared his throat, tracing the ridge of them, skimming beneath them to tease her flesh.

Her nipples tightened to sharp peaks, hard and ready for his mouth. The vision of his head bent at her breast made a soft moan escape her lips.

Drew's fingers whispered over her flesh again and again until they reached his apartment complex, teasing her, torturing her with anticipation. It was a race to see who could fling open the door and reach his apartment door first.

They were both laughing and out of breath when he jammed the key in the door, dragged her inside, and slammed it shut without bothering to turn the lights on.

Instantly, his hands were on her, lifting her to wrap her legs around his waist. "Christ, I want you, Mel," he murmured, his breath hot against her ear while he flipped his shoes off and settled them on the couch.

She bracketed each side of his face with her hands, driving her fingers into his hair, and pulled him down for a kiss, relishing his heavy weight on top of her. The thick press of his cock, hard and insistent, made her lift her hips to grind against him with a level of desperate need that was bigger than the last.

Clothes came off in a heated rush until her hands were on his bare chest and he was dragging her dress up and over her head.

He stopped cold when he realized she had no panties on, only a garter and some thigh-high nylons. His appreciation was a thick groan.

Mel reached down to unsnap them, but his hand was quick to thwart her as he hauled her to him, their chests pressing tightly together. "Don't you dare take those off. You had no panties on all night and I had no idea. I think punishment is in order," he ground out against her mouth, thumbing her hard nipples.

Her lips sought his, craving his tongue in her mouth. She felt naughty and wanton. "I thought I'd surprise you. You like?"

Drew sat her up, capturing her gaze with his intense blue one. "I like everything about you, Mel, but I especially like your idea of lingerie. They stay. Now, turn around," he ordered thickly.

Mel obeyed on a shiver, her stomach quivering, her legs weak when she leaned over the back of the couch. She felt the heat of Drew's naked body behind her, heard his hiss when he wrapped his arm around her waist and laid a cheek against her spine.

He let his hand slide between her legs, driving his way through the damp curls at the apex of her thighs and spreading her swollen lips while he pressed hot kisses along her spine.

Mel arched into his lips and thrust against his hand, her chest heaving. The anticipation of what was to come made her grip the edge of the couch with shaky hands as Drew slipped over the globes of her ass, licked and nipped them until she was quivering.

"Spread your legs, Mel," he demanded from beneath her, slipping between her thighs and licking at the sensitive flesh of them.

Her heart began to crash and blood raced through her veins, hot and electric when he said, "I've waited all week to taste you. I can't wait anymore," just before he thrust his tongue deep inside her.

Mel battled a scream at the hot, wet invasion, bucking against Drew's mouth and clinging to the back of the couch. His head, dark, the silky feel of his hair against her thighs, all lent to the most erotic vision she'd ever experienced.

Drew was relentless, driving his tongue against her clit, swirling it along the swollen bud, lapping at her until the sweet sound of her flesh being driven to climax became an erotic level she'd never attained before.

When Drew's hands kneaded her ass, when he pulled her to his mouth so tight, she gripped his hair and came hard, the release a hot wave of sweetness, sharp and heavy.

Tears sprung to her eyes it was so mind-blowing. She slid down his body, weak and shaking to fall into his embrace and curl her head into his neck.

He cradled her against him with one hand while the other reached for his discarded pants. He pulled the foil wrapper of a condom out and tore it open with his teeth, slipping it on then settling her in his lap, his back against the couch.

Mel straightened, whimpering when he pulled a nipple into his mouth and teased it with his tongue. She lifted her hips, wrapping a hand around his cock and positioning him at her entrance.

She drove downward with force, hearing Drew's growl of pleasure, savoring the grip of his hands on her hips.

He pulled her forward so their flesh met chest to chest and drove his hands into her hair. "I can't get enough of you, Mel. Never enough," he rasped.

Their lips found one another's, clamping together in a molten blend of lips and tongues while their hips crashed together. He filled her, stretched her, pulsed within her as he stroked, thrusting again and again.

Drew was the first to clench his muscles; they flexed then tightened beneath the palms of her hands. Her nails dug into his rippling flesh, clinging, begging him to come with her.

His last thrust was forceful and filled with the growl of his release, and then Mel let go, too, lost in the ache of spiraling need. It coiled deep in her belly then let go like a spring of heat. Her teeth clenched at the intensity, the realization that she didn't know how she'd gone half her life without experiencing this kind of lovemaking. It was unthinkable to never have it again.

With that last racing thought, she came, too, driving downward one last time to the tune of their flesh connecting and the bliss of completion.

They sagged against each other, their chests crashing together while they fought for air. Mel smiled into his neck when he said, "Wow. Maybe we should wait a week more often."

"This is me wholeheartedly protesting."

He tangled his fingers in her hair. "Just can't get enough of me, can you?"

"No. It's your lumpy couch I can't get enough of."

Drew slapped the cushion's worn fabric. "This is a great old couch I got at a garage sale. Don't hurt its feelings."

"I wouldn't dream of it, but do you think we could move to the less lumpy, not as easily upset by my insensitive comments bed. My back is killing me. Besides, if we're having an overnight, we can't be up all night doing that thing we do. We have to be at your mother's by noon for Thanksgiving dinner. My father's thrilled he doesn't have to defrost a turkey."

Drew rose from the couch, pulling her with him to wrap his arms around her waist from behind. "And then you have to leave on the red-eye for your audition."

Her stomach tangled in a knot. "I do." They hadn't discussed the topic at length since she'd found out she was a candidate for the job. Yet, she never failed to sense a thread of tension in Drew's voice when it was merely mentioned, and she didn't quite understand it.

She swung around to capture his gaze, running her hands over his chest and hoping to gauge his feelings on the subject. "We still on for that ride to the airport?" she asked, smiling up at him.

Instead of returning her gaze, he pulled her close, pressing his lips to the top of her head. "You bet."

Again, there was that hesitance in his tone, one she was reluctant to address. She didn't want to spoil this thing they'd created—this warm intimacy. She'd never had this with Stan and wasn't willing to disrupt it at any cost. "Well, okay, then. I say we get some shut-eye. Myriam said I was expected to work in the kitchen just like everyone else. I think that means I have to peel potatoes, and I want my eyes wide open for that."

He chuckled against her hair, the vibration of it soothing. "I think you should limber up your fingers so you can peel all those potatoes."

Mel smiled against his chest and shivered. "And how do you propose I do that?"

He hitched his jaw toward the bedroom with a grin. "Come with me. I'll show you."

They both laughed as they made their way toward the bedroom, Drew's laughter lighthearted and hers colored with a smidge of worry.

~ ૭ ~

"There they are!" Selena shouted, her cheeks flushed from working in the kitchen. "We thought you two would never get here," she chided with a sly grin when they entered the front door.

The McPhees' house was swarming with children, smelled of every good thing Thanksgiving dinner should smell of, and was filled with sound and motion.

She gave Mel and Drew each a kiss then put on her stern face. "You," she said, pointing at Mel, "have dough to roll, and you," she smiled up at her son, "are needed in the living room. Your father seems to think your presence will bring his football team good luck."

Drew shook his head in mock defeat, sighing. "My work here is never done."

Mel made a face at him. "Hey! How come your job is to sit on the couch and mine is to roll dough, pal?"

Selena leaned in to her. "Because you do not want to see my Drew in the kitchen. It's like setting loose a man who's just discovered fire."

Mel winked at her and said, "I dunno, McPhee—you don't dance, you can't cook. How are you a catch again?" she teased.

Drew hauled her up against him, leaving her toes dangling, and whispered, "Did you already forget last night? I have skills that can't be denied. Surely they make up for my lack of talent in other areas?"

"I heard that!" Selena sang on a chuckle, climbing over assorted grandchildren to make her way back to the kitchen.

Drew pulled her into the small entryway and planted a long kiss on her lips, making her sigh. "I have to go make dough—you get to watch TV. Don't try to schmooze me with your kisses."

"I was only trying to make up for our lack of playtime last night because you voted sleeping over mad passionate sex."

"Yeah, yeah. And I have to go home and pack after dinner to leave—which blows our chances of having a sleepover tonight."

Instantly, Drew stiffened, just enough that it was only noticeable to someone who'd come to know his body so well. "Right."

She cocked her head up at him, hoping he'd tell her why he'd been so quiet all morning. "You okay?"

"Right as rain." He swatted her butt. "Go make me some dough, woman." He gave her one last kiss and skirted around her, heading for the living room where boisterous yelling could be heard.

Tonight before she left for her audition, they had to talk about what his feelings on the subject of the show were.

An ominous dread stole over her while she contemplated the

wooden turkey welcome sign hanging on the McPhees front door, but she shook it off.

She had dough to roll.

Before she headed to the kitchen, she popped into the living room to say her hellos before beginning her slave labor.

The blare of the football game followed her to the kitchen where the scent of roasting turkey, women's laughter, and clouds of flour welcomed her. Drew's sisters and Myriam stood in a line at the long kitchen counter, each completing one task or another. Mel rolled up the sleeves of her imitation blue silk shirt and nudged Myriam to press a kiss against her warm cheek. "Put me to work, ladies."

In moments, she had a flour-covered counter and a wad of dough to roll. As she kneaded the soft concoction, Mel fought another niggle of worry about leaving tomorrow. The opportunity was huge and, no doubt, a gift of pure luck, but there was a definite reluctance to return to the place where she'd been officially shunned when she'd become Stan's ex-wife. The glitz of Hollywood, the lure of fame and fortune had long since waned for her.

She loved it here in Riverbend. She loved her job, teaching boys who were as reluctant to dance as they were to skip an episode of *The Big Bang Theory*. She loved that Nate had accepted her so willingly and that their private sessions had given her the chance to get to know him on a one-on-one basis.

She loved being closer to her father and regretted that she hadn't taken a firmer stance with Stan about seeing him more often. She loved her new independence and making her own decisions.

And she loved Drew. Whether he liked to dance or not.

A tingle of awareness skittered along her arms. She was in love, and she didn't want to move to L.A. for a job when everything she'd ever wanted was right here in Riverbend.

Mel loves Drew. She let the phrase repeat in her brain. It was terrifying and exciting and mostly terrifying to feel this way so soon.

But the question was did Drew love Mel? If he did, he hadn't copped to it. She wasn't the only one new to the idea of a relationship after a divorce. Drew had told her, she was his first serious encounter since he'd divorced Sherry. But maybe he wasn't as serious as she was? She'd never know until she asked, and while that would take all the courage she possessed, she was going to ask anyway.

And even if the outcome weren't what she hoped for, would that really affect her choice to take a job on *Celebrity Ballroom* if it was offered? Did staying in Riverbend mean Drew had to love her in return?

No. Because she'd come to love this new life, and if Drew McPhee didn't love her in return, that was fine. He'd be a stupidhead.

Okay, it wasn't fine, but it would be because while she loved nothing better than to be with him and Nate, she'd survive if things went wrong, and she'd do it while she stood on her own two feet. It might hurt like hell to be rejected by Drew, but she could withstand anything now that she knew who she was.

A smile spread across her face. She'd go to L.A. simply because Jackie and Frank had gone to so much trouble to get her an audition, and if they offered her the job, she'd tell them she already had one.

One she loved.

Myriam pinched her cheek with affection. "What's so funny?"

Her head tipped back. "Life. Life is funny, Myriam."

Myriam chuckled, taking the dough from her inept hands. "Yep. Sure is. So I heard you're goin' on an audition for *Celebrity Ballroom.* Me and Selena almost wet ourselves, we're so excited for you!"

Mel's return smile was bright. "I wouldn't get too excited. I'm up against some stiff competition. Lucy Vega to name one," Mel listed a well-known ballroom dancer.

Myriam waved a flour-covered hand at her, leaning into Selena who'd joined them. "As if Lucy Vega could ever be as pretty as you. Have you seen her feet? They're like hooves."

"Whose feet are like hooves?" Drew asked, popping a stalk of celery from a platter on the counter in his mouth.

Mel shook her head, wiping her hands on a nearby towel. "Oh, no one."

"Lucy Vega," Myriam provided. "Mel thinks she'll lose the audition for *Celebrity Ballroom* to that horse. Hah! No way can she out dance our Mel, and no way is she as pretty. Mel's gonna be the new judge on *Celebrity Ballroom*. Count on it." She said with a firm shake of her head and a warm smile in Mel's direction.

Drew said nothing, but the dark expression crossing his face made her pause. His disapproval was crystal clear. Why she hadn't seen it sooner was a mystery.

Her palms grew sweaty with her new now-or-never approach. She rinsed her hands at the sink and dried them, taking deep breaths of air.

It was time to figure out exactly where she stood with Drew.

Where such a resolute stand had come from, she couldn't say. She just knew it was time to sort this through so there were no misunderstandings.

And whatever the outcome—she'd get through it.

Hopefully, she'd do that without a can of chocolate frosting and some sprinkles.

CHAPTER EIGHTEEN

Dear Divorce Journal,

Blow me. Blow me hard. I'm never, ever writing in you again. You only make things worse when I have to see my pain in black and white. Thanks for that. Really.

She tugged on Drew's sleeve. "Got a minute?"

"For someone as sexy as you, I can spare two." His smile warmed her, giving her the courage to push forward.

She folded her hands behind her back. "Meet me in the tree house?"

"It's cold out there. You don't really want me to get frostbite just because you can't keep your hands off me, do you?"

"Funny. You're very funny. I need to talk to you. Meet me in the tree house when the coast is clear," she said with a smile, heading for the door off the laundry room and out into the overcast, cold day.

Grabbing the rope ladder, she climbed to the top and took another deep breath. It would be all right. It had to be all right. *Please let it be all right.*

Mel chalked the foreboding dread up to nerves when she heard Drew's feet climbing the rope. His head appeared in the entrance of the tree house, dark and handsome. He climbed in, sitting on his haunches to work his way over to the bench she sat on.

His face held a question. "Mind telling me what couldn't wait until I'd had a dozen or so of those baby quiches?" He wrapped an arm around her and grinned.

Mel turned to face him, her hands trembling. "I need to know something."

"Well, hurry up, woman. I hear there's clam dip. If I miss that, it's on."

"How do you feel about me going to audition for *Celebrity Ballroom*?"

His chin lifted, and the hand in his lap clenched. "How am I supposed to feel?"

"Happy for me." Yes. Drew was supposed to be glad she'd been offered an opportunity of a lifetime whether he knew she wanted to take it or not.

His jaw tightened. "Okay."

Mel cocked her head as if she hadn't heard right. "Okay? Just okay?"

"I'm not sure what I'm supposed to say here, Mel."

She paused a moment to gather the right words and then she thought, *The hell with the right words.* There'd be no more walking on eggshells for anyone. Not even for the man she loved. "Are you angry because I'm going on this audition? You haven't said a single word about it since I heard from Jackie, and every time I mention it, your jaw clenches. Something's up. I want to know what it is."

Pulling away from her, he leaned back against the bench, his body language unreadable. "'Angry' isn't exactly the word I'd use."

Her heart crashed against her ribs, but she had to know. "Then what *is* the word you'd use, Drew?"

"It's probably more of a phrase than a word."

"Then what's the phrase?"

"I'm just waiting to see if the other shoe drops."

Her next question was filled with hesitation. "The other shoe?

What does that mean? I didn't know there was even a shoe to drop. This is a huge opportunity for me, one I'd like your support in because I'm sick with nerves about it, and I don't want to disappoint Jackie and Frank after they went to all this trouble to get me this audition."

"But you don't mind disappointing me and Nate?"

"*What?*"

Drew's lips, lips that had kissed hers over and over, thinned. "What happens if you get the job, Mel? Wait, no, don't say it. I know what happens. You move off to L.A. and go back to living your lifestyles of the rich and famous. That's what happens."

Mel's mouth fell open. She could abort the mission now by simply telling him she had no intention of taking the job if they offered it to her, but that would make it too easy on Drew.

She needed him to support her choices, barring murder charges, and know she'd never do anything to hurt him no matter what her decision was.

This was about trust.

She was never going to have the kind of relationship where she did all the off-stage work while her partner expected nothing but a bottomless pit of go-get-'ems from her. "So you've figured this all out. All of it. Without ever saying a word to me?"

"I was sort of in wait-and-see mode."

An angry claw of disappointment scratched at her heart. "Wait and see what? Wait and see if ex-pampered-trophy-wife Mel can resist the lure of the bright lights and hardcore greenbacks because she missed her chance at fame and fortune by marrying some rich guy? Maybe have a do-over to reclaim all she lost? But you weren't going to share your misgivings with me, were you, Drew? You know, like normal people in a relationship do. Maybe say, 'Hey, Mel. Let's talk about what'll happen if they offer you the job and you have to commute to L.A.'? *Noooooooo!* You were plenty happy to test me to see if I'd fail without me ever even knowing I was taking the test. You just assumed I was going to choose a new life in L.A. over the one I've made here. *Who the hell do you think you are?*" she fumed, pushing her way past him to climb over his legs and off the bench.

He swung around to fully face her, his face was tight and his eyes were narrowed. "Why else would you want to do *Celebrity Ballroom*, Mel? Because of the things it'll buy you. The exposure it'll get you. You're not going to do it for free, are you?"

How dare he make her out to be some money-grubbing twit? Her mind raced through some of their past conversations and it made her visibly shake her head. No. She'd never ever given him the impression money and being in the limelight was all that mattered to her.

Now she was incensed. That he had no inkling of the person she really was stung like nothing ever had. "No, I'm not going to do it for free, but I would, Drew McPhee! Maybe I want to do it because I love to dance. Because I want everyone to love to dance the way I do. Because this could be a dream come true for me. That there's a paycheck involved is an added bonus."

His lips thinned into an angry line. "A paycheck that'll cost you everyone in your life because you want *things*."

"What is it with you and your ridiculous notion that anyone who has money or hopes to have money is evil incarnate? Yes, Drew—I like *things*." She grated with a harsh rasp. "I like shopping and clothes and shoes. So what? Do they define me? Are they all I aspire to? Didn't I do a bang-up job of surviving without them? Wasn't it me eating a chili cheeseburger with you and Nate when it was zero below? Have you heard me whine even once because I couldn't have whatever I wanted whenever I wanted to? I didn't even do that when I was married to Stan. Damn you for making me sound like I'm frivolous and money hungry!" she yelled on a wheezing breath. The calm approach she'd hoped to take on this escalated to a new height.

His response was dry and cold as ice, his body language a direct reflection of his bitter view of her. "That'll all change once the money starts rolling in again. Forgive me for having a bad taste in my mouth about it. Or have you forgotten what it did to me and Nate?"

A red-hot flash of fury shot up her spine. She backed away from him, the top of her head scraping against the ceiling of the tree house. "Don't you dare compare me to Sherry, Drew! *Do. Not.* I'm nothing like her, and I won't defend possibly taking this job because she did something bad to you. *Things* don't ruin a marriage, Drew—people do! Addictions do. You know who needs to suck it up here, Drew? You do! That you would even consider that I'd do something as horrible to you and Nate as Sherry did makes me want to shove my fist down your throat. I love Nate, and I—"

"Love a big paycheck," he finished for her on an angry snarl, frozen in his place on the bench.

It was as if he'd slapped her in the face.

Her gut clenched in pain, her heart followed suit. So this was what it boiled down to. All this time she'd thought Drew knew she was nothing like the women he so despised, only to find he'd just been laying in wait for her true colors to show once she got her hands on some cold, hard cash. Like he was somebody to pass her impoverished time with until the money train rolled back into the station.

Drew's voice was like a block of ice when he said, "If you took the job, you'd have to move to L.A. I don't want a relationship with someone who only lives here part time. I want one that involves helping me raise Nate."

Tears stung her eyes, but she was determined not to make the same mistakes again. Never. Again. "And I don't want a relationship that means I have to sacrifice my dreams, big or small, filled with bags of money or not, just so I can prove I'm not like your ex-wife!"

Mel took one last look at Drew—angry, cold, and unmoving—before escaping down the rope ladder and running toward the front of the house.

That's where her father found her when he arrived for Thanksgiving dinner.

Hiding in the bushes, red-eyed, and freezing.

But pride and self-esteem still intact.

She made a discovery in those bushes, though. Pride hurt like a bitch and self-esteem blew chunks.

~ ℓ ~

Drew lost track of how long he sat in the tree house. The smells coming from inside didn't tempt him, and neither did the call of a cold beer and his mother's pumpkin pie.

Mel was gone. She wanted what she wanted; and he wanted what he wanted.

Now the twain would never meet.

Fuck.

Her father reached over and ran his finger down her cheek while the flash of headlights passed them by. "You okay, butternut squash?"

Mel tucked her purse under her arm and gave him a grim smile, her eyes sore from crying. "Well, that I didn't buy chocolate frosting in bulk must mean I'm better this time than I was the last, right?"

Her dad nodded his head while he drove her toward the airport. "I suppose so. Sure couldn't tell from all the cryin' you did while you were packing, though."

Yes. She'd cried. Maybe sobbed like a two-year-old was more on target. Yes, Drew's rejection had been an agonizing splash of cold reality. But at least she knew where he stood. He'd painted her with the same brush Sherry had handed him, and there was no changing his mind.

So, okay. It was done. Mel repeated the word over and over in her head so the pain would ease.

Yet, it clung like some kind of venereal disease.

But it would fade. While she hadn't fallen in love with Stan the way she had with Drew, she knew it would fade. Oh, God, please let it be sooner rather than later.

"You sure you still wanna do this?"

Leaning her head on the truck's window, she nodded. "Yes, Dad. I'm sure. Jackie and Frank went to bat for me in a big way. I called Jackie and told her how I felt, but she said maybe I'd change my mind after I heard what the producers had to say. Plus, she said it was a great way to see each other on the studio's dime. The least I can do is show up. But I'm also still pretty sure I won't take the job. Being married to Stan gave me a front-row seat to a lifestyle I never really wanted to be a part of. I just don't think I was meant to be the star I thought I would be back when I was eighteen."

"You're still my star, Puddin' Pop."

"Well, it's good to know I'm someone's star."

Joe cleared his throat, the rustle of his jacket when he reached for her hand penetrating her ears. "Drew'll come around, Mel. He'd be stupid not to. I gotta tell you, though. I don't believe his hang-ups are just about money. Somethin' just isn't right about that. Maybe it's because he's got a lot on his mind from what Myriam says. Maybe that's what the trouble is."

A lot on his mind. So much on his mind he'd labeled her shallow? No go. It was too damned bad if there was more to his issues with her than the idea she was some cash whore. She wasn't a mind reader. If he didn't tell her what the real problem was, if there really was something more to it than what he'd hurled at her, she couldn't address it. "I don't care what he has on his mind. He can't shoot me down, Dad. I'm not going to let that happen again."

"When your kid's involved, you get tunnel vision, kiddo."

She turned to face her father in the passenger seat, her fingers trembling in his. "Nate? What does this have to do with Nate?"

"Myriam was talkin' the other day at Ping-Pong Paradise night at the rec center. Said she was worried sick Nate wouldn't be able to finish out the school year because tuition went up at that fancy joint you both work at. Drew already works for half the kid's tuition as it is. He's there on a scholarship 'cause he's so smart. Myriam said Drew was a stubborn shit. According to her, he's had a couple of offers to go and work for some pretty big contractors for big money, but he won't do it 'cause it sacrifices his time with Nate. Bet he sure wishes he'd taken one of those job offers now."

Her heart pounded. Why hadn't Drew told her? "Nate might have to leave Westmeyer? Dad, do you have any idea what that'd do to a kid like him? He needs what Westmeyer offers. He's brilliant. He'd get lost in public school."

"Then your Drew should rethink his game plan, huh? 'Specially when there's a perfectly good paying job he could take to do it."

Anger replaced the emptiness in her heart. "Drew thinks money and all people with money are evil. In his warped mind, Sherry, his ex-wife, drank because of it. He thinks his marriage was ruined by it. I'm sure he thinks money's responsible for volcanoes blowing and the *Titanic* sinking, too."

Joe ran a hand over his face with a slow pass. "In some cases, I guess that's true, but sometimes it's just that people are weak. They like a good excuse for their vices."

"Well, not in my case," she responded, tears welling in her eyes again. "He was just too much of a Neanderthal to consider I might be different."

Joe's lips pursed. "I can't help but feel like there's something more to this."

Mel made a face. "Well, then he should spit it out, shouldn't he? That's what adults do. Communicate. Maybe if Stan had communicated his wish to dabble in other women, things would have been different for me in the end. But he didn't—and look what happened. Stan blindsided me. That's not happening again. Drew never said a single word about any misgivings where *Celebrity Ballroom* was concerned. Sure, he didn't bring it up ever, but he definitely didn't clue me in to the idea that I was some money-hungry, vapid human being because I considered the job either."

"Sometimes men just aren't as good at expressing their feelings, Melli."

She snorted, slapping her hand on her thigh in exasperation. "That's a great excuse and about as old as dirt, Dad. If Drew isn't new-age enough—man enough—to own whatever the problem is, money or otherwise, too bad." She gritted her teeth with her last words.

Her father clenched her shoulder with his big hand. "He hurt you."

Mel clenched her teeth. "Darn right he did, but I can't give in, Dad. It would be just like doing what I did with Stan. Stan may not have said as much, but he expected me to let him have the spotlight, and I did, for many years. I might not want the kind of spotlight he wanted, but I want one that's mine. The one where I have control of my life."

Joe pulled to a stop at the departures terminal and turned to smile at her. "I'm proud of you, Mellow-Yellow. You've come a long way."

Yeah. Long. Big flippin' deal. "Thanks, Dad. So wish me luck."

Mel gave him a wan smile and opened her door, giving him a quick kiss before she hopped out onto the curb.

"You be safe, and call me when you get to Lala Land."

"I will. You be safe, too." She hurled her purse over her shoulder and dragged her carry-on bag from the backseat. Mel stood back and waved as her father drove off, keeping a smile on her face for as long as she could manage it until he'd driven out of sight, and only then did a fresh batch of tears arise.

Piss and fuck.

No more tears. As it was, her eyes were puffy and shadowed from lack of sleep. HDTV was not gonna love her, if she kept this up.

Trudging through the airport doors, it occurred to her that she'd come full circle. Mel Cherkasov had left L.A. broke, humiliated, and afraid.

She was returning not as broke, and employed, but more broken-hearted than she'd ever been when she'd been dumped by Stan.

Boo-yah.

She pushed her way through the crowd, trying to locate the security checkpoint when someone crashed into her, knocking her purse from her shoulder and stealing her breath.

"Sorry, lady," he muttered, but didn't stop to help her gather the strewn contents of her purse.

Mel made a mad dash for her belongings. God, she needed to organize her handbag. Drew had once joked that she probably could hide an elephant in it.

Drew. Damn you, Drew.

Her hand went to an envelope, and then she remembered her father had left it on the kitchen table for her and she'd never bothered to open it. She'd totally forgotten about it. The return address caught her eye, making her gasp.

Finklemeyer, Westin, and Garrett.

Stan's attorneys. Why would Stan's attorneys send her anything? Hadn't they taken everything already? Was there something left other than belly-button lint and her dental floss?

Angry, Mel tore open the manila envelope with trembling fingers. Damn Stan for poking his head out of the sand today of all days, when her heart ached with every painful beat.

Mel yanked the letter out of the envelope, walking toward the lounge area to find a seat. Her legs began to wobble. She rubbed her eyes to be sure she was reading correctly.

No.

But her eyes said yes when she scanned the letter again.

Yes.

She grabbed the arm of the seat, clinging to it to keep from pitching over face-first.

Yes.

Finklemeyer, Westin, and Garrett had been directed to issue her a check in the amount of ten million dollars.

From Stan.

Drew sat on his parent's front steps, a beer growing warm in his hand. Nate slapped him on the shoulder and nudged him over so he could sit, too.

Drew sighed. The last two days had been hell. He'd gone over and over his conversation with Mel, and just today realized what a total ass he was. "I did a bad, bad thing."

Nate shrugged, the rustle of his jacket crisp in the silence of the night. "I sort of heard a little. But I promise I went inside as soon as I heard it was a serious convo. Swear."

Remorse and shame took alternate stabs at him. "I blew it."

Nate's nod was as solemn as his blue eyes. "I'll say. But I have an answer for why you did what you did. It's a lot like post-traumatic stress disorder, I think."

"Meaning?"

"Meaning Mom's alcoholism traumatized you. It made you suspicious of all women."

"You think?"

"No, Dad. I know. I read it in *Psychology Today*."

"You need to lay off the smart, young man," Drew teased, bumping his thigh.

"Well, I would, but you need my help too much right now. Wanna hear what I have to say—or are you going to ground me for life for telling you how big you messed up?"

"I'm all about honesty."

"Swear it?"

"On my life."

"I have a question, then."

Drew nodded. "Go."

"Didn't you send me to Westmeyer so I'd be challenged by tougher classes, graduate, and eventually attend an Ivy League school?"

He sipped at his piss-warm beer. "That was part of the intent, yep."

"Why would you want me to go to an Ivy League school, Dad?"

Drew shrugged. "Because you deserve the best education, one that'll earn you a solid living."

Nate nodded. "And make me a lot of money . . ."

"That, too. What's your point?"

"It's okay for me to be rich but not Mel? You don't want me to go someplace like Harvard or Stanford to earn minimum wage, right?"

Drew's nod was slow and muddled by Nate's words. "I'd still love you if that's what you decided to do."

"But will you love me if I choose to make more money than Bill

Gates? Will it make me a bad person if I choose to drive a Lamborghini and not a Honda?"

"Don't be ridiculous. I'd like to think I've taught you to be a good person no matter what your bank account balance says."

Nate gave him a "duh" look. "So what makes Mel different? You just can't seem to grasp the concept that just because a woman likes nice things, she can also be a good person. Just because Ms. Cherkasov says she likes an expensive dress, doesn't mean she's going to sell her soul to the devil to buy it."

Drew frowned. "That's a little dramatic, isn't it?"

Nate's eyebrow cocked in a condescending manner. "Not in your case. You seem to think Ms. Cherkasov would give up everything just to have back what she once had, and she's never given you any indication to think something like that, has she?"

"No."

"Exactly, and know what else?"

"There's more?"

"Yep. You wanna know what it is?"

Drew's nod was somber. "Full-on honesty."

"This isn't about money, Dad. That's not the real issue at all. This is about you feeling like Ms. Cherkasov's going to choose her dancing and a career over you. Mom chose her art and then her alcohol over us. You want Mel to love you more than she loves to dance, or at least as much, and you want to make her prove it by not taking that job—which is a little stupid." Nate winced at the word. "Sorry, but it is."

Yes. It was. He'd flung ugly words at Mel. Words that implied she was shallow, and he'd known it at the time because admitting he wanted to be as important to her as her passion for dancing was made him feel spineless and worthless. Looking Nate square in the face,

Drew said, "That's absolutely the truth." And he was a shithead for not telling her that from the start.

"But did it ever occur to you that she might love to dance, but she loves you, too, and maybe she'd find a way to work things out with you even if she did get the job on the show? Why can't she want both things and still be a good person? I don't get why she has to sacrifice one thing for the other. She can still love you in L.A."

Why indeed. Fuck. "I got a little crazy with my baggage, didn't I?"

"I'll say. Mom is Mom. Ms. Cherkasov is Ms. Cherkasov. They're two different people. Your case of transference is transparent. Logical thinking says you'd at least recognize that, but you can't seem to grasp the concept. Though *Psychology Today* doesn't account for being blinded by love and matters of the heart."

Drew cracked a smile. "I wasn't just looking out for me and my heart, bud. I was looking out for you, too. I don't want anyone to hurt you ever again." Never again would he let someone tear up his kid's world like Sherry had.

Nate leaned back, placing the palms of his hands on the steps. "That's crap. Statistics have proven I'll be hurt more than once or twice in my life, and you'll just have to let it happen because that's life, but I can only be your excuse for so long. Someday it's gonna have to be sink or swim. I think Ms. Cherkasov's at a place in her life where she won't tolerate anyone dictating her decisions to her, and it took her a long time to get there. She's drawing a line in the sand, for lack of a better euphemism, and you pushed all her hot buttons by trying to take control of her life. If I'm reading the situation right, this is your test, Dad. It wasn't one she intended, but it is a test. You have to show her you trust her enough to love everything in her life equally. That's the nuts and bolts of it."

Grim. Jesus Christ. He'd been a shit more often than not since they'd begun seriously dating. "There's a lot at stake."

Nate crossed his arms over his knees. "There's a lot at stake just crossing the road. Look, Mel was rich before, and she still taught kids who were underprivileged. She might have had a nice house and a hot car to drive, but what was really important to her was how much she loves to dance and how much she wants to share that with everyone else. Have you ever really watched her teach a class?"

He had, and he understood now. Remembering her that night with Neil brought with it a certain peace. "She's beautiful."

"She isn't just beautiful, she's passionate about what she loves to do. Mom loved painting and alcohol more than us. But I think Mel has room for both. You just didn't give her a shot at working things out. Instead of explaining your *real* fears, you hid—"

"They weren't fears," he bristled.

Nate's eyes rolled upward in his head. "We can call them whatever you want. How's 'misgivings'?"

He nodded his consent. "A fine word."

"Okay. You didn't tell her about your misgivings. You created a fight about something that wasn't the real issue at all. Unfair."

Yep. It was official. He was a total ass. "You really like her, don't you?"

Nate grinned in the darkness, his white teeth flashing. "Yeah, I do."

"You're really smart."

"A genius, in fact."

"I might have ruined things for good."

"That would so suck. For both of us."

Drew rose, his mind racing with ideas for Mel's return. "So I think it's time I show Ms. Cherkasov that even Neanderthals can be reformed. We have a week. You in, son?"

Nate stood, jamming his shoulder against Drew's. "All the way."

CHAPTER NINETEEN

Dear Divorce Journal,

I've heard it said that whatever doesn't kill you will make you stronger. Well, look at that shit, would you? I'm still breathing. Which so sucks, but short of slitting my own wrists with a butter knife—I live. Bleh.

"I can't believe you turned *Celebrity Ballroom* down," Jackie said with a forlorn tone as they drank wine in her enormous kitchen with the gourmet stove and shiny refrigerator the size of a Sherman tank. The girls surfed in and out on feet with wings, chatting and giggling while assorted animals looked for stray hands willing to stroke them with love and attention.

Jackie held up her glass of wine and pointed it at Mel. "If anyone was perfect for the job, it was you, my friend. You were gorgeous on camera. You had that shit in the bag. Now those poor spray-tan people are going to have to suffer the wrath of Lucy Vega, and I want you to know, they hold grudges."

Mel's smile was equally forlorn, but it wasn't because she'd turned down the offer to be a judge. It was because she missed Drew, and Nate, and she hated that she missed him. She hated that she'd checked her cell phone two hundred times since she'd left Jersey only to find that the jackass hadn't called.

"I guess I just discovered that I'm not cut out for this kind of life. I told you that before I left to come here."

Jackie waved a hand at her. "I know, but I thought once you got into the studio, threw on a hot, slinky sequined dress, you'd change your mind. At least, that's what I hoped you do."

"That was what cinched the deal for me. Everyone poking and prodding at me made me want to scream." She shook her head at the irony of it all. "I always thought I wanted to be a superstar. With Stan, that dream faded, but it didn't fade as much because of Stan as it did me. If I'd wanted recognition that much, I could have gotten it via Stan. Now, I like just being Ms. Cherkasov who teaches kids, who hate the craft, BTW, to dance."

"Speaking of Stan—did you talk to his attorneys?"

Mel was still in a state of shock over the letter she'd opened in the airport. "I did, and it's true. I'm a multimillionaire. Don't ask because I sure don't get it."

"I think the fuckerly fuck discovered himself in some monastery while surrounded by goats who told him he's a huge shit via some goat mind-meld in a sweathouse, and he decided to relieve some of his guilt by paying you off. No one knows where the hell he is to ask him."

It was true. Stan's attorneys wouldn't disclose his location, nor would they reveal Stan's reasons for giving her such an enormous amount of money. "It makes no sense at all. Why, after all this time, would he order his attorneys to dole out such a huge chunk of change to me? Guilt?" She'd wanted no part of it at first. The thought of taking Stan's money appalled her, but then an idea had formed, and she'd decided she needed at least some of it.

Jackie's sleek shoulders lifted in indifference. "Maybe he had a near-death experience. I don't care what it was. You deserve the money. If you even consider returning it, I'll break all your limbs."

She grinned. "So how are we going to spend it, darling? Wanna hit Louis Vuitton? I, for one, could use a new purse."

If she was sure before money wasn't the key to happiness, not wanting to buy a Louis V. cinched the deal. Her sigh was long. "No. I'm not going to spend it on things like purses. I'm going to go back to Jersey and teach the boys how to dance just like I was going to do before I came into all this guilt money. I'm also going to buy my dad a place we can share, and I don't have to sleep on a bed fit only for Thumbelina."

Jackie cackled, cupping Mel's chin in her hand. "Did you call Dean Keller?"

Her nod was slow and filled with sadness. "I didn't, but Stan's attorneys did, and I made sure a check was made out to cover Nate's tuition until he graduates Westmeyer."

"Whaddya suppose your Drew will have to say about that?"

She toyed with her pasta vodka in an absent motion. "I think we can officially declare him no longer mine, and I can guarantee he'll never suspect impoverished Mel was responsible. He'd be livid if he knew I'd gone from just barely making ends meet to rich girl by proxy. It would only enforce his conclusions about my evil intent to rule the world one cha-cha at a time."

Jackie's spiky hair gleamed under the soft fluorescent lighting of her kitchen. "And that'd be stupid. Which I don't get. I really liked Drew, and I'm usually good at pegging a guy who's decent. I just feel like there's something else . . ."

Mel snorted, pressing her fingers to her temple. "Both you and my dad think that. Right now, he's just going to be stupid."

"Well, we can't exactly accuse him of being too bright, seeing as he let a catch like you go, now can we?"

Mel's sigh was a shaky shudder. Thinking about Drew hurt her from the inside out. "I can't believe I'm sitting here crying over man number two in just under a year. Second time is a charm, huh?"

Jackie's eyebrow cocked upward. "Ah, well, there's a huge differ-ence this time. This time you're crying but you're not unemployed, honey. Oh, and you're richer than shit. Best of all, you took care of you and stood up for what you want in a relationship. I'm proud, and Drew's a dick."

A big one. Blue whale big.

"Jackieeee!" Frank howled.

Jackie's head swiveled in the direction of Frank's media room just off the kitchen where he sat amidst a multitude of exotic green banana plants and pictures of the stars who'd made him famous hung on the walls. "If he's yelling because he wants a scotch, I'm going to kick his ass. I ain't the maid." She turned in the direction of the media room. "What, honey? Christ. Can't you see I'm consoling my friend with expensive wine you'll regret we wasted because you couldn't wait two seconds?"

"Get in here now, and bring Mel with you!"

Mel and Jackie shared a hesitant glance before scurrying off their stools and heading toward the media room. "What the hell, Frank? Did Clooney jump off a bridge? Brangelina have a three-way with live streaming video?"

He held out his beefy hand to her from the leather sectional that sprawled across half of the room. "Sit. Mel, you, too. I think you'll want to see this." Frank, a large man with an even larger heart, pat-ted the sofa. His wide face, typically never without a smile, held a frown that revealed the wrinkles on his broad forehead.

Frank clicked the remote and Stan appeared on the screen, hand-some as ever, tall, and lithe when he took a chair and seated himself across from Nora Phillips, one of the most respected reporters of all time.

Mel's breathing stopped, seeing him after so long. He looked pained, as though every movement he made was an effort. His hands shook a little, undetectable to most, Mel supposed, most everyone but her. She knew Stan. She knew when he was simply using his artistry as a guise and when he was in real pain.

Jackie groaned and flapped a hand. "This is what the big deal is? Why would Mel want to see this? He's probably going to spill his bullshit about finding himself at some Palm Beach spa confessional style. His ratings have been down since he shit on Mel and hooked up with that gold digger Yelena. He needs public sympathy like a crack whore needs change." She elbowed her husband. "I can't believe you dragged us away from some girl talk for this."

Frank clicked the pause button on the TIVO before putting his hand over Jackie's mouth, which was probably the only way to shut her up. "Hush, my love slave. Shut your yap and listen."

Mel watched as Nora Phillips thanked Stan for coming to "share" his very emotional journey. She listened with half an ear as Stan droned on about his life, his marriage to her, which she gave him kudos for mostly portraying with accuracy, and she listened with two ears while he told Nora with watery blue eyes why he'd chosen her to reveal his tortured secret to.

Nora could be trusted to ask the right questions. She could be trusted not to edit things with her own personal slant. She could be trusted not to leak his interview until he gave her the thumbs-up. She was an icon in the business.

Blah, blah, blah. Stan may have given Mel blood money, but it didn't mean she liked him more because of it. He'd left her to fend for herself with packs of vicious reporters and had never looked back while she sat in the rubble of their marriage.

Mel was a second shy of getting up and leaving to find a bucket to vomit in until Frank clamped his hand over her thigh and made her stay.

So she could hear Stan, with his Russian accent noticeable only in times of great stress, tears streaming down his face, throat clogged with emotion, confess.

That he was gay.

~ℓ~

Drew hung up the phone and shook his head. Dean Keller had personally called on a Sunday morning to tell him an anonymous donor had paid for Nate's tuition for the remainder of his schooling at Westmeyer.

Who did he know that had that kind of money? Why would someone do something so generous? How could he ever thank this faceless person for lifting the weight of a huge burden from his shoulders?

Since Mel had gone to L.A., not only had he spent the better part of her absence kicking himself, he'd spent the other half wishing he hadn't shunned the job offers he'd turned down to work for major corporations because he didn't want to get caught up in the rat race again.

He'd wanted to teach Nate to put family above all else—that no job, no amount of money was worth sacrificing your family time. In the process of that lesson, he'd become a zealot in the way that he lived—in his judgment of everyone around him—even in something as simple as buying a couch.

Now he was going to try and make things right. He had a few calls in to some of the companies that had once expressed interest in him with the hope they'd pan out. Yet, now that Nate's immediate future was secure, he could breathe a small sigh of relief.

Rubbing his hands over the scruff on his face, he sank down on the couch Mel had called lumpy and stared off into space, missing her, wishing he could take back the crappy shit he'd said so he wouldn't have to hear it on repeat when he closed his eyes at night.

A warm mug pressed against his hand startled him. He looked up to find Nate, grinning down at him. "You need coffee."

"Did you just hear what I heard, kid?"

Nate nodded, shoving his hands under his T-shirt. "Yep. Somebody likes me—a lot."

"But who?"

"For all my genius, I have no answer for this one. But promise me something?"

"What's that?"

"That your pride won't keep you from letting me use the tuition."

"You know me well, grasshopper. I'm not saying I didn't think about saying no." Because he had, almost immediately, until he caught himself and remembered he and Nate's conversation.

"I bet you did. That you didn't is like some huge revelation of self-discovery," Nate said with a grin.

"Do you know what this means, son?"

"It means your salary is your salary and we can buy a new couch?"

Drew barked a laugh of pure relief. "Yeah. It might be time for a new couch."

"And maybe a picture or something. Poor people have pictures, too."

Drew smiled. Since their chat when his twelve-year-old son had set him straight about an adult matter he should have seen clearly all alone, they'd put their heads together with a mission to win Mel back. They had a week until she returned from fall break, and he had a plan.

It was a pathetic work in progress, but Drew was determined to make it happen.

The phone rang again, shrill and irritating so early on a Sunday morning. Nate jumped up and grabbed it. "If it's Grandma, tell her no time for chocolate chip pancakes today. I have work to do."

The look on his son's face might have had him worried until he saw him smile.

He handed the phone to Drew. "Today is a very strange day in the McPhee household."

"Who is it?" Drew asked, setting his coffee on the end table.

Nate thrust the phone at Drew. "Just take the phone, Dad, and give that thing we talked about a shot. You know, trust?" His grin turned mischievous.

Drew gave his son a perplexed glance before taking the phone. "Hello?"

"Is this Drew McPhee?"

He stared at the phone while Nate did a touchdown dance. "It is."

"Wonderful!" the cheerful voice, loud and boisterous yelped into the phone. "I'm so glad I caught you, and forgive my calling you on a Sunday, but . . ."

~~ℓ~~

Sunday morning dawned bright and sunny, but Mel couldn't enjoy it as she stared at the horizon over the green, green grass of Jackie's manicured lawns, sipping freshly brewed coffee that she couldn't taste.

Jackie joined her on the patio and plunked down beside her, patting her arm. "You okay this morning, kiddo?"

Mel's stare was blank, her eyes moist and burning. "Why? Why would he live a lie for so long, Jackie?" she croaked, torn between sympathy and fury over Stan's public confession.

Even Jackie, usually at the ready with a smart-ass quip, had been rendered speechless. They'd all gone to bed glassy-eyed and overwhelmed, but Mel had enjoyed little sleep. She'd spent the better part of the night reliving her marriage to Stan. Now revealed as a total sham. She'd gone over and over conversations and lost moments to find even a small clue—a hint—that he was hiding something so huge, but she'd come up dry.

Jackie stared out over the lawn with her, her eyes bewildered and shadowed. "I don't know, Mel. Fear of rejection? Mockery? Being different than what everyone dubs the norm is harder for some than others. It does strange and sometimes horrible things to people. Frank said he'd heard rumors occasionally over the years, but he never had anything solid—or you know he would have come to you, don't you?"

Mel shook her head hard, focusing on row after row of colorful gardens filled to brimming with various palm trees. "Damn him, Jackie. Damn him for using me to cover for him. Like he's the first ever gay dancer in the world? If I ever see Stan again, I'm going to shove a bowl of borscht right up his ass! He lived a lie and he took me with him. He could never love me the way I should have been loved, deserved to be loved because I'm just not his type," she spat, running a hand over her tired, sore eyes.

Jackie brushed a strand of Mel's flyaway hair from her face. "You're right. You deserved better. So much better, and Stan's a bigger ass than I thought. It explains the money. He felt guilty for stealing all those years from you."

A tear slipped down Mel's face and dropped to her lap. "He damn well should."

"Ms. Jackie?" Jackie's maid and right-hand man Melda took a tentative step out onto the patio from the string of French doors off the kitchen. "Ms. Mel has a visitor."

Jackie scowled, her eyes narrowing. "It better not be some asshole reporter. I'm just in the mood to beat some vulture and cook him for breakfast."

Melda folded her hands together, her warm face composed. "Oh, no. It's a Neil Jensen. So handsome!" she twittered, then sobered, wiping the excitement off her face.

Mel brightened, if only a little. Neil had promised to come to support her at the audition, but he hadn't shown up, and she'd forgotten about it in all the chaos of Stan's admission. "Send him in, Melda, please."

"Immediately." Melda left them to go get Neil with a soft hush of footsteps and the swish of her white apron against her jeans.

Jackie reached out a hand to her. "Two BFFs in one place—the universe is looking out for you today, girly."

Mel clung to that, shaky and tired when Neil strolled in. One glance at his face, and she knew he was as upset for her as Jackie. She jumped up, expecting him to engulf her in his embrace, but instead, he looked to Jackie. "Could we have a minute alone?"

Jackie's eyes darted from Neil to Mel in sharp awareness. "Everything okay?"

Neil's gulp was visible, his next words thick. "I just need a minute."

Mel waved her friend off before shooting her a watery smile. "It's okay, Jackie. Go check on the kids, then we'll all sit down and feel sorry for poor Mel together."

"I'll go make some freshly squeezed orange juice." Jackie swept out of the room in a cloud of silk bathrobe and her signature perfume.

Her gaze met Neil's. "So you saw, I guess? Stupid-ass question, right? Who didn't see? Can you even believe it?" she squeaked, fighting another batch of tears. "I don't know how I didn't know—"

"Maybe because you can't always tell who the fag is just by looking at him?" Neil shifted on his feet, jamming his hands into his pockets.

Mel stopped the beginning of her tirade dead in its tracks, her stomach tight. "*What?*"

"I said you can't always tell who's gay. Gaydar is as accurate as craps."

Mel was appalled at Neil's apparent nonchalance. "We lived together for twenty years, Neil! And I never once suspected. Not once. How could I not have even had an inkling?"

Neil's eyes fell to the beautiful slate of the patio and muttered, "Sometimes you just never know."

Mel's lips thinned when she tightened her bathrobe around her with a jerk of her shaky hands. "Oh, I bet people knew. You can't tell me he wasn't unfaithful in one capacity or another. Someone knew and they pitied stupid, stupid Mel behind my back!" The rage she felt over that made it almost impossible to breathe. She'd accused Stan of being wrapped up in his own little world, but she'd been just as wrapped up in hers.

"I knew, Mel. I knew." Neil finally looked at her, his eyes stricken with the kind of pain she'd never seen in them before while he waited for her to process what he'd just stated.

His words rocked her to the core. He couldn't mean what she thought he meant. Her hand went to her chest to ease the ache there. *"You what?"*

"*I knew.* I've known since the day I met him."

Disbelief gave way to a searing pain in her gut. She tightened the belt of her robe around her waist. "So you've always known Stan was gay?" Twenty fucking years of her fucking fucked-up life and Neil had always known there was nothing she could have done to save her marriage because you can't beat the kind of competition that's a whole other gender.

Still, the raw misery that lined his face tore at Mel's heart, warring with her disbelief. "I tried to tell you at your bridal shower, Mel. I swear to Christ."

She flapped a quick hand upward, the mounting pressure in her skull just looking for a reason to explode. "Wait—I remember that night. You were obliterated, but you kept telling me I shouldn't go through with it. I thought it was just because you were drunk. So that was all because you knew even then Stan was gay, wasn't it?"

"Y-yes," he cried the words in a stutter. "Christ, Mel. I'm sorry. I'm so sorry. I couldn't believe it either. Well, no, that's not true. I could believe it, but he had me so convinced he really loved you, and that it was all a big mistake that would never happen again . . ."

Dread climbed her spine. Dread and a hot wave of fear. She forced her knees together to keep them from wobbling. "What was all a big mistake, and why would Stan try to convince you of anything, Neil? You two hated each other. You said it yourself!" None of this made any sense. Everything for the past twenty years was a lie—all a lie.

Neil's head hung to his chest, his breathing shuddered in and out, pushing the fabric of his polo shirt outward.

Mel gripped his chin, tipping it up to search his pain-riddled eyes. Whatever this was about, whatever was making Neil so miserable that he couldn't even look at her, she needed to know. "Say it. Just say it!" she yelled, filled with equal parts frustration and fear.

He clenched his jaw into a hard knot, as though the next words were too excruciating to speak, and then he spat, "I knew he was gay because I slept with him."

The words, words that ripped through her like sharp knives, landed with a sonic boom. She backed away from Neil, her heart hammering her from the inside out.

This was Neil. The Neil she'd always trusted. The Neil who'd been by her side through every dance competition since they were twelve years old. The Neil who'd loved her no matter what.

And he'd betrayed her.

Her head whirled with a whizzing sound. Her heart clamored with the erratic beat of betrayal. "When? When did this happen?"

she screamed, tears falling down her cheeks to land on the slate in salty drops.

Neil grabbed her by the shoulders, pressing his fingers into them with an almost desperate force. "It was just before the two of you announced your engagement. You guys kept everything so hush-hush, I wasn't even sure you were definitely a couple, and you sure didn't confide in me until after the fact."

Mel's hands slapped his from her shoulders with sharp cracks. "Because of the press, Neil! Even back then we had to be careful."

"I know that now, but I didn't then. I swear it, Mel. One minute we were all in a show together, and the next he was announcing your engagement. Look, what happened between Stan and me . . ."

Her stomach lurched; she pressed the back of her hand to her mouth. "Don't."

"I *have* to."

"Why?" she roared in his face. "So you can feel better? Cleansed? You know this cheating thing? It's pretty fucking selfish. Why is it the cheater gets to not only unburden himself, but feel relieved that he has while the cheated on suffer? You were my best friend! The moment you knew we were getting married, you should have told me!"

Anguish streaked his face, but it was as if he was possessed by some entity compelling him to purge all the pent up years worth of lies. "I'd had a crush on Stan forever. Just like you. But I had no one. It's not like I could ever talk about it with my girlfriends like you could . . ."

A fury so sharp it literally stung her shivered along her length. She shoved him hard, catching him by surprise and making his body jolt. "Don't you put that on me, Neil! Don't you dare. I loved you no matter who you wanted to have sex with, and you damned well know that. I never, ever would have judged you because I didn't and don't care what your sexual preferences are unless they involved my husband!"

He ran a hand through his hair, clenching it into a fist. "I didn't mean it like that." His head fell back on his shoulders before he lifted it, and in his eyes, Mel saw anger at its most raw. "Yes! For fuck's sake, yes! It was a cross I chose to bear because I was afraid to tell anyone. I've always been afraid, Mel. You know what my father was like. It was enough that I wanted to dance, but to factor in my homosexuality? He'd have killed me, old Big Dan the truck driver and his sissy kid, Neil the Dancer!"

Yes. Neil's father had hated that his son danced probably more than he'd hated most anything else in his miserable life. But Neil's mother, Flora, she'd adored Neil. She would have understood.

"Big Dan's dead, Neil," she whispered, her throat raw. "What happened to all the time in between when you could have told me? I can't remember a time when you didn't have a woman on your arm—even now at forty years old you're still dating starlets and socialites when you really want to be dating a linebacker. So what about that, *friend*?" Her words were meant to hurt—meant to make him suffer in the way he'd let her suffer.

Neil winced at her harsh attack, but he plodded ahead. "I just couldn't admit it. Own it. The further away I was from it, from you, the easier it was to hide from what I'd done to you and to me. I did go to Stan after you announced your engagement. I told him he should tell you what happened between us, but he said it was a huge mistake—that he loved women and he loved you. He'd never done something like that in his life, and he'd never do it again as long as he lived. He said it was because he was drunk—we both were. When I found out what he'd done to you in the divorce, I was ready to spill it all to whomever would listen. I had Theresa trying to track him down since I came to Riverbend, and I almost had the bastard, but the son of a fucking bitch beat me to it!"

Mel held up a hand that trembled while the other covered her mouth. "I can't hear any more of this."

He made a grab for her arm. "Mel, wait. *I loved him back then, too!* You have to at least listen to me. *Please.*"

Oh, God. The desperation in Neil's tone, the sheer agony all over his face only served to incite her. If she didn't get away from him, she'd likely claw his eyes out.

And then an eerie calm took over, leaving her feeling a little dead inside. "No. No, I don't, Neil. You knew Stan and I would never work. It's a fucking miracle we worked as long as we did, and I'd bet most of the time he was screwing around anyway. When he went off with Yelena, it crushed me. He took everything, Neil. My studio, my house—*everything*. Looking back on it now, I realize as I got older, I didn't love Stan the way I should have. But I wasted twenty years of my life, married to a man I'd never be able to please because he isn't even attracted to women, and *you* let me. To top it all off, you slept with him and didn't tell me even after you knew about the two of us. Or after you *knew* I was going to marry him. What else is there to wait for, Neil?"

Stumbling, Mel made a break for the French doors and flew inside on feet that were numb, with a raw sob that tore from her throat.

CHAPTER TWENTY

Dear Divorce Journal,

What am I, some kind of priest? I think the next time the confessional is full and someone needs to share, they'd better find a new church. I'll take the zero, thank you.

"Oreo cookie? There's someone here to see you." Joe poked his head around the door of the guest bedroom where she sat perusing the real estate ads online with her new laptop with tired eyes.

She'd cut her trip to L.A. short after Neil's admission, unable to bear the idea they were even in the same state. What Stan had done was unforgivable. What Neil had done was unthinkable. He'd known her marriage would never survive from the moment it began. He'd known just days before she and Stan announced their engagement. That her marriage had lasted as long as it did was nothing short of a miracle.

Yet it explained so much about him. The facets of Neil she'd never been able to relate to. It was an almost excruciating ache knowing he'd never felt comfortable enough to be honest with her. As the days passed, that notion troubled her almost more than Neil sleeping with Stan.

Mel groaned at her dad's cheerful smile, running her hand through her tangled hair. "I don't want to see anyone, Dad. Tell whoever it is that I *vant* to be alone," she teased in her best Greta Garbo imitation.

"I'm afraid this is someone you have to see, Mel. For closure. In fact, I'm gonna have to insist." He shook a warning finger at her.

Mel frowned, rubbing her temples, sinking back into the comfort of her pillows. "For closure? I think I've closed a bunch of doors these past four days, don't you, Dad? I'm exhausted from all this closure. I found out my ex-husband of twenty years was gay on a television show, which shouldn't surprise me because it seems like the new way to communicate. My best friend told me he's always known about my ex-husband and that even he wasn't able to resist Stan's charms, and to top all this closure off the man I fell wildly in love with is a jerk with a son I miss so much, it hurts. But to make things really special, I miss the jerk, too. Crazy, right? But at the moment, I'm distracting myself by looking at real estate—because I can—because Stan's check from his guilty account actually cleared and we're rich. I'm looking at real estate so, you know, you can live your twilight years in comfort and I can sleep in a bed my feet don't hang off of? So whoever it is, tell them to come back tomorrow when I'm more appropriately dressed for a nervous breakdown."

"Melina," a voice rumbled from behind her dad.

Her head popped up and her relaxed posture went from slumped on some pillows to on her feet in seconds. "Stan . . ."

But Joe planted himself between her and Stan. "Now before you go gettin' your back up, Mellow-Yellow, I let him in. He has somethin' to say I think is worth listening to. I'm gonna walk Weezer and Jake while you two do your thing."

He shook his finger in Stan's direction. "One yelp outta my kid, and don't forget I can still kick your butt, Twinkle Toes," he growled the warning, pushing past Stan who saluted him.

Despite how far she'd come, despite her steel resolve to never allow anyone to intimidate her, she still felt small next to Stan. His presence no longer awed her, but it did leave her tentative. "Can we talk, Melina?" he asked, his eyes tired, but with a glimmer in them she'd never seen before. His tone was gentle and not at all demanding or impatient as in the days of old.

Her fingers twisted behind her back, clenching and unclenching. "I'm not sure what we have to talk about, Stan."

"Oh, come now, Melina. Don't you owe me a good, what is it they say, *bitchfest*? Surely you have words you want to pummel me with."

Or her fists. Yet, she found, she was too wrung out for angry words or the blame game. Now she just wanted to get back to the life she'd begun before Stan and Neil were gay and Drew thought she was a whore for cash.

Her sigh was raspy. "Is this like some kind of homosexual's anonymous exercise where you atone for all your wrongdoing? You know, apologize for lying to me for twenty years? For using me as your cover? I want no part of it, Stan. None. I want to forget it ever happened. I've been through the ringer this past year, and a lot of the blame falls on you, but I'm tired now. I just want some peace." Her throat tightened. Peace. That would be so lovely.

His head dropped, some threads of grey mingled with the once raven-black of his hair glistening in the late November sunlight. "No, Melina. This is me, coming to you heavy of heart. I did wrong. I took advantage of your idol worship and in the ensuing years, I stole from you what you truly deserve from a husband."

Her chin lifted, her lower lip trembled, and she found his soft tone left her compelled to ask. "*Why*, Stan? Why didn't you just tell me? Why did you expose me to so much humiliation? The press . . ."

He shook his head. His regal posture slouching. "I am a selfish, impulsive man, that's why. When I found out what Yelena was going to do, expose me for who I am if I didn't pay her off, I reacted."

Confusion riddled her face. "Yelena?"

His sigh was ragged, his face littered with disgust. "Yes, Yelena.

The plan was never to tell you the way you found out—not on TV. Yelena . . ." He cleared his throat, swallowing hard. "She found me in a compromising position, Melina, if you know what I mean. I was cornered, and she epitomizes the word 'greed.' She threatened to tell the world if I didn't marry her and, naturally, provide her with the kind of prestige that would include being my wife. Oh, she had it all figured out. I could have as many affairs as I wanted, as long as she could have all the houses and cars, pool boys named Rico, and whatever else she wanted."

"But you were kissing her in that picture, Stan. I saw it with my own two eyes. You know, when the reporter shoved it in my face while I was trying to get into my *locked* studio?" Remembering that moment in time again didn't make her want to huddle in the corner of the room anymore—it made her angry. It made her want to sucker punch him. Which could still happen . . .

Stan reached for her hand, taking it whether she liked it or not. He held it to his heart. "I was sick over that, Melina. When we were in Wisconsin for the auditions for the show, Yelena took matters into her own hands because things weren't moving quickly enough for her cold, calculating heart. I'd promised to tell you I wanted a divorce, but it wasn't enough for Yelena. She hired this supposed fan of the show to follow us, knowing he'd make a great deal of money if he sold the picture, and then it all went to hell. She kissed me, Melina. I can assure you, I would never kiss her." He shuddered with obvious distaste, his elegant features distorting.

Relief flooded her veins—so much so, she had to cling to his hand to stay upright. "So you were willing to tell the world you were leaving me to marry Yelena in order to keep your homosexuality hidden, not to mention, keep her in the style she seems to think she deserves, which, PS was gonna cost a whole lot more than I ever did, yet, you couldn't tell me? Your wife?"

He pulled her hand to his cheek, his eyes glistening. "I have no excuses for what I did, Melina. You were the lesser of two evils. The only defense I have is that your emotions were involved, and Yelena just wanted the money and the prestige. That I could deal with. Hurting you by telling you I was gay and telling you you'd been loyal to a man who'd let you waste your life, your youth, with him seemed far worse than confessing to you I was leaving you for another woman. I toyed with telling you once or twice over the years, but I just couldn't."

Anguish rushed through her, rooting her to the spot. "But to live a lie . . ."

Stan's face grew bitter, his jaw tense. "I've lived with it far longer than you. I lived with the shame, the stigma our world seems to perpetuate. There were times when I hated myself, and when I refused to see you after the divorce, I was simply being the coward I've always been. I knew the divorce had gone through, but I didn't know everything had been taken from you. Especially the studio. Jesus, I'm sorry about the studio. I would have never done that, Melina. I know I was cross and impatient with you about its upkeep, but as I grew older, my secret was eating me from the inside out. I was unjustifiably angry with you, and I had no right to be. I lashed out in my resentment for a predicament I created, and for that, I'm sick with grief."

Mel watched myriad emotions play on Stan's face. Fear, sadness, but most importantly, deep regret. "Then why did we have to go so far wrong, Stan, to make this right? Where have you been all this time?"

"I was in Europe with that man-eater, mostly hiding out—out of touch with almost everyone and everything, and you know what it's like with me and anything that has to do with my accountants and lawyers. Jerry handled everything. I'd forgotten all about the prenuptial, which, if you recall, I didn't want you to sign in the first place."

Mel nodded her affirmation with a slow bob of her head. "Oh, I remember. Jerry wanted me to sign it, and to prove I didn't want your money, I did. Wow—stupid that, huh?"

Stan cracked a wry smile, the lines of worry on his face deepening "Ah, no, stupid me, Melina. All the while I let Jerry handle everything, he was stealing from me. He was who had your money. Money I'd expressly directed him to write you a check for from my personal account."

Her eyes widened in surprise. "What? Jerry was stealing from you? How did you find out?"

"I'd been suspicious of Jerry on and off over the last five years, but it was my divorce lawyers who found the discrepancy." He shook his head in apparent regret. "I don't know the exact details of the numbers. You know I'm not good with them. However, they alerted me about three months ago when some papers had to be filed for one reason or another, and I confronted Jerry." Stan's lips thinned with the memory.

"Do you think Jerry needs to share my cardboard box with me?" she joked.

Stan's head fell back in laughter filled with relief. "Jerry will never work again, if I have a hand in it. He threatened to tell everyone about my secret if I didn't keep my mouth closed. It was the catalyst for my interview with Nora Phillips. I'd reached my limit in my gay closet."

"So Jerry knew, too?" God. What an idiot she must look like.

Remorse filled his features once more. "He did, Melina. I'm sorry. So sorry."

Mel smiled up at him, wanting to forgive. "I always thought Jerry was a worm."

"I didn't know, Melina. I swear I had no idea he was siphoning money from me, and I had no idea you were left with nothing until this mess with Jerry happened. I signed the divorce papers he faxed to me, and that was that."

But that he'd left her with such disregard for her wellbeing still stung. "Did it ever occur to you to check on me—even once, Stan? If for nothing more than the years we shared together?"

"Ah, Melina. I'm a selfish, selfish man. You've always known that about me. I was so wrapped up in my misery, so disgusted with myself that I'd ever agreed to Yelena's blackmail, I couldn't face you. I was so wrong to assume Jerry would take care of you like he promised. When he threatened to expose me if I went public with his embezzlement, something inside me snapped, and for the first time in my life, I felt free. So instead, *I* went public."

"That explains the ten-million-dollar check."

He winked, popping his lips. "Before you accuse me of it, yes, it was guilt money. The guilt I felt when I found out how Jerry had locked you out of the studio, despite the fact that I never liked it to begin with, then took the house and everything else we owned. I was sick with guilt."

"You know, I didn't think I could cash that check, but I changed my mind."

He took her by the shoulders and gave her a light shake. "As well you should. You earned it, Melina. For the years I stole. For the beauty I took from the world when I married you and hid you away instead of letting you be the star I knew you could be. For all the good years you gave me that I just couldn't give back. You'll take it, and you'll like it."

Mel's throat tightened again, for what Stan's destructive lies had done to both of their lives. "Did you ever love me, Stan? Or was I always just a cover for your homosexuality?"

He surprised her when he asked, "Did you ever love me, Melina?"

She paused, sucking in a breath. "I've had a lot of time to think about this. You know, while I was broke and living at my father's?" she taunted. Though, she meant it to tease rather than scorn now.

Stan made an invisible dagger and pretended to plunge it into his heart with his artful flair for drama. "I'm sorry, Melina. So, so sorry. But you haven't answered the question."

She reached a hand up and cupped his weathered cheek, searching his eyes. "In the beginning, I loved you like a teenager loves her idol. Toward the middle, I wanted to love you. I tried to love you. I reassured myself often that if nothing else, we shared a mutual love of dance, and if our relationship wasn't passionate and all the things I'd heard it should be, then at least we had that."

"Unlike your stupidhead of a boyfriend who doesn't dance, yes? Drew, is it? He loves you the way a man should love a woman, I hear." Stan winked suggestively and smiled.

Hearing his name out loud made her heart thump in longing. "How do you know about Drew?"

He shot her a smile. The one he used when he was pleased by a dancer's routine on the show. "Your father told me all about your boyfriend troubles, but only after he threatened my life."

Mel laughed, but it was tinged with bitterness and a yearning so sharp, she ached to the tips of her fingers. "He's not my boyfriend anymore. Anyway, in the end, when our marriage was over, I was so hurt by what happened with Yelena, I didn't realize that I'd fallen out of love with you long ago."

Stan gathered her in his arms, placing the top of her head under his chin. His familiar scent, the way he rocked to and fro, soothed her as tears stung her eyes. "I loved you, Melina Cherkasov. I loved the way you danced; the fire in your eyes when you took a stage was like no other. Your presence stole my breath. I loved many things about you. The difference is, now I love myself enough to know I'm not *in* love with you."

But there was something else. "What about Neil? He told me about what happened before our wedding. He also confessed to having a crush on you much like me. You hurt him, too . . ."

Stan stroked the top of her head. "I didn't know he felt that way. I thought . . . For me it was just—"

"A one-night stand," she finished for him. She'd suspected as much. She suspected there had been many one-night stands for her ex-husband during the course of their marriage. She just couldn't allow herself to ponder them for long.

Stan's long sigh made his chest expand against hers. "I've done some horrible things to protect my secrets, haven't I?"

"And in turn put Neil in the position of risking our friendship all these years."

"Each time you saw him over the years, I worried he'd tell you, and there were times I wished he had."

"Because it was easier than telling me yourself." Mel sighed. "You do know how cowardly that was. To leave Neil with your secrets?"

Stan sighed again, too. "You can't call me anything I haven't called myself, Melina. I know what I did, and this is me owning it. All of it. But I took advantage of Neil's youth by putting him in that position, and as impulsive and reckless as it was, it was far more my fault than his. I hope you'll see he was as starry-eyed as you and consider forgiving him? If you can forgive me, surely, you can forgive him?"

Mel tweaked the fabric of his jacket. "No one said I've forgiven you, not totally. But I want to—because holding onto the bitterness is exhausting. Give me some time on that, okay?"

Stan's nod was of understanding. "But Neil?"

Sadness deep in her soul swept over her. For the losses Neil had suffered, too. "Of course I'll forgive him. It's just going to take time. Neil and I were best friends, and by being my best friend, he could have prevented the worst mistake of my life—marrying you."

"Ouch—that hurts." Stan rubbed his chest.

Mel chuckled against his tweed jacket. "It's just the truth. I'm not going to candy coat this and say you didn't do something you most definitely did do, Stan. I've learned a thing or two since we got divorced, and one of them is to be truthful with yourself and keep everything real. You lied for a long time—that sucks. But there were good things, too. Things that I'll always appreciate."

The rumble of his ironic laughter settled in her ear. "Jesus, Melina. You're a better person than I am."

Mel snorted. "Nah—wait until you get home and read my e-mail."

"I deserve whatever you said in that e-mail."

"Yep. You sure did. Be warned the e-mail that has the subject header, 'You Scum-Sucking Pig' in your inbox."

He set her from him, smiling at her like he had so long ago. Gone was the angry scowl he'd greeted her with over the last years of their marriage. "Do you think we'll be friends, Melina? Maybe in the future?"

"Can a girl ever really have enough gay friends," she teased, feeling lighter than she had in a long time. "I mean, if it wasn't for you and your constant nagging about my ass, I wouldn't look like this, now would I?"

His head shook back and forth. "I was just acting out because I was angry, Melina. Your ass was fine."

"No. It was out of shape and tired. It might not be a hundred pounds anymore, but it's in shape, and best of all, it's healthy."

"So what will you do about your Drew? You love him. I can see this on your face."

Mel shrugged, hoping to keep indifference in her tone, but her throat clogged with tears once more. "There's nothing to do. He wasn't the man I thought he was. I had an opportunity to do something I love, and it's a love he just won't or can't understand. He thought I was in it solely for the money."

Stan wagged a long, graceful finger of admonishment at her. "But you didn't really want to do the show, Melina. I know. My contacts told me you turned them down because you wanted to 'go home to your kids' was the quote, I believe."

Her sigh was wistful, her heart tight. "I was a little in love with the idea, flattered, too. But here's the catch. Drew had to let me go because he wanted to see me happy and trusted that I'd find a way to work it out with him if I did do *Celebrity Ballroom*. But he didn't, Stan. Drew may not necessarily understand my passions. He doesn't even have to relate to them. I definitely don't get his love of some piece of wood, but I respect what he makes from it. What he does have to do is let me have the freedom to do them because they're mine, and I won't let anyone take them from me again. I want the freedom to make whatever choices I want and have him trust I would never do something to hurt him or Nate."

Stan cupped her chin, running his thumb over her bottom lip. "You've learned much since our divorce, eh, my little borscht?"

Mel smiled at the use of his old endearment. "You know what I learned, Stan? How to buy chocolate frosting in bulk at discount prices."

Stan barked a laugh. "I'm proud of you, Melina, and this Drew? He's an idiot to let you go. That's all I'll say on the matter. Now," he pointed to her laptop on the bed, "I hear a house on me is in your near future. What do you say to allowing me to help you look? I have immaculate taste."

Stan plopped on her bed, dragging the laptop over his knees, his body relaxed, and Mel grinned at him amidst the pink pillows her father had bought her to make the room feel more like hers.

An invisible burden she hadn't realized existed fell off her shoulders then. The weight of Stan's betrayal eased like a piece of deadwood dislodging from some invisible place inside her. The anguish of her lost youth let go with a gentle release.

Peace settled inside her.

And it was good.

⁓ℓ⁓

"Your father, he's a clod, no?"

Nate laughed at the man who watched while his dad attempted to follow the steps his Aunt Myriam showed him, but he kept tripping over his big feet.

Nate kicked at the sawdust in the basement of his grandparents' house, making designs in it with his sneakers. "Yeah. It's like his feet refuse to do what his brain tells them to. He just keeps fumbling around with his tongue sticking out of the corner of his mouth like some dork."

The man stuck his hands inside the pockets of his trousers and nodded. "This is because he doesn't *feel* the music."

"Yeah. That's exactly what Ms. Cherkasov says, too."

"You're this Nate she tells me about? The one who holds such promise?"

"Yes, sir."

"You don't really love to dance, do you?"

Nate let his eyes drift from the man's to the floor in shame. "No, sir. I don't like it at all."

"Aha. But your intentions when you lied, they were good, weren't they? I know this after speaking at length with your lovely grandmother tonight."

Nate clucked his tongue, jamming his fists into the pockets of his jeans. "Oh, totally, but if you don't mind me saying, everything's gone to hell in a hand basket now. I blew it."

"Blowing it has degrees of severity."

"Tell that to my dad."

"Yes. He behaved quite irrationally."

"Yep. That's why we're here. But I think we can forget it. He sucks."

"Do you know who I am?"

"Yep." Nate behaved as though he wasn't impressed, but if Aunt Myriam saw this dude, she'd flat-out faint.

Placing a hand on Nate's shoulder, he asked, "Do you think I might offer to help so we can win your father the woman of his dreams? I owe that to her, you know."

"That would be bigger than any words I got," Nate said, fighting the urge to high-five the guy and come off like some lame fan.

"Then shall we?" He swept his arm in the direction of the middle of the basement floor.

Just then, his Aunt Myriam spun around on what was supposed to be a 3/8 turn.

And fell with a screech.

Into a real-live faint, all limp limbs and pale face to go with it.

Which Nate was relieved to find was okay to think was cool because his dad did catch her.

No harm. No foul.

CHAPTER TWENTY-ONE

Dear Divorce Journal,

Have you heard the saying, "What a difference a day makes"? Do you suppose I could have at least that much notice before you tip my world upside down? Clearly, someone in your office missed my memo on the appropriate amount of time required to give me a heads-up, and quite frankly, I'm not as young as I used to be.

"Mel!" Frankie yelled from the corner of the diner, waving her over to their table where her pity party awaited.

She dragged her feet toward Max, Jasmine, and Frankie with a heavy thud and dropped her purse on the table with a dejected thump.

"Darling?" Jasmine said on a glance upward at her. "You look like utter crap."

Mel flashed a wan smile at them—these women who'd taught her so much. "Crap is the new pink, Jasmine. You, above all else, should know that." She slid into the booth beside Maxine who threw an arm over her shoulder and gave her a hug.

"We heard and saw," Frankie said. "So who do we bash first, honey? The bashing pile, she is big. So, Stan, Neil, or Drew? Who's up first?"

Mel closed her eyes and dragged her fingers over them. They were grainy from lack of sleep and, yes, the occasional crying jag. "No one."

Maxine tilted her chin up. "This is me telling you, you've taken my motto on forgiveness too far, Mel. I'm all for a healthy attitude, but you've gone overboard. It really would be okay if you got one good freak on."

Cupping her chin in her hand, Mel looked at them. "I'm okay. I really am. I'm not in love with the fact that my ex-husband stayed married to me to cover for his homosexuality. I also not in love with the fact that Neil didn't stop me from marrying him—or that for all these years he knew not just Stan was gay, but he was, too. And I'm really not in love with the fact that Drew called me some crappy things. Yet, I'm still standing, and I haven't once considered booze or drugs. Okay, once I did. It was a long night of chocolate-frosting withdrawals. But I didn't consider it for long. Swear it."

Jasmine's beautiful smile was filled with sympathy. "We tried to call you a million times, honey."

Frankie nodded, reaching across the table to squeeze her hand. "We did. We've all suffered betrayal, but Jesus, Mel. You got the market cornered. So how can we help if bashing isn't the chosen show of solidarity?"

Mel's smile was of gratitude. "Just keep reminding me that breaking up with Drew was the right thing to do."

Each woman sighed.

Mel eyed them. "What? It wasn't the right thing to do? Wouldn't that contradict everything you preach, Maxine?"

Max nodded. "You know, we've all said the same thing to ourselves over and over. Yet, every one of us thinks that it doesn't make any sense and there's something more to it that Drew's just not sharing. But none of us can put our fingers on it. Don't ask us why we think that, it was just an immediate hunch on all our parts."

Mel gripped her napkin. She was sick of hearing that, and she said as much. "Here's something you can do. Quit saying there's something else. You guys, my dad, even Jackie said that, but if there's something else, that 'something' is as elusive as my once twenty-two-inch waist.

So leave it alone, please?" *Please, please, please leave it alone.* She was exhausted from hoping Drew's "something else" would magically reveal itself.

It was over between her and Drew, and unlike her slowly coming to terms with what Neil and Stan had done, she was having a hard time coming to terms with what Drew had done—said.

Jasmine's hands went in the air like two beautifully manicured white flags. "Consider it left. We were just throwing out the possibility."

Maxine and Frankie nodded in unison. "So Nikos says his mother's meatloaf cures even the most painful of heartbreaks," Frankie joked with a smile. "Want some?"

Mel squeezed her eyes shut then popped them open and forced a smile. "You bet I want some—and supersize it." Because if meatloaf was the answer, she was going to need a Dumpster-sized portion to cure this heartbreak.

～⦿～

"Why am I here, Nate?" Mel toed what she suspected was the edge of a curb.

"Please, Ms. Cherkasov. It's a surprise I made just for you. Just keep your eyes closed and hold my hand."

Nate's plea and her genuine affection for him were the only things keeping her from ripping off this crazy blindfold and hitting the ground running. "I willingly got into a car with you and your Aunt Myriam, who shouldn't drive unless someone else is doing it for her. Now I want to know what's going on," she demanded, fighting a surly tone.

When Nate had shown up at her father's door tonight, Myriam in tow, and told her he had a surprise for her, she'd been happy, and skeptical. Happy because she'd missed seeing him, skeptical because what kind of surprise could Nate possibly have for her? Had he re-created the atom bomb with toothpicks and Krazy Glue?

After checking with Nate to be sure his father knew where he was, they'd gotten into the death trap Myriam called a car and only broke out when it was a special occasion.

Before they'd arrived at this secret destination, Nate had insisted Mel put on a blindfold while Myriam careened down winding roads, which was just as well. If she were going to die, she'd just as soon do it not seeing the Mack truck that took her out.

Five minutes or so later, Myriam screeched to a halt and told her and Nate to get out. A creak of a door, with Nate's hand around hers, and she heard the sound of an engine roaring back to life and leaving them wherever they were standing.

"I don't like this, Nate," Mel fretted, rubbing her arms for warmth.

"I worked really hard on this, Ms. Cherkasov. *Please*, just trust me."

Mel's ears pricked to the plea of frustration she was hearing in Nate's voice and softened. "Okay, okay, but if I break a leg, I can't teach in a cast and on crutches. So keep that in mind, partner."

Nate placed his hands on her arms from behind and moved her somewhere warmer, taking her jacket from her shoulders, and said, "Just stand right there, okay? I'm going to leave you for a sec, but swear you won't take the blindfold off."

"I'd pinky swear it, but I can't see your hand."

Nate laughed, his chuckle easy and light. "Just promise."

"Promise."

"Be right back."

"Don't be long. I'm not a huge fan of the dark, or surprises in the dark. Did I mention I don't like the dark? I'm only down with this because I sort of like you."

Nothing. Silence. Mel's nostrils flared. Was that the scent of freshly cut wood? A tear threatened to slip from her eyes beneath the blindfold. The smell reminded her of Drew—his shirt off that warm fall day—naked from the waist up as he varnished an end table for his mother under the oak tree in the McPhee's front yard.

She took a deep breath, fighting the urge to break her promise and rip off the blindfold. "Nate?" she squeaked into the room.

Her ears pricked when the music to "Come Away With Me" began to play. Always, when she heard this song, it would remind her of her and Drew, swaying in the dark of his bedroom, wrapped in each other's arms.

Was Nate trying to rip her heart out?

Of course not. He had no idea.

He only knew that this was one of her favorite songs to waltz to. She'd told her class that when they'd snickered the first time she'd played it for them. Nate wouldn't know the meaning of the song went much deeper for her now.

The shuffle of feet, more than one pair, sent a shiver of fear along her spine until Nate said, "It's okay, Ms. Cherkasov. Gimme your hand and walk forward."

Mel did as she was instructed, following Nate's innate lead. He placed her hand on something warm and hard, covered in something crisp that felt like the material for a man's suit. She hissed a breath at the uncertain texture.

Nate pulled the string from the blindfold, then let it fall to the floor. Mel heard it flutter to the ground. As her eyes adjusted, she let out a small gasp.

Lights, so many twinkling lights—the room was illuminated in a soft, dreamy haze—strung from each corner, ending in a spiderweb leading to the center of the room where they connected.

The floor shone, buttery soft with nary a scuff on it. Her feet instantly moved to test the glide of it beneath them. Mirrors lined one long wall. There were no cracks like at Westmeyer, just a smooth surface with her reflection in it.

And Drew's.

The world had officially stopped turning and she barely heard Nate say, "Good luck, Dad," before he gave Drew a slap on his shoulder, shot Mel a shy smile, and escaped through the side-door exit.

Drew's deep, blue eyes held hers, defying her to look away.

His sharp jaw, defined by the crisp white shirt under his black tie, made her eyebrow raise. It was the only outward emotion she'd allow. On the inside, her heart ached its pounding was so fierce and her knees were like jelly.

"What . . ."

He held up a single finger in front of his lips, and then held out his hand.

Mel cocked her head in question, tamping down the rush of nervous anticipation touching every part of her body. His handsome length in a black tux with tails stole her breath.

Drew remained silent. Instead, he covered the distance between them and pulled her into his arms.

Into a waltz hold . . .

Okay, and it was one of the most awkward holds ever. Like right up there with R.J. and Emilio's kind of awkward, but it didn't matter.

Because it was Drew. Strong, handsome, and so obviously completely unsure, she had to fight a chuckle while she bit back tears.

"Isn't your head supposed to be tipped up and back or something?" he asked, his deep voice a rumble of determination.

"Oh, right. Sorry." She corrected the angle of her head on command, taking her questioning eyes from his gorgeous face.

And then Drew's feet began to move, slow, sluggish, but with the kind of resolve Mel saw by the tic in his angular jaw. She watched as he counted the rhythm in his head, stopping himself each time his lips wanted to move, and she fought another giggle.

Their toes cracked together when he lost his footing. Yet he continued. "Sorry. I forgot where I was, and stop looking at me like that. You're not supposed to be looking at me from that angle if your head's supposed to be tilted the other way. I'm the frame and you're some kind of artwork. Be the artwork, or something, and help a guy out," he muttered, focusing back on the point over her shoulder.

"The picture. Yes. I'm the picture," she acknowledged quietly, reveling in the clench and release of his tense fingers, forcing herself to keep a straight face.

And the music played, the cool air of the foreign studio doing nothing to ease the dampness of Drew's tux now clinging to her bulky sweater.

Whatever this was about, Drew wasn't giving up.

He didn't lead her around the floor; he pushed her like a shopping cart. Yet, with each thrust of his arms, each failed rise and fall of his obviously uncomfortable feet and stiff knees, Mel fell more in love with him.

"Aren't you supposed to be pressed closer to me?" he chastised through clenched teeth. "You're messing up this frame thing. We could park an elephant between us. What kind of ballroom instructor are you?"

Her shoulders heaved in another attempt to keep from laughing out loud. "Absolutely. I forgot this isn't the circus," she teased. Mel immediately straightened, closing the gap.

As the music swelled, and she internally prepared for what she was sure was going to be a natural spin turn, tears slipped down her cheeks, blurring her vision and almost tripping her.

Drew's upper torso tensed, and he forgot to look over her appropriate shoulder, making following him an exercise in trust, but his effort was all that mattered to Mel.

Nothing else mattered but this moment.

The music stopped before Drew did, though he clearly needed to end this with a waltz pose if it was the last thing he did by the way he forced her body to bend to his will.

Their bodies warred momentarily, Mel's frame fighting for the proper, instinctual position. Drew's making a hasty decision then correcting himself in the middle of everything.

Mel ended up sort of draped across his arm, but not quite. She clung to him when he gazed down at the awkward line her body was in and winced. "I forgot when to stop. Damn, that's been driving me insane."

It was all Mel could do not to throw her arms around him and lavish him with the swell of love she felt for him at this very second. This was about Drew now. It was about him choosing to understand something she needed to breathe. Something he'd never quite understand but had so clearly gone to extreme lengths to try.

Was there really anything else a woman could ask of the man she'd fallen so desperately in love with?

Sweat glistened on his forehead as she hung there and waited until he was ready to speak. "I clearly suck at this dancing thing."

She cocked her head, forcing herself to bite back more giggling. "'Suck' is so harsh, Drew."

"But so true."

She tipped her head and winced. "There are levels to suckage."

"Of which I've scaled."

She couldn't take it anymore. She caved in a fit of laughter, snorting and snickering. He did suck. Period. But he sucked in a way that made sucking seem like the most romantic gesture in the world.

Drew hauled her upward, lifting her off her feet and forcing her to wrap her arms around his broad shoulders. Her neck arched backward, capturing his gaze so deep, so intense.

"You want answers, right?"

"Only when you're ready."

"Stan taught me how to waltz. Stan, Neil, and Nate."

Her eyes widened in shock even as her heart thrummed. "Stan? You're kidding me."

"Would I joke about letting your ex pretend to be you while he threw me around a dance floor and snapped words at me in a language I'd need the Rosetta Stone to understand?"

Mel's giggle squeaked when she summoned up an image of that in her head. "Stan can be a hard taskmaster. So wanna tell me why? Why would you do this? Why would Stan help?"

"He said he owed you, and after he explained what happened, I thought he was right. He stepped in and saved Myriam's hip and her toes. Never thought I'd say it, but he's an okay guy, your ex-husband. So is Neil."

Mel's nod was fond without a trace of bitterness. "Yeah. Yeah, he is. So you know everything?"

Drew nodded his consent. "I know. I saw the Nora Phillips show, and after I said what I said to you, it made everything that much shittier. Stan told me all about Neil and . . . what happened before you married Stan."

Mel smiled up at him, her heart fluttering in her chest. "I didn't know it, but when I saw Stan again a few days ago and we talked, it was like this huge weight had been lifted. I hated thinking I'd been married to someone so callous because there was good in our marriage and it turned it all so ugly. Turns out, I was just married to someone who was too afraid to be who he really was."

"It's a pretty grim way to live."

"Did he also tell you what happened with his manager, Jerry?"

Drew brushed a strand of her hair from her face with tender fingers. "Over pumpkin pie and coffee. Myriam invited him back to the house, but not before she gave him a ration of shit for hurting you he'll probably never forget, after we practiced this waltz thing for the hundredth time. I think I could do it a million times and never get it right. He told us everything. Yelena, Neil, everything."

Mel bit her lower lip. "Did he also tell you I'm very rich? Because you can drop me right here if we're going to fight over money again, Drew McPhee."

Drew pressed his nose to hers. "He told me, and I'm an ass."

"Baby got back kind of ass," Mel agreed on a hopeful giggle.

His smile was warm—the smile she'd hoped to see just one more time every night when she'd closed her eyes this past week. "I was wrong."

"You were way beyond wrong."

"I said some shitty things, Mel."

"The shittiest."

"But the things I said weren't the real issue."

"Is this going to be the 'something more' thing I've been trying to figure out?" she asked.

"The what?"

Mel shook her head with a wry grin. "Forget it. Just tell me what the real issue is."

"Nate set me straight."

Her surprise was genuine. "Nate?"

"Yeah. He used big words like 'transference' and 'post-traumatic stress disorder'—or something. What it boils down to is I couldn't trust you to love me as much as you love to dance."

Hmm. "Couldn't?"

She sensed the struggle in Drew to find the proper words and express them without sacrificing his manhood, and it made her tingle from head to toe. "Fine. I was *afraid* to trust you, and I took it out on you because of my marriage to Sherry and the fact that she chose her passion for her career, and eventually her drinking, over us. It was unfair and unjustified, and I used the money thing as a cover for the

real issue at hand, which was you potentially putting your career
before Nate and me. I said those things to you to keep you from finding out what an ass I was being."

Ahh. So *that* was the "something else." "So the real truth is you
felt threatened by my career possibly turning into something much
bigger than just being Ms. Cherkasov from nine to five?"

His eyes hardened, but only for a moment before he winced. "It
consumed Sherry once . . ."

"But my name is Mel," she whispered. "And here's something to
think about. I'd never make you choose between me and a piece of
wood."

"But my love for making things isn't going to take me away from
my family or put me on TV across the country."

Mel smiled sympathetically. "I get it, and I can see it took a lot out
of you to admit your feelings, oh ye of the demand for communica-
tion," she taunted with a teasing grin.

Drew's laugh was husky. "You have no idea. This past week has
been like one long therapy session of discovery."

"No kidding," she acknowledged with a coy smile. "So wanna tell
me what this is all about, Mr. McPhee? The dancing—this studio?
Whose is it?"

His lips came to rest on her cheek when he whispered, "I wanted
to prove to you that I get this dancing thing. Not on the level you
do, obviously. You once said dancing freed you to express emotions
you didn't even know existed. I don't feel free when I dance. I feel
like an idiot with really big feet. But I get why it's more than just a job
to you."

Warmth flooded her and made her fingers tighten on him. "Really?"

"Honestly?"

"Please."

"No," he said on a laugh. "I don't understand it at all, but it makes you happy, and that's really all that matters to me. Plus, if I'm honest, when you do that stretchy thing to warm up, it's pretty hot."

Mel's heart tightened and released as she clung to his neck and lifted her lips for a kiss she'd missed more than any words could express. "So where are we?" She craned her neck to take a peek around.

He set her down and took her hand to walk her toward what would eventually be a door. Drew pointed to the wall. On the bare sheetrock hung a sign that read "Ms. Mel's Office."

Mel gasped when she read it, but remained speechless, still confused.

Drew pulled her to him, molding her body to his in a gesture that was possessive. "Stan. He bought this for you, to make up for losing your studio in L.A. Nate and I and my brothers-in-law have been here all week trying to get the floor and mirrors in on time to surprise you. Add in my dance lessons, and we've been busy."

"*Stan* bought this?" she squeaked.

Drew's head bobbed. "He did. There was no talking him out of it either. He couldn't stop worrying over you losing the studio, so he called up a real estate agent, and bam. Things happen damned fast when you're rich. It's going to be a few months before it's up to code, but it's all yours."

Excitement swelled in her at all the possibilities, the doors having her own dance studio opened. "I don't know what to say . . ." It was too generous.

His lips found her ear, hot and sweet, making her shiver. "You'll figure it out, Mel. I'll help you figure it out, if you help me figure out my new job."

She pulled back from his mouth with reluctance, her eyes wide. "Your new job?"

"Yep. I start next week. Corporate offices of Reiner and Sons."

"Wait, isn't that apartment complexes or high rises or something?"

"It is. Subdivisions, too. Meet the new project manager."

She was overwhelmed—with surprise—with happiness. "*Who* are you? Won't that job make you the all evil, nothing but trouble, money?"

Drew's eyebrow rose, but his grin was wide. "It will, a great deal more than I'm making now, too."

"Did you take the job because Nate's tuition's going up? Because you don't have to worry . . ." Hoo, boy. Cat officially out of the bag. She winced when she looked at him, waiting for the thundercloud of doom to cross his face.

Instead, he smiled, smug and confident as the first day she'd met him. "I know all about it, Mel."

"But how? I did it anonymously through Stan's lawyers."

"Nate. It was easy to put two and two together after Stan told us about the substantial amount of money he gave you."

Mel was prepared to stand her ground on this—at all costs. Her eyes narrowed, ready to do battle. "Is your pride going to keep Nate from earning the kind of education he needs because let me tell you a thing or two, McPhee. I won't stand—"

Drew's lips landed on hers with force, thwarting all protest as he scooped her up and kissed her, letting his tongue slide between her lips to the tune of her blissful sigh. She relaxed against him, clinging to his muscled arms. "I took the job because it's high time I do what I love. I love to build houses in subdivisions and buildings. Big, tall buildings. Know what else I love?"

Her fingers lodged in his hair, reveling in the silky strands. She grinned. "Chili cheeseburgers? The Giants? Elvis? The Dallas Cowboys Cheerleaders. Don't pretend you don't. I saw it with my own eyes. I even saw drool at the corner of your mouth."

"I love *you*, Mel Cherkasov. I was a jackass for not saying it sooner—before you left to go to L.A. If you want to take the job with *Celebrity Ballroom*, I'll support whatever makes you happy."

Tears began to slip from her eyes. It was the last piece of the puzzle—Drew's support—no matter what she chose to do. His thumb swiped at her tears. She grabbed hold of his wrist and asked, "Didn't Stan tell you?"

"There's more? I don't know how much more I can take, honey. I'm on confession overload."

Stan hadn't told him because he knew how important it was to her for Drew to trust her. A new respect for Stan blossomed in her, replacing some of the inner turmoil he'd created. "I didn't take the job on *Celebrity Ballroom*."

His eyebrow rose again. "Say again?"

Mel walked her fingers up the lapel of his tux. "I said I didn't take the job on *Celebrity Ballroom*. They offered it to me, but I turned it down."

"Because?"

"Not because of you, pal. You didn't think I was going to come back here just for the torture of seeing you every day, did you? I did it because I'm happy at Westmeyer. I love the boys, and even if they don't love to dance, they like me. I discovered if I'd wanted the spotlight so badly, I'd have found it through Stan. I guess, in the end, it just wasn't as important to me as I thought it was back when I was fresh off the turnip truck."

"So you're staying at Westmeyer?"

"Wild horses couldn't drag me out of there. Though, I'm a little sad you won't be there. Lunch just won't be the same if you're not sneaking me a Ring Ding."

"Whaddya say I bring you a Ring Ding every day at lunch? My office is just down the road."

Happiness settled deep in her heart, right beside contentment. "Deal."

"Did you hear that, everyone? I think we have a deal!" Drew yelped.

Mel's head swiveled as bodies poured out of every available nook and cranny still unfinished in the studio. *Her* studio.

Nate jumped out from behind the big speaker and thumped his father's back. "Wow, you sucked, Dad," he said on a grin and a laugh. "But nice try." He gave Mel a quick hug before taking off to grab a plate for food that had suddenly appeared on a folding table in the corner of the studio.

Stan approached them, his face relaxed and happy. He slapped Drew on the shoulder with a laugh. "You are the worst dancer I've ever seen. Thousands of lifetimes of lessons couldn't make you any better."

Drew stuck out his hand in Stan's direction and smiled wide. "Couldn't have done it without you, my man."

Stan threw his head back and roared with laughter. "If you ever tell anyone you're the product of my instruction, I'll shoot you."

Someone turned the music back on as Myriam and Selena gathered Mel up in a warm hug, kissing her cheeks, while Joe gave Drew the father-to-boyfriend speech.

"I take back all the horrible things I said about Stan. He's not a crusty wiener after all," Myriam chirped.

"What's this about crusty wieners?" Stan asked over her shoulder.

Myriam's face turned red. "We didn't know you were so nice," she sputtered.

Stan cocked an arrogant eyebrow at her when he held out his hand. "I think you can make your off-color remarks up to me. May I have this dance?"

Myriam's eyes widened as Stan swept her away to twirl her on the dance floor while William gathered Selena in his arms and pulled her into an awkward box step.

Drew wrapped an arm around Mel's waist and pulled her to his side. "There's someone over there in the corner you need to talk to, honey."

Mel's eyes swept the room and spotted Neil in the far corner, somber, shadows under his eyes, his hands in his pockets.

She gazed up at Drew, hesitant. "Do you mind?"

Drew let his lips touch hers briefly, the promise of the night to come on them. "As long as you remember when this is done—I have plans for you. It's been a week, and you know how I feel about waiting longer than a week."

Bracketing his face with her hands, she shivered against him. "Be right back." She pressed a kiss to his jaw before sifting her way across the dance floor.

Neil eyed her with hesitance, but he lifted his chin in her direction, clearly fighting to maintain his composure.

Mel held out her hand to him. "Come here often?"

He took it, clasping it in his, his palms sweaty and cold. "Not as of late, but I hope to in the very near future."

Mel smiled a warm smile, more of that peace she'd found wending its way through her veins. "So I hear you dance. Is that true?"

Now Neil smiled, too, and rolled his hips. "I got a couple of moves."

She rolled her tongue in her cheek. "Oh, yeah," she challenged. "Care to show them to me?"

He threw his arm around her waist and hurled her over his arm, bending her spine. He gave her his *Celebrity Ballroom* smile and cocked an eyebrow down at her. "Is that a challenge I hear in your voice?"

Mel placed her hand on his opposing shoulder like she had a thousand times before. "You bet your ass it is."

He rolled his neck. "Well, then, it's on," he said, cocky and husky before lunging her body upright and taking her sailing across the floor into a Viennese waltz.

And they danced—like they'd always done—as one.

In those moments when everything but the rhythm of the music and the swift movement of their unified feet was all that mattered, Mel found forgiveness.

Neil was her best friend, and instead of blaming him for keeping Stan's secret from her, she saw his position all these years from his eyes. He'd wanted to protect her.

It was what every best friend wanted.

When their dance ended, Neil pulled her close, their chests rising and falling in choppy breaths.

She gazed up at her best friend and wiped a bead of sweat from his brow with affection. "I love you, Neil. I just want you to be happy, okay?"

He returned her smile, a smile that didn't have any reservations. "Me, too, Mel. Me, too."

Mel gave him a hard shove toward Stan. "Then maybe you should go try and find some happy, huh?"

He blew her a kiss before escaping through the crowd of Drew's family to find Stan.

Drew came up behind her, dragging her close to him. He bent down and whispered in her ear. "All's well?"

She snuggled into him, warm, undeniably happy. "All's well."

"Did I tell you how amazing you looked out there with Neil?"

Mel swung around. "I don't believe you did."

"What kind of boyfriend am I?"

"The kind who'd better excel at covert ops. We need to get out of here pronto, Double O Seven. It has, after all, been a whole week," she said suggestively, letting her lower body press into his.

He settled her hips against his, kissing her lips in swoon-worthy fashion. "Well, then, we'd better bust a move, huh? I'll lead," he said, beginning a slow sway to the music, inching his way toward the door.

When the coast was clear, they ran outside into the freezing night, the sky filled with dozens of stars. Drew pulled her around back to the parking lot where his truck waited and unlocked the passenger door, helping her inside.

Then he backed away, crossing his arms over his chest. "You know, there's just one little thing we need to clear up before I take you back to my place and ravish you from head to toe."

She shivered, but it wasn't entirely from the cold. "Well, hurry it up, dancer. It's freezing."

"I don't recall you returning my declaration of love. Now how can that be, Ms. Cherkasov?"

Mel put a finger to her chin in thought. "You know, it must've slipped my mind."

He shot her a cocky grin. "I can wait as long as you can."

She wagged a finger at him. "C'mere."

He pointed to the space between her legs. "There?"

She nodded. "*Riiight* there."

He took the two steps in seconds. "Here?" he asked, slipping his arms around her back.

"Yeahhh," she cooed. "That's good." So. Good.

"I await."

Wrapping her legs around his waist, she drew his mouth to hers. "I love you, Drew McPhee. I love you. I love you. I love you."

His chuckle against her mouth left her tingling. "One more time. Just so I'm sure I heard right."

Her eyes met his—confident and bright. "I. Love. You. Drew. McPhee."

Running his knuckles over her cheek, he replied. "Well, woot to that. Let's go home and celebrate."

And they did.

Oh, did they ever.

EPILOGUE

Dear Journal,

Do note, I no longer call you my "divorce journal." That's because I don't consider myself divorced anymore. Nay. In fact, I proudly wear the label "married"—and the label Mrs. Drew McPhee. Score!

One year and five months later

"Drew, if you don't stop now, we'll never make the dance. I'm the teacher. I kind of have to be there."

Drew didn't stop. Instead, he kissed his way up her thigh and pressed his hot lips at the line of her panties. "You don't really want me to stop, do you, dancer?"

When his fingers moved her panties over an inch and his mouth found her core, she shuddered against him. "Noooooooooo. I really don't want you to stop, but we'll be . . ." She gasped at the touch of his tongue on her clit. "Late. We'll be *late*."

His moan against her flesh vibrated, making her leg lift higher over his shoulder. Still warm and damp from his shower, his skin stuck to hers in a delicious suction. Replacing his silken tongue with his fingers, he slid up her body. "I can't help it. You look so hot in that dress, I had to have a piece of that," he joked, capturing her lips.

She clung to his shoulders, pulling him with her as she hopped up on the bathroom counter in their new home. The home Drew had designed for her and Joe.

The home, one year down the road and a Vegas wedding—Elvis-style—later, she now shared with not just her father, but Nate, Weezer, Jake, and a stray cat named Amos.

And Drew, always Drew.

Drew's job, though more demanding than his position at West-meyer, allowed him plenty of time to spend with his family, and he worked from home one day a week. He and Nate had continued working on the dance studio, and it was almost ready.

Which meant it was time to branch out by handing in her resignation at the end of the school year. She was sad to leave the boys, but they'd know where to find her if they wanted a good dose of Ms. Cherkasov, and she'd welcome all of their left feet with open arms.

Mel gave him her best smoldering gaze, then spread her legs wide. She wiggled her finger at him. "We've got all of five minutes. Make me smile, McPhee," she teased.

His groan when she wrapped her hand around his cock and placed it at her entrance never failed to make her dizzy with lust. She tilted her hips, letting them rest at the edge of the counter when Drew drove upward into her.

Her sigh was one of completion when he filled her. He never failed to make her want to consume him. She kneaded the hard planes of his back, enjoying the ripple of them under her palm. Her legs went around his waist and her hands left his back to rest on the cool marble of the sink. Mel's head fell back on her shoulders when her nipples tightened at the sound of their lovemaking.

Drew cupped her ass, driving into her in slick, hot thrusts, pulling her to him. Her cry was primal when release clawed its way to the surface of her desire.

She dragged him close, using the strength of her legs to keep him flush to her, burying her face in his strong soap-scented shoulder.

"Christ, woman," he gritted, just before his muscles flexed and he climaxed, too.

She fell back on her elbows and sucked in gulps of air when she caught sight of her silk dress. "Now look what you've done," she chastised lovingly, sitting up and winding her arms around his neck. "My dress will never be the same."

Drew nipped at her neck. "I'll buy you another dress. All I can say is you brought it on yourself. If you'd just stayed downstairs and waited in the kitchen where all good women belong, maybe baked some cookies or something, I wouldn't have had to get you seminaked. It's those damn thigh highs, honey. They're smokin' hot."

She kissed his jaw and giggled. "Hah! This bathroom will see more action than our kitchen ever will, and I wore them just for you, but the plan was to have you take them off me *after* we were done at the dance with the boys."

Drew growled in her ear, low and husky. "I can do that, too." He stood up. "Hey, you think you're ready for this? Are the boys ready for this?"

"Are you questioning my teaching skills? Didn't I teach Nate's class to dance, only to find out Nate hates to dance? I've done this twice now. I'm an old pro, and Nate graduated his first year in my class just fine."

He lifted her off the sink. "You're a hot pro. So, you think Stan and Neil will make it? Last e-mail we got from the happy couple, they were off in Bali."

Mel grinned. So much had changed. The road to forgiveness had gotten easier with each day that passed.

And somehow, through so much hurt, not one, but two happy

couples had been produced. Stan and Neil had begun dating a few months after that night at the dance studio, and they'd made the news of their love official just two months ago. "I know they wouldn't miss it, if they could help it."

Drew placed her on the floor and made his way into their bedroom of grays and blues with every available wall space covered in family photos, the bedroom where they spent many nights making love, laughing, talking. "I'm surprised Nate's as excited as he is," he said, slipping into his shirt.

"Well, a little birdie, cough, Aunt Myriam, cough, told me that a certain girl, whose name is Mercedes—but you didn't hear that from me—is going to be there. I'm sure hormones and puberty play a huge role in his desire to show off his waltzing skills."

Drew winked laciviously. "Aha. Damn women'll get you every time."

Sitting at the edge of the bed, she gazed up at her husband. His handsome frame still took her breath away. Watching him dress was one of her favorite things to do. "Sherry's going to be there, too . . ."

His face hardened momentarily, then eased. "She should be. She's his mother."

"She's been sober five months, that's longer than any period in her alcoholism. Nate's so proud." Inspired by Nate, who'd finally made the choice to not see his mother again until she was sober, Sherry hit rock bottom.

It had been an ugly night in the emergency room for Nate and Drew, when they'd gotten a call five months ago that she'd been in a serious auto accident. With Stan's help, and his resources, Mel had convinced Drew that Sherry could be helped—if she'd just reach out.

She'd done just that, and now she was in a sober living facility, painting again, happier, and making plans to spend more time with her son.

Stan continued to make gestures, small and large, in order to prove he needed Mel's forgiveness—like helping talk Sherry into rehab—a facility Stan knew well from the occasional dancer's bout with addiction. And though she'd told him time and again, it wasn't necessary, Drew had reminded her that this was Stan's way of helping all the lives he'd turned upside down, sit right side up again. He was trying to earn her forgiveness, and there was something to be said for the amount of time and effort he was putting into it.

She hadn't completely forgiven Stan. There were still moments when something reminded her of her old life, the things she'd never experience because she'd been wrapped up in Stan, and they still stung. But lately, she smiled more than frowned when she thought about him. And that was a huge leap from wanting to set him on fire.

Drew finally shot her a smile. "I'm glad for Nate. He deserves the best mother she can be."

Nate poked his head around the doorway, hands over his eyes. "Can I come in?"

"Wowww! Somebody looks pretty handsome." Mel rose on tiptoe and sniffed. "And is that cologne I smell?" She whistled her appreciation.

"Whatever," he drawled in his usual teenage disinterest. "Hurry it up, Dad. We have to go. Stan and Neil are downstairs with Grandpa Joe, and Grandma, Grandpa, and Aunt Myriam are already there."

Drew gave Mel a wicked smile. "What's the rush, pal?"

Nate gave them a dramatic sigh. "You know exactly what the rush is, Dad. I know you know about Mercedes, and do I have to explain the flux of hormones to you again?"

Mel's snort was a sputter. "Okay, okay. We get it. I don't need another speech on the species known as teenager. Go get Stan and Neil into the truck. We'll be right there." She gave him a peck on his cheek and watched him head down the hallway to the stairs.

She swatted her husband's gorgeous backside. "You heard him. Hurry it up. Mercedes awaits. You wouldn't want to be responsible for thwarting young love, would you?"

Throwing on his jacket, he nipped at her lips. "Oh, the horrors."

Just as Mel rushed to their bedroom doorway, Drew grabbed her hand, dragging her close to him. "Hey, in all the chaos, find the time to save me a dance, would ya?"

She straightened his tie, yanking on it to pull him to her lips. "Did you really just say that to me, Drew McPhee?"

"Nate and I have been practicing at the studio. I think I finally nailed that running finish in the quickstep."

Yeah. He'd nailed it—when he'd slid into the wall like he was sliding into home plate. "I can't wait to see."

"Just do me a favor."

"Anything," she cooed up at him, her eyes warm with love.

"Make sure you clear a path. I'm good at the starting. Not so much on the stopping."

Mel laughed until tears stung her eyes. She cupped his face in her hands, loving that while he continued to be the worst dancer ever, he tried at every given opportunity to learn. "I love you, Drew. Crappy dancing and all."

"You can tell me all about it tonight when I take those thigh highs off." He wiggled his dark eyebrows suggestively at her.

Mel threw her leg around his hip. "Promise?" she purred.

He rubbed her chin with his thumb. "That's a promise, Mrs. McPhee."

A promise she knew—as sure as she knew the steps to a cha-cha—was one he'd keep.

Forever.